Secrets o...

KATHERINE GARBERA
ANN MAJOR
KAT CANTRELL

ley is to use papers that are natural, renewable and recyclable
n and made from wood grown in sustainable forests. The logging
facturing processes conform to the legal environmental regulations
try of origin.

ted and bound in Spain
Barcelona

A CASE OF KISS AND TELL

BY
KATHERINE GARBERA

Katherine Garbera is a *USA TODAY* bestselling author of more than forty books, who has always believed in happy endings. She lives in England with her husband, children and their pampered pet, Go-diva. Visit Katherine on the web at www.katherinegarbera.com, or catch up with her on Facebook and Twitter.

This book is dedicated to Rob, Courtney and Lucas.
I love you guys.

Acknowledgments:
There are many people to thank for their help and
support during the writing of this book. First of all, my
husband for giving me the freedom to just write—there
truly aren't words to thank you for that. Also to my kids
for just making me laugh when I was stuck on the plot
and couldn't figure out where to go. And last, to my
editor, Charles Griemsman, for being a great sounding
board for ideas and of course for his deft editing.

One

Conner Macafee was used to reporters snooping around his family. His great-uncle had been a confidant of John F. Kennedy, and Conner's own family were considered American royalty in politics and business. Of course, they had more than their share of scandals as well, which had always kept the press interested in them.

But Nichole Reynolds, the society reporter for the national newspaper *America Today,* was going about it in an entirely new way. She'd crashed his family's Fourth of July party in Bridgehampton and was doing her best to fit in, but so far she'd done little but stick out. She'd tried to blend by faking an ennui with the dignitaries and A-list celebs who were in attendance. But Conner couldn't help but notice her gushing more than once to the model and polo star Palmer Cassini.

Conner had gone to school with Palmer and knew him to be a fun-loving partier. He was an intense athlete, but also a hell of a fun guy, and Conner counted Palmer as one of his closest friends. But Palmer didn't hold his interest the way the redheaded reporter did.

He knew why Nichole was here. He'd turned down numerous interview requests from her and her bosses. He understood that she was a friend of Willow Stead, the producer of *Sexy & Single,* the reality television show that featured his company, Matchmakers, Inc. With the TV show under way, Nichole intended to write a series of articles on the matchmaking service his grandmother had founded. But he didn't trust reporters and never talked to them. That's why he had a marketing manager, Zak Levy, who was handling all the promotion and press releases. Conner had been very careful to keep out of the spotlight.

"Who is she, Conner?" his mother, Ruthann Macafee, asked, coming up next to him.

"Who, Mother?" he asked, pulling his gaze away from Nichole. He assured himself that keeping an eye on the reporter was the only thing that interested him. Not her lush red hair, which flowed in waves past her shoulders, or the stunning white sheath dress she wore. But he knew that he was lying to himself. He wanted her and if he'd had any idea how potent the attraction would be, he would have granted her an interview at his office weeks ago.

"The woman you keep staring at? I don't recognize her so I suspect she doesn't run in our circles," she said. His mother was sixty-five but looked at least fifteen years younger, thanks to her active lifestyle. She played in a tennis league and ran a charity. She'd never been the type of woman to sit at home, and Conner admired her for it. Even when a plane crash had taken his father's life and revealed a scandal that would have broken many women, she'd carried on in that quiet strong way of hers.

"Nichole Reynolds—reporter," Conner said.

"Oh, dear. I wonder why she's here." He heard a hint of fear in his mother's voice. She didn't like reporters, and with good reason. He wrapped his arm around her shoulders in a quick hug.

"That reality TV show I'm doing…she wants to interview me."

"Truly? Are you going to do it? It's so gauche to talk about your private life." Conner bit back a smile at his mother's attitude. To say she was old school was a major understatement.

"I'm well aware of that," he said, leaning down to kiss his mother on the forehead. "I think I'd better get rid of her before she makes any problems for us."

"Good idea. Do you want me to ask Darren to escort her out? How did she even get in here?"

"The head of security doesn't need to be bothered with this," Conner said. He'd been handling women like Nichole since he'd turned fourteen. "She probably came as a plus one."

"Next year I'm going to make sure that the invitations are better vetted," his mother said. "I don't want her kind getting in here."

"Whose kind?" his sister, Jane, asked, joining them.

Jane was a posh and trendy woman who had her own cooking and lifestyle show on TV. She didn't shy away from the media the way Conner and his mother did, but then Jane had been sheltered from most of the fallout from their father's infidelity.

"A reporter."

"Scourge of the earth," Jane said, winking at him. "Where is she? I'll go take care of her."

His sister was a troublemaker, and Conner knew the only way to deal with her and their mother was to end this conversation. "I'm handling it."

"Which one is she?" Janey asked.

"The redhead," his mom said.

"Oh, I see why you want to 'handle' her. Go for it, big bro," Jane said.

"Mom, I think you should have disciplined Janey a lot more when we were younger. She's a complete brat."

"She's perfect," their mom said as Jane stuck her tongue out at Conner.

He shook his head and walked away from both women. He worked his way through the well-heeled party crowd, picking up a firecracker mojito—Janey's creation—from a uniformed waiter on his way to Nichole and Palmer.

She glanced up as he approached, and Conner saw the guilty look in her eyes a moment before she masked it with a brazen smile.

"Conner Macafee," she said, with a little too much enthusiasm. "Just the man I've been wanting to see."

"Nichole Reynolds," he said, matching her energy. "Just the woman I don't remember inviting."

"With women there is always some sort of intrigue," Palmer said.

"Indeed," Conner agreed. "Are you enjoying yourself?"

"I always do," Palmer said.

Nichole looped her arm through Conner's and led him away from Palmer. "If I waited for an invitation from you, I'd never have the chance to talk to you in person."

"That's because I don't do interviews." Conner's father had been very involved in politics. Even after he'd left office, he'd been in a high-profile business that had demanded lots of press and reporters having access to his life. As a teenager Conner had been photographed and interviewed by every society magazine. He'd hated living in a fishbowl and had vowed never to allow it to happen again once he was an adult. Something he'd been very successful at, even though he lived a jet-set life and had a reputation as something of a player, he didn't give interviews and was seldom, if ever, caught by the paparazzi.

"I think you're reacting negatively to someone in the past," she said, dropping her arm from his once they were far from the crowd. "I promise it will be painless."

"Maybe I like pain," he said, primarily to bait her but also because there were times when pain was the only reminder he had that he was alive.

She narrowed her gaze as she stared at him; he knew she was trying to guess if he was telling the truth. "So how about answering a few questions?"

"No, ma'am."

"I'll do anything to get this interview, Conner."

The hint of determination in her tone intrigued him. It had been a long time since anyone had been so dogged to get something from him.

"Anything?"

"Yes," she said. "I'm known as the girl-who-gets-her-story and you're making me look bad at work."

"We can't have that now, can we?" he asked, stepping closer into her personal space and letting his hands fall lightly on her shoulders. She was tall for a woman—probably five-eight—but she only came to his chest and he liked the feeling of power he had looking down at her.

"You do know I don't give interviews," he said.

"But this is different. You're doing a television show."

"Not me, my company. There's a very big difference," he said.

"Your dad didn't see it that way. He practically lived on the pages of the *Post*."

And that was precisely why Conner wouldn't. "I'm not my dad. And the answer is still no."

"Please," she said, tipping her head back and pouting up at him.

Her luscious red lips made him want to groan out loud. He felt a zing of lust shoot straight through him.

"I might do it, but the price will be high," he said, knowing he'd never sit for an interview with her. But he wanted her and didn't see why he couldn't indulge the fantasy a bit.

"Name it," she said.

He lifted a strand of her hair and wrapped it around his forefinger. She held her breath as a blush spread over her neck and cheeks. Her creamy skin with the light dusting of freckles was smooth under the fingers of his other hand.

He wanted her.

But he knew he'd never have her. He couldn't be with a woman he couldn't trust, and at the end of the day her loyalties would always be with her newspaper. But he wasn't about to let her go without stealing at least a kiss from her. He suspected the shock of what he was going to say would drive her away and maybe even cost him that kiss he wanted so badly. But that was his intention. Self-preservation won out over lust…well, sort of.

"Be my mistress for a month and I'll answer all your questions," he said.

Nichole stared up into the bluest eyes she'd ever seen and tried to make sense of what he'd just said. She'd never imagined she'd be so turned on by someone so…well, conservative. She would have to call him that. To be honest, he was so far out of her league, she knew he must be toying with her.

She was used to doing whatever it took to get a story but this was…risqué and daring and she wanted to say yes. But ethics made her back down. She suspected he'd said that to push her away and that made her mad.

"A month?" she asked. "What kind of secrets are you hiding, Mr. Macafee? I had only planned on asking you about Matchmakers, Inc. But for that kind of price, I'd have to have full access to every part of you."

She knew he wouldn't negotiate with her. Why would he? She'd read the papers back when his father died. She knew the scandalous stories of the second family that Old Jed Macafee had kept hidden and she remembered seeing the photos of Conner and his sister, Jane, as they'd been caught leaving the country on a private Learjet owned by a Greek billionaire. There had been something so sad about the once-press-friendly teenagers suddenly donning dark glasses and refusing to look at the cameras.

Conner was never going to let her interview him. She'd known it was a long shot from the beginning, but she'd gone after it anyway. Her dad always said you had to break a lot of eggs to make an omelet.

"No, you wouldn't," he said. "If you agree to this, I will specify the parameters and if you break one of the rules outlined for you, then you leave and never bother me again."

She shook her head. "If I agree, then we will hammer out an arrangement that works for both of us. Why would you even suggest this?"

"Because I know you are going to say no," he said with the confidence of a man who knew he held all the cards. "Though I would really like to kiss you."

She knew the offer of an interview had been too good to be true. She'd never be able to be someone's mistress. Her mother would have a cow for one thing. She raised all her daughters to be strong and independent. But that didn't mean that Nichole didn't long to feel Conner's arms around her.

"One kiss, one question?" she suggested.

He arched an eyebrow at her. "And that would be enough for you?"

"Is one kiss really going to be enough for you?" she countered. She had never felt instant lust for a man before. Well a man in real life. There was no denying that the first time she'd seen Daniel Craig as James Bond she'd been in instant lust. But this was real. Conner was touching her and she didn't want him to stop touching her.

"No," he admitted.

"Good. Then we keep the kiss-question ratio?"

He shook his head. "One kiss is all I want. More than that and you'd have to agree to being my mistress."

His mistress. That sounded oddly exciting to her as she'd always secretly wanted to be Gigi and have Louis Jourdan take a look at her and decide he wanted her. But could she do it?

"I want to do a series of interviews about dating and the way that our society is dominated by online dating sites and services like Matchmakers, Inc. I hadn't planned on asking you anything personal, Conner," she said.

"You wouldn't have asked me if I ever used those services?" he asked.

She shrugged. "Okay, I would probably have asked you some personal questions, too. I'm a good reporter."

She was dying to know if his father's secret family was the reason why he was still single. And she knew that if she got this story from him, she could name her own price and sell it to the highest bidder. But the price was high. Could she still look at herself in the morning if she agreed to this kind of arrangement?

Newspapers paid for interviews all the time, but paying with her body…well, it didn't feel right to her. Could she string Conner along? Make him think she'd sleep with him and sort of give him enough kisses to get what she needed without going through with it?

Ugh! She had no idea. Especially since the spark of lust that had ignited from the first moment she'd seen him was now growing inside her.

Conner was asking her for something she'd never given any other man—control over her body. But he was offering her something he'd never given any other woman—entrée into his very private and secluded life.

"I thought so. What will it be, Nichole? Do you want to come with me and be my mistress or should I signal one of the security staff and have you escorted from the property?"

She tipped her head to the side, weighing the matter carefully. Of course she should say no. There was no other answer that made any sense. But being sensible wasn't at the forefront of her mind just now.

She was intrigued. Turning away, she led him to a bench surrounded by high hedges so they had some privacy.

His hands were on her shoulders, the waves of his body heat engulfed her and the scent of his one-of-a-kind aftershave enticed her. She wanted, at the very least, one kiss.

"I can't decide until I've had one kiss," she said. She'd always been a gambler who wasn't afraid to take a chance and maybe get the big payoff. A kiss shouldn't be that big a deal. But there was something in Conner Macafee's eyes that made her believe it was.

"Why?"

"So I know exactly what I'm bargaining for. Sexual chemistry doesn't always add up."

He stroked one hand down her bare arm until he reached her waist. Wrapping his hand around her, he drew her closer until they were pressed against each other. His other hand slid deeper into the hair at the back of her neck. He positioned her so she was off balance and she had to grab on to him. She held him at his waist and looked up again into those blue eyes of his.

He lowered his head slowly, watching her the entire time, and she licked her lips, which felt dry. But Conner didn't move any faster. He had thick lashes that were as dark as his black hair. They were pretty, she thought, but then everything about this man seemed to be pleasing to her.

She felt the brush of his breath over her mouth a second before his lips touched hers. His were moist and hard and perfect. The caress of their mouths was light and made her lips tingle. He angled his head and then she felt the tip of his tongue slide over her lips and into her mouth.

He rubbed his tongue over hers and she forgot to breathe as the tingling from her lips spread down her neck and chest. Everywhere he touched her became a hot spot of intense feeling and she leaned more firmly into him. She pushed her tongue against his and tasted the inside of his mouth.

He pulled back, but continued to hold her. She knew that walking away from Conner Macafee was the only sensible thing to do. But her body was aching, her breasts felt full and she wanted to rub them against his firm chest. His eyes were narrowed as he studied her and she saw a hint of indecision in those eyes.

That hint was enough to convince her that Conner was as thrown by their embrace as she was. She held on to him, lifting her head and rubbing her lips over his one more time before stepping back.

"So, is it question time?"

"Yes. And that counts as a question," he said.

Damn. She should have realized that playing games with

him was going to be a challenge and winning wouldn't be that easy.

"Let's talk," she said. "I didn't realize you'd be so tricky."

"Not tonight," Conner said. "I have to get back to the party."

She wasn't about to let him walk away…not like this. She stopped him with her hand on his arm. He half turned toward her and she stepped in front of him and put her hands on either side of his face and kissed him for all she was worth.

His hands went to her waist, holding her to him as his mouth fell to hers. This kiss was brazen and bold, earthy and sensual. It tore her apart at the moorings, leaving her nothing to hold on to except Conner. And she clung to him.

She was shivering as he lifted his head and came back for nibbling kisses before he gently disengaged from her.

"So yes to being my mistress?" he asked. His tone was arrogant, but she knew he had every right to feel confident.

She'd just thrown herself at him. "Not so fast. I have a question for you and no cheating like last time."

"Why do you want to ask me another question?" he asked.

"I need to be sure the information you're giving me is worth the price I'm paying for it."

"Very well," he said. "Ask your question."

"Why are you still single when you own a very successful matchmaking service?"

"I prefer to be," he said.

"That's cheating."

"How do you figure?"

"That's a nonanswer," she said.

"That's the only one I have…so are you still interested?" he asked.

"Maybe. But your answers are going to have to be better," she said.

"I'm holding all the cards," he said.

"Are you?" she asked, knowing he wanted her. She went back over to him and this time she didn't kiss him. Instead she leaned in close, letting her body brush against his. Her breasts were against his chest as she put her hand on his shoulder and leaned close to his ear to whisper directly into it.

"I think I have something you want."

His hands came to her waist and drew her hips forward until his nudged her. She felt his rock-hard erection pressing against her center and shivered.

"We will hammer out the details in the morning," he said. "Be at my office at eight."

She nodded, but he'd already turned on his heel and was walking away. All she could do was watch him leave, but she knew she'd won a victory of a sort. The chemistry between them wasn't something that could be denied and she wasn't going to let him keep pushing her away.

There was no need for her to stay now, so she headed for her car. She knew that it was risky, but she was going to take him up on his bargain—she wanted both the story and the man.

Two

The next morning Nichole dressed to the nines before leaving her apartment on Manhattan's Upper East Side. She caught a glimpse of herself in the mirrored elevator on the way down and the wolf whistle she attracted getting in the cab confirmed she was rocking it.

Normally she would have walked the few short blocks to Conner's office building, but she wasn't taking any chances with messing up her hair or her heels. She'd had one get stuck in a subway grate just last week. If she was bargaining with a master like Conner, she had to bring her A game.

She gave the cabdriver the address and sat back, forcing herself to relax. But her mind was a jumble of last night's kisses and the questions she wanted to ask. She was going to be like Ann Curry—friendly and seemingly open to him but asking the hard questions he didn't want to answer.

She needed to show him that she was here to win. That

she was a serious reporter…but the fact that she'd bargained a question for a kiss might have jeopardized that. She'd just needed entrée, though.

The cab pulled to a stop in front of Conner's building and she paid the driver before getting out. She took a deep breath as she stood and walked toward the revolving door. The street was busy with commuters on their way to the office. She didn't hesitate as she walked boldly into the lobby.

She smiled at the security guard as she told him her name and he got so flustered he dropped his pen. She gave herself a mental high-five and took the guest badge he handed to her. He directed her to the middle bank of elevators.

She got on the elevator and was surprised to find she was on her own on the ride up. When she got to the correct floor, she exited and saw the large logo for Macafee International. When she entered the office, the receptionist took her name and directed her to have a seat in the guest lounge, which she did.

She was offered coffee but she declined. She wasn't here for beverages. She was here for Conner Macafee.

"Ms. Reynolds, please follow me," the receptionist said after a couple minutes.

She was led down a long hallway to an office with Conner's name on the door. It was open and she stepped inside. The first thing she noticed was the size of the office. It was huge, with a wall of windows that overlooked the city. She stood there for a minute with the sun casting a shadow over Conner so she couldn't see his reaction to her.

She walked into the room and found he'd stepped around his desk to offer her his hand.

"Morning, Ms. Reynolds."

"I think we've moved beyond formalities at this point, Conner. Please call me Nichole."

He shook his head. "Bold as ever."

"Did you really think I would have changed overnight?" she asked. "Maybe you aren't as savvy as I gave you credit for being."

He laughed, and the sound made her want to smile. He was fun. If they'd met under different circumstances... maybe. Maybe, what? she asked herself. They would never have met if her friend Gail Little hadn't decided to go to a matchmaker, which had ultimately led to the TV show.

Gail had decided to give matchmaking a try after she'd struggled to find a guy she wanted to really date. As the owner of a PR firm she was busy and didn't have time. When she'd told Willow and Nichole about the service, Willow had jumped on the idea of filming Gail's experiences for her next TV show.

"I'm sure I'll still surprise you," he said.

She was sure of that, as well. "So have you decided to give in to me and just do the interview? Think how refreshing it will be to get it out of the way."

"Please have a seat," Conner said. "I think you must be getting light-headed if you believe that an interview would be refreshing for me."

She walked to the leather armchair placed in front of his desk and sat down. She leaned back and crossed her legs while he watched her. She shifted on the chair and let the hem of her dress ride a little farther up her thighs to see his reaction.

His pupils dilated and he leaned forward, resting his elbows on his desk. Now she knew that she hadn't imagined the attraction between them last night. It had been so strong and so potent she was almost afraid that she'd been dreaming.

"Have you thought more about being my mistress?" he asked.

"I thought I made it clear that I wouldn't do that…I was hoping you'd have come to your senses," she said.

"There is nothing wrong with any of my senses…I'm a man who goes after what he wants, Nichole, and I always get it."

"You've met your match," she said. "I never lose."

"Never?"

Not unless she counted her rather nasty childhood, but Nichole never did. That was the past and she'd been too young to know how to deal with it.

"Not in recent memory," she said. "I'm sure we can come up with something—"

"I already have. I want you. You want me. We both have something the other desires. Now it simply comes down to figuring out how far each of us is willing to go to get it."

She knew he was serious. She could see it in his eyes. "I'm willing to keep the kiss-to-question ratio."

He shook his head. "I'm not. I can't believe you'd be satisfied with that scenario. I'm not the kind of man who multitasks that way. When I have you in my arms I guarantee that you won't be thinking of questions."

A warm shiver slid down her spine. She wanted to be in his arms and she knew it would take very little for him to do what he'd said. She could just give up on the interview and have an affair with him. It would be like lightning hitting dry ground, striking hot, causing a fire to burn out of control until it was put out.

Then he'd go his way and she'd be left alone. She leaned back in the chair, uncrossing and recrossing her legs because she knew it would distract him and give her time to think. But the extra time didn't make her path any clearer. She wanted more than an affair.

She could find white-hot sex if she wanted it, but this interview was once in a lifetime. And she doubted that

Conner would want her if she just gave in. She was going to make him chase her.

"I don't think so, Conner," she said. "You seem like a very competent man and I am more than confident that if you put your mind to it you could answer my questions easily...unless you're afraid of what you might reveal if your guard is down."

She saw that her comment hit its mark as he leaned back in his chair and crossed his arms over his chest. Where before he'd been leaning forward to engage her, now it was as if a barrier had come down between them. Here was the Conner Macafee she'd expected to find.

He didn't like that she'd already found a chink in his armor. He knew the only way to handle Nichole was to show her the door and get on with his life. But he wasn't used to losing and didn't intend to start now. She wanted him and she wanted her interview and he thought it was about time she learned that Conner Macafee didn't back down.

He was going to have her and she was going to acquiesce to his demands. No other solution would satisfy him.

"I have no weaknesses, Nichole, but you are welcome to keep looking for them."

She shrugged delicately and uncrossed her legs again. His eyes immediately tracked the movement. He liked the bit of thigh he kept glimpsing with each shift she made in the chair. He sensed that she was doing it to distract him and probably to turn him on, but he didn't mind.

He liked that feeling of being on the edge of control. It made him work harder to keep his focus and not let her win this round.

Or any round. He didn't like losing and he hated that she was using her innate femininity as a weapon. He knew she was aware of it—well, at least suspected she knew how much she affected him. Duh, right? He'd offered to make her his mistress. She knew he wanted her.

"Everyone has weaknesses, Conner, and I've already figured out one of yours," she said.

"And that would be?"

"You like to be in charge, and if someone threatens that control you don't like it," she said.

He shrugged. "That's not an unusual reaction."

"No, it's not. But you know that I have something you want and I'm not going to give it up easily," she said.

"I'm very glad. I don't like things that are easily attained."

She smiled at him then and he knew that she was savoring the sparring as much as he was. In another world he would have enjoyed knowing her as a woman, not just as a sex partner.

"Good. So here's my thought. We start with my questions—"

"Not happening, honey. No matter how many times you cross and uncross your legs, you aren't going to get me hot enough to agree to that."

"What would get you hot enough?" she asked.

He shook his head, unwilling to reveal that her flirting with him would be enough. "Become my mistress and you'll find out."

"I'm trying to avoid that," she said.

"Why? We both know it's what you want," he said.

She nodded. "It is. But I have my professional integrity to think about."

"Integrity. I didn't know that crashing a party had any high moral value."

"I came as a plus one," she said.

"Whose?"

"Um…"

"That's what I thought. I admire that you're willing to go to any lengths to get this interview," he said.

"How can you be sure of that?" she asked.

"You are sitting here," he pointed out. "As I was saying, I admire your guts. But I think you need to acknowledge that all of your cards are on the table and I'm holding an ace up my sleeve."

"Are we playing for high stakes?"

"Yes, I believe we are. I don't want you to think that my offering to make you my mistress means I don't respect you."

"Sure you do."

"I definitely respect you and I want you. It's the easiest way for us both to get what we want. It's a business arrangement."

"I'm not interested in that," she said. "Perhaps if you knew what I was writing about, it would make you see there's nothing to fear and we could try to have a normal relationship after I write the article."

He wasn't interested in that. He knew from his own feelings on the matter of relationships that he would never marry or settle down. And though he'd never formally had a mistress, in general the women he involved himself with knew he wasn't in it for the long haul.

"I doubt that would work," he said.

"Why? Because I'm not from your echelon?"

He shook his head. "Not at all. It's just that I'm not relationship-minded. Never have been. I saw the dark side of it from my parents' marriage, of course, but also from friends. It's just not to my taste."

"I'd love to quote you on that."

"Well, you can't."

"Honestly, Conner. That is the type of article I want to write. I think even you can see that it's not invasive at all."

"I've already offered to let you interview me if you become my mistress."

"What if I just ask you about the business?"

"You can do that through my marketing department."

"But your marketing department isn't you. I want to know why someone who's so disdainful of relationships would try to set people up."

"In a word?"

"If that's all you will give me," she said.

He bit the inside of his cheek to keep from smiling. He liked that she never just gave in. "Money."

"Money?"

"That's right. There's a lot of money to be made from people looking for that special someone."

"That's so cynical."

He gave a wry shrug of his shoulders. "Obviously I don't run around telling our clients that, but that's my feeling. If the company didn't make money I would have cut it from my portfolio a long time ago."

She leaned forward. "I thought it was a family business."

"That's all you're getting out of me until you agree to the terms."

"What terms?"

"I will answer your questions and you will be my mistress."

"For how long?" she asked.

"A month," he said. "Long enough for us both to still enjoy each other."

"You're not listening to me," she said quietly. "I'm not going to just bow to your wishes."

He stood up and walked around the desk, stopping right

in front of her and leaning back against it, his long legs stretched out so that his well-shod feet were on either side of her. "I won't hold it against you when you do."

She wanted to scream. He was frustrating and so arrogant she wanted to take him down a peg or two. She was tempted to agree to his deal and then back out of it when she got what she wanted. Could she string him along for enough time to get a story?

Could she live with herself if she did that?

She had been brought up in a family where lies—not outright lies but lies of omission—were routine. That was one of the main reasons she'd become a reporter—to expose the truth. So, no, she couldn't lie to him or herself in hopes that she'd get a story without having to pay the price.

"I can't do it," she said. "I have to look myself in the mirror each morning."

He crossed his arms over his broad chest, the sides of his jacket parting so she could see his dress shirt underneath it. This would be so much easier if she wasn't tempted by him. If she didn't want him.

But she knew that anything worth having was worth sacrificing for and she was just going to have to push on and stick to her guns. She'd meant what she said: She had to look at herself every morning and she couldn't do that if she sold her body in exchange for an interview—even if it was a once-in-a-lifetime chance.

"Have you ever paid for an interview?" he asked her.

She sensed where he was going with this. "It's not the same thing."

"Answer the question," he said in that forceful way of his.

"I'll bet you were never spanked as a child," she said.

"What makes you say that?" he asked.

"You are way too arrogant," she replied. "Yes, I've paid a source for an interview."

"Then how would this be different?"

"I get your point—I really do—but we're talking about sex, and there has always been a stigma to paying for it or doing it in exchange for something."

He nodded and leaned forward, putting his hands on either side of her chair so that she was now surrounded by him. His face was just inches from hers and she could see those thick dark lashes of his and the compelling blue of his gaze.

His masculine scent—clean, crisp and spicy—surrounded her. "If I asked you to hire painters to do the walls of this office in exchange for the interview, would you?"

She bit her lower lip. A part of her wanted him to talk her into this. That way she wouldn't have to accept all the blame for the fallout—and she wasn't about to fool herself that there wouldn't be a fallout.

"Of course I would. But I wouldn't just give in. Tell me something. Give me some information that is going to make it worth my while. Sweeten the pot for me," she said.

"I want you."

Those bald words sent a shiver down her spine and made her lean a little bit closer to him. She wanted him, too, but that wasn't the issue. The issue was ethics and pride. She wanted him to want her enough not to make it a business deal.

She licked her lips and noticed that he tracked the movement with his eyes. His nostrils flared as he leaned in even closer and brushed his lips over hers. Just that touch of his mouth on hers sent a pulse of desire through her entire body.

She turned her head to the side. "I want you, too, but I'm not going to give in to physical desire."

"That sounds like a challenge," he said.

"You can try to make it one," she said. "I need to talk about the interview. How about I agree to be your mistress after the interview is done?"

"How could I trust your word?"

She frowned at him. "I'm not known for lying."

"Yet, the day we met you'd snuck into a party to which you weren't invited," he said, stepping back to lean against his desk again.

"True, but that wasn't lying. No one asked to see my invitation."

"Semantics. I want to know I can trust you and the only way I can be assured of that is if we are both giving up something we normally wouldn't."

"God, I'd hate to sit across the bargaining table from you," she said.

He flashed a wicked smile. "I do win a lot, but mainly because I just don't back down."

"I stand my ground as well. How about a little friendly necking in exchange for an interview about the business and the reality TV show? I'll forward you the article before it's published and you can read it to see that I'm keeping my word."

"I'm not interested in making out with you. I want the entire woman when I take you in my arms again. Nothing else is going to satisfy me."

"Okay, we're making progress here," she said, crossing her legs again. "I have something you want very badly and I'm willing to negotiate with you for it. But you have to give a little ground here. What's the bare minimum you are willing to take in exchange for an interview?"

"You bare naked on my desk for fifteen minutes and I'm allowed to do whatever I want to you," he said.

She blushed. She should have been prepared for his

brazen words, but she hadn't been. "Um…no. That's not happening. I don't have the kind of body that would stand up to that much scrutiny."

"You look very fine to me," he said.

She shook her head. Looking good with clothing on was way different than looking good naked, something she realized again and again when she got out of the shower and caught a glimpse of her out-of-shape body.

"Maybe you won't be happy with what you see if I got naked," she said.

"If I'm not satisfied, you still get your interview," he said. "But I know that I'm going to enjoy every inch of you."

She nibbled her bottom lip.

"Come on, red, you know you want to do it. Just give in and say yes, and everything you dreamed of can be yours."

She wasn't too sure she believed that, but a part of her wanted to. She wanted to put her faith in this man who didn't believe in anything, but that seemed like the surest way to broken dreams and a broken heart as well. Because she knew she couldn't separate her heart and soul from her body.

Three

Nichole wasn't a woman who ever veered from a path once she stepped on it. She'd decided to be a journalist and pursued it wholeheartedly. Not just in the workplace, but in her personal life. She'd made choices that kept her single and free to be the workaholic she was today.

She loved her life and didn't regret any of her decisions. But now…she was tempted to make a big change. The kind of change she knew could potentially harm her and her career. She had to be very certain if she agreed to this arrangement with Conner that no one ever knew the details. And she had to be sure she could get her story and keep herself from falling for him.

A tall order. Not impossible exactly, but not easy, either. She just needed time to think and that was out of the question while she was with Conner.

"I can see that your method of negotiating is one of squeezing water from a stone, but I am not going to be pushed into accepting your position as the only one. I know that we can come to terms that will be suitable to both of us."

He walked back around his desk and took his seat again. "I've put all my cards on the table. I'm not going to budge."

"I don't see why not. I'm the one with everything to lose," she said, nibbling her lower lip. She was losing him and she didn't want to.

"Come on, you must see that talking about my personal life in any way isn't easy for me," he said.

She stared at him, feeling a pang of sympathy, remembering coverage of him as a teenager, and she started to soften toward him. But then she glanced up and met his gaze with her own and realized that he was playing her.

"That's not going to work. You're only going to let me see the side of you that you're comfortable with. We both know that you play your cards close to your chest."

"I do. And that's not going to change. Yet, you're an anomaly. I haven't wanted a woman as much as you in a long time, but that could be a danger in itself. I've made my offer and I'm not backing down. If you walk away, I'll probably always have a wistful what-if feeling toward you, but that's life."

She walked over to his desk, perching on the edge of it right next to where he was seated. Though he'd been glib and tried to play her, she knew that he was vulnerable as far as his father was concerned. He didn't want to answer any questions about the past, but she was already seeing how it had defined him.

"If I agree to keep the personal questions to a minimum and just use my own observations…"

"No."

"Conner, you have to give a little."

"I already have," he said, reaching over to put his hand on her thigh.

He rubbed one long finger over the inside of her thigh, tracing a pattern that made sensations flow up her leg to the very core of her. She wanted this man. And all the justification she was trying desperately to find wasn't going to make a bit of difference. She simply wanted to stay. And that was the bottom line.

She could tell herself that she was after the story of a lifetime, but she knew her motivation was rooted in something much more primal.

"I am not going to write something that is scandal-ridden or sensationalized. I think that a lot of people are struggling with finding a mate in today's society, and I'd really like your take on that."

His hand skimmed down her thigh to her knee. She'd had no idea that it could be that sensitive. His touch was warm and brought her an intense awareness each time he moved his hand over her. She stood up and stepped away from him.

"I don't know that you are going to answer any of my questions."

"What do you want me to say?"

"Tell me something, give me a preview of what kind of story I'll be getting so I know I'm not just giving in to your will at my own peril."

He arched one eyebrow at her. "Your peril? That sounds very Victorian and just a tad melodramatic."

"Dang, I was going for more than a tad," she said with a grin. "But seriously…"

"Seriously," he said. "I decided to keep the matchmaking company for two reasons. The first is because it makes me a lot of money. And that's really the only reason that counts. You can't be a businessman in this economy and not give serious consideration to something that is keeping you solvent."

"I agree," she said. This was the kind of information she wanted. He was talking about matchmaking as if it were a widget being made in a factory, and to him it was. "What was your second reason?"

He leaned back in his leather chair and steepled his fingers over his chest. "I want to use it as a vetting tool for my friends. One of my cousins was the target of a gold digger and I hated what she did to him. I didn't want to see anyone else in that situation. Given my own past with my father and the secrets that people keep in relationships, I think having a firm like Matchmakers, Inc. involved in setting up dates is the safest way for people to meet."

She had gotten more from him than she had expected. "That is so cynical. A lot of people meet without doing a background check or having their likes and dislikes tallied and are actually happy with each other."

"I'm willing to bet that they aren't in my socioeconomic bracket. And I'm not saying that to be snooty. There is a different set of variables when you are talking about old money and family fortunes."

"Tell me more about that," she said.

"I'm afraid that's where your sneak peek ends," he said. "If you want any more material for your story, then you're going to have to agree to be my mistress."

She swallowed hard. He had given her just enough to make her want to ask more questions. Her instincts had been right in pursuing him. Conner had the potential to be a career-changing interview.

"What does being your mistress involve?" she asked.

Conner had barely given her any insights that he hadn't shared with friends over the years and was relieved to see that it was enough for her. He understood what she wanted from him and he knew that there were lines he'd always been afraid to cross. Lines that he didn't want to chance letting her know existed because Nichole had proven this morning in his office that she was more than equal to him.

She was willing to sacrifice to get the story and he knew that being in his bed wasn't exactly a hardship. But he also knew that because he'd pushed her into this position he was asking her to do something that was hard for her.

"Being my mistress will involve a lot of pleasure," he said.

She flushed. "I'm not asking for a rundown on what kind of sexual pleasures you will be pursuing with me. I mean, from a logistical standpoint, I have no idea what makes a woman a mistress."

He had no idea, either. He'd never had a mistress before, though his friend, Alexander Montrose, did all the time. Alexander believed that money was at the root of all relationships and the only way to manage relationships was to make them business deals.

"You will move into my penthouse apartment here in the city and be available to me whenever I want you."

"I have my own place and a job."

"For the duration of our arrangement I'd want you to live with me. As you know, I'm the busy CEO of a huge multinational conglomerate, so even though I said you'd be available whenever I want you, we're not talking every hour of the day. Though I think I would want to have you to myself for the first twenty-four hours so I can sate the hunger that has been riding me since I first laid eyes on you."

His words were nothing less than the truth. He had to give Alexander props for the mistress thing. It was so much easier than dating. No coy games or subtleties—just full-on lust. He liked it. He didn't expect to be keeping mistresses full-time in the future, but the more he thought about the idea, the more he liked it.

"I want you, too. What else?"

"I will pay your bills. I might need you to accompany me to a few social events, but given that you are writing an article about me perhaps we should keep that to a minimum?"

"Why? Reporters follow their subjects all the time," she said. "But if I agree to this, I don't want anyone to ever know about our arrangement. I think moving into your place would be a bad idea. There will be doormen and maids who will know I've stayed there."

"What's the alternative?"

"You can come to my house," she said.

"You have neighbors, right? The risk of discovery is just as great. Perhaps you should just disclose that we are dating and let the cards fall where they may after that."

"I'd have to ask my boss," she said. "Actually, that sounds like the best option. Most people won't guess that we have any other arrangement."

"Exactly. A win-win. You get your story, I get your body and we both leave happy."

She tipped her head to the side, staring at him askance. "Happy?"

"I think so," he said. And he'd be in control of the article. He didn't know why he hadn't thought of this before.

"Okay, so I want two different stories from you. The first is strictly about the dating industry and your involvement with the venture. I'll include the stuff you mentioned earlier about vetting gold diggers, that sort of thing."

"Fine. That's no problem at all," he said, glancing at his calendar to see what would have to be moved so he could spend the rest of the day with Nichole. In her arms. It looked like the mistress deal was in the bag.

"The second story will be about the effect your father's betrayal has had on your own dating habits and maybe your sister's. I think it's interesting that she is the home guru yet single."

"No."

"No? To what part?" she asked.

"All of it. I'm not talking about my father. I'm certainly not talking about Jane."

"I want two stories," she said.

"I will not talk about my private life," he said. "There's no merit to it other than gossip and you said you weren't that type of reporter."

"I'm not. I think it's a human-interest story. There are readers out there who want to know what happened to you. They watched you grow up—"

"Too bad. I'm afraid that's a deal breaker for me," he said.

She retreated around the desk, back to the guest chair. He could tell her mind was going one hundred miles an hour trying to come up with something else to tempt him. But he knew the mistress deal was over. He wasn't going to talk about his father—ever.

He never had and never wanted to. His father was nothing more than part of a past that Conner had already forgotten. "I think we're through here."

"Are we?" she asked. "I'm willing to settle for a different type of story."

"The one on dating?" he asked.

"Definitely, but also one on you. Maybe as a corporate raider," she said. "You have done some amazing things with failing companies."

"Yes, I have. But that type of article is more suited to the business pages than the lifestyle section that you write for," he said.

She sighed.

"What's your decision, Nichole? Will you be satisfied with the one article from me in exchange for being my mistress?" he asked.

At this point it was all down to her. He'd live up to his end of the bargain, but he knew there were lines that he'd never allow her to cross. And seeing the way she interviewed him he knew that he'd have to be careful not to reveal too much. He also knew that he was playing a dangerous game by bringing her into his home because reporters were never really off the record.

She wouldn't be satisfied with just one interview with him and one article. But she knew there was more than one way to get what she wanted. And for now it seemed that she should retreat and give this some thought.

It was easy to say that it didn't matter to her if she slept with Conner in exchange for the information she needed. She was a sophisticated, new-millennium woman, but the truth of the matter was she was a bit old-fashioned. And though she often told her friends that she liked to keep her personal life light, so it didn't interfere with her professional life, she knew that deep inside she was afraid to let anyone too close to her.

Living with Conner, even for only a month, would jeopardize that. She was afraid that once she saw what she'd been missing all these years, she might want more.

"I have to think this over," she said. "It's not a decision I can make easily."

"I can respect that," he said. "To be honest, I didn't expect you to agree to it."

"Then why did you make the offer?" she asked.

He shrugged. "There's something about you that brings out impulsive instincts."

"I feel the same way about you," she said. He was different than other men. It wasn't just the wealth and the upbringing that he'd had. It wasn't just that she thought she'd known him from the background research she'd done. It was that she'd been surprised by how different he was than she'd expected.

He gave her a half smile that she was coming to realize was his only way of smiling. He didn't give much away when it came to emotions. He'd admitted to wanting her, but that was lust and she suspected he'd put it down to chemistry. But his real feelings he kept buttoned up.

She glanced at her watch, surprised that she'd taken up thirty minutes of his time. It felt like she'd just arrived. That should be another warning to her. She wasn't herself around him.

"I should be going. I'll get back to you in a few days to let you know my decision."

He stood up and came around his desk, holding his hand out to her. She took it in hers, realizing that although they'd kissed they'd never shook hands. Unsurprisingly, his handshake was firm, conveying confidence.

But it also made her want more. She wanted him to touch her as he had earlier on her leg. She couldn't believe she was going to walk out the door when she wanted him as badly as she did.

"Are you sure I can't change your mind?" he asked as he rubbed his thumb over the back of her knuckles.

"No, I'm not at all sure. But this seems like the kind of thing I really need to think about," she said.

"Thinking is going to overcomplicate it. No one has to know what's between us. How is it any different than a relationship?"

"The agreement. We'd both know that we aren't just dating," she said.

"It's more of a commitment than most relationships."

"Most of yours?" she asked.

"Yes."

"How many dates do you usually have?" she asked. Thinking that she wanted to know personally, but also testing her theory that his father had damaged some relationship skills in Conner.

"Two. You?" he asked.

"Um…about the same. I tend to seek out men who aren't looking for anything long term."

"Why?" He still held her, his thumb making those maddening circles on the back of her hand.

"My career. I don't want anything to derail it."

"Interesting that you are going to walk away from me and the interview that could rocket your career to the next level," he said.

"It is interesting," she said. "But I'm not sure that we'd be okay even if my boss knew we were dating. I can't take a chance of losing everything that I've worked so hard for."

She pulled her hand away. "I…would you reconsider the one-kiss-to-one-question ratio?"

"Not for the long term," he said.

She arched her eyebrow at him. "What does that mean?"

"I don't want you to walk out that door without having one last kiss with you," he said. "I know that once you get back to your office and have time to mull my offer over— you'll more than likely decide I'm not worth the risk."

She suspected by the way he'd worded it that he'd heard that at some time in his past. Was it only his father's secret family that had soured Conner on relationships or was there more to it?

"I doubt I'd ever think you weren't worth the risk," she said impulsively.

"You already do. Or you wouldn't be leaving," he said.

"Touché," she said. She wanted so much more than what he'd offered her. She saw in him a man she could invest herself in. He was a mass of contradictions and she knew that she shouldn't take a chance on him. Shouldn't let him into her heart and mind, but she was afraid it was too late.

"So one last kiss," she said at last.

"Yes," he said, pulling her off balance and into his arms.

Her handbag fell to her feet as she put her hands on his shoulders and looked up into that bluer-than-blue gaze of his. She let herself get lost in his eyes. Forgot that she'd come here for business, but was going to leave with only pleasure.

It was worth it. This little forbidden delight that was Conner Macafee and his kisses.

She leaned up toward him as his mouth slowly descended to hers. He was taking his time, she realized. He didn't want this to end, either. And that made her like him a little more than she already did.

She tipped her head to the side as his mouth moved over hers. His hands caressed her back before settling on her waist and drawing her ever closer to him. He wrapped his arms around her shoulders and drew her closer so they were chest-to-chest. Her nipples hardened as his tongue traced the seam between her lips.

Just that little touch made everything in her body clench as she moistened in her core. Her hands clutched his shoulders as he deepened the kiss. It was demanding and passionate and most of all it said goodbye.

Four

Conner felt more than a little regret as he held Nichole in his arms for what would probably be the last time, but he knew that he had to say goodbye to her. Though she stirred him as no one else had in a long time, she wasn't the right woman for him. And despite owning a match-making business, he wasn't even looking for someone.

Her lips under his were soft and her mouth tasted like the most exotic flavor he'd ever sampled. He was addicted to it, he thought, as he plunged his tongue deeper and deeper. He wanted to sate the hunger for her in this one kiss, but that didn't seem possible.

He craved more. Why didn't he just take what he wanted? It was clear that she wanted him, too, and though she was trying to use that desire as leverage to do a deal with him, in his arms she didn't seem to remember that she was a reporter.

He swept his hands down her back, lingering at the

small span of her waist. He lifted her off her feet and held her against him, feeling her almost melt into him as all plans of deals went out of his mind. All he wanted was for this kiss to never end.

She clung to his shoulders and her breasts rested so softly against his chest. He took two steps backward so he could lean against his desk and continue to hold on to her. Her legs parted and she brushed against his erection as she wrapped those long legs of hers around his hips. He moaned deep in his throat and heard an answering mewling sound from her.

He slid his hands from her knees up to her thighs as he'd been longing to do since she'd walked into his office and perched so femininely in his guest chair. She moved against him, her legs moving around his hips to find purchase with her knees. But the position was awkward and he cupped her butt in both his hands and turned them so she was sitting on the edge of his desk and he was standing between her spread thighs.

The movement pulled their mouths apart and she braced her hands on the desk behind her, looking up at him with those wide, fathomless eyes of hers. Her lips were wet and glistening from his kisses and there was a pretty pink flush of desire on her neck and upper chest.

"One more kiss and then I'll ask my question," she said.

He nodded, not even listening to her words beyond… *one more kiss*. He wanted their next kiss to end with him buried hilt-deep in her sexy body.

He lowered his head again and she started to lean up toward him, but he liked her spread out before him like a sexual offering and stopped her with a hand on her chest. "Stay like that."

"Like this?" she asked, leaning back on her elbows again.

"Yes," he said, his voice sounding guttural to his own ears.

He leaned down over her, taking his time, his hands slowly moving up from her waist to her breasts. He skimmed the edges of them at her side and then moved farther up, tracing the line of her collarbone and the skin underneath. "I love your freckles."

She scrunched her nose up at him. "I don't. They aren't sexy."

"On you they are," he said, lowering his head to lap at one of them. "Are they all over your body?"

He felt her skin heat under his hand and he glanced up, surprised that she was blushing. "Yes."

He growled as an image of her completely naked on his desk, covered only in those freckles, danced in his mind. He reached for the zipper at the side of her dress, but she stopped him with her hands on his and he realized he was in his office.

He stood up and started to walk away from her to cool down, but she pushed her fingers through his and drew his hand to her mouth where she kissed his palm. Then she lifted herself up into a sitting position.

She shifted forward, wrapping her arms around his shoulders, and the motion moved her feminine core against his hardening shaft. She lifted her free hand to his neck and urged his head down toward hers.

The next moment their lips met and once again he found that the only thing that mattered was Nichole and this moment. This time she didn't just let him devour her mouth, she was aggressive and passionate in the kiss as well— more of a participant this time. He felt her move his hand to her breast and then her hand fell away and he was cupping her through her bra and dress.

He had a realization that Nichole was bold and brash in her reporter mode, but the woman was a bit shier and softer. He liked that. He wanted to have that woman in his arms. But he knew that he could never separate the two.

This was goodbye and he needed to remember that. He wanted this complex woman, but these stolen moments in his office were all he was ever going to have.

He rubbed his forefinger over her breast as he plunged his tongue deep into her mouth and when he felt her nipple bud against his finger he concentrated his touch there. She shifted in his arms and then he felt the strong suck of her mouth on his tongue.

His hard-on strained against the front of his trousers and he used his other hand at her waist to draw her closer to him. He rubbed himself against her and felt her rock her hips against him.

He tipped his head to the side to take more of her mouth, wanting to see this through to climax. Nothing could stop them now. Their bodies knew what they wanted and now that they were touching their minds had stopped arguing for anything else.

He pulled the fabric away from her body and slipped one finger under to feel the softness of her skin.

There was a loud rap on the door and Conner stepped away from Nichole. He realized that he couldn't let his body take over. This was probably how his father had gotten into the mess he'd made of their lives.

"Just a minute," he called, turning back to see that Nichole was struggling to get up off the desk. There was a strong blush on her face and she looked unkempt. He gestured to his washroom. "Why don't you take a minute to repair the damage I did."

She nodded and walked across the room. As he watched her go, he knew that he'd had as much of Nichole as she could afford to give.

* * *

Nichole was losing control. She realized how little she had over herself and Conner. He was making a mockery of her and the entire interview. She had to stop compromising herself this way. She closed the door of the executive bathroom behind her and locked it.

She saw herself in the mirror. Her hair and clothes were disheveled and she hardly recognized the woman staring back at her. She met her own gaze and gave herself a frown.

"You worked hard for your career and you are about to let a man derail you," she said to herself sternly, reaching into her purse for her makeup bag.

"Dammit, Nic, you can do this. You can beat him." She reapplied her lipstick and put some powder on her nose. Then she straightened her clothing, turning to make sure she looked as good from the back as she did from the front.

On the plus side, she could definitely count on the fact that she had kept Conner off balance. But her plan to beat a strategic retreat had almost backfired. She'd underestimated her own desire for him. And that ticked her off. She'd always been in control in her attractions with other men.

She'd learned early on to keep a level head, but Conner somehow had gotten through her guard. She knew that she'd never be able to sleep with him and still be the calm, cool reporter she prided herself on being.

And without that who was she?

She leaned in close to the mirror, searching for the answer, but the woman looking back had no answers. She realized that she was taking too long in here. She didn't want Conner to think that she was scared to come back out or to even let him guess he might have gotten the upper hand in their negotiations.

Which, even she had to admit, he had.

She opened the door and found that he was standing across the room staring out the plate-glass windows at the city below. She walked over to stand next to him. Having grown up in Texas with lots of wide-open spaces, she always found it a little breathtaking to see the cityscape spread out before her.

"I think you owe me one answer," she said.

"I believe I do," he said. His voice was firm and calm, but he seemed subdued around her now.

She wondered if their embrace had shaken him as well. It was easy to look at him and see a man who was always in control of his life and his environment, but she had seen little chinks in that facade.

"Fire away," he said.

But she was still muddled and the questions she wanted answers to had nothing to do with an article. She wanted to know why a normal relationship was out of the question with him. Why he'd only consent to take her as a mistress when it was clear he wanted her. But that wasn't the question to ask now.

She cleared her throat. "Let me grab my notebook."

"By all means," he said, walking back to his desk and sitting down.

It was hard to believe he'd been kissing her so passionately only a few minutes ago. Sitting before her was a totally different man…the man she'd been expecting him to be from the beginning.

Given that this might be her last chance to question him, she wanted to make it count. She took a deep breath and asked the question she really wanted an answer to. One that was highly personal and one that, depending on the answer, could give her the backbone for her entire article.

"I've read finance magazines that say your business acumen is very much like your father's. Are you still single today because that's not the only area in which you and he are the same? Do you fear making the same mistakes he did?"

His mouth tightened and she knew that her probing questions were making his hackles rise, but he owed her. She'd given him much more than the one kiss he'd asked for. And she was fairly confident that he was an honorable man.

"I'm not going to answer that other than to say that many people have said my business instincts and my father's are the same, and aside from the fact that we both have helmed Macafee, I can't see any other similarities."

"My question isn't really about the business, Conner. I want to know if you're afraid of being too much like him."

His mouth tightened and for the first time she felt a shiver of something almost like fear running down her spine. He wasn't a man she wanted to be at odds with.

"No comment."

"No comment?"

"Did I stutter?" he asked flippantly.

She stood up and walked to his desk. Placing both hands on the surface of it, she leaned over toward him. "We had a deal. I more than held up my end of the bargain."

He steepled his fingers together and stared at her over the top of them.

"You did, red. I never expected for things to…get so hot, so fast."

"Me neither."

He gave her a little half smile as he dropped his hands to the armrest on his chair.

"I'm not asking for much. I won't print a direct quote from you on this in my article, but I do want to know because I think that is part of the cornerstone of who you are today."

He shook his head. "I'm afraid I can't answer that."

"*Won't* is more like it. You owe me," she said.

"Ask a different question," he said. "I'll allow you time to come up with one."

"I have asked my question and I expect an answer. You didn't bargain for any approval over the question I wanted to ask. I'm a reporter. I need the answer."

"Reporters are only privy to certain parts of their subjects' lives. As I'm sure you know."

"Yes," she said. "But certainly a mistress has more rights."

"No," he said. "I'm afraid she doesn't. You only have the access that I grant you."

She was stunned speechless. And so angry she wanted to punch him. He had tricked her. She doubted that if she went to bed with him he'd hold up his end of the bargain he'd wasted her morning trying to get her to agree to.

"Excuse me?" she said. For the first time he heard the tang of her Texas accent coming through.

"I'm not giving you carte blanche," he said.

"I didn't set any limits on that embrace," she said.

"But you did," he pointed out, remembering his strong desire to see the expanse of her creamy, freckle-covered skin.

"We're in your office," she said. "We can't go too far."

"Yes, we are," he conceded. "But I believe you were attempting to do what I'm doing now. We are each limiting the access the other has to what they want. Trying to give away just enough to keep this going."

She nibbled on her lower lip. "I can see where you're coming from, but what you just said makes it almost impossible for me to trust you. I want this to work. I think that readers have an interest in *you* and not just your company."

"I don't care about the personal aspect. How would you feel if I asked you personal questions?"

"Go ahead," she said. "I'm an open book."

"Why are you still single?"

"I told you—I'm a workaholic. I love my work."

"Me too," he said. "There's your answer."

"Ha! That was my answer. We both know there is more to you than that."

"And I know there is more to you than what you said. Something must have hurt you in the past to make work your sanctuary."

He saw by the way she narrowed her eyes that he'd hit the nail on the head with that observation. "So? I'm not in the public eye."

"Neither am I," he said.

"That's not true. You're in the newspapers all the time and your sister has a cooking show…I think if we walked out on the street right now you'd be instantly recognizable. No one would know who I am. And that's the reason why this article is so relevant."

"I don't believe there is any interest in me beyond gossip," he said. "I've given you the answers I am going to."

"You can be a hard-nose, can't you?" she asked.

"And you can be a pit bull when you aren't getting your way," he said. "We are too similar. We both expect to win and in this situation it's simply not going to happen."

"I guess you think you're the winner?" she asked.

"I intend to be," he said.

"Well, then, there isn't anything more to say, is there?" she said, standing up and gathering her bag.

He knew immediately that he'd made a huge mistake in how he'd worded that last bit. But she'd struck a nerve with her question. It was exactly as he'd feared when she'd asked to interview him. The information she wanted was too personal and he wasn't about to let anyone—even someone as rocking-hot as Nichole—have that kind of access to him.

"You didn't win," she said, opening the office door and looking back over her shoulder at him. "I'm not giving up."

"I wouldn't expect anything less," he said.

She walked out, hips swaying, making him wish his secretary hadn't knocked on the door when she had. But there was no going back and changing the past; he knew that better than most. God knew there were a lot of things he'd change.

He sat back in his office chair and wondered if their encounter would affect her coverage of the show and of Matchmakers, Inc. He hoped she was professional enough not to let it.

He knew she was. She wanted the interview with him and she was going to keep working on different angles to get it. There was a part of him that was looking forward to her next move.

There was a knock on his door. "Come in."

"Your next appointment is here," Stella said. Stella was in her mid-forties, a single mother of two college-aged boys. She'd been his secretary for the last ten years and he relied on her a lot to make sure the office ran smoothly. "Shall I send him in?"

Conner glanced at the calendar on his computer screen. He wanted to groan. It was Deke, one of his old boarding school buddies whose family fortunes had been tied to a Ponzi scheme. Now he was in need of a job.

"Yes, please do," he said. "Stella, don't let this meeting run more than thirty minutes."

"Yes, sir. I never do," she said with a smile. Which was why she'd knocked on the door earlier.

Conner didn't know what to do about his old friend. A part of him understood Deke way more than he wanted to. He knew what it was like to see your family name in the papers with scandal attached to it.

He stood up as Deke entered. He was six foot and had dark curly hair. He'd rowed crew at boarding school and still had the upper-body strength of an athlete. But Deke's family money had meant that he'd spent the last fifteen years jet-setting around the world. He had no real-world skills.

"Hello, Deke," Conner said, holding out his hand.

Deke shook it. "Hey, man. Thanks for seeing me today."

"No problem. I meant to call you, but I've been busy. What can I do for you?" Conner asked.

Deke looked uneasy for a moment, then gave him a smile. "I have an investment opportunity for you."

Conner suspected as much, which was why he'd put his friend off as long as he had. He walked back to his desk, gesturing for Deke to take a seat in the chair that Nichole had recently occupied, and then invited his friend to explain the opportunity to him.

While Deke talked, Conner's mind wandered back to the time of his life when he'd been in Deke's shoes. Luckily, Conner had been young enough to readjust, but Deke was an adult, used to a certain standard of living.

"I don't have many skills, but I'm damn good at sailing and my wife suggested we start up one of those barefoot-type vacation cruises. All my assets have been seized, so I don't have my old yacht, which is where you'd come in. If you agree, I'd like you to invest in one yacht that I can use for these high-end sailing vacations."

Actually, it was a great idea. Conner asked a few more questions and Deke produced a business plan with some solid numbers in it. Seemed Deke had married a woman from a working-class background who wasn't afraid to help her husband out of a bad situation.

Conner agreed to invest in the company from his private funds and not Macafee International's. Deke was a happy man and once he left Conner felt strangely alone.

He knew it was his own choice to be where he was, but hearing Deke talk about his wife and her ideas had made him long for something he never had before.

Conner wondered if Nichole would react the same way if her man got in trouble. He didn't know. But then he didn't know anything about her except that he wanted her.

CATHERINE GEORGE

Five

Nichole dropped by the set of *Sexy & Single,* the reality matchmaking television show featuring Conner's company. She had been writing a blog about the daily goings-on of the show behind the scenes. Lots of information and maybe just a little gossip.

The producer of the show was one of her closest friends, Willow Stead. Willow came over the moment she walked on the set, which today was a private balcony near Central Park West. The other part of their trio, Gail Little, had been the first bachelorette on the television show. And Nichole had been happy to report that Gail had tamed her match, the Kiwi billionaire Russell Holloway, and they were engaged.

The second couple featured on the show, fashion designer Fiona McCaw and billionaire game developer Alex Cannon, were also engaged. Willow said her show was on a roll.

But Gail was back to her job in PR and the weekly drinks were the only excuse the three women had to get together anymore. Which was to be expected. A part of Nichole wished that she and her friends had more time for each other, but life was busy.

"Hey, lady!" Willow said, coming over to hug her.

"Hey, you," Nichole said, trying for her usual cheeriness but it was hard since she'd only just come from Conner's office and he'd...well, he'd left her shaken.

"Rikki Lowell is a handful. I can't imagine how she runs a successful party planning business. She's so demanding," Willow said about the show's latest bachelorette. She linked her arm through Nichole's. "I'm so glad I'm not the matchmaker."

Nichole smiled. "She has a reputation for demanding perfection."

"I've seen it. I don't think Paul is going to measure up in her eyes."

"He's a partner at one of the top corporate law firms in the country. He should meet at least some of her standards," Nichole said. She'd interviewed him and found him to be charming, smart and very sweet. "Is he too nice for her?"

Willow threw her head back and laughed. Nichole noticed that Jack Crown, the celebrity host of the show, glanced over at them. He'd gone to the same high school as the three friends, which made them all meeting here a bit of a small-world type thing. But he'd been two years ahead of them and Nichole hadn't remembered him at all. "Don't look now, but Jack Crown is watching you."

"Is he?" Willow asked without turning around.

"Yes, he is. Why is he watching you?"

"I have no idea," Willow said.

"Liar."

Willow blushed. "We can chat later."

"We will. I'm going to call Gail and tell her to bring a bottle of wine and we are coming to your place tonight."

"Fine, but anything I say must be kept off the record," Willow said.

"It always is," Nichole reminded her friend. Her comments made Nichole wonder if that was part of why Conner thought he couldn't trust her. Was he afraid that she'd reveal all sorts of intimate personal details about him in her article?

"Do you ever worry that I might slip something you said to me into an article?" Nichole asked Willow.

Willow wrinkled her forehead. "No. I know you wouldn't do that. I was just teasing."

Nichole nodded. "I guess we've been friends for so long we trust each other."

"We do indeed. I don't trust him though," Willow said.

"At least he's cute."

"Ha. Like cute counts for anything."

"Can you believe we went to high school with him? I certainly don't remember him roaming the halls. But then I was pretty much in the library all the time and something tells me Jack didn't even know the school had one."

Willow laughed, but there was something quiet about her as she turned to stare at Jack. "I did know he was at our high school."

"I'm going to ask you more about that later," Nichole warned as Jack started to walk over to them.

"I've got to run," Willow said and left before Jack joined them.

Nichole smiled up at the show's celebrity host. "What's new?"

"I got to fly with the Blue Angels last weekend," he said with that big toothy grin of his, which she noticed didn't quite reach his eyes. And his eyes…well, they followed Willow as she walked away.

"For one of your shows?"

Jack was the host of nearly half a dozen shows that aired on three different networks.

"Yes. *Extreme Careers,*" he said. "Want an exclusive interview with me?"

"Ha, you talk to every reporter. There's nothing exclusive with you."

"What can I say?" he asked, again with that grin. "I liked the article you wrote about Gail and Russell. I was worried the backstage stuff might be sensationalized…"

Nichole shook her head. "Gail is one of my closest friends. I'd never print anything to hurt her."

"I didn't realize that. So you're from Frisco, Texas, too?"

"Yes. I don't remember you at all, so if that's what you're thinking, we're in the same boat," she said.

"I wondered about that. Why didn't we ever run into each other? A pretty redhead like you…I definitely should have noticed you in high school," he said.

"Probably because I spent most of my time in the library or in Mr. Fletcher's classroom. And I don't think you did either of those things."

"Did you write anything I might remember?"

"Only if you found the weekly lunch menu fascinating," she said.

He laughed. "Oh, that was you. I'd like to talk to you later for *Extreme Careers.*"

"Okay, but being a society reporter isn't considered 'extreme' at all."

"I know. I was hoping you could use your contacts to help me find a war reporter."

She nodded. "I know a couple of guys who've been to

the Middle East. I'll ask around and see if they'll talk to you about it."

"I don't just want to talk to them, Nic. I'd like to go over there with a reporter and do some frontline shooting, too," he said.

She didn't think that any of the reporters she knew would want to be on a reality television show, but she'd been wrong about Gail wanting to be on one. "I don't know if anyone will agree to that."

"Let me talk to them. I can be very convincing and, if not, there's more than one way to get the story I want."

Jack left and she talked to the bachelor and the bachelorette for a few minutes before leaving herself. One of the things Jack had said continued to resonate with her. There was more than one way to get a story and if Conner wouldn't talk to her, she might have to look into the other members of his family, especially Jane Macafee. She was in the spotlight and might have some insights into Conner that Nichole could use for her story.

Conner sent three calls from his sister to voice mail and narrowly missed her when she showed up at his office for a surprise visit. Finally, when she tweeted about him, he couldn't ignore her anymore. He picked up his office phone and dialed Janey's number.

"It's Conner," he said when she answered.

"I know it is. Why are you avoiding me?" she asked. "I wanted to find out what happened with that redhead reporter."

"Nothing," he said. Jane was as bad as could be when it came to snooping into his personal life. Besides, Nichole was the last person he wanted to discuss with anyone in his family.

"Nothing? You spent a lot of time with her for nothing."

"She was…difficult," he said.

Jane chuckled. "Good. Sometimes I think life is a little too easy for you."

He wished. "Did you just call to harass me?"

"You called me," she pointed out. "I tweeted about you."

"Which I have repeatedly asked you not to do," he said. Whenever she mentioned him on the internet or on her show he got slammed with emails through the company website, asking if he was on Twitter or Facebook.

"Sorry, bro, but if you ignore me you must face the consequences."

"So what did you want?" he asked.

"I'm having a dinner party tomorrow night and have an odd number of guests so I need you to come. It's at eight so you'll be done with work."

"Are you filming it?" he asked. One time she'd been doing her cooking show and he'd shown up unaware that the dinner was going to be taped. He had left without saying a word to her, but they'd had a huge fight over it later. Janey didn't understand why he still had such an aversion to the press. In her mind what had happened with their dad was over years ago. But it was different for Conner.

"No. I think we both remember what happened the last time I did that."

"Thanks, Jane. I'd love to come to dinner then. Eight?"

"Yes," she said. "Did you talk to the reporter?"

"Only to get her to leave. She wanted to do a story on Dad and that old scandal," he said, which wasn't quite true, but he didn't want Jane talking to Nichole. His sister could be stubborn once she had an idea about something.

"Oh, that's too bad. I thought she was doing a piece on the television show that Matchmakers, Inc. was part of."

"She is. But she also wanted to delve into the personal

side of it. Stuff like why do I own a matchmaking firm if I'm determined to stay single."

"A question Mom and I have pondered many a time," Jane said.

"Um…you're single, too. Would you like to delve into your reasoning on that?"

"I haven't met Mr. Right," she said.

"I don't think you're even looking," Conner said. "I do want you to be happy."

"I am happy. And I suspect you are, too. We aren't like other people who need a spouse to be fulfilled," she said. "We learned a long time ago to depend on ourselves—and each other, of course."

"Of course," he agreed. He hadn't realized that Janey felt the same way he did. He'd tried his best to shield her from the worst of the fallout with their father. "I thought I protected you from most of the family drama that made me such a loner."

"You did. You have always been the best big brother a girl could ask for."

"The best…that's not what you tweeted a few minutes ago."

She laughed as he'd hoped she would. It bothered him that his sister was as closed-off to interpersonal relationships as he was. He'd adjusted to living alone and not letting anyone get too close, but Janey was gregarious and always had a group of friends around her.

"Love you," she said.

"Love you, too, brat. Is Mom coming to this soirée of yours?"

"No, she has a board meeting for her charity. She said if you didn't agree to come she'd call and put the screws to you."

"You two always team up, don't you?"

"If we didn't, you'd stay shut away in your office like some sort of hermit and then, when we finally did see you, who knows what you'd look like."

"Now you're just being silly," he said. He liked that Jane had retained most of her upbeat personality. She'd always been a giggling little girl, but after their father left and the scandal broke there were times when Conner thought he'd never hear his sister's laughter again. Luckily, over the years they'd moved on and slowly that specter of pain from their father had dulled.

"Yes, I am. See you tomorrow night," she said and hung up the phone.

Conner spent the rest of the afternoon in meetings and pretending that he didn't notice that Nichole Reynolds had tweeted about him right after Jane had. He knew that social media was the wave of the future, but personally didn't care for it.

Which was why he continued checking to see if Nichole tweeted anything else. He didn't know why he was so obsessed with that woman. Sure, she could kiss his socks off and just the thought of her in his arms gave him a raging hard-on, but otherwise she was just like every other woman and reporter he'd ever met.

He was kidding himself. He knew that she was different and he wanted to see her again. Except that he'd done everything in his power to make sure she didn't come back.

He knew that he'd said some callous things to her the last time they were together. A better man would call and apologize or send flowers or jewelry, but he couldn't be that man...*wouldn't* be that man. As Janey had said, life was easier when he only depended on himself, and he wasn't about to risk that for Nichole Reynolds, no matter what her effect on him.

* * *

Willow lived in Brooklyn in one of those brownstones that were going for millions of dollars back before the beginning of the recession. She had waited and watched the property she wanted until the market had gone soft and she'd been able to buy it. That was one thing about her friend that Nichole envied. Willow had patience. She would wait as long as it took to make something happen.

Nichole knocked on Willow's door just as another cab pulled up and Gail Little stepped out. Gail smiled and once again Nichole was struck by how happy her friend looked. The two women hugged and said hello. Willow opened the door with her cell phone to her ear. She gestured for them to come in.

"So why did you call this emergency meeting?" Gail asked as they both entered Willow's foyer and walked down the short hall into the kitchen.

"Willow is keeping a secret about Jack Crown," Nichole said, opening the cabinet to get out three wineglasses. Gail opened the bottle of chilled Chardonnay she'd brought and poured three glasses.

"She is?"

"I'm not," Willow said, entering the room. "I knew him in high school."

"How come you never mentioned it before now?" Nichole asked.

Willow sighed and took a long swallow of her wine. "Let's sit down if you're going to grill me. I ordered a pizza and it should be arriving in fifteen minutes."

"Good," Gail said with a big smile. "Plenty of time for you to tell us all about your Jack."

"He's not my Jack…I tutored him when he was a junior."

"What year were we in?" Nichole asked.

"Freshman."

"That must have been humiliating for him," Gail said.

Willow flushed and looked down at her glass. "I have no idea. He needed help in English. That was all."

It didn't take reporting skills for Nichole to know there was a lot more to the story than Willow was letting on.

"Yeah, right," Gail said.

"Why didn't you ever mention him to us?" Nichole asked.

"Because he was just another kid I was tutoring. You guys didn't want to hear about that."

"Was he cute back then?" Nichole asked. "He had to be. He has what scientists call the golden triangle. His face is perfectly symmetrical. He is beautiful," Nichole said.

"Don't let him hear you say that. His head might explode," Willow said.

"That sounds like a lot more than just his old tutor talking. What happened between the two of you?" Gail asked.

Willow finished her glass of wine and poured another. "He...he was just a teenage boy and I was a stupid teenage girl who thought that just because he was nice to me in private we were friends in public."

"Oh, Will, I'm so sorry," Nichole said, putting down her glass to go and hug her friend. Gail joined them, rubbing Willow's back.

"That's too bad. He seems like a fun guy now," Nichole said.

"You'd probably like him," Willow said. "He keeps things light, the way you do."

Nichole wasn't too sure she kept things light anymore. She certainly hadn't been able to do that with Conner. She wanted something more with him, but wasn't sure she trusted herself.

"He's not my type," Nichole said, mentally comparing

Jack to the clean-cut handsomeness of Conner. He'd suddenly become her fantasy man. No surprise there, given the chemistry that sizzled between them.

"Since when?" Willow asked.

"You don't understand what I liked in my boy toys," Nichole said.

"*Liked?* Do you want something else now?" Gail asked. "This is exciting. Do you have a man in your life? One you're serious about? I think you were grilling Willow to keep us from asking you about your life."

Nichole bit her lower lip. "Truthfully, there is a guy, but it's complicated and I really don't think anything is going to come of it. But I sort of wish something would."

"How could it be complicated?" Willow asked. Then she gasped. "Oh my God, is he married?"

"God, no. Do I seem like the kind of woman who'd date a married man?"

"You said it was complicated, and you don't let anyone get too close," Gail said gently.

"I meant—never mind, I don't want to talk about it," she said, feeling hurt that her friends thought she'd get involved with someone who was married.

"I'm sorry," Willow said. "I guess you cut a little too close with your questions about Jack and I wanted to strike back. I know you'd never have an affair with a married man."

Nichole nodded but she wasn't ready to forgive yet.

"Don't be mad, Nic. We can't always choose the people we're attracted to. We never thought you'd do anything with a married man, but that doesn't mean you wouldn't fall for one," Willow said.

"You're right about not being able to choose who we fall in love with," Gail added. "I never thought I'd fall in love with a playboy. I mean Russell just wasn't my kind of guy…but then somehow I started caring for him."

"He *was* your kind of guy. You just couldn't see it because of all the flashbulbs that surrounded him," Nichole said, letting go of her hurt.

"I had a crush on Jack in high school," Willow blurted out. "It ended badly and I've been wanting to get back at him ever since."

"Get back how?" Nichole said.

"Some kind of humiliating revenge. I thought I'd gotten past it, but I haven't."

"Oh, dear," Gail said.

"Oh, dear? What are you, ninety-two?" Nichole asked. "Our BFF is contemplating revenge. We need to use stronger words here."

Gail shook her head. "Willow isn't going to change her mind no matter what we say, and I have a feeling it's going to be—"

"Complicated!" Willow said. "Just like Nichole's situation."

The women laughed as the doorbell rang. Once the pizza was on the table, talk turned to the TV show and Nichole let Conner and how he complicated her life dominate her thoughts. There had to be another way to get her story and still get him. Because she wasn't ready to let him slip away just yet.

Six

Conner worked up until the last moment when he could leave and get to his sister's apartment but still be fashionably late. If Nichole had been here to see him, she'd have realized that he wasn't a social animal. He dreaded parties and other social gatherings because he didn't do small talk.

Yeah, right. He didn't like them because he hated being around strangers who might know too much about his past. He didn't know how Jane was able to survive her life in the spotlight. There were always people who wanted to prod her about the past and ask questions about how it had felt to go through that public humiliation.

Something that Conner hoped never to relive. When he was a block from Jane's apartment, he remembered that he hadn't picked up flowers and didn't have a bottle of wine. And there was no way he could show up at the home of America's leading hostess without a hostess gift. Janey would nail him for it.

"Stop at the corner, Randall," he said to his driver. "I need to get a bottle of wine."

"Yes, sir," Randall said.

Conner ran into the corner store and bought the best bottle of wine they had available. It wasn't a pricey vintage, but he knew it was one his sister liked. As he was waiting in line to pay, he caught a glimpse of Nichole's face next to her byline in *America Today* that the woman in front of him was reading.

Glancing over the woman's shoulder he saw that the article was about Jack Crown's latest daredevil stunt. Conner had met Jack since he had been brought in to host the reality TV show, but he hadn't had a chance to get to know the other man.

"Why don't you buy your own copy?" the lady said, folding the paper in half and putting it on the counter.

"My apologies," he said, embarrassed to be taken to task by the woman. But he wasn't going to read the society column of any paper. It was little better than gossiping and he wouldn't do it. Though, if he'd been pressed about it, he would have had to admit that Nichole's writing style was very inviting. He'd wanted to read more.

But not today. He paid for his wine and shoved the sexy, redheaded reporter out of his mind as he got back in his car. Randall drove the rest of the way to Janey's high-rise but when he pulled up to the curb, Conner was reluctant to get out.

"I'll text you when I'm ready to leave," he said. "It might not be too long."

Randall laughed. "I'll be in the garage waiting for your text."

Conner took the elevator to the penthouse, entering the code that would take him straight to his sister's place. When he exited the elevator, he had the uneasy feeling that he hadn't timed his entrance to be as late as he'd hoped. The first person he saw when he walked into her hallway was Palmer Cassini.

"So, she roped you into this as well," Palmer said.

"Sadly, yes. But I was corraled because of an uneven number of guests."

"She used a different technique to get me to come tonight. How have things been?"

"Good. Business is business, but we're turning a profit and in this economy that's all anyone can ask for."

"You say it like you're blasé about it, but I know that you're in the black because of your savvy and leadership," Palmer said.

Conner tucked his hands into his pockets and tried to look nonchalant, but Palmer had hit the nail on the head. Conner wasn't about to let years of hard work go down the drain because of a downturn in the economy.

"Where's my sister?"

"In the kitchen with another guest. One I suspect she may have invited for you," Palmer said.

"Should I leave now?" Conner asked jokingly.

"I wouldn't. She's a very sexy woman."

"Do you wish she'd invited this mystery woman for you?" Conner asked. He'd be more than happy to bow out of the dinner and let Palmer go after her.

"Not at all. I shouldn't tell you this, but I'm very interested in your sister," Palmer said.

"You are?"

"Yes, but she's stubborn and refuses to let me get too close."

"Don't mess around with Jane," he said. "If you hurt my sister…"

"You'll come after me, I know. But it is she who hurts me. She doesn't want anything serious to develop between us and every time I get too close she shuts me out…the way she did at the Fourth of July party."

He sympathized with his friend. It was hard to court a difficult woman. And though he wasn't courting Nichole, she was difficult and he did want her. He clapped a hand on Palmer's shoulder. "If it's meant to be, it will happen."

"I'm not sure I want fate on my side. She can be a cruel mistress," Palmer said with a laugh. "Come on, let's go join the women."

Conner wasn't too sure he wanted to, but hopefully whoever Jane invited would take his mind off Nichole, even if it was only for tonight. He needed to put the attraction to her in perspective. He'd been working too hard. That was probably why he'd been so consumed with her lately. She was, after all, the only woman he'd kissed and held in his arms recently.

Of course, he was going to be thinking about her all the time. In fact, he was doing it again, he thought. The woman in the kitchen even sounded like Nichole as he walked toward it. But as soon as he crossed the threshold and entered the kitchen he realized it wasn't his mind playing tricks on him.

Nichole was standing next to his sister, helping her assemble some kind of hors d'oeuvre and laughing at something Jane had said.

Remembering the last time he'd seen her, only a day ago, and how she'd left his office, he couldn't help believing that she was here for revenge. She had gone after his sister when she hadn't been able to get the dirt on him.

Of course a woman like Nichole would never understand that Jane wouldn't give him up. His sister was very loyal and knew better than to talk about their past with any reporter, no matter how charming she was.

"Uh-oh, my brother doesn't look happy to see you," Jane said.

"I told you he wouldn't be," Nichole said.

He handed the bottle of wine to Jane and gave her a kiss on the cheek. "Nichole, I'd like a word with you in private. Jane, I'm using your study."

He turned on his heel and walked out of the kitchen. He heard the sound of Nichole's carefully measured footsteps behind him as he entered Jane's study and waited for her to follow him in.

He gestured for her to enter the room and carefully closed the door behind them. Then turned to her. "What the hell do you think you're doing here?"

Nichole had suspected that Conner wouldn't be pleased to see her here, but she'd never guessed that he'd be so angry. "Having dinner."

"Don't be flip. It was cute the first time we met but now, not so much," he said.

"I'm not being flip. I'm here to have dinner," she said. "I had no idea that you'd be here."

"I'll bet you didn't."

"What exactly do you think I'm plotting to do?" she asked. "Your sister is friends with one of my BFFs…actually you know her, too. Willow."

"So you asked Willow to get you close to my sister?" he asked.

"Not at all. I want an interview with you, Conner, not with your sister. She's funny. She thinks that we'd make a great couple but that you're letting the fact that I'm a reporter keep you from seeing my charms—her words," Nichole said.

"I can see your charms," he muttered under his breath,

rubbing the back of his neck. "So you're not here to dig up dirt on me?"

"Nope," she said. "And I'm insulted that you'd think I'd do something like that. I'm a reporter with ethics. I don't make up stories or dig through trash cans to find leads. When I write my story on you, it will be because you gave me an interview," she said. To be honest, she was insulted, and who wouldn't be. But more than that, she was hurt. She had the feeling that Conner was doing everything he could to keep from being attracted to her, and if that meant that he had to make her into the bad guy, then she guessed that's what he'd do.

"I'm not going to stay for dinner. Your sister is delightful, but you are not the man I thought you were," she said, turning to walk away.

He grabbed her elbow and tugged her off balance until she fell back into his arms. "I'm sorry."

"What?"

"I'm sorry," he said. "I felt cornered by Janey and then seeing you just added fuel to the fire. I was happy to see you, I *am* happy to see you. Dammit, Nichole you are a complication."

"I said the same thing about you earlier. I don't know why you can't simply agree to the interview and then we can get it out of the way."

"I can't do that. I've sworn I'd never give an interview."

"But you can bargain with me?" she asked.

"It's the only card I have," he admitted. "It's the only thing I can say to keep you interested in staying here with me."

"You could try asking me to stay."

He shook his head. "I can't. Then you'd know how much I really want you."

She wrapped her arms around him and hugged him

close, putting her head on his shoulder. "You make things so hard."

"I do, don't I?"

She pushed away from him, taking a step back. "Why is it so hard for you?"

"Just between us?" he asked.

She nodded, realizing that he was more vulnerable than she ever would have guessed.

"You're not like the women I've dated," he said.

She arched one eyebrow at him. "That sounds like a line."

"It isn't. You are so fiery and passionate about your work. You don't let anything stand in your way, but when I hold you in my arms I can tell that you are equally passionate with me. I want that, but…"

"But what?"

"You can also seem all-consuming," he admitted.

She understood what he was trying not to say. She suspected that he was afraid, just as she was, of letting him get too close. They were both, in their own ways, used to being alone, and meeting someone of the opposite sex with this much chemistry was a threat.

There was a knock on the door before it opened. Jane stood there with two cocktail glasses in her hands. "I'm sorry I didn't tell each of you that the other was coming."

"It's okay," Nichole said.

"We'll talk later," Conner said.

But Jane just handed a cocktail glass to Nichole and then hugged her brother. "It's your own fault for refusing to say what happened between the two of you. I knew there was something going on."

She saw Conner's face tighten and though Nichole knew Jane had been trying to help, she'd just done the one thing guaranteed to drive Conner further away from her. He prided himself on being aloof, but he couldn't be if everyone saw them as a couple.

Dinner wasn't as awkward as he'd feared it might be. First of all, the only people at the party were the four of them and since Palmer and Jane were two of his favorite people, Conner found it easy to relax. But that just kept him on guard a little more. He didn't want to inadvertently give anything away to Nichole that she'd use later.

Once the meal was served, Jane was in her element at the head of the table. As the hostess, she kept the cocktails flowing and the conversation moving.

"So, Nichole, inquiring minds want to know. Why did you decide to become a reporter?" Jane asked after Palmer finished telling them a hilarious story about his first polo game when nerves had gotten the better of him and he'd fallen off the horse.

"I always wanted to be one. I think I saw myself as a Nancy Drew type when I was little," she said.

"Oh, I liked Nancy Drew, too," Jane said. "But solving crimes isn't the same as being a reporter."

Nichole put her fork and knife down and took a sip of her drink before she leaned forward. "When I was in high school, I had Mr. Fletcher for freshman English and he was the sponsor of the school newspaper. He liked my writing and told me I should join the newspaper staff. I did. I liked it," she said.

"What did you like about it?" Conner asked, fascinated at learning more about her. Suddenly she wasn't just a nosey reporter—hell, she'd never really been just that—but now she seemed more real to him.

"My family had a lot of secrets growing up. Stuff we didn't talk about with each other or with anyone outside the family. That's not healthy. I liked the fact that my job was to find out the truth, to report and let everyone know what was going on. It was such a change from my home life that I was addicted to it, I think."

"Sort of like me and making this perfect lifestyle on television," Jane said. "In real life I'm so not perfect."

"I'd have to disagree," Palmer said.

"You don't know me well enough to disagree," Jane said, wrinkling her nose at Palmer.

"I'm trying to," he said with a laugh.

Nichole picked up her fork and toyed with the asparagus on her plate. Conner wanted to know more. What kind of secrets had she learned to keep? He doubted it was anything like the ones his father had kept. But when she looked up and caught him staring at her, he smiled gently in her direction and she blushed.

"What made you decide to do a cooking and lifestyle show?" Nichole asked.

"I always liked to make my room a retreat. So I started learning how to sew and craft things. And then when we had to leave our home in the Hamptons there was a six-month period where we didn't have a cook—do you remember?" she asked, turning to her brother.

"I do," he said. "You started cooking for Mom and me."

"Well, Mom is an excellent fund-raiser and bridge player, but the woman cannot cook," Jane said with a laugh.

"Sounds like you found your calling," Nichole said.

"I did," Jane admitted. "I just liked the feeling I had when Mom and Conner ate my food. I made them happy and life was good while we were sitting around the table."

Conner wished Janey wouldn't talk like that in front of Nichole. He had no idea what she'd print about him or his sister. He had nothing but her word that she'd only use what she learned in an interview.

"I feel the same way about being at my mother's kitchen table," Palmer said. "We have a cook but my mama likes to cook for me and my brothers. There is such a feeling of love in the dishes she prepares."

"What about you, Nichole?" Jane asked. "Are you like me or your mom?"

Nichole nibbled her bottom lip, something he realized she did when she wasn't sure what to say. "I don't know. It's just me at home and I don't cook much for myself. But I think maybe someday, if I have a family, I'd like to create something special like you or Palmer's mom do."

He didn't like the thought of Nichole having a family someday and he didn't want to acknowledge why it disturbed him. He knew he wouldn't be the man in her life and he didn't like the thought of another man being with her.

"That's sweet," Jane said.

"What about you, brother?"

"What about me? I'm never getting married. I like my freedom too much."

"I don't believe that's true, but that's a conversation for another night," Jane said.

"What about me, darling Jane? Don't you want to know what I'd want?"

"No. I know what you want and it sounds like someone else's dream," she said. "How about some dessert?"

Jane pushed her chair back and stood up. Palmer watched her go and Conner had to admit that he felt sorry for his friend.

"I'll help Jane with the dishes," Nichole said, gathering the remaining plates before she went into the kitchen.

"Why is your sister such a stubborn woman?" Palmer asked, his Brazilian accent heavier than normal. "I could make her happy."

Ordinarily Conner wouldn't have offered any advice. He

made it a policy to stay out of Jane's personal life so that she'd stay out of his. But he liked Palmer and he wanted his friend to be happy. "She doesn't trust happy."

"What do you mean?"

"The last time she was truly happy and trusted someone, it blew up in her face."

"You mean your father?" Palmer asked.

"Yes."

"There's been no man since then?" he asked.

"Not that I know of," Conner said.

"Then I will have to work twice as hard to show her that she can trust me," Palmer said. "That I am nothing like your father was."

"That's going to be hard," Conner said. "Our father did a lot of damage."

The door to the dining room opened and Nichole was standing there. He knew she'd heard his comments and he hated that. If she were just a dinner party guest, he could pretend it meant nothing, but she was a reporter bent on digging up his past.

Jane came back with a coffee tray and a fake smile. She was overly animated and it was almost painful to watch her pretend to be the perfect hostess now when they'd seen her genuinely enjoying herself earlier. The tension between Palmer and Jane was palpable.

Nichole must have felt the same way because as soon as dessert was eaten, she glanced at her watch and said she had an early morning and had to go.

"I'll walk you out," Conner said. He hated that years later his father still had the power to hurt both him and his sister. It wasn't fair that neither of them had found a way to heal from those lies.

"Okay," Nichole said. "But I don't think it's necessary."

"Maybe he wants to be in your company," Palmer

said. "Sometimes a man just wants to prove himself to a woman."

"Or maybe I'm ready to leave as well," Conner said.

He got that Palmer was talking to Jane, but he didn't want Nichole to get any ideas about what he had in mind for them.

Seven

Nichole was tired and just wanted to get home. What had started out as a fun and interesting night had become a little tense as she rode down in the elevator with Conner. Especially when he reached out, pushed the stop button and turned to her.

"Everything that Jane said tonight was off the record. I don't want to see that showing up in your column tomorrow morning," he said.

She sighed and wanted to punch him hard in the stomach. "I already said I have ethics. When are you going to get it? I don't write about what my friends say at their dinner parties. Your warning shows me that I was completely wrong about you from the beginning."

"What do you mean?" he asked.

"I thought maybe we could have a chance as a couple."

"I don't want to be a couple. I want to have you as my mistress," he said.

"I know," she said, reaching around him to start the elevator car in motion again. "I really do have an early meeting and since we've had the mistress discussion before, I hope you won't mind if we skip it now."

He leaned back against the wall of the car and stared at her with that bright blue gaze of his. "Don't be offended. I can't take any chances."

"Why not?"

He crossed his arms over his chest. "When I was nineteen and just starting to take over the reins at Macafee International, *Business Week* sent a reporter to interview me. He was about my age and easy to relate to. He spent a week or so following me around at the office and I let my guard down and talked openly with him. He printed things that weren't part of the interview itself and I learned the hard way that there is no such thing as *off the record*."

She was angry with the reporter who had abused Conner's trust and a little sad for the young man he'd been at that time. "I'm not like that."

"You say that, but then you also told me you'd do anything to get this story. And then I show up at my sister's house and there you are…it doesn't look good," he said.

"She invited me," Nichole said carefully, enunciating her words, though the anger she'd felt earlier about his attitude had disappeared. She had caught a glimpse of the private side of Conner and she wasn't about to let that slip away. He was a man with a lot of complicated emotions. Tonight had proven that. And though he was arrogant and demanding, she was beginning to suspect that was all a ruse he used to keep from being hurt again.

"Why are you looking at me like that?" he asked.

"Because I'm just getting the feeling that I've barely scraped the tip of the iceberg that is Conner Macafee."

"Iceberg? I thought I'd proven I was anything but cool as far as you were concerned."

"Oh, you're red hot when I'm in your arms, but you seem so forceful and solid underneath that it'd be easy to accept you as just a man who wanted a mistress. But then the water moves and I see something hidden in the depths of you…"

"That's pretty deep. I'm really not all that. I'm just a guy who likes to get his way and right now my way would be you in my bed."

"If only that were all you were asking," she said.

"Would you have a one-night stand with me?" he asked.

That point-blank delivery struck her the same way his initial demand that she be his mistress had—with a thrill she couldn't deny, at least to herself, and then a bit of sadness because she genuinely liked him and wanted so much more than just one night.

"Would you sit down to an interview with me?" she asked.

He shook his head. "You haven't changed my mind."

"Are you sure?"

The elevator doors opened and they stepped out into the lobby of the building. There weren't many people there and Conner took her arm and drew her to a quiet corner.

"Actually, I'm not sure. Tonight when you were talking about secrets…I want to ask you about your childhood. Would you be willing to open up to me about it?"

"Maybe," she said. She didn't like talking about her own secrets. It made her mad at herself that she still couldn't break the habits that were ingrained in her since childhood.

"What if I gave you a kiss?" he asked.

She had to smile at him. "You can be a scamp, you know that?"

"Yes," he said. "If sheer willpower won't convince you to give me what I want, I'm not afraid to use charm."

"Is this still a game?" she asked, because she needed to know before she let herself fall any deeper for him.

He pulled her closer to him, wrapping one arm around her waist and leaning in so that his breath brushed her cheek when he exhaled. He smelled the way she remembered him, spicy and delicious, and she wanted to rest her head against his chest and just let him wrap her senses in comfort.

"I'm not sure," he admitted.

With another guy that wouldn't be enough of an answer, but with Conner it was more than she expected. He was so guarded. So used to protecting himself and keeping everyone at arm's length that she felt even that tiny admission was a treasure.

"I'm not, either," she said, looking up at him.

"How are you getting home?" he asked.

"A cab, why?"

"I have my driver waiting. Can we give you a lift?" he asked.

"Why would you offer?" she asked.

"I'm not ready to say good night yet."

"Why not?" she asked.

"You sound so suspicious," he said with a laugh. Pulling out his cell phone, he typed a quick message.

"Well, with you I've learned to be."

"Don't be," he said, cupping his hand under her elbow and leading her to the exit. "I just want a chance at uncovering your secrets."

Conner was happy that Nichole had accepted the offer of a ride from him because he wasn't ready for the evening to end. Randall said nothing as Conner gave him Nichole's address; the driver just piloted the car through the evening Manhattan traffic.

Nichole sat back against the leather seats of the Rolls Royce Phantom. Conner stretched his arm out along the back of the seat and toyed with a strand of her hair, wrapping the silky lock around his finger and then letting it unravel.

"You're making my life difficult," she said at last, turning toward him.

"I know," he said. If he'd let go of his convictions and say yes to having an affair with her, life would be easier, but he didn't know for how long. He suspected it would only last until he got her into his bed and then he'd be back to the same distrust he had now.

"What kind of secrets did your family hide?" he asked. He wasn't going to play around and pretend that he didn't want to know about her past. Knowing the person she was might make it easier for him to trust her. But it would also make it easier for him to figure out what kind of pressure to apply to make her cave in to his desires.

"You still want to know about that?" she asked.

"Stop stalling. You know I want to know every detail about you. And I tried researching you on the internet the other day and couldn't find anything but your column and the articles you'd written."

"You researched me?"

"My attorney advised me to," he said, deadpan.

She narrowed her gaze on him and then started laughing. "Dated a few crazies?"

"No, I was joking with you. I wanted to know more about you. Find out what made the woman behind the reporter tick."

She shifted around in the seat, turning so she faced him.

"There isn't much to tell. My family's secret isn't too bad or too dark. It was more damaging the way we dealt with it."

The way she downplayed it told him that wasn't true. "What was it?"

"Depression. Severe depression that makes the person feel like they should kill themselves," she said.

"Which family member?" he asked, not liking the sound of her secret.

"My mom. She has medicine she can take to control it, but it makes her sort of a vegetable so she hates it. My childhood was a roller-coaster ride and we could never discuss Mom's periods of blueness. That's what she called it."

"What about your dad? Surely, he said something to you," Conner said.

"Not really. He was at work most of the time and he was the one we'd hide it from. I'm an only child, so it was just my mom and me at home," Nichole explained. "When I was little my dad traveled a lot for business and that always brought on my mom's depression."

Conner remembered the one thing she'd said earlier that he'd let pass. "Did she ever try to kill herself?"

Nichole pursed her lips and turned to look out the window. He could see the reflection of her drawn face in the car window as they passed under the street lights. "Once. My dad had to be called home. I was fourteen. He didn't travel after that and my Aunt Mable moved in with us to watch her while he was at work."

"Did that help?"

"Yes. She's much better now," Nichole said. "See, it wasn't so bad. It's not like she hit me."

"Well, it's good that you weren't physically abused, but you still saw things that no child should. Who found your mom?"

"When she tried to kill herself?" Nichole asked.

Conner nodded. He suspected that she had, but he wanted to hear the story from her lips.

"I did. I...I thought she was sleeping and tried to wake her. When I couldn't I panicked and called my dad. I told him everything. He took control and called 911. I just sat on the floor next to my mom holding her hand. It was really horrible," Nichole said.

Conner put his hand on her shoulder to comfort her and then drew her into his arms. "I'm sorry."

"It's not your fault, but thanks. Dad and I had a long talk about everything and after that Mom was much better. You know," she said, turning to look up at him, "it was then I realized if he'd known from the beginning how bad Mom was when he was gone, he would have stopped it sooner. That helped me decide to be a reporter. Maybe I can find out some facts that will spare someone else."

Conner wondered about that. It had been a reporter who'd uncovered his father's second family and that had hardly helped him or Jane. The only thing that could help in those situations were adults who behaved like adults. Parents who understood that their first duty was to their child. Something his father hadn't ever understood.

"I'm glad that you found a career that could help you," Conner said and he meant it. Though it was the one thing that was keeping her from being his.

The car slowed to a halt in front of a walk-up apartment building.

"We're here," she said.

Conner grabbed her wrist before she could open her own door to get out. "I've tried to get you out of my mind."

"Me, too," she said.

He smiled. "Would you please consider negotiating with me again? I don't think I'm going to be able to sleep or even have a moment's peace until we get this resolved."

She nibbled her bottom lip and he leaned in to kiss it.

"Stop chewing your lip to bits. You know you want to figure out something between us."

"I do. Want to come up and have a drink? We can discuss it in my living room instead of in the backseat of your car," she said.

"Yes, I would like that," he said.

Randall got out of the Rolls and opened the back passenger door. Nichole slid out of the car. Conner joined her on the sidewalk, telling Randall he could have the rest of the night off.

"Um…how do you plan on getting home?" she asked.

"A cab."

Conner followed Nichole up the three flights of inside stairs to her apartment. When she unlocked the door and opened it, she stood there, hesitating for a minute. He knew that once they moved forward into her place, something would change between them.

This would be the first time they'd been somewhere private together. Not his mother's party or his office or his sister's apartment, but Nichole's home. And there was the promise of intimacy in that.

Nichole figured that of all the men she'd invited back to her place, Conner was the most dangerous. He wasn't one of her just-for-fun guys, that was for sure. She couldn't even blame that on him. She was the one who wanted something more.

She'd like to say it was because of the chemistry between them, but she knew the mere chemistry was for boy toys. What made her want more with Conner was the depth she'd glimpsed in him. She knew there was more to him than met the eye and her subconscious was driving her to uncover this man's mysteries.

She led him into her apartment, which was a respectable size for New York but not nearly as large or glamorous as Jane's had been. She put her keys on the table in the hallway and as soon as he entered she closed the door behind him.

"Welcome to my home," she said. "I've had enough alcohol tonight so all I'm serving is soft drinks or coffee."

"Coffee sounds great," he said.

"The living room is through there," she said, pointing down the very short hallway. "Make yourself comfortable while I get the coffee. Do you take cream or sugar?"

"Both," he said.

She walked away without looking back. She needed to regain her focus, maybe recall that she was trying to find out about him, not tell him every detail of her own life. But she knew that, somehow, if talking to him about her past helped him relax and eventually trust her, then she'd bare it all.

Hell, she'd seriously considered becoming his mistress for the story. Now she thought it might have been easier to sleep with him than to reveal the parts of herself she'd rather keep hidden.

She had one of those Keurig machines and absolutely adored it. She made coffee at all hours of the day and night now, and she could change blends without having to throw out the entire pot of coffee. Willow called the Keurig her dealer. And Nichole had laughingly agreed that coffee was definitely her drug of choice.

She made two cups in the matching I ♥ New York cups she'd bought when she'd first come to the city as a student. She put them on the serving tray that had been her grandmother's, then placed the sugar dish and creamer next to the cups, along with spoons and napkins, and finally made her way to the living room.

She'd heard if you didn't look at a full cup it wouldn't spill, but the path of coffee stains on her carpet from the kitchen to her home office proved otherwise.

She had expected Conner to be sitting down on the couch or in her recliner. Instead, he was standing up studying the pictures that hung on the wall of her living room. He was in front of a photo of her with her parents on graduation day.

Though he didn't say anything, she could almost sense that he was remembering what she'd told him about her mom earlier. "Seeing her like that, it's hard to believe she has any problems."

"Absolutely," Conner said. "She looks happy and proud of you. They both do."

"As I said, I'm an only child so I was always their entire world."

"That's good. I can stop thinking of you as the Little Match Girl."

"Thank God. I never want you to think of me that way. Come and get your coffee," she said.

She set the tray on the coffee table and then sat down in her recliner so she wouldn't be seated right next to him. His arched eyebrow told her he knew what she was up to.

He added milk and sugar to his drink while she wiped up the coffee that had spilled out of her cup and pooled on the tray.

"Do you?" he asked, holding up the coffee mug.

"Huh?"

"Love New York?"

"Oh, yes. I do. I was so terrified when I first got here, but that quickly faded," she said. "What about you?"

"I don't especially love it. More like tolerate it," he said. He took a sip of his coffee and then leaned against the back of the couch, crossing his legs.

As he settled in there in her house, Nichole knew the last thing she wanted was for him to go home tonight. She wanted to be curled up next to him now and then make love to him in her queen-sized bed later. But the only way she could do that was if she figured out how to get her story *and* her man.

She thought about the night and the dinner they'd shared. She hadn't minded talking about her past when she'd known that it was only Jane, Palmer and Conner who would know about it, but if she'd thought that one of them might blog or tweet about what she'd said she would have felt differently.

"I think I get what you meant when you asked me how I'd feel if everyone read about my personal life," she said.

"Do you? Given your past, I think you'd want to keep it hidden," he said.

"That's what I mean. But most of the people who know me can guess that there is something in my past that keeps me from being in a committed relationship."

"And that has any bearing on this how?" he asked.

"Give me a second. I'm fiddling around with the problem between us. If we can find a way for me to write the story without asking you any direct questions about your past, would that be okay?"

He leaned forward, resting his elbows on his knees. "I thought the golden ticket was me talking about the past."

"It is. But I can see now that you'll never do that and I don't know if I even want to write that story anymore. I'm thinking more that I can interview you about the TV show and then just observe your interactions with your family. I won't ask them any questions and anything they say to me will be off the record, but my own personal observations might make interesting reading."

Conner stood up and walked over to her chair, resting

his hip on the arm as he leaned down over her. "Let me get this straight. You'll observe me and my interpersonal relationships with my family but only interview me about the show?"

"Yes," she said, tipping her head back to meet his eyes with her own.

"In exchange for being my mistress?" he asked.

She hesitated. She'd hoped to just have a relationship with him without the mistress arrangement, but it looked as if that was something Connor had to have.

Eight

Conner was reluctant to agree to anything with Nichole, but at this point she'd become such an obsession that he had no choice but to figure out a way to have her. He knew nothing else would satisfy him. He stood up and walked away from her chair.

Her apartment revealed a woman who had deep roots and connections to the people in her life. Every photo was genuine. No staged smiles, no fake emotions. He wanted to trust her, but the desire he felt for her made it harder for him to do it.

Was he giving her a free pass because he wanted her in his bed or was he seeing the signs of a woman he could truly trust? He just didn't know, and he was afraid to make the wrong choice.

He had no problems acknowledging his own fears. He knew that he had weaknesses; if you pretended you didn't, you were only fooling yourself and headed for a big fall.

He turned to look over his shoulder at her. She chewed her lower lip and stared pensively at him. He should just let go of the mistress thing, but he couldn't. He wanted her to be his completely and only as his mistress would he have the freedom to make their every meeting about sex.

In his head it seemed like sex was the way to go. The one thing that would make a relationship with her manageable. Otherwise, he'd be tempted…hell, he already was tempted by everything about her. And he knew that he didn't want to allow her to mean too much to him.

"You haven't answered my question," he said.

She shook her pretty head, the red hair brushing over her shoulders and her bangs falling forward to cover one eye before she tucked the hair back behind her ear again.

"I'll do it," she said, "but only if you agree to let me capture my own observations about your family and that dynamic. I think that will add a personal touch and that's what my readers expect."

He turned back to look at the wall of photos in her apartment. If he agreed to let her observe his family, he'd leave them all vulnerable. That wasn't acceptable. How could he manage it?

He was so close to having Nichole and everything he wanted. And he was a damn smart man at the bargaining table, no matter who sat on the other side of it. He knew there had to be a way to make this work.

"How would you observe my family? With me present?" he asked.

"Yes, when we went to functions they were also attending. I assume you'd bring your…"

"Mistress," he said. "If you can't say it, how can you agree to be it?"

"I'm going to say *girlfriend*. We can both pretend it means mistress."

"Don't do that, Nichole," he said. "Make sure you know that what we are going to have will be temporary. It's stamped with an end date."

She nibbled her lip again.

"You're going to chew your lip raw," he said.

She stopped. "You're right. Why does it matter what I think about our arrangement?"

"Despite what you might think of me," he said, "the last thing I want is to see you hurt."

"That makes two of us," she admitted.

"Good," he said.

"So you'll do it?"

He would be able to control the amount of access that Nichole had to his family. He didn't know for sure if that would be sufficient, but in the end he knew he was going to agree to this. He would manage her and her access to his life. He'd been doing that with the media since he'd turned seventeen, so he wasn't too worried about that.

"Yes," he said.

"Okay…now what?"

He laughed at the way she said it.

"Well, we have to seal our deal."

"In writing?"

"I don't think so. That kind of document could end up in the wrong hands," he said. "How about with a kiss?"

"A kiss…just one kiss?" she asked, standing up and walking over to him. "One kiss is never enough."

"No, it's not. So let's say a kiss, but take whatever we get," he said.

She nibbled her bottom lip again when he opened his arms to her. She just stood there staring at him and he wondered if now that he'd agreed she was going to back out.

"Second thoughts?"

"Yes," she said softly. "And third and fourth thoughts. It

all comes back to you and the story. I want you both. But a part of me is sure I'm going to regret this."

He closed the gap between the two of them and pulled her into his arms. He hugged her gently, trying to reassure her, yet he honestly had no idea how this would turn out. He hoped by making her his mistress he'd be able to control the influence she had over his life and ensure that his emotions didn't get engaged. But this was Nichole and nothing had gone according to plan since she'd shown up uninvited at his family's Fourth of July party.

"I will do my best to make sure you have nothing to regret," he said.

She tipped her head back and stared up at him with that pretty gaze of hers. "That's the worst part. I know your intent isn't to hurt me, just as mine isn't to do any damage to you, but I'm not sure that as much as we are trying to make this a business arrangement that we'll succeed."

She had a point, but he'd made up his mind and she'd agreed to his terms. He wasn't letting her go or giving her a chance to back out.

"We'll both just have to do our best," he said, lowering his head and taking the kiss he'd wanted all evening.

Nichole was glad to stop thinking and just enjoy Conner's embrace. Tonight hadn't gone exactly the way she thought it would but she'd gotten the one thing she'd set her mind on. Why, then, wasn't she happier?

She was in Conner's arms, enjoying his ravishing kiss, but her mind was reluctant to let her relax and just enjoy it.

"I can tell you're still thinking," he said. "I'm insulted that my kiss hasn't distracted you."

"You shouldn't be. I'm just…oh, I don't know. This is crazy. I spent my entire adult life building my career and trying very had to expose the truth, and I've just agreed to do something that feels like a back-alley deal."

"There's nothing back alley about it. It's inevitable that you and I are going to have an affair. I don't know about you, but I don't feel this kind of chemistry with every woman I meet."

She had to admit that was true. "I guess that's part of why I'm so shy about seeing this through. I know you said by making it a business agreement we could mitigate the possibility of both of us getting hurt, but I don't know—"

"You can't worry about the ending right now when we are just at the beginning," he said.

He'd kept his arms around her and his words were dissolving her fears. She tipped her head back and he lowered his mouth to hers once again. This time, as their lips met, she let her fears melt away.

She wrapped her arms around his shoulders, as his hands slid down to her hips, drawing her closer to him. They were pressed chest to chest, hip to hip, and she wished they were even closer.

His tongue thrust into her mouth. She sucked on it and then let her hands find the buttons of his shirt. First she loosened his tie and then she undid the first few buttons so she could slip her hand under the cloth and touch his warm flesh. There was a faint dusting of hair on his chest and it tickled her fingers as she caressed him.

His hands were busy cupping her butt and drawing her closer to his groin. She felt him hardening against her as he thrust his hips into the notch at the top of her legs. She moaned in the back of her throat.

He tore his mouth from hers and she felt his lips against the side of her neck. He dropped nibbling kisses down the column of her neck, lingering to suckle the spot at the base where her pulse raced.

She tugged his shirttails from his pants and wrapped her arms around his bare torso. She wished she was bare-chested as well, wondered what it would feel like to have him pressed against her right now. She lightly scratched a pattern down his back along the line of his spine, touching him with growing passion as his mouth found hers again.

She let him control her. As if there was any other re-action she could have toward him. He was dominant and that came through in his embrace. He sucked her lower lip into his mouth and gently rubbed his tongue over it. She was trembling with passion. Sensations radiated from the kiss to the tips of her breasts and then lower as moisture pooled between her legs.

"I want you," he said, in a husky whisper into her ear.

"Me, too," she said.

He lifted her in his arms and carried her toward the couch. He sat down and set her on his lap. Her legs were to one side, one hand on his stomach, her other hand on his shoulder. He tipped her head up and kissed her again.

His hands swept over her body, pulling her blouse up until he'd exposed her midriff. His hands were warm as he rubbed them over her lightly. She shifted around so that she was reclining on his lap like some kind of sexual offering. Then he shifted their position on the couch until she was lying beneath him and he straddled her hips.

His shirt swung free, both sides falling away from his long, lean chest. She massaged his pectorals before she traced the light line of hair that tapered across his stom-ach to where it disappeared into his pants.

He moaned her name in a way that made it sound like ecstasy. She felt an answering tingle deep inside her own body. She shifted her legs until she could sprawl them open and then grabbed his hips to draw him down toward her. But he held fast.

"Not yet," he said. "There is still so much of you I haven't explored."

She didn't want this first time to last forever. She wanted him to continue overwhelming her senses until she came hard and repeatedly.

"I don't want to wait."

"Too bad," he said. "You're my mistress. What I say goes."

He leaned down and bit lightly at the flesh just above her left breast. She glanced down to see that he'd left a tiny mark.

"I don't want you to forget you're mine," he said.

"There's not a chance of that happening," she said. She reached between them for his belt and started to undo it. But he stopped her by wrapping his hands around her wrists. He drew them up above her head and held them there.

"Not yet," he said, firmly. He pushed her blouse farther up her body until her breasts were revealed encased in a flesh-colored bra. It was more practical than sexy, but the way that Conner looked at her told her he didn't need lace to be turned on by her.

Her nipples were hard and beaded against the material. Conner plucked at her right nipple with his free hand then lowered his head to put his mouth over her left one. She felt everything inside her clench at that touch. Her hips arched up toward his and, as he continued to suck on her nipple through the fabric of her bra, she arched her hips. Desperately trying to reach his.

She tugged on her arms, trying to free her wrists, but Conner held her firmly without hurting her. There was such decadence in the way he held her and touched her. She was shivering on the edge of an orgasm and she wasn't sure what she wanted at this point.

One thing she wanted was to feel his erection pressing against her, but she knew he wasn't going to lower his hips until he was good and ready.

"Conner…"

"Yes…"

"I'm going to come."

"Not until I tell you to," he said.

"I can't wait," she said, her words gasped out as she kept lifting her hips. He lowered his mouth to her breast again and let go of her hands as he thrust his hips against hers. Even through their clothing, the tip of his erection hit her clitoris and she shuddered as her orgasm washed over her.

Conner hadn't meant for the kiss to go as far as it had, but he'd been wanting her for so long it was all he could do not to open his pants and thrust himself deep inside her straight away. Holding her while she came was a double-edged sword that made his desire even stronger.

But he hadn't come to her house prepared to make love to her and he wasn't about to chance accidentally getting her pregnant. He wasn't thinking too clearly when he felt her hands between his legs and her fingers moving over his fly. She'd undone his belt and the next thing he knew her hands were on his hard-on.

She slid her fingers over the tip and his hips jerked forward, a bead of moisture slipping out. She rubbed her finger over it and then brought it to her lips to lick it away.

Her other hand pushed his pants and underwear over his hips and then he felt her cupping him. She squeezed gently as she rose up and found his mouth with hers. She kissed long and slow and deeply.

He leaned down over her, letting his bare chest brush over her bra. He reached underneath her body and undid the catch and then pushed the fabric off her breasts. Her skin was lightly freckled and he leaned down to kiss each of the freckles before slowly making his way to her strawberry-colored nipples.

He tongued them as she continued to caress his erection. He wanted her and could think of nothing but getting inside her silky-smooth body.

He let his hands skim lower to the waistband of her skirt and unzipped the side fastening before pushing it down her legs. She shifted underneath him until the skirt was completely off.

He thrust his hips forward and felt the smoothness of her skin underneath him. She felt so soft and womanly and as he stared down into those chocolate-brown eyes of hers, he felt something else change inside of him. Something more emotional, and that jarred him. Nichole was the one woman he'd met who made him react this way. This strongly. And he didn't know if making love to her was such a smart decision after all.

But his body wouldn't let him back down now. Wise or not, he wanted her. He wasn't going to be able to breathe again until he was buried hilt-deep in her curvy body with those long legs of hers wrapped around his waist.

He also knew he didn't want to rush this first time with her. He stood up, toed off his shoes and stepped out of his pants and underwear.

Before he reached down to lift her in his arms, he asked, "Where's your bedroom?"

"Down the hall," she said, gesturing to the left. He held her high in his arms and walked the short distance to her room. "In here." She reached out and hit the light switch as he entered the room. It was flooded with soft light from two bedside lamps. Her bed was queen-sized with an aqua-blue comforter on it. He set her on her feet and slowly finished undressing her, taking his time to enjoy each new patch of skin revealed.

"Do you have a condom?" she asked.

"Yes."

"Thank God," she said.

Once she was naked, he lifted her onto the bed and laid her back against the pillows. The aqua comforter was the perfect backdrop for her red hair and her creamy freckled skin. She kept her knees bent, but he saw the red hair that covered her most intimate secrets. He shrugged out of his shirt and stood there looking down at her.

He took her ankles in his hands and drew her legs down and apart from each other. She bit her lower lip.

"You can't be nervous now," he said, slowly drawing both hands up her legs, caressing her soft, smooth skin. He lingered on her knees and watched as gooseflesh spread up her legs as he moved his touch slowly higher toward her center.

"I'm not," she said. "I just expected you to be on me quicker."

"I don't like to rush things, even pleasure," he said.

He took a moment to put on the condom, then crawled onto the bed between her spread legs. He put his hands on either side of her chest and leaned down over her. He kissed her softly on the side of her neck and then moved his mouth lower to trace the globes of her breasts, first with his kisses and then with his tongue.

Her hands came up and tunneled through his hair, holding his head to each breast as he tongued one nipple then the other. Supporting his weight on just his right elbow, he used his left hand to draw a line down between her breasts over her ribs to her belly button.

He traced a circle around and around it, watching the red flush to her skin deepen. Her own hands were busy caressing him and he enjoyed every pulse of desire that she drew from him seemingly effortlessly.

He was on the knife's edge and he knew that no matter how much he wanted to prolong the moment until he entered her, he was fighting his own instincts. He wanted her with a red-hot desire that was hard to contain.

It was only the fact that he also wanted to taste every inch of her that allowed him a modicum of control. He lowered his head and traced the circle of her belly button with his tongue.

Her hands were back on his head as her hips rose on the bed.

"I need you," she said, her words raspy and drawn out.

They sent a shiver down his spine. She writhed underneath him as he shifted his position so he lay between her legs, his elbows on either side of her body.

He slid one hand up to caress her shoulder and neck before pushing his fingers into that thick red hair of hers. He kissed her deeply, pushing his tongue into her mouth as he pulled his hips back and then slowly thrust his hips forward.

He slipped slowly into her. Inch by inch, he went as slowly as he could and it felt so good. Finally his willpower gave way to his body's demands and he pushed himself all the way in. He was buried in her silky-hot body and it wasn't enough. He needed more. He started thrusting harder and deeper, urged on by her cries for more.

Her legs came up and wrapped around his hips. Her nails dug into his shoulder blades and she cried out his name as he felt her tightening around him. His own guttural cry of release followed a second later.

He kept thrusting, spilling himself inside her until he was spent. He collapsed against her chest, careful to keep her from bearing his full weight. Sweat covered both their bodies and he felt the minute kisses she dropped on his shoulder. He wrapped his arms around her and, keeping their bodies together, rolled to his side so he could hold her properly.

He kept his eyes closed, knowing he was hiding, but at this moment he didn't want to see her face or talk to her. He needed the silence to pretend that nothing had changed between them when he knew that everything had.

Nine

Nichole slept restlessly. She wanted to blame it on not being used to having someone else in her bed. But what weighed on her mind was the fact that Conner had only agreed to be her lover because of their bargain. She had vivid dreams of her boss finding out how she got Conner's story and firing her.

She finally got out of bed at six, just before her alarm went off. Conner appeared to be sleeping. She slowly went to the bathroom, trying to be extra quiet so as not to wake him. She didn't want to face him this morning. She knew she shouldn't leave without waking him, but she wanted to.

Part of her was very afraid of what he'd say to her. Of what she'd say... Last night had been more intense than she'd expected. But then nothing with Conner had gone exactly according to plan since the moment she'd met him.

She carefully closed the door to her tiny bathroom and reached over to turn the shower on to get the water hot.

She glanced at herself in the mirror and shook her head. She didn't look any different.

Maybe she was overthinking the entire arrangement with Conner. There was nothing tawdry about having slept with him. She'd had one-night stands before and she knew that as long as both she and her partner were on the same page, no one would get hurt. So why then was this bothering her so much?

Steam started to fill the tiny room and she pulled back the shower curtain and got inside. She started to wash when she heard the bathroom door open.

"Morning, Nichole," Conner said, his voice sounding raspy with sleep. She stood there frozen with her loofah in one hand and the shower gel in the other.

She shook her head. He knew she was in there and probably had guessed that she was naked. Why was she being so silly?

"Morning," she said. "Sorry if I woke you. I have an early meeting."

"Not a problem. I would normally leave you in peace in here, but this is the only bathroom and I, too, have an early meeting so I need to wash up."

"That's fine," she said. Oh, man, she'd come in here to hide from him and now he was here. But at least she didn't have to face him. *Not yet.*

"What's your day like?" he asked.

"Just the usual… Do you even know what a reporter does?" she asked.

"Meddle in other people's lives and make trouble for them?" His tone was light. She pulled the shower curtain back to peek out at him. He was bent over the sink washing his face. He was naked and his body looked good, with tan lines on his legs and arms.

He straightened up and she closed the curtain so he

didn't catch her peeking at him. "Ha! No, that's not what I do. Mostly I spend my time doing research and making calls trying to get recalcitrant people to talk to me."

"And if that doesn't work, then you crash their parties."

She shook her head. His easy banter was making her relax. She'd been worrying about what was going on between them, but Conner wasn't treating her any differently than he had before.

"That was only for you," she said. She finished washing her body and though it was an odd-numbered day of the month and normally she didn't wash her hair on those days, she went ahead and did it anyway.

"I'm honored," he said. "Would it bother you if I joined you in the shower?"

She hesitated. She'd been hiding in here so that she wouldn't have to face him, but now she didn't want to anymore.

"Not at all," she said. "In fact, I'm almost finished."

"Good. I'll be quick."

He opened the shower curtain and stepped in. She couldn't resist reaching out to touch him. He gave her a sexy smile.

"I can't make love this morning," she blurted out.

He shook his head. "Okay."

She handed him her loofah and the shower gel and then switched places with him. "I'm going to leave you to it."

"Are you nervous?" he asked.

"Of course not," she said. But she knew she was acting like a ninny. She never let anyone shake her, but Conner was. "I just don't want to tempt you when I know there isn't time to do anything about it."

"I'm always tempted by you," he said, and leaned against her, putting his hand on the wall behind her head and kissing her.

She closed her eyes and tipped her head back. His mouth on hers was soothing and arousing. It made most of her doubts fade away, and she was suddenly very glad that Conner was here with her this morning.

He canted his hips forward and she felt his erection nudge her stomach. Then his hands slid down her body to caress her breasts.

She ran her hands over his wet body as well, finding his hard-on and caressing the entire length of him. He continued kissing her and then put his hands on her waist to lift her off her feet. He leaned back against the wall and she wrapped her arms around his shoulders and her legs around his waist.

"I thought you didn't have time," he said.

"Stop gloating," she said.

She shifted until she felt him poised at the entrance of her body. She slowly took all of him and then rocked her hips against him. He kissed her deeply, driving her on, the tips of her breasts brushing against his chest.

He thrust up into her hard and deep until she felt her orgasm wash over her. She pulled her mouth from his and lowered her head to his shoulder as she felt him jetting his own completion into her body.

She slowly let one leg fall to the floor of the shower. She was dazed by the passion that seemed to flare so effortlessly between them. He pulled himself from her and kissed her softly on the forehead before he gently washed her body and then his own.

She opened the shower curtain and grabbed her towel from the rack, drying off quickly. Then she went back into the bedroom, leaving Conner alone in the bathroom.

She could no longer pretend that last night hadn't changed everything.

* * *

Conner knew she'd been hiding from him in the bathroom. All night long she'd tossed and turned next to him. Neither of them had had a good night's sleep. He knew that, for him, it was second thoughts about what he'd agreed to let her write about him and his family.

But he hadn't made a success out of all his business ventures by backing down once a decision had been made. He'd see it through and manage it so that he was in control.

And that was what this morning had been about for him. Making sure that she didn't have too much time to think about her story. He meant to ensure that she kept her focus on Conner as her lover, not the subject of an interview.

He turned off the shower and realized that he smelled sweet. Glancing down at the bottle of shower gel she'd given him, he groaned when he saw it was "birthday cake"–scented. Damn, he didn't want to walk around all day smelling like this.

He got out of the shower and found a clean towel in the small closet. He dried off and then wrapped it around his waist. He needed a shave and didn't have deodorant or a change of clothes, but that was okay—he'd already sent a text to Randall asking him to pick up those items and bring them over.

The telephone rang and he hesitated for a moment before leaving the bedroom. He heard the muffled sound of Nichole's voice.

When he entered the bedroom, he found Nichole standing in front of her closet with a cordless phone tucked between her shoulder and her ear.

"Yes, Mom, I'm doing fine. I'm sorry I didn't call you last night," she said.

Nichole listened again as she pulled a dark sapphire-blue sheath dress from her closet. She hung it on a hook and then turned, but stopped midstride when she saw him standing there.

"No, I wasn't out on a date. I just went to a dinner party at Jane Macafee's."

She smiled at something her mother said.

"She's just as charming in person as she appears on the show," Nichole said. "I have to go. I'll call you at lunchtime."

Nichole listened again.

"Love you, too."

She hung up the phone and tossed it onto the bed. It seemed to Conner that she and her mother had a really good relationship. But how could that be, based on her past?

"My mom calls me if I don't talk to her every day. Even though I've been living here for more than ten years, she's still afraid something bad will happen to me," Nichole said.

"My mom is the same way," Conner said. "She pretends she's calling to ask me about business or other things but she manages to talk to me every day."

She walked over to her dresser and pulled out a matching bra-and-panty set. This one was cream-colored and had a lace trim on the edge. He knew he should be getting dressed as well, but he enjoyed the intimacy of watching Nichole slowly clothe herself.

"Are you going to keep staring at me?" she asked.

"I can't help myself. You're gorgeous," he said.

She gave a quick curtsy. "I'm so glad you think so."

She was funny and quirky and every second he spent with her made him want more.

And that made her dangerous.

Who would have thought that this woman would be able to rock his world the way she had? He was used to dealing with powerful, beautiful women, but Nichole was different.

She dressed quickly and he went over to his own clothes and began putting them on. When she was seated at her vanity table, he glanced over at her and noticed that she had been watching him in the mirror.

She quickly picked up a makeup brush and drew it across her face, refusing to meet his eyes in the mirror. He understood that she was a complicated woman and that no matter how much she'd enjoyed the sex with him, there were bound to be some heavy emotions inside her this morning.

"Are you okay?" he asked, thinking he probably sounded pretty inane. "I guess we can see that I'm definitely not a reporter given my lame questions."

She gave him a sad half smile. "That's for sure. And I'm fine. A little tired."

"Tired sounds like an excuse," he said as he buttoned his shirt. "Do you regret last night?"

She shook her head. "Not at all. Since the first moment we talked at the Fourth of July party, I've thought of nothing else but getting you into my bed."

"Me, too. But that doesn't mean that this morning you might feel differently. When I was first starting out in business, I set all these financial goals for myself and in my mind I thought once I have this amount of money I'll feel secure. But the truth was the money didn't make a difference."

She turned on her vanity stool to face him. "What did make the difference?"

"A sense of confidence in myself. I had to trust that I would continue making the right decisions and that I didn't need to stop at one good deal to ensure the future."

She nodded. He'd told her something personal that he hadn't meant to. Dammit, he needed to be more on his guard around her. And this wasn't even her fault. He had to watch himself because she mattered to him.

He suddenly realized that he cared about her and not in the general way he'd thought he had. She mattered to him. Her happiness mattered to him.

"Thank you for sharing that," she said.

"You're welcome." He finished dressing quickly. Now he was the one who felt awkward and that wasn't like him. His cell phone beeped and he glanced down at the screen to see he had a text from Randall saying he was waiting downstairs.

"I'm going to get out of here. Are you free for lunch or drinks tonight?"

"Lunch would be better. I have to drop by the set of *Sexy & Single*."

"Lunch it is—does the Big Apple Kiwi Klub at noon work for you?" he asked. "We can discuss the details of your moving in with me then."

She nodded.

He stood up and walked over to her, pulled her into his arms and kissed her softly. "Have a good day, red."

Then he turned and walked out of her bedroom, but he knew he couldn't walk away from the new emotions that were flowing inside of him.

Nichole's morning flew by. Her editorial meeting was long and boring as usual, but she was preoccupied with thoughts of Conner and the previous night. A couple of her coworkers mentioned that she seemed distracted and she told them that she was on a new story and that was all that was on her mind.

But part of her knew that Conner was definitely a distraction. She'd always been 100 percent focused at work and today she wasn't. Instead, she remembered the way he'd felt inside her this morning in her shower. And she hoped that tonight she'd sleep a little better, but doubted it.

She was his mistress now. She didn't know what the reality of that would entail, but she did know that there was going to be a lot more of Conner in her life. And she had to get it together to focus on the story she wanted to write or else she was going to find that she'd wasted this time with him.

But part of her just wanted to revel in being in a new relationship. That scared her. Especially since Conner had made it clear that he was moving on when their month of being lovers was up.

She glanced at her iPhone and saw that she had fifteen minutes to get across town to meet Conner for lunch. She wanted to be prepared to ask him a few interview questions or at least schedule some interview time so that she didn't get distracted by being his lover.

Just as she was about to walk out of the office, her phone rang. She glanced at the caller ID and saw that it was Gail.

"Hey, girl," she said, forcing herself to sound cheerful, even though she was in the midst of her greatest moral dilemma ever.

"Hey. Are you free for lunch today? I wanted to talk to you and see how things were going," Gail said.

"I can't. Why do you want to talk to me?"

"You seemed a little…*lost* is the wrong word, so don't get mad, but just unsettled about the entire thing with Conner Macafee," Gail said.

"I *am* lost," Nichole admitted. "But only because he's not like other guys and I don't know exactly what to do to handle him. I could use a sounding board."

"I thought so. I'm busy tonight, but I can do breakfast or lunch tomorrow," Gail said.

"Maybe breakfast. I'm supposed to drop by the set of

the TV show tomorrow, so if you tag along maybe we can rope Willow into joining us."

"I'm already on it," Gail said. "I'll text you the details later. Bye."

"Gail?"

"Yes?"

"Thanks for calling," Nichole said. She knew that she wasn't comfortable reaching out to her friends because she never wanted them to think she was whiney, but she needed someone to talk to.

"No problem. You and Willow are my soul sisters and we have to look out for each other."

"I know that, but it's hard when we're all so busy."

"I'm never too busy for you," Gail said. "Take care, honey."

"You, too."

Nichole felt less alone when she hung up the phone. She left her office and hailed a cab. Traffic was heavy and she sent a text to Conner that she'd be ten minutes late. He replied right away.

I'm running late, too.

I'll get a table if I'm there first.

I have one reserved. See you soon.

Nichole was unsure if she should answer back. She knew it would just be something like *okay*, but she hated to not respond to a message. When she IMed with Gail and Willow, they teased her that she had to have the last word. And she knew it was true. Finally, she just texted back *Okay* and put her phone away.

The cab pulled to a stop in front of the Big Apple Kiwi

Klub, which housed a hotel and nightclub in one facility. The hotel had a Michelin-starred restaurant and featured a traveling exhibit of Gustav Klimt's work. The Klubs were an international chain, owned by Gail's fiancé, Russell Holloway.

Nichole exited the taxi and headed to the restaurant on the third floor. She gave Conner's name to the maître d' and by the time their table was ready, Conner had arrived. He put his hand on the small of her back as they followed the seating hostess to their table.

No one looking at them would think that they weren't involved. Nichole realized that she needed to have a chat with her editor and let him know that she was "dating" Conner before the story ran so that it didn't look like anything inappropriate was going on.

That was just another complication to this deal she'd made. She knew the stakes were high and she'd gambled everything on this being a story that could take her career to the next level.

Once they were seated, she noticed that Conner had found time to shave and change his clothes after he'd left her apartment this morning.

He ordered sparkling water for both of them and told the waiter they'd signal him when they were ready to order. "We need a few minutes to talk."

"No problem, sir," the waiter said and backed away.

"I hope you don't mind, but I wanted to talk to you before we order our food."

"Not at all. What's up?" she asked.

"I wanted to give you a chance to back out of our bargain," he said.

"Why now?" she asked.

"It seems as if it's weighing heavily on your mind and I don't want you to feel that you have to continue on with it."

"Will you still sit down for an interview?" she asked.

He shook his head. She felt angry that *he* might want to renege on their deal now that she'd slept with him. "I'm not going back on my word, Conner. Are you?"

Ten

Conner immediately realized his mistake, but he had wanted to give her a chance to back out. "I didn't mean it at all the way you've taken it."

"How did you mean it, then?"

"Just that I can tell how much our bargain is troubling you…and I wanted to give you an out."

"I appreciate that, but I'd only take it if you still intended to pursue a relationship with me as well as letting me talk to you about Matchmakers, Inc."

"I understand. Let's put my question behind us. Shall we order lunch and then discuss the details of our arrangement?"

She nodded, but there was a tightness to her features that told him he wasn't forgiven. And he couldn't blame her. He'd worded his idea in the worst possible way.

And he'd forgotten something extremely important: She'd slept with him last night and undoubtedly felt a little vulnerable as far as he was concerned this morning.

They both ordered and once they were alone again, Nichole pulled a notebook from her purse and a fountain pen. "I would like to get a couple of interviews scheduled."

"I understand. I think for both our sakes, maybe we should draw up an agreement between the two of us."

"Like what?"

"Just what I expect from you and what you expect from me," he said.

She wrote their names next to each other on a blank page in her notebook then drew a line down the middle. Under her name she wrote the word *mistress* and under his *interviews*.

"That's just the start," she said. "We agreed last night that you would do an interview about the matchmaking service and that you would allow me to observe you with your family."

"Yes, we did," he said.

She added those to the column under his name.

"*Mistress* is a vague term," he said. "But I'd like you to live with me in my apartment for the duration of our time together."

"I don't know about that. Will you allow me to check with my boss this afternoon?" she asked. "I'm going to say simply that I've interviewed you and we are dating. Let him know about the relationship and make sure that he's cool with it."

"Shouldn't you have already checked?" he asked. It sounded like there were details she hadn't covered and that didn't seem like Nichole.

"I have to check it out. There are other reporters who have written about their significant others, but I just want to let my editor know we are dating. If we hadn't been seen out in public together we might have a chance at remaining under the radar, but I'd rather not take any additional chances."

"Agreed," he said. "Barring any problems with that, I think you should move into my apartment this evening."

"Isn't that quick?" she asked.

"It's a little late to think of that now. You're mine, red, and I want you under my roof."

She shivered with sensual excitement at the way he claimed her. Her mind tried to warn her not to let it go to her head, though. She had to focus on the interview. That should help her keep cool as far as he was concerned. Not so easily agitated by everything he said and did.

"Sounds good. Do you have time to meet with me tomorrow for the interview?" she asked.

He pulled out his iPhone and after a few minutes said, "I can give you thirty minutes tomorrow."

"That's not enough time, but it will do for a start. When?" she asked.

"Ten-thirty," he said.

She jotted that under the column for his name.

"I'd like to do one interview at the Matchmakers, Inc. offices," she said. "Do you keep an office there?"

"I don't. I'm not all that involved with the everyday operations of the company."

"Do you ever go down there?"

"Occasionally, for board meetings. We can use the boardroom at Macafee International if you don't feel like using my office," he said. "Are you afraid of a repeat of what happened last time?"

She was. But then they could be riding together in a cab and she'd want him. What was the hold he had over her? If past experience had taught her anything, once she'd slept with a man usually the lust started to wane, but the opposite was true with Conner.

She seemed to want him more. Even now, sitting across from him and writing down details of their indecent agreement, she was thinking about the way his hands had caressed her body last night and the way his mouth felt against hers when he kissed her.

"Not unless you are," she said, leaning forward and taking his hand in hers.

"Hell, I'm not afraid it will happen—I'm counting on it," he said.

She almost smiled, but Conner was too self-confident to begin with. She didn't need to react to everything he said and let him know that she was under his spell.

Damn. She hadn't thought about it that way before, but that was the truth. She was truly under his spell. No other man had made her feel this way. Which was why she'd been a serial dater with her little boy toys.

But now, as she sat across from Conner and stared into his blue eyes, she realized that she wanted so much more from him. She wanted something that felt scary. Something she'd never tried before.

She wanted something permanent and solid. And she knew that she had no idea how to make that work. It was a good thing she was writing down the details of this arrangement because maybe seeing those stark facts would help her remember that Conner was just a story and she was his mistress, not his girlfriend. He had been very clear on what he wanted from her and that was sex—not forever.

Forever had never been that important to her because, after her childhood, she'd always believed that it would be smart for her to live alone. But there was something about Conner that made her rethink that. Or maybe it was all the stories she'd been doing on matchmaking. She was forgetting the realistic woman she'd always been and dreaming of things she wasn't sure she wanted.

* * *

Conner had booked the lunch right before another meeting so he wouldn't be tempted to linger too long with Nichole. When his iPhone beeped to remind him it was time to go, he signaled for the check.

"Text me as soon as you find out from your boss if you can move in with me. From my side that is one of my must-haves."

"You made that clear. I'll let you know as soon as I can," she said.

"I have a meeting in fifteen minutes," Conner said as he handed his credit card to the waiter. "I'm sorry we didn't get to finish talking over the details, but I feel as if we got the main things out and on the table."

"I do, too," she said.

"Great. I'll be looking forward to hearing from you about tonight."

"Not a problem," she said, closing the notebook and putting it in her purse.

Conner signed the check, then stood up and followed Nichole from the dining room. He was very aware that most of the men in the room watched her as she walked. She was one of those women who drew men's gazes. Conner felt a spark of jealousy and reached out to grab her hand. She glanced up at him.

"What's the matter?"

"Nothing. I just wanted to make sure that every man in the room knows you're with me," he said.

"I guess I should be glad you didn't pull me into your arms and kiss me," she said.

"I thought about it. But one kiss is never enough with you and me," he said.

She shook her head. "You're very arrogant, you know that, right?"

"I'm not being arrogant," he said. "I'm being possessive. You're mine by our agreement."

"I know," she said.

As soon as they exited the restaurant, he did drop a light
kiss on her lips, but then quickly stepped away.

"I knew you wouldn't be able to resist," she said.

He arched one eyebrow at her.

"Me. I have a power over you," she said.

"You do? We can talk about this power tonight," he said.

"Yes, we can," she agreed. "I have a lot of things I want
to talk to you about."

"I'll bet you do," he said.

The elevator arrived and they both got in and rode it
to the ground floor. Once they stepped outside the lobby,
Conner saw his car waiting. "Do you want me to have
Randall take you back to your office after he drops me at
my meeting?"

"No, thanks. I'll take a cab," she said.

He couldn't resist kissing her again and for that very
reason almost didn't do it, but he was in control of this arrangement and his own body. So he kissed her to prove to
himself that he could stop if he wanted to.

"Until tonight."

He got in the back of the waiting Rolls Royce Phantom
and glanced back only once as Randall drove away. He
saw Nichole standing there with her hand on her mouth
watching his car. Then she shook her head and turned and
started walking in the opposite direction.

His cell phone rang and he glanced at the caller ID. It
was his mom. Probably the last person he should be talking to right now when he was feeling…not any particular
thing, just feeling emotions. For so long he'd pretended that
he was aloof and didn't feel the same way other people did.

Often he felt superior by his ability to keep his emotions out of his daily life. But he knew now that it was only the fact that he'd never met a woman like Nichole before. She tempted him in ways that had nothing to do with sex.

He answered the call. "Hi, Mom."

"Are you busy, Conner?" she asked.

Even though he'd told her he wouldn't answer if he couldn't talk, she always asked him that. "No. What's up?"

"I'm having a charity open house in Bridgehampton this weekend and I want you to come."

"What day?"

"Saturday, but I was thinking you could come down Friday night and stay until Sunday and you can bring that reporter you had dinner with at your sister's house the other night."

"How do you know about that?"

"Janey. She doesn't mind talking to me every day."

He was annoyed with his sister for telling their mom about Nichole. "Did she mention she's dating Palmer?"

"Is she? No, she didn't. I guess I'll include him in my weekend invitation, too. Oh, this will be so nice. Both of you home and with—"

"Mom, I will come to the event on Saturday but I can't make it for the entire weekend."

"Oh, really?"

"Yes, is there anything else?"

"Jane said you and Nichole Reynolds really hit it off. Did you?"

"Yes, we did. But it's not serious," he said.

"It never is with you," she said with a forlorn sigh. "I would like grandkids one day."

"Janey can give them to you, too," Conner said.

"I think she's waiting for a sign from you that life is okay," his mom said.

That couldn't be true. "I don't see why. She's better at making a home than I ever was."

"You both have created what you felt was missing when everything happened with your father. You created financial security for all of us and Janey the perfect house. But it's not enough, and I don't know what to do to show you both that."

Conner didn't like hearing what his mom had to say. He knew that he put money first and had made interpersonal relationships a distant second. He hadn't gotten to be thirty-five by not knowing what made him tick, but it hurt to hear his mom sum it up that way.

"I'll be there on Saturday," he said. "And I will be bringing Nichole Reynolds. I've got to go now, Mom. Love you."

He hung up before she could say anything more. After the lunch with Nichole, the last thing he needed was an emotional discussion with his mom. He wasn't sure how it had happened, but his tidy little life had suddenly been thrown upside down. Actually, he did know how it had happened and exactly who was to blame—Nichole Reynolds.

Nichole had taken the subway back to her office, hoping that by being around other people she'd be less likely to get stuck in her own head. But it didn't work. She was still unsure of what she'd agreed to with Conner and the more time she spent thinking about it, the worse that knot of tension in her stomach became.

She had had a number of uncomfortable conversations with people over the years. She had gotten to be such a good reporter by asking tough questions, but she'd never had to discuss her personal life with her boss before and she knew she was going to have to do that today.

She had the distinct feeling that her own knowledge of

what she'd agreed to with Conner was coloring her feelings on the issue, but she couldn't help that.

She took the stairs up to her floor instead of the elevator, no doubt to put off the inevitable. But as luck would have it, her boss was in his office when she stopped by to see him.

"Do you have a minute?" she asked.

"I've got a few. What do you need?" he asked.

She stepped into his office and closed the door behind her. Ross Kleeman had started as reporter a long time ago and he'd managed to keep *America Today* vibrant and profitable. Many newspapers hadn't made the transition to the web-based editions as skillfully as *America Today,* thanks in large part to Ross.

"Well, two things. The first is that I got an interview with Conner Macafee. I see this as a two-part story. The first will focus on his matchmaking company, featured in the new *Sexy & Single* television show. And the second will be a color piece on how the scandal with his father influenced his business and personal choices."

"Wow. How'd you get him to agree to that? And what do you mean by color piece?" Ross asked.

"How I got him to agree kind of ties into the second thing I wanted to tell you—Conner and I are dating. Is that going to be a problem?"

Ross leaned back in his chair and crossed his arms over his chest. "We can disclose your relationship when we print the articles. That should take care of any ethics issues. So he agreed to let you write about that because you're dating?"

Nichole nodded. "For the second piece, I'm going to rely on my own observations, since he won't talk to me about the scandal with his father. But I can see how it has influenced the choices that Conner has made. To some extent I can see that in his sister, too."

"Interesting. Depending on the type of story you end up writing, we might be able to run it in the *Weekend Magazine* edition."

"Okay. I don't intend it to be an exposé. It'll be a longer version of my usual column," she said.

"See what you come up with. And think feature piece instead of column when you're writing," Ross said. "Was that all?"

"Yes," she said, heading out of his office.

She walked back to her cubicle and stowed her purse in her desk while turning on her computer. She got out her cell phone to text Conner.

No problems with my boss. I can move in tonight.

A few minutes passed before she got a reply.

Good. I have a 5 pm meeting so I can't meet you until 8. Will call when I'm done here.

OK

Do you have to get the last word in all the time?

Yes. ☺

OK

TTYL

You win.

Good.

There was no other response from Conner and Nichole smiled to herself. That was the part that always surprised her about him. He was fun. He shouldn't be because he was arrogant and too used to getting his own way. But he made her smile a lot of the time.

Part of her was worried about how she was going to be able to manage to live with him and not fall in love with him. It was bad enough that they had this bargain. She wished she could keep her emotions out of it.

She wondered what other men's mistresses did. When she was in college, she'd done an article on a study that was conducted at NYU on brain chemistry and sex, and she knew that no matter how sophisticated society was, at its most basic level everyone was still programmed to find a mate and procreate.

If she tried, maybe she could use science to protect herself, but she doubted it. Conner just didn't fit in the nice little mold she'd always used to make sure that she didn't fall in love with anyone.

What she needed to do was somehow figure out how to make every time they were together about the articles she was writing instead of their attraction.

But she knew it would be next to impossible because she wanted him.

It hadn't taken much prodding on her part to get him to kiss her after lunch. She'd needed it. She needed to know that she wasn't the only one who was helpless in this infatuation. Conner seemed so much in control—both of himself and the world around him. Something she'd always assumed she was, but he put those beliefs to shame.

Her career had only been so super-important to her because the men she'd dated in the past had been boys. She hadn't realized that the fun she was having had been designed to shield her commitment until this moment.

She put her head in her hands and stared at her desktop. In her mind's eye she saw the list she'd written at lunch with Conner and she knew that she'd left one very important thing out of her column.

Don't fall for Conner.

He'd told her he didn't want to hurt her, and he'd been honest from the beginning, so she knew if she did get hurt she'd have no one to blame but herself. But that still didn't help her figure out how she was going to get her story, be his mistress and not fall in love with him.

Eleven

Conner had expected Nichole to need more time or try to make up some reason why she couldn't move in with him, but she seemed determined to live up to the bargain she'd struck with him.

His respect for her grew a little bit as he realized that. The more he knew about her as a person, the less fearful he was of anything she'd print about him. But that was a foolish way of thinking. He had to remember that she was here for a story and he was going to make sure that she got the information he allowed her to have and nothing more.

His apartment was a penthouse in a building on the Upper East Side. It ran the entire length of the building and had a glass wall overlooking his patio. He'd spent a lot of money on decorating and it felt like home when he opened the door.

Conner ushered Nichole into his apartment. He was carrying her small overnight bag, leaving her with her computer and purse. Randall was bringing up the rest of her bags, but overall, she hadn't brought a lot of stuff.

"Welcome to my home," he said as they walked over the threshold and into the big open-plan living room.

"Thank you. I had to tell my parents I was staying with a friend while my building had some work done," she said, blurting it out. "My mom calls on my house phone all the time."

Her demeanor was the only clue that she was at all nervous about moving in with him. As she looked around his apartment, he tried to see it through her eyes. He knew it was stylish and well decorated, but he wondered what she thought of it.

"Okay, do you want to give them my home phone number as well?"

"Yes, if you don't mind. That will make both of them feel better. I don't want them to know about you, though," she said.

"What do you mean?"

"If they know that I'm living with you, they'll want to meet you and then, when we break up in a month, they'll be disappointed for me and for themselves and the grandchildren they are dying to have."

"My mom is a little bit like that, too."

"So you can sympathize," she said.

"I'm going to give you your own bedroom so that you can have some privacy. I know you were worried that my insistence that you live here might have taken that from you."

She nodded. "Thank you. I actually do a lot of my writing at home because our office is so noisy."

He led her to a large guest bedroom that was next to the master bedroom. "This room has a desk in it. We can bring the one from your apartment over, if you'd prefer that."

"This will be fine," she said.

He put her bag on the bed and then stood there for a minute. He'd never had a mistress before. He had some image in his head of himself as a sheikh and her as his harem girl, but he knew better than to tell her to get naked.

"I'll leave you to settle in," he said. "Have you had dinner?"

"No," she said. "My day was busier than I expected it to be."

"I haven't, either. Would you like to join me on the patio in twenty minutes? My housekeeper left dinner waiting for us."

"Yes, I would."

He walked out of the room before he gave in to his instincts and swept her into his arms and onto the bed. He had thought about this moment all day long. What he would do once he had her here in his home. He had decided he'd keep her off balance. But he hadn't counted on her keeping him off balance as well.

He went to his own bedroom and changed from his suit into a pair of khaki shorts and a plain black T-shirt. He reviewed his email on his cell phone and responded to the urgent ones. Then sitting back in the wingback chair next to his bed, he realized that he was excited that Nichole was here.

Sometimes when he was here, he felt alone. He'd never invited anyone to spend the night here before and having a companion appealed to him. The only trepidation he felt was that he had to be on guard not to say anything detrimental she could use in her articles.

There was a knock on his door and he pocketed his cell phone as he went to open it. Nichole stood there in a pair of skintight jeans and a tank top. Her feet were bare and she'd pulled her hair up into a high ponytail.

"So this is your room?" she asked, brushing past him to enter.

"Yes," he said. He couldn't take his eyes off her as she walked around his room. He'd intended for sex to be the thing that kept her from asking him too many questions, but he hadn't thought that she could distract him in the same way.

She walked over to the walnut dresser and ran her finger along its polished surface. There was a small watch box on the surface and a picture of his mom and sister from the previous Christmas. Otherwise, the room was devoid of personal mementoes.

"Kind of sterile, isn't it?" she asked.

"I don't like clutter," he said. "Especially in here. What did you expect to find?"

"Some clues to the real Conner Macafee."

"You'll find more 'clues' to him in bed, red."

"Why do you call me that?"

"I don't know. You're fiery and full of passion. It suits you."

She nodded. "I hated my red hair growing up," she admitted.

"I hated that everyone thought they knew me growing up," he said.

"I'll bet you did. Did you go to a private school?"

"Yes, it was very exclusive. Lots of old-money families. We were pretty much from the same type of background. And our families mostly knew each other."

"But you were different than the other kids?" she asked.

"I thought so, but then I'll bet we all did. It's hard to be a rebel when you have everything," he said.

"But I'll bet when you suddenly lost it all it was much easier," she said.

"You could say that. Let's go to the kitchen. I have a feeling I'm going to need a drink."

Nichole followed him to the kitchen, looking around his apartment along the way. It wasn't sterile, and she realized she shouldn't have said his bedroom was. It was just that he didn't have a lot photos on the walls. He had artwork, though.

"I guess rich people put up artwork instead of personal photos?"

"I don't know. I just put up what I like. My mom and my sister are the only two people I'm close to," he said, going to the chrome refrigerator. "Want a Corona?"

"Yes, please," she said.

"Have a seat," he said, gesturing to the bar area.

She hopped up on one of the stools and noticed that his kitchen was state of the art, with a professional-grade cooktop. "Do you cook?"

"No, but I have a personal chef I use for dinner parties and events I hold here. She insisted that the kitchen must be like this. Mainly I use the microwave to heat things up following Mrs. Plumb's instructions."

"I use my microwave a lot, too. I just don't have the time to cook at home," she said, taking the Corona from him when he handed it to her with a wedge of lime in the top. She pushed the lime into the bottle and then took a swallow of the beer.

"Is Jane the chef you use?"

"Yes, she is," Conner said, coming over to lean against the counter across from her.

"Why didn't you just use her name?" she asked.

"I'm used to never talking about her."

She had known Conner was going to be a tough interview, but she hadn't realized how much he kept up his guard. If he was never going to let her in, how the hell was she going to get the information she needed?

"It's okay to use her name with me," Nichole said.

"I know that. Force of habit," Conner said. He took a long swallow of his beer and then set the bottle on the countertop. "Let's see what we have for dinner."

He opened the bottom warming oven, bending down to see what was inside. She enjoyed the view of his backside and gave a little wolf whistle to let him know. She didn't want Conner to feel pressured to answer her questions and she knew the only way to make sure he didn't was to (1) keep him off guard and (2) keep things light. He expected her to go for the hard questions and she would. But not at first.

"Like the view?" he asked, shaking his hips.

"Yes, I do. So what's on the menu other than you?" she asked.

"Salmon en croute. Mrs. Plumb has been experimenting with some different recipes lately."

"Sounds good. How long has Mrs. Plumb worked for you?"

"Eight years. I've lived here that long, too," he said. Using oven mitts, he removed two dishes from the oven and set them on the countertop.

"Can you carry both our beers?"

"Yes, sir," she said.

He led the way to the glass door with the automatic sensor that opened it when he approached. Once they were outside, he set the plates on the table, which was already set with glasses, napkins and flatware.

"I like that door," she said. "Very high tech."

"I like convenience and I have the money to get what I want," he said. "Be right back."

She set the beers down at each of their spots and then

took a seat and waited for him to come. He returned with two salad plates, setting one next to her dish and one at his place.

"I probably should serve wine with this, but I don't care for it."

"Any wine?" she asked.

"Not really. I'll drink it at dinner parties because it's expected, but when I'm at home I don't touch it."

"I really love a dry wine, but mainly I drink it with my girlfriends when we're hanging out."

"You mentioned that Jane was good friends with Willow and Willow is one of your friends?"

"Yes. Willow and Gail Little and I all grew up together," Nichole said. "We all ended up going to college in New York and just have grown closer over the years. It's really nice having them here with me. It makes me feel like I've got a little bit of home close by."

"I have some good friends, but they are mainly business associates who have the same hobbies I do," Conner said.

Nichole relaxed as dinner progressed and noticed that Conner did, too. It was almost like any other first date, except that they both knew they'd sleep together tonight.

"What are your hobbies?" she asked.

"Sailing," he said. "I love being out on my yacht."

"What do you like about it?" She suspected it probably had a lot to do with the fact that when he was out there no one could bother him.

He shrugged and took a bite of his dinner. She watched him chew and then realized that she was fascinated by everything about this man.

"I guess the solitude. There's usually poor cell phone reception so no one can reach me from the office. I tend to go out alone or with a very small crew so no one bothers me."

She could see why that would appeal to him. Conner

had been shaped into the man he was today by a very intrusive incident in his past. He'd always need to be alone to feel safe.

Maybe that was why he wanted her as his mistress instead of his girlfriend. Maybe that added layer gave him the security of knowing that he'd still have the assurance of being alone when their time together ended.

She knew there was no maybe about it. That was exactly why he'd set it up the way he had. But what did it say about her that she'd agreed to his terms?

She knew she wanted her career to continue to be her focus, but having met Conner, she doubted it would satisfy her the way that he did. Oh, that wasn't right. It was more the way she imagined he would fill her life if she let herself really care for him.

He made her want things that she didn't think she ever would. And no matter how hard she tried to switch back to the way she'd been before, she knew she couldn't. Something inside her had been irrevocably changed by Conner Macafee. That should bother her. Strangely, it didn't.

Conner enjoyed the evening with Nichole. But it felt homey in a way and that bothered him a lot. He didn't want to feel too comfortable with her.

Turned on by her, of course, but comfortable, no way. He needed to keep his edge and his wits about him. She'd thrown him with her casual sexiness and it was time for him to start regaining the ground he'd lost earlier.

She'd asked him questions, but he tried to keep them on even footing by learning just as much about her. Nichole was a mystery to him and each new thing he uncovered only brought more questions. She had a natural elegance to all her moves and she was funny and had a sharp wit.

She was giving him the rundown on the person who

sat behind her at work. A sportswriter who, in Nichole's words, spent most of his time trying to relive his glory days. "The thing is, he's a great guy and a terrific writer. If he didn't talk so much about his failed career in baseball, people would like him. He should be more like Jack Crown."

"In what way?" Conner asked as he made coffee for them both.

"Jack doesn't dwell on the fact that he didn't have the career playing pro football that he should have had. He just lives in the now."

"I see what you mean. That's why I don't like to talk about my past. What's important is what's happening now," Conner said.

She gave him a sardonic look. "Your past influences everything you do today. Being a jock in high school and telling everyone about how you were the reason your team won the state championship is a totally different story."

He shook his head as he added cream and sugar to his coffee and just cream to hers. "It's only different because you want to know about my past. If I was Joe Schmoe and you'd never heard of my dad, you wouldn't care what went on."

"Fair enough, but you're not. So that point is moot," she said, taking her cup from him. "I was very excited to see you have a Keurig machine. I love mine and almost packed it."

"Why?"

"I need coffee and lots of it."

"Doesn't it leave you wired?" he asked, sitting next to her at the counter.

"Not really. I just love the taste," she said, then shook her head at him. "I don't know why I'm going on about coffee. It's really not that big a deal."

"You're cute when you let your guard down," he said.

"Is that what I'm doing?" she asked.

"I think so. I think you've decided the only way to get me to open up is to open up yourself," he said.

"You're a shrewd man, Mr. Macafee, but I'm not going to let you manipulate me," she said. "I could tell from the moment we met that you were too used to getting your own way."

He laughed. "I wouldn't dream of manipulating you. And we all want our own way so of course I'm used to it. I've worked very hard to make sure things happen the way I want them to."

He had spent years designing his life for the best possible outcome. It was no easy task to get to where he was and keep everyone in the world from asking about the one thing they all wanted to know. He'd never fully escaped the salaciousness of his father's scandal. Yet he'd moved through life ignoring the questions and keeping reporters at bay.

How then did he come to have Nichole sitting next to him? He still wasn't clear about that. He'd thought that the reasons he'd given himself were honest.

He had wanted her and here she was.

"Ready to see the rest of the place?" he asked.

"Sure," she said. "Why didn't you move to the West Coast after everything happened with your dad?"

"Mom said it would be too much like running away— like we had something to hide," he said.

"Your mom sounds like a very strong woman. And so is your sister," she said.

"You're a strong woman, too," he said. "I'm used to women who know what they want and aren't afraid to go after it."

He led her up the stairs set to the left of the hallway that led to the bedrooms. "This is my play area."

"I can't wait to see what's up here."

There was a full-sized pool table and a media center. Built onto the other wall was a bar with six barstools and behind it was a fully stocked liquor cabinet. He led her past the game room into a large study. There was a dark wood desk that sat in front of a large plate-glass window. On either side of it were floor-to-ceiling bookcases. The shelves were overflowing with books.

She walked over to the bookshelves and took her time reading the titles. There were some classics and of course there were the business books, but she was surprised to see books by Machiavelli and the Baroness Orczy.

"The Scarlet Pimpernel."

"I was young when I read it. It was my mother's favorite. She told me he was the first Batman."

Nichole had to laugh at that. "Your mother sounds like she's a lot of fun."

Conner had a quiet look on his face. "She's the best. She's always just let me and Jane do what we wanted, but kept us in line at the same time. She's a good parent."

"Are you glad you live so close to her?"

"Yes. Jane and I take turns keeping an eye on her, but she doesn't need the attention."

"What kind of work do you do from home?" she asked.

"Whatever needs doing," he said. "If you weren't here I would have eaten at my desk and answered emails until eleven."

"Workaholic!"

"Yes, I am. But it's impossible to have a successful business and not be. Everyone talks about wanting to have balance, but it takes drive and ambition to be successful and that type of personality doesn't want to spend weeks having downtime."

That said a lot about Conner and she added it to the image of him she was building in her head to write her article. He might have been born with a silver spoon in his mouth, but there was nothing lazy about him. He didn't expect anything to be handed to him and she admired him for it.

"Ready to go downstairs and see the rest of the rooms?" he asked.

"No, but I am ready to see your bedroom again," she said.

He took her hand and led her downstairs to his bedroom, where he made love to her and she stopped thinking about stories and bargains and just enjoyed being in her lover's arms until he carried her back to her own bed in the middle of the night and she was reminded of those very facts.

Twelve

Nichole woke early, showered and left Conner's apartment without seeing him. Unfortunately, once she'd left it was too early for her to meet Gail and Willow for breakfast. But she knew if she stayed she'd feel pushed into saying or doing something with Conner that she shouldn't.

Last night she'd been ballsy and acted like being his mistress was all part of her plan, but being carried back to her bed after she'd fallen asleep wasn't cool, no matter how she tried to make it work in her head. She'd thought she'd been prepared for the reality of being his mistress, but she hadn't been.

She knew that it was past time for her romantic dreams about Conner to be put to bed, but it wasn't that easy. She felt as if she'd won some things from him the night before. He'd answered her questions. Granted, they'd been easy ones, but still.

And this morning, having gotten absolutely no sleep,

she was feeling very emotional. She stopped at Starbucks for a coffee and texted both Willow and Gail to see what time they were meeting. She quickly heard back that if she and Gail were willing to go to Brooklyn, Willow could meet in thirty minutes.

Nichole texted back that worked for her and hailed a cab to get out of Manhattan. They met at a coffee shop that served what Willow called the best breakfast burrito in New York. Gail had to cancel so it was just the two of them.

"Okay, what's up with you? You never can meet this early," Willow said after the waiter had set down their food and coffee.

Nichole might be making her living as a reporter, but she was uncomfortable being the one on the other side of the questions. She knew what she wanted to say to her friend, but not how to say it. Finally, she just took a deep breath and blurted out, "I've agreed to be Conner's mistress in exchange for interviewing him."

Willow stopped midchew and just looked at her incredulously, which made Nichole realize she should have chosen some different words, maybe something that made it sound a little less like what it was.

Willow finished chewing the bite she had in her mouth and then reached across the table to take Nichole's hand. "Okay, first of all why?"

"He wouldn't agree to be interviewed otherwise."

"So he's a pig?" Willow asked.

"No. It's not like that. You know…actually you might not know this, but after he kept avoiding me on the set and refused to take my calls, I crashed his family's Fourth of July party and when he confronted me…well, we had chemistry."

"Okay, this is making more sense now. So he wanted

you and you, being a good little reporter, said no, my story comes first."

"Yes, Willow, it was very *Perils of Pauline* with my swooning and putting my hand on my forehead," Nichole said, getting a little frustrated with her friend.

"I'm sorry," Willow said. "But this is only a problem because…I'm not sure why. How is being his mistress any different than those one-night stands you've had or your vacation boyfriends?"

"It's different because I like him," Nichole said.

"And that's the heart of the matter. You've always been careful to keep men at arm's length and it was easy for you because you picked men who weren't looking for anything serious."

"Conner definitely isn't looking for anything serious. Do you think that's why I like him? The challenge?" Nichole asked. She desperately wanted to figure this out, so she could just go back to how she used to be.

"Maybe, but it's more likely, given the chemistry you said the two of you have, that you've found a real man you're interested in," Willow said.

"That's what I was afraid of. What am I going to do, Will?"

"I guess backing out is not an option," her friend said.

"No. I want that interview. Ross is talking about putting the story in the *Weekend Magazine* edition if it's good enough. You know how long I've waited for that?"

"I do," Willow said. "Well, then, the only solution is to keep things light. See if pretending he's one of your boys—"

"Please stop calling them that. There weren't that many of them and they were men," Nichole said.

"Okay, I guess I was always jealous of your little hotties," Willow admitted.

"You can be jealous," Nichole said with a small laugh.

The conversation drifted to breakfast, which they both started eating, and they finished their meal with gossip about the latest couple on *Sexy & Single*. "Rikki finally lightened up as far as Paul is concerned. I think when you drop by the set this week, you're going to see a different woman."

"What did he do?"

"That's the million-dollar question," Willow said. "It happened off camera, but the ice queen has started to thaw."

The waiter gave them the check and as they both put cash on the table to cover their portion of the bill, Willow glanced over at Nichole.

"Are you going to be okay?"

Nichole didn't know the answer to that. She knew that she had to be because, as her father had said more than once, "Life goes on whether we're ready for it or not." But she had never felt as hurt by any other person in her adult life as she had last night when Conner had dropped her in her bed and left the room.

"I don't know."

"I'm here if you need to talk more," Willow said as they stood up. Willow hugged her and Nichole was grateful for her friend.

"Thanks."

"Nic?"

"Yes?"

"There will be other interviews," Willow said. "If you don't think it's right for you personally, I'd bail and just chalk this one up to experience."

Nichole nodded and held her hand up for a cab as they walked outside. "I will. But I'm not a quitter."

"No, you're not, but that's not always a good thing. You

can't keep at something that isn't any good for you. Just remember that you deserve to be successful and happy."

The cab arrived and those words echoed in her head all the way back to her office. She knew that a lot of times she thought she could have one thing or the other, but she would like to have it all. She wasn't sure if Conner fit that pattern or if he was going to be the reason why she ended up with nothing.

Nichole prepared for her interview with Conner as if she was preparing to interview the President of the United States. She knew she had to have all her questions and follow-ups ready and she knew she had to be on her guard; otherwise Conner would find it easy to distract her.

Her plan—albeit a rough one—was to be professional and not speak about what had happened the night before. But she was tired, and no matter how many cups of coffee she downed, she didn't feel like herself.

The conversation with Willow still weighed on her mind as she got out of a cab in front of the Matchmakers, Inc. offices. She wondered what Gail had felt when she'd first arrived there. She remembered that her friend had decided to go to the matchmaker because she was tired of being alone.

Was that it? Was she tired of being alone too? Was that the reason she was feeling things for Conner she didn't want to? She hoped not. Falling in love didn't figure into her plans until she was closer to forty, and since she was just thirty she had ten years before that happened.

She noticed that most of the professionals she knew lost their edge when they got into their forties. Knowing that, she'd always figured that would be the time she'd settle down. But Conner had shown up now. And he was tempting her in ways she wasn't ready to be tempted.

"Hello, ma'am. Do you have an appointment with one of

the matchmakers today?" the receptionist said as Nichole entered the building.

"No, I don't," Nichole said, pushing her sunglasses up on top of her head. "I'm Nichole Reynolds, here to meet with Conner Macafee."

"Yes, ma'am. He's not here yet, but he said to show you to the conference room."

"Thank you," Nichole said, following the girl down a hallway lined with photos of romantic dates and couples in silhouette.

The conference room had a big picture of a romantic island beach with a couple shown walking away from the camera holding hands. And written on the far end of the wall, in a pretty, scrolling font, were the words *Everyone Deserves to Be Happy Ever After.*

This entire room was designed to make you think of hearts and flowers. Of love and romance and all the dreams that people had when they thought of meeting their soul mate. This room was part of the propaganda of the matchmaking business.

"Would you like something to drink?" the receptionist asked.

"Water would be great," Nichole said. She had dry mouth from all that caffeine she'd ingested today.

The receptionist got her a bottle of water from the refrigerator hidden under the credenza and then left her alone in the room. Nichole used the camera on her phone to take a picture of the room and then jotted down a few notes before the door behind her opened.

She knew without glancing up that it was Conner. It was as if her body had some sort of GPS that notified her when he was in the vicinity.

"Hello, Nichole," he said.

"Hello, Conner. How's your day been so far?" she asked.

"Well, it didn't start off that great since my mistress was missing from my house this morning," he said.

"I had another early meeting," she said.

He stared at her with those shrewd blue eyes of his and she felt as if he could see straight through her. She blinked and glanced down at her notes. "If you'd have a seat, we can get started."

"I don't want to get started yet. Why did you leave this morning without saying goodbye?" he asked.

She chewed her lower lip. She had to play this the right way or she was going to end up saying the wrong thing. But she didn't know how to do that. "I said I had an early meeting. Can we leave it at that? I'll be more than happy to discuss this with you when we are both at your home tonight."

"Very well," he said. He sat down next to her at the conference table instead of across from her. "What do you want to know?"

"Do you mind if I record our interview?" she asked. "That way if I have a question from my notes I can go back and listen to the tape."

"That would be fine," he said.

She took out her iPhone and chose the voice memo app. She set it up between them on the table and hit Record.

"This is my interview with Conner Macafee, owner of Matchmakers, Inc., in their Manhattan offices.

"First of all, how involved are you in the running of the day-to-day operations?" she asked.

"I'm not really involved except from a financial oversight standpoint."

"Why do you own a matchmaking company when marriage is clearly not something you're interested in?" she asked.

He leaned back in his chair and she lifted her phone and

pointed it toward him. "I inherited the company from my maternal grandmother. My original intent was to sell, but I had a friend who was the victim of a gold digger. He ended up with a broken heart so I thought if I kept the company, I could send my friends who were marriage-minded here. Matchmakers, Inc. vets all applicants to prevent the sort of thing that happened to my friend."

"Interesting. So, in a way, in the beginning you were part of the company?" she asked.

"Only as far as my one friend was involved. The matchmakers were already employed and had strong reputations for being good at what they do. I simply added a new step in one of the background checks they were already running."

"The sign on the wall says everyone deserves to be happy ever after. Is that something you want for yourself?" she asked. She knew that this question wasn't just for her interview. Willow had said happy and successful weren't mutually exclusive and Nichole needed to hear Conner's answer so that maybe she could keep herself from falling in love with him.

"I do want that for myself," he said. "I'm just not entirely sure what I need to be happy in a relationship."

The words were unexpected and Nichole glanced up at him to see how intently he was staring at her. He reached over and took her iPhone from her hand and turned off the recording option.

Conner had a sinking feeling that he was losing control of the entire situation with Nichole. Last night he'd had to carry her back to her room because he'd wanted her to sleep in his arms all night and after the night before when that had happened, he knew if he was going to maintain any control over his emotions and keep from letting this mistress thing become a real relationship, he couldn't sleep with her.

Sex was fine, but sleeping with her made him feel things that he couldn't attribute to chemistry. And he knew that was a mistake. From the beginning, Nichole hadn't been like other women and instead of seeing that as a challenge, his mind was saying he should have viewed it as warning.

But he hadn't. And part of him felt as if it was almost too late now. "I want to be happy as much as the next guy."

"I guess that's off the record?" she asked.

"Yes. This is between you and me," he said. "I know you're upset about last night."

She exhaled heavily and put her pen down on the desk. "You are so right I am. But I can't get into that right now. We only have thirty minutes for this interview."

"There's really not much else to say about the company. But I will answer your questions later if they keep coming up."

"Thank you," she said. "So what do you want to discuss?"

He didn't know. Now that he'd pushed to make it personal, he was unsure. Ah, hell, this was a mistake. A big one. He should pretend he'd received a page from the office and leave now.

"I can't sleep with you at night and still be objective about our relationship the next day," he said.

She nibbled on her lower lip and he couldn't resist leaning in to kiss her. She didn't relax into his embrace as she normally did and that was an indication of how upset she still was at him.

"I can't, either. I'm struggling here because I can't tell if what I want is driven by you or by me. I have always had light, no-strings-attached relationships, but with you that doesn't seem to be enough."

He didn't like hearing about her past relationships, even though he knew that was a hypocritical attitude to have. He'd had the same kind of relationships, but he didn't like the thought of any other man touching Nichole intimately. Or knowing her the way he was getting to know her.

"I don't know, either. You are the worst possible woman for me to be in this situation with. You're a reporter—"

"I know. And you are a commitmentphobe," she said. "We aren't exactly each other's perfect mate, but this bargain we struck…it's more complicated than I thought it would be."

He had to admit it was for him, too. He thought they'd have sex, he'd keep her off balance and in a daze, she wouldn't ask too many questions and the month would speed by. Damn, had he been wrong. His objectivity had been compromised as far as she was concerned.

"I'm sorry," he said.

"The worst part is that even after everything that's gone on between us, I'm not sorry."

Those words gave him back the upper hand. He had the feeling that if he was careful in how he handled her from now on, she might be willing to forgive him his shortcomings. And this bargain could still work out for him the way he needed it to.

"We will just have to figure it out as we go along," he said, hoping those words would be enough to keep her happy with him.

"Yes, we will," she said.

"I did have one more question for you," she said.

"Yes?"

"Is there a part of you that wonders whether your parents' relationship would have turned out differently if they had used a service like this one?" she asked.

Just like that, she had the upper hand again. Yes, it was

something he'd debated a million times. When his friend, Grant, had been the victim of a gold digger and Conner had referred him to the matchmaking service, he'd thought of his mom. Would a matchmaker have been able to foresee that his father could create two separate families and never let those lives touch?

He had no idea if that would have mitigated the situation they'd all found themselves in.

"I don't dwell on the past," he said.

"Conner, I gave you access to me in a way I've not given any other man. I expect you to honor our bargain in the same way and answer my questions."

He shoved his chair back from the table and paced away from her. "I can't do that. We didn't agree to how I'd answer your questions. Only that I would."

She stood up as well. "I'm not going to let you push my questions aside. This isn't too personal. It is a simple question."

"It's not simple, as you well know. It's damn complicated and plays on a boy's emotional reactions to a horrible situation with his parents. I'm a man and I run this company for a profit. Sure, it'd be nice to say that I have some kind of romantic delusion about how my parents' marriage could have been saved, but it's simply not true.

"My dad was a duplicitous man—both in how he treated his family and in his shady business dealings. Do I think a matchmaker could have somehow gleaned that about him in a fifteen-minute interview? Doubtful."

Conner knew he needed to stop talking, but the anger he felt at his father was welling up inside him and the anger he felt toward Nichole for making him think about these things and feel the way he used to was huge. He shoved his hands in his pockets and then started walking toward the door of the conference room.

"That last part was off the record—don't print it," he said. "This interview is over for today. I have a dinner meeting tonight and my colleague is bringing his wife. I expect you to attend. My assistant will text you the address and time."

He walked out the door without a backward glance and kept on walking until he was on the street. He ignored the Rolls Royce Phantom parked at the curb and just tried to lose himself in the crowd. He'd like to pretend that the only emotions roiling through him right now were anger, but he also knew there was a bit of sadness tinged with regret when it came to how he'd handled Nichole once again.

Thirteen

Nichole dressed for her dinner with Conner with the most care she'd spent on herself in years. The way he'd left her at Matchmakers, Inc. had shaken her. She intended to follow up with him tonight when they were alone.

But she wanted him off guard. She needed him to be awed by how she looked and to want her to stay in his life.

She was scared because everything he'd said to her made her fall a little more for him. He was wounded and, she had to assume a little threatened by having her in his life. And even though she'd always thought she wasn't one of those women who wanted to heal a man, she did want to help him put his past to rest if she could. She needed to figure out how to fix that for him.

And though she knew there wasn't an easy way to do that, she was tempted to try.

She arrived at Del Posto, the restaurant in the Meatpacking District owned by celebrity chef Mario Batali.

Nichole had never eaten there before. Conner was waiting in the crowded lobby for her.

He smiled when she walked over to him, making her realize he was going to pretend that nothing had happened earlier between them. She leaned up and kissed his cheek.

"Thanks for getting here on time. Cam and Becca Stern aren't going to be meeting us for another ten minutes," Conner said. "I wanted a chance to give you some background on them before they arrived."

"Shoot," she said. "If you'd texted me the names earlier I would have done a Google search on them."

"Good idea. If we do this again I'll definitely do that. Cam is the co-owner of Luna Azul in Miami. It's one of the hottest nightclubs on the East Coast."

"I'm familiar with it. Nate Stern, his younger brother, is my contact in Miami and South Beach for gossip. He used to be a baseball player."

"Good. So you're familiar with them. I'm one of the investors in a second location for Luna Azul here in Manhattan and tonight's dinner is to discuss some of the details of that. But since he's brought his wife, I think it will be more social," Conner said, leading her into the bar area. "Everything said businesswise would have to be off the record."

"I know that," she said. "But thank you for always being so official."

"That was sarcasm, right?" he asked.

"Yup. When are you going to realize—never mind. You're never going to see me as a different type of reporter from the guy who duped you when you were young."

He shook his head. "I'm trying. What can I get you to drink?"

"A bellini," she said. The sweet peach and prosecco drink was exactly what she needed to relax and just let the evening progress. She was beginning to suspect that being a mistress meant pushing emotions to the very bottom. How else did women survive in this position?

She knew she should be thinking of their arrangement as a business deal—exactly what Conner had told her to do in the beginning, but she hadn't been able to. She didn't want to. It was too intimate for that and every time they were together—not just sexually—it was harder for her to keep the line between personal and professional clear.

Conner came back with the drinks. He handed her glass to her and then lifted his own. "A toast."

"To?"

"To you, Nichole, for putting up with me and making me want to be a better man," he said.

Damn, why had he said that? She clinked her glass to his and started to say something when a couple joined them. She took a sip of her drink while Conner shook hands with Cam Stern. They were the same height. Cam was tan, as befitted a man who lived in Miami. He kept one arm wrapped around his wife's waist and she smiled up at him.

"Introduce us to your lady," Cam said.

"Becca and Cam Stern, this is Nichole Reynolds," Conner said.

Nichole held her hand out to each of them and they both shook it.

"I know your name," Becca said. "I read your column online every day."

"Thanks," Nichole said. "I also talk to your brother-in-law frequently to keep up-to-date on what's going on in your neck of the woods."

"I'm confused," Cam said. "Conner, did you know you were dating a reporter?"

"Of course I did, Cam," Conner said.

Cam winked at Nichole. "Sorry, my dear, but he's always said reporters were the scourge of the earth."

"I'm trying to bring him around to a new way of thinking," she said.

"Is it working?" Cam asked.

Conner snaked his arm around her waist and pulled her close for a quick kiss. "She's got her ways of making me forget she's a reporter."

Nichole knew that wasn't true, but quickly picked up on the fact that, for tonight at least, he wanted Cam and Becca to see them as a couple. Not a man and his mistress.

Luckily, the hostess called them and they were seated in a private area. Dinner was a lively affair that mainly consisted of general conversation. As Conner had suspected, the inclusion of the women made it a social evening instead of a strictly business meeting.

Nichole learned that Becca and Cam had a son who'd recently turned two. Becca was a doting mom who thought her son was a genius. Cam was proud of his boy as well and both parents had more than one time during the evening pulled out their cell phone to show off pictures of their child.

"Are you planning for more children?" Nichole asked.

"Yes, as a matter of fact, Becca just learned she's three months' pregnant," Cam said.

"Congratulations," Conner said.

"You thinking about starting a family soon?" Cam said to Conner. "Now that you've found a woman like Nichole."

Nichole looked over at Conner and wondered what he'd say to that. She didn't feel that either of them was ready for a family at this point.

"We're still getting to know each other and enjoying our relationship. We aren't that serious," Conner said and turned the conversation away from them.

Nichole knew that he could have said she's my mistress and we just have sex, so she counted herself lucky that he hadn't. It was the kind of comment she'd made a million times in the past about someone she was dating and she knew the words shouldn't have hurt her, but deep inside they did.

Nichole had been avoiding him for the last five days. When they'd come home from dinner with Cam and Becca, she'd said she had menstrual cramps and rushed off to her bed alone. The next day she'd been gone before he got up again.

He knew something was the matter because she'd even turned down his invitation to the party at his mother's house—he had thought she wanted to observe him with his family. He'd gone against his better judgment in inviting her, hoping she'd see it as the olive branch he'd meant it to be. But she'd declined.

That night, he sent Randall to pick her up after work and bring her back to his apartment. He'd had to cancel all his plans for the evening, but he didn't care what happened. He was going to get to the bottom of whatever was going on between them. If she wanted to back out, well, then, he'd have to think it over.

She had enough to run a story about his involvement with Matchmakers, Inc. and the television show. But she'd always wanted more from him. He'd tried to deliver it, but in the end he didn't know if he'd ever be able to give her what she really wanted.

She walked in the front door of the apartment around 7:30 and put her keys on the table near the door.

"I can't believe you had Randall practically kidnap me," she said, hands on her hips. She wore a pencil skirt with a button-down blouse tucked into it. Her hair was in a high ponytail and she had a pair of designer shades pushed up on her head.

"I asked you to dinner," he said.

"And I said not tonight," she said.

"Well, our agreement was for every night," he said. "And you've been avoiding me. We need to talk. Since you've been doing your level best to avoid me, I had no other choice. Come in and sit down. I've poured you a glass of wine," he said.

She walked across the floor with that slow gliding gait of hers and he watched her move. God, he wanted this woman. The two nights she'd spent in his arms hadn't been nearly enough.

Part of him suspected a million nights wouldn't be enough but he wasn't going to have that many, so he'd have to make do with this time they had together.

She sat down on the edge of the couch and took the wineglass he held out to her. Conner was nervous, and that annoyed him. In fact he hadn't been this nervous since the first time he'd walked into the board of directors meeting for Macafee International and told them that he was ready to run the company.

He took a swallow of the scotch and soda he'd poured for himself and then sat down next to her on the couch.

"Why are you hiding from me?" he asked, point blank. "I'd come to expect you to be someone who would confront a problem, not avoid it."

She took a sip of her wine and then set the glass on the coffee table. "I am normally a person who faces things head-on, but I didn't know how to handle this. We have an agreement, we aren't in a normal relationship, as you sort of stated to your friends at dinner the other night."

He shoved his hand through his hair, something he

knew was a bad habit. "I didn't say anything about us that wasn't true."

She frowned a little. "I know. I guess I had started thinking that we might have something more between us."

"Like what?"

She took another sip of her wine and then put the glass down. "Despite the agreement, I'm starting to care for you, Conner."

"I care for you, too."

She smiled at him then. She took her sunglasses from her head and tossed them on the table. "I hoped you would. I didn't know how else to deal with this. I've never been in a relationship where I was so concerned about making it work, but I am with you."

"That's flattering and I'd love to see this work out for us, too, but I'm not sure…"

He stood up and walked to the windows to look down at the city. He knew something about himself that he'd never shared with anyone else. He was very afraid that he was like his father in more than just business. He might be the kind of man who was incapable of loving anyone.

He cared deeply for his sister and his mother, but that didn't feel like love. And though he had to be honest and say that Nichole mattered more to him than he'd ever thought any woman could, he didn't see it developing any further.

He wanted her. He lusted after her as if he'd never been with a woman before and had just discovered sex. But it was more than that.

"What aren't you sure about?" she asked him.

"I'm not sure I have any more to offer you than what we have right now," he said.

"I don't know that I do, either. Why don't we both try it together?"

He was tempted by what she was offering, but he knew he'd be lying to her if he let her in any further. "Red, I would love to say yes and become that happily-ever-after guy you asked me about at the Matchmakers, Inc. office, but I'm not that kind of guy."

"You're just afraid to take a chance," she said. "You can love. I'm scared, too."

He wasn't afraid of her or of caring for her. "I'm not afraid."

"Yes, you are. Whatever is going on inside you is fear. I know you can love. I've seen you with your mom and your sister," she said.

"You're grasping at straws," he said, shutting down all his emotions instead of letting her get through to him. He wasn't going to give that kind of power over himself to anyone, especially Nichole.

"I can't," he said. "I like you, you're sexy and you amuse me, but that's all this can ever be. I don't feel that deep bond with you that could be love."

"I don't believe you."

"Then you're fooling yourself. Love is a superficial emotion that people use to make excuses for their own lack of control. I'm not one of those people."

Nichole saw how sincere Conner was as he confessed that he couldn't love her because love was superficial. But she didn't believe it. She could see fear in him because it was the same thing she had inside of her.

She didn't know what the future held. She'd seen her parents stick together to their own detriment early in their marriage, but then they had figured out a way to make it work. And her father had always said it was the love he felt for her mom that had helped them survive as a couple.

"Love isn't superficial," she said. "I don't think you be-

lieve that, either. That's the reason why you didn't throw
me out of your office that first day. And it's also why you
invited me to go to your mom's party this weekend. You do
care about me, Conner. And there isn't anything you can
say that will change my mind. Why not give us a chance?"

She could see the conflict within him as he watched her.
There was a longing in his eyes that made her want to say
just forget it, but she knew she couldn't keep on this way.
From the beginning, the illicit thrill of thinking of herself
as Conner's mistress had been exciting, but the reality had
always made her hurt deep inside.

She wasn't sure if it was just that she had recognized
him as…her soul mate. They were so similar in many
things, especially in how both of them were afraid to let
anyone too close. Yet Nichole was willing to take a chance.
Willing to give Conner entrée into her life and into her
heart. Clearly, he wasn't willing to do the same.

"I can't," he said at last. "When my dad left, the way he
left, I decided that no one would have that kind of power
over my life. No one would hurt me that way again or disappoint me the way he did."

"I won't—"

"You have no idea if you will or not. The thing I learned
from that is that I have to control who I let into my life.
And what I've found to be true is that I function better
when I'm not involved with anyone.

"I thought that by making you my mistress, by keeping
in mind that you were a reporter, I'd be able to keep you
in one neat, safe corner of my life. We would make love
and enjoy superficial conversations, but that's it. That's
where it would all end."

"But it didn't work out that way, did it?" she asked. His
words were like a dagger in her heart. He was telling her he
was too afraid to take a chance on love. And Nichole had

just realized with Conner that she was the kind of woman who needed to take a chance on love to really experience it.

It was only standing here with him that made her see that all the light, fun relationships she'd had were meant to safeguard her heart. By keeping it light, she'd stayed safe until she met the one man she didn't want to keep out.

And he was afraid to take a gamble on her...on them.

"We already have found more than that. Well, I have," she said. "I think that you have, too. Otherwise, you wouldn't be so worried about letting me sleep in the same bed as you."

He thrust his hands through his hair until it was disheveled. He was agitated and she could tell that she was making her point with him. She felt a little ray of hope deep inside that she might be able to get through to him. Might be able to convince him that a real relationship was what they both needed.

"Don't read too much into that," he said carefully. "You are my mistress and it is important that you have your own living space."

"Too late. I already have," she said. She realized that she was seeing Conner the way she wanted him to be and not at all sure she was seeing him as he really was. "Tell me that you care about me."

"Why?"

"I need something to hang my hope on. I will stay with you and wait for you to get comfortable with having me in your life, but I need to know that you are capable of feeling something for me."

He paced around the room behind the couch and she watched him walking back and forth. It seemed to her that he was weighing his decision very carefully. She could see the tension inside him and had never seen him like this before.

"Conner."

"Yes?" he asked, looking at her.

She had the feeling she might have asked him for too much. Might have pushed him too far in her bid to get to the heart of what he really felt for her. But she also knew she had no choice. She couldn't keep living with him and pretending that it was okay that she was his mistress.

She wanted to feel safe enough to fall in love with him. Hell, who was she kidding? She was already in love with him, and now feeling so vulnerable she was looking for him to let her know she hadn't fallen alone.

She walked around to him and wrapped her arms around him. She hugged him close, trying to let her feelings surround him. "I'm not sure of this, either, but I'm willing to take a chance."

He hugged her close and she felt the terrible fist in her stomach start to loosen. He lowered his head and breathed in the scent of her hair and then he tipped her head up and she met that blue gaze of his, but she couldn't read any emotion in his eyes.

His mouth descended to hers and his tongue swept over her lips into her mouth. The kiss was long and sweet and as he pulled back from her she realized it was goodbye.

"I can't give you more than this," he said, tracing the line of her cheekbone with his forefinger.

She felt a stab of disappointment and, if she was honest, pain that he'd rejected her love. "I can't do this any longer. I'm going to leave."

"Don't do that."

"I have to," she said.

"What about your story?" he asked.

She felt how desperate he must be to keep her here to use that as a reason for her to stay. And that made the hurt in her heart that much keener. "I have everything I need to write my story."

She picked up her purse and walked slowly to her bedroom where she packed up her overnight bag and got her laptop. Conner didn't follow her and when she came back into the living room he stood in the exact same place.

She walked as slowly as she could to the door, hoping he'd call out that he'd changed his mind and stop her from leaving, but he didn't.

She got to the elevator and realized that she was crying and felt stupid that she was. She hadn't cried like this since the day she'd found her mother lying on the floor next to her bed. She hadn't hurt like this since then, either. And part of her wondered if Conner even knew what he was doing. Was life safer when you kept everyone out?

Fourteen

The next week was the longest of Conner's life. He focused on business, staying long hours at the office because when he went home it felt empty. Even though Nichole hadn't been in his home for that long, she'd left her trace in every room of the apartment.

He'd dealt with this kind of feeling before, but it had been a long time ago. He knew he'd made a mistake when he'd let her go, but given the way he felt now he also knew that it had been the right decision. As hard as it was, he was dealing with her absence in his life and he would just soldier on.

He'd had Mrs. Plumb pack the remainder of her belongings and then Randall had taken them back to her house. There was no sign of her left anywhere in the apartment, but he still felt her there. He spent too much time late at night standing in the doorway of the guest bedroom and wondering how much his carrying her back to her bed had contributed to her leaving.

His iPhone rang and he glanced at the screen to see it was his sister. He didn't want to talk to her so he ignored the call. He left his office and headed downstairs to the gym in his building. Maybe running would take his mind off Nichole.

He'd been reading her column every day, telling himself it was to see if she'd written her article on him yet, but he hadn't seen it. And part of him hoped it took her a while to write it because as long as she didn't he'd have the excuse to go and look at her picture.

She was a good writer, something he'd known since they'd first met, and he was surprised at how much she made him laugh when he read about the different people she reported on. Part of it was the way she captured the people that he knew pretty well; the other part was her wry take on life.

The current couple being taped for *Sexy & Single* were finally falling for each other and reading her columns about their love was just a tad painful. He knew that it was his own perception coloring what he read, but also felt that she was directing some jabs at him.

This morning's column, in particular, had hit a nerve, when she wrote about how Paul wasn't afraid to take a chance on letting Rikki into his life.

Those were practically the same words she'd said to him when she left. He still remembered how slowly she'd walked to the door. He wished he'd stopped her.

He got changed in the locker room and then walked into the main gym. His phone beeped, sending him an alert that he had mentions on Twitter. His sister was tweeting about him again.

But he didn't call her. He wasn't ready to talk to Jane

or his mom. He'd been avoiding both of them for the last week because he didn't want to deal with their questions about Nichole and he knew they'd have them.

He switched his iPhone to airplane mode, put on his exercise playlist, which featured lots of heavy metal from the '80s, and started running.

As AC/DC's *Back in Black* blared in his ears, he tried to put some distance between himself and his feelings for Nichole. But her face was there in his mind as he ran. The harder he pushed himself, the more he saw her. That impish, sexy grin on the Fourth of July. How earthy and sensual she'd looked that first night in his apartment in those damn skintight jeans and that tank top. The way she'd looked when she'd told him the terrible secret of her past. That vulnerability that she hadn't hidden from him, even though she didn't have to share what she was feeling with him.

Thirty minutes later he slowed his pace to a cool-down run, no closer to getting Nichole out of his mind than he'd been when he started. He got off the treadmill, switched his phone back on and found he'd missed three calls from Jane. He was planning to continue ignoring her until he got her text.

I'm worried about you. Call me.

He didn't want her worrying about him. He showered and then called her back.

"It's about time," Jane said. "Where the hell have you been?"

"Working, Janey."

"Mom is driving in from the Hamptons because she hasn't spoken to you in over a week."

"She doesn't need to do that," Conner said. "Let me call her and talk to her."

"Too late. We're descending on you. What's up?" she asked. "You haven't been like this...I can't remember the last time you completely shut down this way. And don't say it's business because I know you don't have any big deals going on right now."

"What do you mean descending on me?"

"We're coming to your place," she said.

"I'll come to you," he said. He didn't want to go to his apartment right now himself, nor have either of them there for that matter. "I'm on my way as we speak."

"Conner, are you okay?" she asked.

"Yes. I've just been really busy at work," he said.

"Okay. Are you bringing Nichole with you?" she asked. "I liked her and Mom wants to meet her."

Of course his mom wanted to meet her. Thanks to Jane's blabbing, she thought that Nichole and he were a couple. And thanks to his own blundering, that wasn't true anymore. "No, I'm not. We're no longer dating."

"Oh," Jane said. "Why not?"

"She wanted something from me I couldn't give her," Conner said after a long pause.

"What did she want?" Jane asked.

"Probably the same thing that Palmer wants from you," Conner said.

"What's wrong with us?" Jane asked. "Why can't we fall in love?"

"I don't know, Janey. I guess we're both afraid of the consequences."

"I think you're right," she said. "I wish we weren't."

"Well, it's not too late for you to change. Palmer isn't like Dad."

"You know the scary part is that I get that. But I'm still afraid to trust him."

Conner knew exactly what his sister was feeling in that regard. "I know."

Conner didn't want to think about how different Nichole was or how much he cared about her. He just wanted to find a numb place in his emotions and figure out how to keep living without her. The price of having her back in his life was too high, and one he wasn't willing to pay.

The first week after leaving Conner had been the hardest. She spent a lot of time at work writing about the lives of others. The hardest thing to write about was the progress of Paul and Rikki on the set of *Sexy & Single*.

It was amazing for her to see how much Rikki had changed over the course of their dates. They were at the halfway point in their televised dates and Nichole could see the couple falling in love. And seeing what a healthy relationship looked like made her wish that Conner could be a different kind of man. But in her heart she knew she wouldn't have fallen for him if he'd been anyone other than himself.

She'd found herself subsisting on coffee mostly. The second week after she left him, she woke on a Sunday morning and decided she didn't want to leave her apartment.

She moved her Keurig machine into the living room, put *Romancing the Stone* into her DVD player and sat there crying, wishing that Conner would unexpectedly show up on her doorstep and tell her that he loved her.

A knock on her door startled her because she rarely... okay, *never* had guests. She couldn't help the hope that blossomed in her heart as she walked to the door. She knew she looked terrible with her hair unbrushed and still in her PJs at three in the afternoon, but she didn't care.

She looked through the peephole and saw Gail and Willow standing there. She patted down her hair, undid the security locks and opened the door.

"I told you she must be sick," Gail said, coming into the apartment and looking around the room.

"She's not sick," Willow said. "She's hiding."

"Why are you two here?" Nichole asked.

"You missed brunch," Willow said. "You never miss brunch unless you text us and you didn't. Are you okay?"

She had forgotten it was the fourth Sunday of the month. "Oh, God, I'm sorry. I just lost track of the days."

Gail put her hand on Nichole's forehead. "You don't have a fever, but your eyes are watery and your nose is red."

Willow was walking around her small living room and saw the coffee machine on the end table and the pile of tissues on the couch. "Why is the Keurig in the living room?"

"I didn't want to have to walk to the kitchen," Nichole said.

"Is this about Conner?" Willow asked.

Nichole thought about lying to her friends, telling them that she had been working hard and needed a pajama day, but they'd both listened to her to as she'd tried to figure out what to do with him so they'd know she was lying. "It's over with him and me."

"Why didn't you call us?" Gail asked. "I know how hard it was for you to decide to live with him."

Nichole went over to the couch and sat down. Gail and Willow did the same. "I didn't want to talk about him. I'm still trying to figure out how I feel about everything."

"Tell us what happened," Will said.

"I fell in love with him. I should have known when my

instincts were telling me not to agree to be his mistress that it was because I cared about him.

"He isn't the type of man who feels safe being in love. He's afraid, I think. Oh, I really don't know what he thinks, but I asked him to give us a chance and he said no."

"Why?"

"He doesn't believe in love," Nichole said. "I get why. I mean his father did a number on him when he left in the middle of a scandal. And Conner never had a chance to talk to him because of that plane crash that killed him."

"He has issues," Gail said. "Can you get him to talk to you about it?"

"No. He doesn't want to. He likes the way his life is. He likes being alone. I thought I did, too, until I met him."

"I'm sorry," Gail said.

"Me, too. Do we hate him?" Willow asked.

"No, we don't hate him. I feel sorry for him. And I'm trying very hard to fall out of love with him," Nichole said.

"Is it working?" Willow asked.

"Not so far…I was hoping you guys would be him."

"I'm sorry we weren't," Gail said. "You need to get out of this apartment if you're going to forget him."

"I do?"

"Yes, as long as you stay home all you'll do is think about him. Russell and I are going sailing this afternoon. Why don't you come with us?"

Nichole loved her friend dearly, but the last thing she wanted to do was spend the afternoon with a couple who were clearly in love. Especially not sailing, when she remembered that it was Conner's favorite hobby.

"No, thanks," Nichole said. "I'm watching *Jewel of the Nile* next."

"No, you can't watch romantic movies now. It will just keep feeding your hopes," Willow said.

"I know, but I want to. I need to do this," Nichole said. "I'm going to be fine. It's just a broken heart. Hopefully, over time, it will heal."

"Do you want to be alone?" Gail asked.

"Today, yes, but not forever. I think I'm mourning what might have been and the sad part is I know that it's just my dreams of what might have been. Conner never did or said anything to make me believe he'd be different."

"None of that matters, does it?" Willow asked.

"Nope," Nichole said. "Have fun sailing this afternoon, Gail."

"Are you sure you'll be okay?" she asked.

"Yes, I'm fine. You both can go," Nichole said.

"I'll stay," Willow volunteered.

"You hate *Jewel of the Nile* and I don't want to hear your snide comments about the plotting," Nichole said.

Willow laughed and Nichole felt a little better knowing that she had these women as her friends. "I just need to feel sorry for myself for today. I'll snap out of it soon and be back to my old self."

Her friends left and slowly she found that she did start to feel better. She still missed Conner, but the reality of knowing he was truly out of her life forced her to start adjusting to living without him. She'd write her story about him and then hopefully be able to move on.

Summer had finally waned and it was fall. Conner would like to say that with the passing of time he'd stopped thinking about Nichole all the time, but he hadn't.

He was alternately annoyed at himself and angry with her for making him still feel something after all this time. She'd written her column about Matchmakers, Inc. and he'd enjoyed reading it, but she'd never written the story about him and the past. The one that he'd feared she'd write. He saw that as proof that she had more integrity than he'd thought she did.

He wished that he could find a way to meet her again and start over, but he knew that he'd never do it. He hated that even though it had been two months since she'd walked out his door, a day hadn't gone by when he didn't think of her.

He'd been invited to the finale of the third couple's matchmaking episodes on *Sexy & Single* and he was attending. He told himself and his assistant that he was going because it was expected of him. But the truth was he knew that Willow was a good friend of Nichole's and he hoped that either Nichole would be there or he'd be able to bring her name up to Willow and find out how she was.

The finale was being held as the first one had been, in a large ballroom in the Big Apple Kiwi Klub. Russell Holloway had allowed the *Sexy & Single* TV show to shoot there in exchange for some free publicity. Conner couldn't help but remember the lunch he'd had at the Klub with Nichole. It was on that day that she'd agreed to be his.

A big part of him wished he'd taken better care of how he'd kept her. He wondered if she'd still be in his bed—no she wouldn't, he thought. He'd only asked for her to be his mistress for a month.

He knew now that a month wouldn't have been long enough. He was starting to think a lifetime wouldn't be long enough, but he knew that wasn't in the cards. Hell, he didn't want it to be. He didn't want her back because she made him vulnerable and yet all he thought about when he wasn't working was how to get her back.

He walked into the ballroom and saw his friend, Russell, standing off to one side. Russell waved Conner over and he walked across the ballroom, scanning the crowd for Nichole. He didn't see his sexy redhead.

But she wasn't his. He'd kicked her out of his life—rather, let her walk out of his life—and he had to move on. He was starting to feel as if he was obsessed with her.

"Hey, Conner, how's things?" Russell said as he joined the other man.

"Can't complain," Conner said.

"I haven't seen you at the yacht club lately," Russell remarked.

"I've been busy with work," Conner said. And he had been. His staff were all complaining about the hours he'd been putting in because he'd been demanding they work just as hard as he did. He knew he'd become a tyrant at work, but it was the only time he stopped thinking about Nichole, so he had to stay there longer.

"I know how that is. I'm leaving next week to break ground on my first family-destination resort."

"How's that going?" Conner asked.

"Good. It's a totally different market and I love the challenge of figuring it out," Russell said.

"Is Gail going with you to the groundbreaking?" Conner asked. He remembered that Gail was one of Nichole's good friends, too.

"She is. I told her I needed my fiancée by my side," Russell said.

"Yes, he did," Gail said, joining the men. "And since the first resort is in L.A., I thought I could combine it with a work trip. I have some clients I'm going to meet with out there."

Conner wanted to play it cool and try to ask some innocuous question about Nichole, but he couldn't. "Hi, Gail, how is Nichole?" he blurted out.

"She's good. But you should ask her yourself," Gail said. "She's over there."

Conner turned his head to see that Nichole had entered

the ballroom while he'd been talking to Russell. She looked good. She was thinner than he remembered, her cheek-bones more pronounced. Her hair seemed thicker than he remembered, too. He stood there staring at her, his eyes slowly skimming over her body until his gaze dropped to her stomach and he noticed a small bump.

He started walking toward her, wondering if he was seeing things. But he knew her body intimately and she hadn't been like this before. She glanced up as she saw him walking toward her and broke off her conversation.

"Can I have a word with you in private?" Conner asked.

She nodded and pivoted on her heel, walking out of the ballroom and down the hall where there was a bench tucked into a small alcove.

He followed her, thinking how much he'd missed seeing her. His mind was also going over the possibility that she might be pregnant. He remembered that the second time they'd made love, he hadn't used protection.

"What can I do for you?" she asked, stopping at the bench.

"Are you pregnant?" he asked.

"Yes."

"Why didn't you call and tell me?" he demanded. He couldn't process everything at once and clung to some anger to see him through this encounter. He was conflicted. He wanted to pull her into his arms and kiss her, but he also wanted to know why she hadn't let him know about the baby because that would have been enough of a reason for him to demand she come back into his life.

"Why would I?" she asked.

"I am the father of your child," he said. He didn't ask, because he knew Nichole well enough to know she'd never move on to another man that quickly, despite the serial dating he knew she'd done before him. He'd been as different for her as she'd been for him. And she'd said she loved him.

He hadn't forgotten that. Hell. Dammit to hell. He suddenly realized that the reason he hadn't been able to forget about her was that he loved her. But now it didn't matter. She'd think he was telling her what she wanted to hear for the baby's sake.

It was too late.

Fifteen

Nichole didn't know what to say to Conner. How could she put into words that she wanted him to come back to her for her—not for a baby? She just hadn't figured that out, and no matter how many late-night gab-fests she'd had with her girlfriends, she hadn't come up with a solution.

"I didn't think you'd care," she said at last. She should have been better prepared to see him, but she hadn't been. She noticed that he'd had his hair cut and she longed to run her fingers through his hair. He was cleanly shaved, but looked tired.

She'd missed him. Couldn't help but sleep hugging the pillow he'd slept on that one night he'd spent in her bed. She often thought of what she'd say to her child when that child asked about his father, but she didn't have words for that yet, either.

"Why wouldn't I care?" he asked.

"You said that you didn't need me in your life. I'm pretty

sure when I walked out the door you planned to never see me again. Why would a child make any difference?"

"Because it's my child," he said.

He put his hand out to her, but she stepped back. If he touched her, she was either going to start crying or jump into his arms and neither of those actions was something she wanted to do right now. She needed to keep her cool and let this play out.

"So you want me in your life for the child?" she asked. "That's not acceptable to me."

She could see how conflicted he was and wanted to offer him some kind of emotional help, but she knew herself well enough to realize that she couldn't put him first. From the moment she'd found out she was pregnant, she'd stopped moping around with her broken heart.

She'd never expected a child to give her hope. But that's what her pregnancy had done for her. All the unwanted love she had for Conner she could pour into the child that was growing inside her. And that was what she'd done.

"I'm sorry you feel that way, but I do want my child," he said.

Nichole realized that part of her had been hoping he'd say he wanted her, too, but she knew she had to stop hoping that Conner would react the way she wanted him to. "We can discuss that some other time. I need to get back into the ballroom."

"No," he said. "We need to finish talking about this now. I want you to move back into my apartment so I can take care of you while you're pregnant."

She shook her head. "Why do you need me to do that?" she asked.

"I...for the baby, of course."

"Oh, for the baby," she said. "Then my answer is no.

We can discuss some kind of custody arrangement once the child is born."

She turned to walk away and Conner grabbed her arm and stopped her. "Why won't you at least try to work this out with me?"

"Because I need something from you that you can't give me. You said you couldn't trust someone to be there for you. I don't mean *someone,* I mean me. And when it was just me you couldn't love or care for, then I probably would have gone back to you. You have no idea how much I've missed you," she said. Admitting out loud what she'd felt for him was so cathartic.

"I've missed you, too," he said.

"You have?" she asked.

"Yes."

"Why haven't you called me?" she asked, suspecting that Conner was going to say whatever he had to to get her to do what he wanted. She hated that that was her first reaction, but until he gave her some sign that he really cared for her, she wasn't going to just blindly trust him. She couldn't.

If he broke her heart again, she knew she'd never recover from it.

"I was getting on without you," he said.

"What's changed?" she asked, hoping for just a tiny sign that he loved her.

"Seeing you today. Knowing that you're going to have my baby," he said.

The baby. This was why, despite Gail's urging her to tell Conner, she hadn't. He didn't want her and if she wasn't pregnant, he wouldn't be here trying to talk her into coming back now.

"I'm sorry, Conner, but that's not good enough," she said.

He pushed his hands through his hair the way he did

whenever he was agitated and stared at her. She sensed for a minute that he might understand what she needed from him and she waited, hoping one last time that he'd say what she needed to hear.

"This is all I have," he said at last. "I can't be someone I'm not."

She knew that. She reached up and squeezed his shoulder before pulling her arm out of his grasp. "I know you can't. Please don't blame me for hoping that you could be."

She walked away and this time wasn't any easier than the first time she'd walked away from him. It was what she needed to do, so she kept on walking without looking back at him.

When she entered the ballroom and saw all the trappings of romance, it hit her hard. Why hadn't she fallen in love with a man who could love her back?

What was it about her that led her to men who only wanted fun and no commitment? And why, when her own desires had changed, hadn't fate sent her a man who wanted the same things she wanted?

She realized that she was on the verge of crying and tried to find a quiet place to retreat, but when she turned toward the door she saw Conner standing there. They stared at each other for long minutes and Nichole felt her heart beat so heavy in her chest. Finally, Conner lifted his hand and waved at her before turning and walking away.

And Nichole realized there was something worse than that long lonely walk she'd just taken down the hall away from Conner.

Watching him walk away from her. She knew that no matter what the future held for their child, this was the moment of finality between the two of them and he wasn't ever coming back to her.

* * *

Saturday morning Conner was woken up by a call from his mother. "Good morning, Conner. Have you seen the *America Today Weekend Magazine?*"

Conner sat up in bed and looked at the clock with bleary eyes. After seeing Nichole last night, he'd come home and hit the bottle heavily. It was only 7:00 a.m. His head was pounding and he felt like hell. What had his mom asked?

"What?"

"There is an article about us in *America Today,*" she said. "Have you read it?"

"No. What do you mean us?"

"Our family…well, sort of you. Do you want me to read it to you?"

"Sure," he said. Dammit, he thought…what the hell had she written?

"'Behind the Scenes with the Rich and Famous, by Nichole Reynolds.

"'Like many of you I grew up reading about the wealthy and the powerful. As a teenager, I envied their lives of privilege, their cars and clothes. As I got older and established myself as a writer for *America Today,* I started to gain some more insight into their lives.

"'I saw that behind the privileged facade many of them had worries and concerns that never really touched my life. But it wasn't until I sat down to write an article about Conner Macafee that this was driven home.

"'Like the rest of you, I often wondered what was hiding behind his frosty blue gaze and how the scandal that had surrounded his father and his father's death had affected him. I wanted to know this not because it would bring me anything I could use in my life, but simply because it was a juicy story.

"'I never thought about the impact writing about the rich and famous has on them. Now, some people court publicity, but Conner always shied away from it and that whetted my appetite to know more. When I did finally have a chance to talk to him, I was surprised to find him relatable and human.

"'His family wasn't the dysfunctional mess that many of ours would be if something similar had happened in our lives. His mother, sister and he are very close, with a tight bond of love that flows between them, and they've moved on with their lives the way that true families do by supporting each other.

"'And this reporter has figured out that leaving their past in the past was the best thing that I could do. Examining his life taught me an important lesson in dealing with moving on. I can only hope that I would deal with that kind of incident with as much dignity as the entire Macafee clan has.'

"That's it. What a nice piece," his mom said. "Why did you let her go?"

Conner was still taking in what Nichole had written. It wasn't about them at all, but about him. And he almost felt as if it was written to him. "I was afraid of keeping her in my life."

He heard his mother sigh. "I made a mistake all those years ago, son. When everything happened with your father, I ran away and took you and Janey with me. I stopped going to charity events, I tried to hide, but that wasn't smart of me."

"You did the best you could, Mom," Conner said.

"I put myself first and set a bad example for you and your sister. Instead of staying put and figuring out how to move on, I hid from my own heartbreak and made the two of you afraid to take a chance on love. That was never my intent."

"I don't blame you at all."

"You blame your father," she said. "And I did, too, but the fact is he's gone and we all should leave him in the past, as Nichole said. And I want you to have a shot at a real future."

Conner did, too. "Mom, what if I'm like Dad and one woman isn't enough for me?"

"You have never been serious about any woman and I'm guessing from what Jane said that you are about this one. Just her, am I right?" his mom asked.

"Yes."

"Your father always loved all women. I had to fight for him and it was a constant battle to keep his attention on me. Don't think you are anything like him."

He hadn't remembered that until his mother said it. His father had been a world-class flirt, and there hadn't been a woman in their lives that he hadn't tried to charm. "I guess I don't want to let her in. What if I can't make it work?"

"Being in love is the greatest feeling in the world, and even if it doesn't work out, no one can ever take that from you. But you have to take the chance on it first," she said.

Her words set something free in him. "Thanks, Mom."

"You're welcome, son. Am I going to meet Nichole soon?"

"If I have anything to say about it, you will," Conner said. His head was still pounding, but he didn't feel quite so tired. He hung up with his mom and got out of bed, knowing he had to come up with a plan to get Nichole back.

He showered and shaved and stared at himself in the mirror, but he still had no idea what to do. He only knew that he wanted her back.

Finally he did the only thing he could do. Picking up the phone, he dialed her number and waited.

She didn't answer, so he left her a voice mail. "This is Conner. I read the article in *America Today Weekend Magazine* and we need to talk."

He hung up and waited five minutes before he called back again, but when she didn't answer, he simply hung up. He needed to get other things in place, as well.

He loved her and he wanted to make sure she knew it. He left his apartment and went to the jewelry store to buy her two pieces of jewelry. The first was an engagement ring, because he couldn't tell her he loved her and then not ask her to share the rest of his life with him.

The second was a charm bracelet, which he hadn't intended to buy, but when he saw the Swarovski crystal fireworks charm, he thought of her and the day they'd met. How fireworks had sparked between the two of them. He imagined he would fill the bracelet with other charms as their life together progressed.

He ordered flowers and champagne and then went back home to wait for her call. She finally called him at three in the afternoon, just as he was about to go to her place and find her.

"Hello, Nichole," he said.

"Hi, Conner. What's up?" she asked.

"I need you to come to my place to discuss the article you wrote."

"I don't know if that's a good idea," she said.

"Please," he said. "I think after everything we've been through you could come over here."

She sighed. "Okay, it might take me some time to get a cab."

"Randall is waiting outside your building for you," he said.

He hung up and glanced around the room to make sure everything was just as he wanted. Then he sat down to wait out the longest fifteen minutes of his life. When he heard the elevator bing and then her footsteps on the tile outside the front door, he wiped his sweating palms on his pant legs and hoped that she still loved him enough to take him back.

Nichole couldn't believe she'd returned to Conner's apartment. She wanted to pretend she was doing it for their unborn child, but she knew that part of her still hoped things could work out between them.

He opened the door before she got to it and she stopped in her tracks. Seeing him standing there just reminded her of the painful way they had said goodbye the last time. And she realized that no matter how much she hoped it might be different, this meeting would more than likely end in the same painful way.

Was she some kind of masochist to keep doing this to herself?

"Come in," he said, stepping back.

She started to walk over the threshold, but as she brushed past him, Conner pulled her into his arms. He held her so tightly to him that she felt that glimmer of hope deep inside her again.

He tipped her head up to his and kissed her slowly. His hands slid down her back and he pulled her so close to him that she couldn't help but believe he'd invited her here today because he finally realized he cared about her.

He lifted her into his arms and carried her into his apartment. She saw that roses were covering every surface in the living room as he set her down on the couch. Instead of sitting down beside her, he stood next to her.

"Thank you for coming here today," he said.

"You're welcome. I'm sorry I didn't send you an advance copy of the article."

"That's fine. I didn't call you to talk about that."

"Why did you call me, then?" she asked.

He shoved his hands through his hair in that trait of his that she was coming to know meant he was going to tell her something that was hard for him. He only did that when he was nervous.

"I asked you to come here today because I realized what a fool I'd been. Letting you walk out of my life once was stupid, but twice was completely unacceptable."

"I agree," she said. "What changed your mind?"

He got down on one knee by the couch and reached out to touch the bump of her pregnancy belly. "I don't want our child to grow up the way we did. Shrouded in secrets and living with lies. And that is what will happen unless I tell you something today."

"What?" she asked. "I can't live with a man who doesn't love me."

"I know that and you don't have to. I love you, Nichole."

"Are you sure? A few days ago, you didn't think you could love me."

Conner nodded at her. "I'm very sure. It didn't take me long to figure out that I loved you and that I was afraid to let myself admit it. But not admitting it didn't mean it wasn't true. I've missed you so damn much the last two months. I've thought of nothing but you.

"I love you and I hope that you still love me, but if you don't I'm determined to be the man you need so that I can win your love again."

"I do love you," she said, reaching out to touch his face, then putting her hand over his on her belly. He got to his feet and pulled her into his arms, holding her as close as he could.

"I can't live without you," he whispered in her ear. "I know that you could have an easier life with a man who is more open to emotions, but you won't ever find a man who loves you more than I do."

"I don't want to live without you, either," she said, kissing him solidly.

"Good," he said, going down on one knee again. He pulled a small ring box from his pocket. "Nichole Reynolds, will you do me the honor of being my wife?"

She got down on her knees in front of him and took the ring from him, putting it on her finger. "Yes, Conner, I will be your wife."

Conner hugged her close and then scooped her up and set her on the couch. "I know you're pregnant, but can you have a small sip of champagne to celebrate our engagement?"

"I think one sip will be okay," she said.

"While I open the bottle, why don't you open this?" he asked, handing her another jewelry box.

"You're going to spoil me," she said.

"I think I'm entitled to. I'm the man who loves you, after all," he said.

For a man who'd said he had a hard time admitting to his emotions, now that he had he seemed to be unable to stop.

Nichole was delighted by the charm bracelet and the fireworks charm. "I guess I'm not going to have to crash the party next year?" she asked.

"No, you're going to have unlimited access to my life for all of eternity," he said.

After they toasted their love, Conner carried her into his bedroom where he made love to her. Then he held her in his arms all afternoon while they talked about the future and made love again.

Nichole fell asleep knowing she'd gotten it all: the story of her lifetime with the man of her dreams.

* * * * *

A SCANDAL SO SWEET

BY
ANN MAJOR

Ann Major lives in Texas with her husband of many years and is the mother of three grown children. She has a master's degree from Texas A&M at Kingsville, Texas, and is a former English teacher. She is a founding board member of the Romance Writers of America and a frequent speaker at writers' groups.

Ann loves to write—she considers her ability to do so a gift. Her hobbies include hiking in the mountains, sailing, ocean kayaking, traveling and playing the piano. But most of all, she enjoys her family. Visit her website at www.annmajor.com.

A special thank-you to Stacy Boyd, my editor, for her
patience and brilliance.

A special thank-you to Nicole, a fan who sent me an
email encouraging me while writing this book.

And a thank-you to Ted.

Prologue

A man's life could change in a heartbeat.

Seven days ago Zach Torr had been in the Bahamas, elated to be closing the biggest deal of his career. Then he'd received an emergency call about his uncle.

The one person who'd held Zach's back these past fifteen years was gone.

Now, still dressed in the suit he'd worn to give his uncle's eulogy, Zach stood on the same narrow girder from which his uncle had fallen. He stared fearlessly down at his contractors, bulldozers, generators, cranes and men, big tough men, who appeared smaller than ants in their yellow hard hats sixty-five stories below.

Zach was a tall man with thick black hair and wide shoulders; a man his competitors swore was as ruthless as the fiercest jungle predator. The women he'd left behind agreed, saying he'd walked out on them without ever looking back.

Normally, his eyes were colder than black ice. Today they felt moist and stung. How had Uncle Zachery felt when he'd stood here for the last time?

A shudder went through Zach. Men who walked iron were no less afraid of heights than other men.

The chill breeze buffeting him whipped his tie against his face, almost causing him to step backward. He froze, caught his balance…hissed in a breath. A sneeze or a slip— was that how it had happened? Up here the smallest mistake could be fatal.

Had Uncle Zachery jumped? Been startled by a bird? Been pushed? Suffered a heart attack? Or simply fallen as the foreman had said? Zach would never know for sure.

As Uncle Zachery's sole heir, Zach had endured several tough interviews with the police.

The newspaper coverage had been more critical of him than usual because he'd stayed in the Bahamas to close the deal before coming home.

He hated the invasion of the limelight, hated being written about by idiots who went for the jugular with or without the facts.

Because the fact was, for Zach, the world had gone dark after that phone call.

When he'd been nineteen and in trouble with the law for something he hadn't done, Uncle Zachery had come back to Louisiana from the Middle East, where he'd been building a city for a sheik. Uncle Zachery had saved him. If not for his uncle, Zach would still be serving hard time.

Houston-bred, Zach had been cast out of town by his beautiful stepmother after his father's death. Her reason—she'd wanted everything. His father had naively assumed she'd be generous with his sixteen-year-old son and had left her his entire fortune.

If it hadn't been for Nick Landry, a rough Louisiana shrimper who'd found Zach in a gutter after he'd been beaten by his stepmother's goons, Zach might not have survived. Nick had taken Zach to his shack in Bonne Terre, Louisiana, where Zach had spent three years.

It was in Bonne Terre where he'd met the girl he'd given his heart and soul to. It was in Bonne Terre where he'd been charged with statutory rape. And it was in Bonne Terre where the girl he'd loved had stood silently by while he was tried and condemned.

Fortunately, that's when Uncle Zachery had returned. He'd discovered his sister-in-law's perfidy, tracked Zach to Louisiana, gone up against the town of Bonne Terre and won. He'd brought Zach back to Houston, educated him and put him to work. With his powerful uncle behind him, Zach had become one of the richest men in America.

His cell phone vibrated. He strode off the girder and to the lift, taking the call as he descended.

To his surprise it was Nick Landry.

"Zach, I feel bad about your uncle, yes. I be calling you to offer my condolences. I read about you in the papers. I be as proud as a papa of your accomplishments, yes."

So many people had called this past week, but this call meant everything. For years, Zach had avoided Nick and anything to do with Bonne Terre, Louisiana, but the warmth in Nick's rough voice cheered him.

"It's good to hear from you."

"I've missed you, yes. And maybe you miss me a little, too? I don't go out in the boat so often now. I tell people it be because the fishin' ain't so good like it used to be, but maybe it's just me and my boat, we're gettin' old."

Zach's eyes burned as he remembered the dark brown waters of the bayou and how he'd loved to watch the herons skim low late in the evening as the mist came up from the swamp.

"I've missed you, too, yes," he said softly. "I didn't know how much—until I heard your voice. It takes me back."

Not all his memories of Bonne Terre were bad.

"So why don't you come to Bonne Terre and see this old man before he falls off his shrimp boat and the crabs eat him?"

"I will."

"We'll go shrimpin' just like old times."

After some quick goodbyes, Zach hung up, feeling better than he had in a week.

Maybe it was time to go back to Bonne Terre.

Then he thought about the Louisiana girl he'd once loved—blonde, blue-eyed, beautiful Summer, with the sweet, innocent face and the big dreams. The girl who'd torn out his heart.

She lived in New York now, a Broadway actress. Unlike him, she was the press's darling. Her pictures were everywhere.

Did she ever come home…to Bonne Terre?

Maybe it was time he found out.

One

Eight Months Later
Bonne Terre, Louisiana

Zach Torr was back in town, stirring up trouble for her, and because he was, a tumult of dark emotions consumed her.

Summer Wallace parked her rental car in front of Gram's rambling, two-story home. Sighing because she dreaded the thought of tangling with her grandmother and her brother over Zach, she took her time gathering her bag, her purse and her briefcase. Then she saw the loose pages of her script on the floorboard and the slim white Bible she kept with her always. Picking them up, she jammed them into her briefcase.

When she finally slammed the door and headed toward the house she saw Silas, Gram's black-and-white cat, napping in the warm shade beneath the crape myrtle.

"You lazy old thing."

A gentle wind swayed in the dogwood and jasmine, carrying with it the steamy, aromatic scent of the pine forest that fringed her grandmother's property. Not that Summer was in the mood to enjoy the lush, verdant, late-August beauty of her childhood home. No, she was walking through the sweltering heat toward a sure argument with Gram. About Zach, of all people.

Fifteen years ago, when she'd run away after her mother's death, she'd felt sure he was out of her life forever.

Then Gram had called a week ago.

It had been late, and Summer had been dead on her feet from workshopping an important new play.

"You'll never guess who's making a big splash here in Bonne Terre, buying up property to develop into a casino," Gram had said in a sly tone.

Gram had a habit of calling late and dropping her little bombs in a seemingly innocent way, so, wary, Summer had sunk into her favorite chair and curled up to await the explosion.

"And who do you think bought the old Thibodeaux place and hired your brother Tuck as his pool boy and all-around gopher?" her grandmother had asked.

Tuck had a job? This should have been good news. Gram had been worried about him after his latest run-in with Sheriff Arceneaux. But somehow Summer had known the news wouldn't be good.

"Okay! *Who?*"

"*Zach* Torr."

Summer had frozen. Her brother, who had poor judgment in nearly every area of his life, could not work for Zach, who couldn't possibly have her family's best interests at heart. Not after what had happened. Not when their names would be forever linked in the eyes of the media and, therefore, the world.

She'd become too famous and he too rich, and their tragic youthful love affair was too juicy. And every time the story was rehashed, it always surprised her how much it still hurt, even though she was seen as the innocent victim and he the villain.

From time to time, she'd read about how hard and cold he was now. She'd never forget the story about how ruthlessly he'd taken revenge on his stepmother.

Any new connection between Zach and her family was a disaster in the making.

"You're not the only former resident of Bonne Terre who's famous, you know."

Summer's breath had caught in her throat as she'd struggled to take the news in.

"Zach's a billionaire now."

Summer had already known that, of course. Everybody knew that.

"Even so, he's not too busy to stop by to play Hearts with an old lady when he's in town…or to tell me how Tuck's doing on the job."

Zach had been taking the time to play cards with Gram? To personally report on Tuck, his pool boy? *This was bad.*

"Gram, he's just trying to get to me."

"Maybe this isn't about you. You two were finished fifteen years ago."

Yes, it had been fifteen years. But it *was* about her. She was sure of it.

Summer had tried to make Gram understand why Tuck had to quit his job, but Gram, who'd been exasperated by all the stunts Tuck had pulled ever since high school, had refused to hear anything against Zach, whom she now saw as her knight in shining armor. Then she'd punched Summer's guilt button.

"You never come home, and Zach's visits are fun. He's awful good with Tuck. Why, the other night he and Nick took Tuck shrimping."

"A billionaire in a shrimp boat?"

"Yes, well he did buy Nick a brand-new boat, and his men are remodeling Nick's shack. And you should see Zach. He's lean and fit and more handsome than ever."

Lean and fit. Rich and handsome. She'd seen his photos in the press and knew just how handsome he was. Oh, why couldn't he be the no-good homeless person her stepfather had predicted he'd be?

"Rich as he is—an old lady like me with a beautiful, un-married granddaughter can't help wondering why a catch like him is still single."

"Gram! We have a history. An unsavory, scandalous his-tory that I'm sure he wants to forget as much as I do! Not that that's possible when there are always reporters around who love nothing better than to rehash the dirt in celebrities' lives. Don't you see, I can't afford to have anything to do with him."

"No, your stations in life have changed. You're both enor-mously successful. Your career would threaten most men, but it wouldn't threaten Zach. Whatever happened to letting bygones be bygones?"

"Not possible! He hates me!" *And with good reason.*

"Well, he's never said a word about that scandal or against you. You wouldn't be so dead set against him, either—if you saw him. The townspeople have changed their narrow minds about him. Well, everybody except Thurman."

Thurman was Summer's impossible stepfather.

There was no arguing with Gram. So here Summer was—home in Bonne Terre—to remove Tuck from his job and, by doing so, remove Zach from their lives. She didn't want to confront Zach, and maybe, if she could get through to Tuck and Gram, she wouldn't have to. All it had ever taken for Summer to remember the secrets and heartbreak of her past, and the man who'd caused them, was to visit Gram.

Nothing ever changed in Bonne Terre.

Here, under the ancient cypress trees that edged the bayou,

as she listened to a chorus of late-summer cicadas and endured the stifling heat, the wounds to her soul felt as fresh and raw as they had fifteen years ago.

Unlike Tuck, Summer had been an ambitious teen, one who'd decided that if she couldn't have Zach Torr, she had to forget him and follow her dreams. That's what had been best for everybody.

She'd worked hard in her acting career to get where she was, to prove herself. She was independent. Famous, even. And she was happy. Very happy. So happy she'd braved coming back to Bonne Terre for the first time in two years.

Summer pushed the screen door open and let it bang behind her.

"I'm home!"

Upstairs she heard a stampede of footsteps. "Gram, she's here!"

Yanking earbuds from his ears, Tuck slid down the banister with the exuberance of an overgrown kid. She was about to cry out in fear that he'd slam into the newel post and kill himself, but he hopped off in the nick of time, landing on his feet as deftly as a cat.

"Come here and give me a hug, stranger," she whispered.

Looking sheepish, with his long hair falling over his eyes and his baseball cap on backward, Tuck shyly obliged. But then he pulled away quickly.

"If I didn't know better, I'd say you were even taller," she said."

"No, you're shorter."

"Am not!" she cried.

"God, this place is quiet without you here to fight with."

"I do have a career."

"It must be nice," he muttered. "My famous sister."

"I'm doing what I love, and it's great," she said much too

enthusiastically. "Just great. I'm here to try to teach you about ambition."

"I got a job. Didn't Gram tell you?"

Gram walked into the room and took Summer into her arms before Summer could reply.

"I was wondering what it would take to get my Babygirl home."

"Don't you dare call me that!" Summer smiled, fondly remembering how she used to be embarrassed by the nickname when she was a teenager.

"Set your bag down and then go sit out on the screened porch. Tuck, you join her. I'll bring you something you can't get in that big city of yours, Babygirl—a glass of my delicious, mint-flavored tea."

Summer sighed. "Gram, I don't want you wearing yourself out waiting on us. Tuck, we're going to help her, you hear?"

Tuck, who was lazy by nature, frowned, but since he adored his big sister, he didn't argue. He trailed behind them into the kitchen where he leaned against a wall and watched them do everything.

"At least you're going to carry the tray," Summer ordered as she placed the last tea cup on it.

Tuck grabbed a chocolate-chip cookie instead.

Then the phone rang and he shrugged helplessly before disappearing to answer it.

As Summer took the tray out to the porch and set it on the table, she sank into her favorite rocker, finally taking the time to appreciate the deep solitude of the trees that wrapped around Gram's big old house. In New York or L.A., Summer's phones rang constantly with calls from her agent, producers and directors…and, especially of late, reporters.

She was A-list now, sought after by directors on both coasts. She'd worked hard and was living her dream.

She had it all.

Or so she'd believed. Then her costar and sometimes lover, Edward, had walked out on her. The night their hit play closed, he'd declared to the entire cast that he was through with her. That had been a month ago. Ever since, nosy reporters had been hounding her for the full story, which she still didn't want to share. That night, back in her apartment after the wrap party, she'd tried to tell herself that Edward's departure hadn't made her painfully aware of how empty her personal life had become.

No well-known Broadway actress was ever alone, especially when she was under contract for a major Hollywood film. Even when she was between shows and movies, she couldn't walk out of her apartment without some stranger trying to take her picture or get her autograph. She was always multitasking—juggling workshops, PR events, rehearsals and script readings. Who had time for a personal life?

She was thirty-one. Forty, that age that was the death knell to actresses, didn't seem quite so far away anymore. And Gram, being old-fashioned and Southern, constantly reminded Summer about her biological clock. Lately, Gram had started emailing pictures of all Summer's childhood girlfriends' children and gushing about how cute they were.

"Where would I be without you and Tuck? Mark my words, you'll be sorry if you end up old and alone."

Gram's longings were part of the reason Summer had let Hugh Jones, the hottest young actor on the west coast, rush her into a new relationship not two weeks after Edward had jilted her so publicly. Had she actually felt a little desperate at realizing how alone she was?

Not wanting to think about her personal life a moment longer, Summer picked up her glass and drank some of her iced tea.

Where was Gram? And what was taking Tuck so long on the phone?

Was he talking to Zach?

She took another sip of tea.

Reporters constantly asked her if she was in love with Hugh. But unfortunately for her, it wasn't Hugh who came to mind at the mention of the word *love*. No, for her, love and Zach would always be tangled together like an impossible knot. Her chest tightened. She'd only felt that exquisitely painful rush of excitement once.

She never wanted to feel it again.

She'd been sixteen, and he nineteen, when their romance had ended in unbearable heartbreak. For a brief moment she allowed herself to remember New Orleans and the terrible, secret loss she'd suffered there, a loss that had shattered her youthful illusions forever, a loss that had taught her some mistakes could never be made right.

Zach was the reason why she almost never came home. Bonne Terre was a small, gossipy Cajun town. If she hadn't forgotten her past, the town wouldn't have forgotten it, either. Even if the town's citizens didn't ask her about him, she always *felt* him everywhere when she was home. She had too many painful memories and…secrets.

Here on this very porch *he* had kissed her that first time.

Just as she was remembering how her mouth had felt scorched after he'd brushed his lips against hers, her grandmother's low, gravelly whisper interrupted her thoughts.

"You're not the only person who loves to sit in that chair."

The sly, mischievous note in her grandmother's tone sent a frisson of alarm through Summer.

"Oh." She didn't turn and smile because her cheeks were still burning.

"Zach always sits there."

Summer stiffened.

"I can't believe you allow him to come over, much less allow him to sit in *my* chair. What if someone tips off the press about his visits to see my grandmother and this causes another nasty story to be published about us? And why is he developing in Bonne Terre anyway? In all these years he's never once come back, until now."

"When his uncle died back in the fall he came to visit Nick. When he saw the land prices, he started talking to people. He already has a casino in Vegas. One thing led to another. The city fathers decided to court him...."

When Summer noticed the ice cubes in her glass tinkling, she set the glass down with a harsh *clink*.

"Careful, dear, that's your mama's best crystal." They paused, as they both reflected on the sweetness of Anna, Summer's dear, departed mother, whom they would miss forever. "Zach's bought up all that land across from our place."

"I still can't believe that with his history, with so many in this town set against him, Zach would come back here."

"He says it's time to set the record straight. He's certainly winning the town over."

How exactly did he intend to set the record straight? Summer thought of the one secret she'd kept from him and trembled. "He's made a fortune in Houston. Isn't that vindication enough? Why would he care what the people here think of him?"

"They nearly sent him to prison."

Because of me, Summer thought with genuine regret.

"Old wounds run deep sometimes...and need healin'. He's got everybody around here excited. His casino's going to be a fancy riverboat."

"Gambling? It's a vicious, addictive sport."

"Gaming will bring jobs.... And jobs will buy a lot of forgiveness. Bonne Terre's fallen on really hard times of late."

"Gram, you sound brainwashed. It makes me wonder how often Zach comes by."

"Well, he dropped by the first time because he wanted to see if I'd sell this place to him."

Summer would watch the swamp freeze over before she let that happen.

"Zach's been by about once a week ever since. We have coffee and cookies. Chocolate chip are his favorite."

Summer took great pains to center her glass in its condensation ring on the coaster. "I hope you didn't tell Zach you might sell or that I was coming to see you about all this."

Her grandmother hesitated. "I'm afraid I might have told him he could make me an offer. And… You know how I can never resist bragging about you. I've shown him my scrapbooks."

Summer frowned. "I can't imagine I'm his favorite subject."

"Well, like I said, he's always ever-so polite. He's been especially interested in your romance with Hugh." Gram smiled. "Asked me whom I thought was more fun—Hugh or himself?

I said Hugh was a rich movie star, who probably wouldn't waste his time on an old lady. I told Zach he had nothing to worry about."

Summer squeezed her eyes shut and counted to ten.

Kneading the knot between her eyes, she said, "Did you or didn't you tell him I was coming home because I'm upset about Tuck's job?"

"It's hard for me to remember exactly what I do or say these days, but if I did tell him, what can it matter? You said that what happened between you two was over a long time ago."

Summer frowned. Yes, of course, it was over. So, why was she obsessing about him?

"I think Thurman had Zach all wrong. I told your stepfather he was too hard on the boy at the time, that you were just youngsters in love. But Thurman doesn't ever listen to anybody."

He hadn't listened when Summer and her mother had begged him to drop the charges against Zach, and the stress of that time had ended her mother's remission. Her mother's death was just one of the reasons Summer was estranged from him. The other had to do with a tiny grave in New Orleans.

But Summer didn't want to think about that. "Okay, back to selling this place to Zach. That can't happen."

"I can't help it if I'm not averse to moving into a modern condo, if Zach comes up with some favorable financin'."

"But I love this house," Summer protested. "I can't believe you've actually gone this far with a deal without once mentioning it to me. What's his next move?"

"He said he'd put an offer together, but so far he's been too busy."

"Maybe we'll get lucky and he'll stay busy," Summer muttered, squeezing her eyes shut.

Somehow she didn't really think Zach, who could be relentless, would leave her grandmother alone until he got exactly what he wanted. Had he hired Tuck to win over Gram? So she'd sell him her home, which had been in the family for more than a hundred years?

"Word has it he closed on that tract across from us just yesterday. That's where he'll build the dock," Gram said. "So he'd like to control this property. He definitely doesn't want me selling to anybody else."

Inspiration struck.

"Gram, I'll buy the house from you. Then you can live here or in a condo. Your choice."

"Oh?"

"I want you to call Zach and tell him you won't sell. Hopefully, when he learns I'm here checking up on you, he'll back off."

Her grandmother watched her intently for a long moment. "You never looked at Edward the way you used to look at Zach. Fifteen years is a long time for you to still be bothered by a man," said her grandmother wisely. "Have you ever asked yourself why?"

"No." Summer yanked her scrunchy out of her hair and pulled her ponytail even tighter. "Because I'm perfectly happy with my life as it is. Can we quit talking about him and not start on your dissatisfaction with my single state?"

"Oh, all right, dear. I won't bring him up again—or the fact that you're an old maid—not unless you do."

"Old maid? Gram, there's no such thing anymore."

"Maybe that's so in Manhattan, but that's definitely not so in Bonne Terre. Ask anybody."

Gram's set expression stung way more than it should have.

Tuck stuck his head out the door. "Zach called and needs me to come in, so I've got to get to work."

"Hey, Tuck, your job is one of the reasons I came home. Can we talk?" Summer said.

"Later. He needs me to run an errand."

Summer ground her teeth as she watched her brother lope out the door.

Tuck refused to quit his job. Summer and he had quarreled about it briefly, but Zach had just promoted Tuck to full-time status and he now spent his whole day running errands for Zach's contractor.

As for Gram, she was as good as her word. Two whole days had passed without her ever once mentioning Zach.

She was the only one silent on the subject, however. The whole town was buzzing because Summer and Zach were both in town. Whenever Summer went shopping, the curious sneaked sidelong glances at her. The audacious stopped her on the street and demanded to know how she felt about Zach now.

"Do you regret what you and Thurman did—now that Zach's so rich and nice and set on saving this town from economic disaster?" Sally Carson, the postmistress, had demanded.

"Your grandmother told me he's been real sweet to her, too," Margaret York, one of Gram's oldest friends, said with a look of envy.

"Well, his return to this town has nothing to do with me," Summer replied.

"Doesn't it?" Margaret's face was sly and eager. "Men don't forget...."

"Well, I have."

"I wonder how you'll feel when you see him again. *We all wonder.*"

One of the worst things about fame was that it made everyone think they had a right to know about her private life. Some things were too personal and painful to share with anyone, even well-meaning neighbors.

So Summer stopped going into town. Instead, she stayed at the house to work on her script and formulate a new way to approach Tuck.

On this particular afternoon she'd set a plate of cookies and a glass of tea garnished with a sprig of mint beside a chaise longue on the screened veranda. She paced in frustration, gesturing passionately as she fought to discover her character, a young mother. The role eluded Summer because, for her, young motherhood was a painful theme.

But today she did something she'd never let herself do before—remember how she'd felt in New Orleans when she'd been expecting her own child. Suddenly, she broke through the protective walls inside her, and grief washed over her in waves.

Her eyes grew wet, and she began to tremble, but she didn't relent. So deeply was she immersed in painful memories, she didn't hear the hard, purposeful crunch of gravel beneath a man's boots until he was nearly upon her.

A low vicious oath startled her. Expecting Tuck, Summer whirled, dabbing at her damp eyes with the back of her hand.

And there *he* was.

At the sight of Zach's hard, chiseled features swimming through her tears, the pages she'd been holding fell to the wooden floor.

"Well, hello there," he said.

"Zach." She hated the way his low, velvet voice made her heart accelerate, made the air feel even hotter. Frantically, she dabbed at her eyes so he wouldn't see her tears. "Gram said you'd been visiting a lot." Her voice sounded choked and unnatural.

"Did she?" Black eyes narrowed as he pushed the screen door open. "She told me you were coming home." Zach scowled. "You're pale, and your eyes are red. Have you been crying?"

"No! It's nothing," she whispered. "I was just acting out a part."

His lips thinned. "You always were damn talented at that."

Good, he bought it.

Tall and dark in a long-sleeved white shirt and jeans, and as lethally handsome as ever, Zach's tight expression told her he wasn't happy to see her.

As she bent over to retrieve her script, his insolent dark eyes raked her body in a way that made her aware of how skimpily clad she was in her snug blue shorts and thin, clingy blouse.

Feeling strangely warm and too vulnerable suddenly, she bristled and sprang to her feet. "I told Gram to tell you. If she decides to sell, she'll sell to me. So, why are you here now?"

"I haven't spoken to her. My secretary arranged my appointment with your grandmother," he said, striding closer. "When I saw you in those shorts, I imagined she told you I was coming and you were lying in wait...."

"As if I'd do—and, hey, it's August. I...I have a perfect right to wear shorts," she sputtered.

"Yes." His gaze drifted over her appreciatively. "You look good in them. Too good—which I'm sure you know."

"Gram didn't tell me you were coming."

"And she didn't tell me to cancel my visit. I wonder why. Maybe she likes my company. Or maybe she'd prefer to sell to me. This old place and that brother of yours are way too much for her."

"None of that is any of your business."

"Your Tuck was running pretty wild, got himself fired from a bar because money went missing...."

"As if you know anything about Tuck. He doesn't steal!"

Zach's black brows arched. "Still thinking the worst of me while you defend everybody else. Your stepfather's been giving me hell, too."

The comparison to her stepfather cut her...deeply. Zach hadn't been there for her when she'd needed him either, had he? He hadn't cared....

Maybe because he hadn't known.

"As a matter of fact, I like your grandmother. That's why I hired Tuck. When I happened on him late one night, he'd had a flat tire. He didn't have a spare or money or a credit card, and his phone was dead. So he accepted my offer to haul him to a service station and buy him a new tire on the condition that he become my pool and errand boy and work it off."

"I see through your Good Samaritan act."

"I was sort of suspicious about it myself."

"You're just using Tuck to get at me in some way. So go,"

she whispered. "You are the last person I want involved with my family, especially with Tuck, who's extremely vulnerable."

"Well, sorry if my return to Bonne Terre upsets you, or if Tuck's being my employee bothers you," he said, not sounding the least apologetic. "But since I've got business in this town for some time to come, and Tuck works for me, I suppose you and I were bound to meet again…sooner or later."

"Gambling? Is that your business?"

"Yes. What of it? You're an actress, someone skilled at weaving seductive illusions. You sure seduced me with your little act. And I let you off easy. You should feel lucky. I'm not known for lenience with people who betray me."

Easy? Lucky? New Orleans lay like a weight on her heart.

"All you see is your side."

"I was the one who damn near got strung up because of your lies," he said. "I'm the one who's still found guilty every time some reporter decides to write another story about us."

"Well, maybe you don't know everything!" She stopped. She would never make the mistake of trying to confide in him. But despite her best intentions, she said, "You…you can't believe I ever wanted to accuse you, not when I begged you to run off with me, and when it was my idea to…"

"To seduce me?" he finished.

His silky whisper and the intense fire in his black eyes rubbed her nerves raw.

"It wasn't like that and you know it. I…I couldn't help it if Thurman hated you for what I did."

"Let's not kid ourselves. You did what you did. I don't give a damn anymore about why you did it."

Shame and some darker emotion she didn't want him to sense scorched her cheeks as she turned away from the coldness in his face. "If I could have undone what I did or said, or what I caused people to believe about you, I would have."

"Hollow words…since you could have stepped up and

cleared my name at any point. You didn't. Like a fool, I waited for you to do just that. I was young. I believed in you back then." His mouth tightened into a hard, forbidding line. "But, no, you ran off to New Orleans where you probably seduced somebody else."

"There was never anyone but you…." She swallowed tightly. "I—I tried to apologize…and explain. You refused to take my calls. I even went to Houston looking for you after your uncle took you away, but you wouldn't see me."

"By then I knew what a talented manipulator you were."

At his dark, unforgiving scowl, she sucked in a tortured breath. "If you hate me so much, why won't you just go?"

"I don't hate you. Frankly, I don't consider you worth the waste of any more emotion. What I'm doing here isn't about you. I've made a name for myself in other places. When Nick called me a few months ago, I realized I'd never let go of what happened here and neither have the people of this town or the media. Maybe I've decided it's time I changed a few people's minds.

"Your stepfather used to be the biggest man in these parts. Not anymore. I intend to be bigger than he ever was. I intend to make him pay for what he did—to kill him with kindness, bestowed upon his town."

"I want you to leave Gram and Tuck alone. I'm buying this property from her because I won't have you cheating her to get back at me."

"You'd better not make accusations like that in public."

"And you'd better stop trying to make me look bad to my grandmother, who's started nagging me about not coming home often enough!"

"Haven't you been neglecting her?"

"Well, if I don't come home, it's because of you. I—I can't forget…when I'm home," she finished raggedly.

Dark hurt flashed in his eyes but was gone so fast she was sure she'd only imagined it.

When he stomped toward the front door, she blocked his way. At her nearness, his hard body tensed. When their gazes locked, a muscle in his jawline jerked savagely. His breathing had roughened.

He wasn't nearly as indifferent as he'd said.

Nor was she.

"Move aside," he muttered.

Hurt, she lashed out. "No—this is my grandmother's house. I won't allow you to use her to get at me. So—leave."

"Like hell!"

When she stood her ground, his hands closed over her forearms. But as he tried to edge her aside, she stomped down on his foot with her heel.

Cursing, he tightened his grip and crushed her against his muscular length.

Despite the unwanted shiver of excitement his touch caused, her tone was mild. "Would you please let me go?"

A dozen warring emotions played across his dark face as she struggled to free herself.

"I don't think I will."

Locking her slim, wriggling body to his made their embrace even more alarmingly intimate.

"You're trembling," he said. "Why? Are you acting now? Or do you feel what I…." He broke off with a look of self-contempt.

"Damn you for this," he muttered. "You're not the only one who can't forget."

Even if she hadn't felt his powerful arousal against her pelvis, his blazing eyes betrayed his potent male need. Then his gaze hardened with determination, and she watched breathlessly as he lowered his mouth to hers.

"I shouldn't do this," he whispered fiercely, bending her

backward, molding her even more tightly to the hard contours of his body. "God help me, I know what you are, what you did."

"You did things, too...." He'd hurt her terribly. Yet she wanted him, ached for him.

"I can't stop myself," he muttered. "But then I never could where you were concerned."

No sooner did his warm mouth close over hers than she turned to flame. If he'd flung her onto the chaise longue and followed her down, she would have forgotten the hurt that had turned her heart to stone for fifteen years. She would have ripped his jeans apart at the waist, sliding her hands inside.

She wanted to touch him, kiss him everywhere, wind her legs and arms around him and surrender completely—even though she knew his need was based on the desire to punish while hers was due to temporary insanity.

On a sigh, her arms circled his tanned neck, and she clung, welding herself to his lean frame in a way that told him all that she felt. She was a woman now, a woman whose needs had been too long denied. When he shuddered violently, she gasped his name.

"Zach... I'm sorry," she murmured as warm tears leaked from her eyes and trickled down her cheek. She feathered gentle fingertips through his thick, inky hair. "I wronged you, and I'm so sorry. For years I've wanted to make it up to you." She hesitated. "But... You hurt me, too."

For fifteen years, she'd been dead in the arms of every other man who'd held her.

She hadn't felt this alive since she'd last been in Zach's embrace.

His hand closed over her breast, stroking a nipple until it hardened. The other hand had moved down to cup her hip.

Next he undid the buttons of her blouse so that it parted for his exploration. For one glorious moment she was her younger self and wildly in love with him again. Back then she had trusted him completely. She'd given him everything of herself. With a sigh, she leaned into him as he stroked her, and her response sent him over some edge.

He rasped in a breath. Then, in the next shuddering instant, he ended their kiss, tearing his lips free, leaving her desolate, abandoned.

Loosening his grip, he let her go and staggered free of her as if he'd been burned. He raked a large, shaking hand through his hair and swore violently, staring anywhere but at her.

"Damn you," he muttered, inhaling deeply. "I see why you do so well on Broadway. You're like a tigress in heat. Is that why Hugh Jones took up with you so fast?"

Summer was about to confess she felt nothing when Hugh kissed her—nothing—but Zach spoke first.

"Brilliant performance," he said. "You deserve an Oscar."

"So do you," she whispered in breathless agony as she dried her cheeks with the back of her hand. She couldn't let him know that for a few magical seconds she'd actually cared.

"I'd better go before I do something incredibly stupid," he said.

"Like what?" she murmured, feeling dazed from his mesmerizing kiss and savage embrace.

"Like take you back to my house to do whatever the hell I want to do with you…for as long as I want."

"Oh?"

"Don't look at me like that! I know what you are. Damn you for making me want the impossible," he muttered.

She clenched her fists, not any happier than he was to realize that she wanted the impossible, too.

He didn't like her. With good reason. Their past was too painful to revisit. What burned inside her, and in him, was lust—visceral and destructive.

Gram opened the front door. Her violet, silver-lashed eyes wide, she peered out at them with excessive interest, causing Summer, whose blouse was still unbuttoned, to blush with shame even as she quickly pulled the edges back together. The last thing she wanted to do was get Gram's hopes up about a romantic reunion with Zach.

"Oh, my go-o-o-d-ness." Gram worked hard to hide her pleasure at the sight of Zach's blazing eyes and her grand-daughter's scarlet face and state of dishabille. "I'm so sorry." In a softer voice directed toward Summer, she said, "And I thought you told me you wanted nothing more to do with him." There was that sly note of satisfaction in her tone again.

"I don't," Summer cried, but the door had already closed behind her triumphant grandmother. "Why didn't you tell me he was coming over?" she called after Gram. Then Summer turned and said to Zach, "Why did I even ask, when I specifically ordered her not to mention you?"

Zach's eyes went flat and cold. "As far as I'm concerned, this never happened. But—if you see me again—you'd better run. You and I have more unfinished business than I realized. Don't give me any more reasons to come after you and finish what you started."

Suspecting he must want revenge, she swallowed. "Don't threaten me."

"It's not a threat. It's a promise, a warning. If you're smart, you'll stay away from me."

As if to emphasize his words, he strode over to her. Reaching up his hand, he ran a calloused fingertip along her damp cheek, causing her to shiver involuntarily.

"I want you in my bed. I want you to pay for what you did. In every way that I demand."

Startled, because the image he painted—of lying under him on a soft bed—aroused her to such a shocking degree, she jumped back. Out of his sensually lethal reach, her voice was firm. "I won't be seeing you again."

"Good. Tell your grandmother I'll call her after you leave town."

His gorgeous mouth curled. Looking every bit as furious and ashamed as Summer was beginning to feel, Zach turned on his heel and strode down the gravel drive, leaving her to wonder how she could have stood there like a besotted idiot and let him touch her again after sharing such an embarrassing kiss.

"None of this happened," Summer whispered consolingly to herself when she finally heard the roar of his car. Too aware of gravel spinning viciously, she sank down onto the steps and hugged her knees tightly.

She felt cold and hot at the same time.

It was all a horrible mistake. Zach didn't like that it had happened any more than she did.

She was glad he felt that way.

She was glad!

Somehow she had to make Gram and Tuck understand that Zach was dangerous, that he'd threatened her.

Tuck, who'd gotten in trouble too many times to count, could not continue to work for Zach, who would use whatever her brother did to his own advantage.

Squaring her shoulders, Summer got to her feet and picked up the remaining pages of her script. Then she ran into the house and up the stairs where she took a long, cold shower and brushed her teeth.

Not that she could wash away his taste or the memory of his touch or the answering excitement in her system.

That night, when she awoke, breathing hard from a vivid dream about Zach kissing her even more boldly, it was impossible to ignore the hunger that was both ancient and familiar lighting every nerve ending in her being.

Wild for him, she sat up in the darkness and pushed her damp hair back from her hot face. "It was just a stupid kiss. It doesn't matter! Zach can't stand me any more than I can stand him."

So, why are you dreaming about him, aching for him, even when you know he despises you?

Two

One month later

Once back in New York, Zach's kiss lingered on the edges of Summer's consciousness almost all the time, despite the fact that she'd willed herself to forget him. Despite the fact that she'd decided it was best not to obsess over things she couldn't control, like Tuck's refusal to quit his job and Gram's support of his decision.

And because the memory of Zach's kiss lingered, she drove herself to work harder than ever.

Summer read every script her agent gave her. She auditioned tirelessly for any part that was halfway right for her. When she was home alone she compulsively cleaned and dusted every item in her already immaculate apartment in a vain attempt to shove Zach Torr and his stupid kiss and his ridiculous threats back into the past where they belonged.

Not that she could stop herself from calling certain gossips in Bonne Terre to get a picture of what he was up to back home or stop herself from reading her hometown's newspaper online to get the latest news about his riverboat gambling project. Everything she read was annoyingly favorable. People were more impressed by him every day. He was the town's favorite son. Rumors abounded about the lavishness of the riverboat he was building and the luxurious amenities and hotels he was constructing onshore.

On impulse, maybe to prove to those blockheads back home how little she cared for Zach, she let Hugh Jones join one of her interviews.

Naturally, the young, bright-eyed journalist went gaga over beautiful, golden Hugh, whose immense ego was hugely gratified at being fawned over.

At first, the young woman's eager questions had been standard fare. Summer tossed off her ritual answers.

Her favorite role was the one she was creating. She was always nervous opening nights. And, yes, the play she was workshopping today was ever-so exciting.

Naturally, when the journalist wasn't entirely focused on Hugh, he grew bored.

Hugh shuffled from one foot to the other and yawned, and the reporter laughed and leaned into him so her breast brushed his elbow.

"Okay, let's talk about this hot new man in your life. Every woman in America is dying to be you, Summer." The woman was staring into Hugh's baby-blues as if she'd been hypnotized.

Idiotically, the phrase *hot new man* put Summer back on Gram's screened porch, in the arms of that certain individual she would give anything to forget.

Again she tasted the sweet, blistering warmth of Zach's mouth and felt his muscular length pressing her close. At the memory of his big hands closing over her breast and butt, the dark, musty corner she shared with Hugh and the reporter felt airless.

"So, what's the latest with you and Hugh?" the reporter asked. "If you don't mind my saying so, you two are *the* most exciting couple these days."

"I'm a pretty lucky guy." Hugh squeezed Summer closer before launching into a monologue about himself.

Summer was wondering if she and Hugh had ever once had a real conversation about anything else.

"I don't think Summer's got any complaints," the reporter said when Hugh finally ended the everybody-loves-me monologue.

Hugh laughed, pulled Summer closer and planted his mouth on hers just as a flash blinded her.

Infuriated at his brashness, Summer thumped her fists on his chest. Luckily, her cell phone vibrated and blasted rap music from her pocket.

"Excuse me," she whispered, desperate for an excuse to be done with the reporter and Hugh.

Sliding her phone open, she read the name, *Viola Guidry.* "Sorry, guys, it's my grandmother. I have to take this."

"So—that kiss makes me wonder how serious you and Hugh are?" the reporter asked.

"We're just good friends," Summer snapped in a flat, cool tone.

"That's all you're going to give me—"

Nodding, Summer smiled brightly as she shook the woman's hand. "Thanks so much." Cupping the phone to her ear, Summer walked away.

"Hey, girls, much as I loved doing this interview, I've got a meeting before I catch my plane to L.A.," Hugh said carelessly, blowing Summer an air kiss. "See you, angel."

Summer waved absently and fought to concentrate on her grandmother's frantic words.

"You have to come home! Tuck's in the hospital. He's going to be okay, but Sheriff Arcenaux says he may have to arrest him!"

"For what?"

"Tuck invited some friends over to Zach's and they got into his liquor. When Zach came home, Tuck was so drunk he'd passed out. Two of Zach's cars were missing, and Tuck's friends were busily looting the place."

"Oh, my God! Did I warn you or not?"

"Zach's threatening to press charges. So—you've got to come home."

Fear was a cold fist squeezing Summer's heart so tightly she could barely breathe. Practically speaking, she didn't have time for this. Her calendar was jam-packed with work commitments. Emotionally, she knew her family needed her.

"Zach wants to meet with you. He gave me his attorney's number and told me to have you call him. He said maybe he'd be willing to work something out with you, instead of pressing charges, if you meet with him. But he'll only meet with you."

Summer felt so frustrated and panic-stricken it was all she could do not to throw the phone.

Zach had her right where he wanted her—cornered.

In a soft voice, she said, "I'm on my way, Gram."

She was late.

Zach hated wasting time, and that was exactly what he was doing as he waited for Summer, a woman he'd spent years trying to forget. His empire should be his focus, not some woman from his past.

Hell, he'd wasted too much time worrying about her ever since he'd seen her on Viola's porch. She'd looked so sad and fragile before they'd spoken. He was almost sure she'd been crying. The pain in her eyes had been so profound he still wanted to know what she'd been thinking.

Then, like a fool, he'd kissed her.

Her mouth had been hot and yielding, almost desperate with pent-up passion. But tender, too. Ever since that kiss, it was as if her lips and her taste and her softness and her sweet vulnerability had relit the passion he'd once felt for her. It seemed nothing, not all the ugliness or news coverage or even reason, had been able to destroy his desire for her.

The woman's kiss had made him remember the girl he'd loved and trusted.

She didn't matter; she couldn't ever matter again.

Summer had been a virgin when she'd given herself to him. His one and only. Never would he forget how lush, lovely and shyly innocent she'd been, nor how her shy blue eyes had shone. He'd been deeply touched that such a beautiful girl with such a radiant soul had chosen him.

For the first two years they'd known each other, his focus had been their friendship and protecting her from her controlling stepfather. Then they'd fallen in love during her senior year, so he'd stayed in Bonne Terre to wait for her to graduate. He hadn't pushed for sex, but somehow, after they'd run away together, she'd gotten through his defenses.

One night when they'd been alone in that remote cabin, she'd cried, asking him what she should do about her stepfather. What would happen if they didn't go back, if she didn't finish school? Would he come to New York with her?

He'd realized then that Summer saw him as part of her future; saw her stepfather and Bonne Terre as something she was finished with forever.

Intending to comfort her, to reassure her that he wanted her in his future as well, he'd gone to the bed, taken her in his arms and held her close. Her hair had smelled of jasmine, so he'd nuzzled it. Then she'd kissed him, her soft mouth open, her body pressing against his eagerly. She probably hadn't understood how she'd tempted him.

He'd stroked her hair, caressing her, and she'd moaned. Her tears had stopped, but she'd clung anyway. Then they'd come together as if it were the most natural thing in the world. Their union had been both sexual and spiritual. He'd believed they'd marry after she graduated, that they would be together forever.

Never again had he felt like that about a woman.

Forget it.

Zach forced his mind to the present. He couldn't afford to reminisce. Time was more precious than money. His uncle's death had taught him that.

Zach had his briefcase stuffed with foreclosure cases he'd intended to review as he sat in his attorney's sumptuous conference room. Waiting for *her.* Plate-glass windows afforded him an excellent view of the bayou four stories below. Not that he was enjoying the scene of cypress and dogwood trees. No, he couldn't stop thinking about her.

Why was she late? Was she remembering their last encounter and his promise to make her pay?

When he heard the desperate click of her high heels in the hall, he glanced up, tense with expectation. Even as he steeled himself to feel nothing, his heart began to race.

The door opened, framing her slim, elegant body before she entered. Her delicate, classical features and radiant complexion were too lovely for words.

He wanted her so much he couldn't breathe.

They looked at each other and then away while the silent tension between them crackled. On some deep level, she drew him. Her incredible blond beauty alone made her unforgettable. Then there was her fame. Hell, how could he forget her when her face was plastered on the covers of gossip magazines and cheap, weekly newspapers?

She was everywhere.

Only a few days ago he hadn't been able to resist reading

the latest about her budding romance with Hugh Jones in one of those sensational newspapers he despised. He'd grabbed it off a wire shelf in a drugstore and jammed it into his brief-case. He'd carried it up to his office and pored over the story that went with the front-page photo of the famous couple sharing a kiss. Summer had claimed they were just friends, but Jones had expounded about how crazy they were about each other. Which one of them was lying?

Probably her.

Zach had wadded the newspaper and thrown it in the trash. In his penthouse suite, staring out at the city of Houston, which was littered with the skyscrapers he'd built and owned, he'd never felt more isolated.

She had a life—perhaps she even loved that famous, ego-tistical movie star—while he had only his fierce ambition and immense wealth. He'd gone through his contact list on his smart phone, called a beautiful blonde who resembled Sum-mer and asked her out. But that night, after dinner, when she'd invited him up to her loft, he'd said he had to work. Driving home, feeling empty and more alone than ever, he'd burned for Summer.

So, he'd seized his opportunity. He'd used her brother to get her here.

"Coffee?" His attorney's pretty secretary offered from the doorway.

"No," Zach thundered without even bothering to ask Sum-mer, for whom he felt irrational fury because she wouldn't stop consuming his thoughts.

He wasn't in the mood for niceties. When the secretary left and Summer's long-lashed, legendary violet-blue eyes flicked in alarm, he felt as if she'd sucker punched him in the gut. Damn her, for having this much power over him.

His heart hardened against her knockout beauty even as other parts of his body hardened because of it. He wished he could forget the softness of her breast and the firmness of her butt and the sweet taste of her lips. He wished he didn't ache to hold her and touch her again. He wanted to kiss her and force her to forget all about Jones.

How many others had there been in her bed since Zach? Legions, he imagined with a rush of bitterness. A Broadway star with a face and figure like hers, not to mention a budding movie career, could have anybody—directors, producers, actors, fans.

Hell, she had Hugh Jones, didn't she? But was she as responsive when Jones touched her? Had Zach only imagined she'd been pushing against Jones, trying to free herself, when that picture had been taken?

None of it mattered. Zach wanted her in his bed with an all-consuming hunger. And he was determined to have her.

As if she read his thoughts, she flushed and glanced down, staring at her white, ice-pick heels rather than at him. Still, her sultry voice made him burn when she whispered, almost shyly, "Sorry I'm late. Traffic. I had to go by Gram's first… to check on Tuck."

"How's he doing?" Zach asked, standing up and placing his hand on the back of the chair he intended to offer her.

He'd found Tuck drunk and unconscious on the living-room floor of Zach's new house. The garage doors had been open, and Zach's Lamborghini and second Mercedes had been missing.

Fortunately, Zach had come home unexpectedly and had caught two of Tuck's friends, also drunk, ransacking his house, or he might have suffered worse losses. Since then, the automobiles had been found abandoned in New Orleans.

Zach blamed himself, in part, for not having hired an appropriate staff for the house.

"Tuck's doing okay." Summer answered his question as she stepped farther into the room, her legs as light and graceful as a dancer's, her silky white dress flowing against her hips. He remembered how sexy she'd looked when she'd bent over in her short shorts on her grandmother's porch.

And why shouldn't she be graceful and sexy? She was a performer, a highly paid one. Everything she did was part of a deliberate, well-rehearsed act. Maybe the kiss they'd shared when she'd seemed to quiver so breathlessly had been a performance, as well.

She sat down in the chair he'd indicated and crossed her legs prettily. He stayed on his feet because staring down at her gave him the advantage.

Even though he knew what she was, and what she was capable of, the years slid away. Again he was sixteen, the bad new homeless kid in school with the sullen, bruised face. Everybody had been scared of him. Summer had been the popular, pampered high-school freshman, a princess who'd had every reason to feel superior to him.

People talked in a town the size of Bonne Terre. Everybody knew everybody. Nobody approved of Nick dragging such a rough kid home and foisting him upon the school. Thurman Wallace had even demanded Zach be thrown out.

Only Summer, who'd been a precocious thirteen and two years ahead of her age in school, hadn't looked down on Zach. Not even when all the other kids and her step-daddy thought she should. No, even on that first day, when Roger Nelson, a football star, had demanded to know what Zach had done to make a guy hate him so much he'd beaten him nearly to death, she'd butted in and defended him.

"Maybe that's not what happened," she'd said. "Maybe Zach was in the right, defending himself, and the other guy was in the wrong. We don't know."

"So what happened, Torr?" Nelson had demanded.

"Why should I tell you?"

"See, he's trash, Pollyanna," Nelson had jeered. "Anybody can see that!"

"Well, then maybe I'm blind, because I can't," she'd insisted. "I see a person who needs a friend."

Not long after that Summer had become his secret best friend.

The memories slipped away, and Zach was heatedly aware of the woman seated before him.

As if she couldn't resist using her power on him, Summer tipped her head his way, sending that thick curtain of blond hair over her shoulders as her blue eyes burned into the center of his soul.

"Zach, thanks for getting Tuck medical attention so fast. They said you had specialists flown in from Houston." Her face was soft, beguilingly grateful.

Clenching a fist, he jammed it in a pocket. He wasn't buying into her gratitude. Not when he knew she'd do anything to keep her brother from being arrested.

"The doctors are personal friends of mine in Houston. It was either fly them here or airlift him to New Orleans. He was out cold. He had a bump the size of a hen's egg on his head and a gash that needed stitches, so I wanted to make sure he was just drunk and that there was no serious head injury involved."

"Thank you," she said.

"I don't see any need for us to make a big deal about something anyone would have done."

"You paid for everything, too. We have insurance. If you'll invoice me, I'll—"

"You'll pay me. Fine," he growled.

He was blown away by his feelings. He wanted her so badly he could think of nothing else, and she was coldly talking money.

"You said you wanted to see me. I've talked to Tuck, and

he feels terrible about everything that happened. He had no idea those boys were going to steal anything or tear up your house. The last thing he remembers is hearing a noise in the garage and stumbling across the living room to check it out. Then he must have tripped."

"Oh, really? What about the money that went missing when he was fired from his last job? Your brother's been running pretty wild all summer. He's nineteen. Old enough to know what the guys he runs around with are capable of."

"He was just showing off. They said they'd never seen a billionaire's place. He wanted to impress them."

"He shouldn't have invited them over or given them my whiskey."

"I agree, and so does he…now. He just didn't think."

"Your Tuck's had too many run-ins with the law for me to buy into his innocence. He's been indulged in Bonne Terre. Maybe because he's a Wallace."

"That's what this is about, isn't it—his last name? You were hoping something like this would happen. You deliberately hired my trouble-prone brother, set him up, so you could get back at me."

He tensed at her accusation. "Since you're so quick to blame others for his actions, I'm beginning to see why he's so irresponsible."

Heat flared in her eyes. He noted that she was breathing irregularly, that her breasts were trembling.

"You have no right to use him this way. He's practically an orphan. I was twelve when he was born. He was two when our father ran off, four when Mother married Thurman and he adopted us. If my stepfather was hard on me by pushing me in school, demanding I excel and graduate two years ahead of my class, he constantly browbeat Tuck, calling him a wimp and a sissy who'd never amount to anything. I was the favorite. Tuck could never measure up.

"After our mother died, he was raised by a stepfather who disliked him and then by aunts who cared more for their own children, and later by his grandmother, who's become too old and lenient. And I admit, I don't come home often enough."

Zach had figured all that out for himself. The kid had no direction. She and Viola were protective of Tuck, but didn't demand enough responsibility from the boy.

"And what do you do—you put him in temptation's way so you can get at me," she repeated in a shaky tone. "Since he's been in trouble before, if you press charges and he's tried and convicted, he could be locked up for a long time. You knew that when you hired him. If this gets out to the media, there will be a frenzy."

Zach paced to the window. "If you believe I deliberately used Tuck to hurt you, you wouldn't believe anything I told you to defend myself. So, I won't bother."

"Oh, please. You threatened me the last time I saw you. I think you've ordered me here because you intend to make good on that threat!"

Yes, he wanted to yell.

I want to sleep with you so badly I'd do almost anything to accomplish that!

But then the intensity of her pleading look made him jerk his gaze from hers.

She was afraid of him.

He didn't want her fear. He wanted her warm and passionate and wild, as she'd been the first time.

He strode back to the table and picked up the legal documents in which he'd accused her younger brother of a felony.

When he saw his grip on the papers made his tendons stand out, Zach knew he was dangerously close to losing control. What was her hold over him?

By all rights he should have the upper hand in this situation. Her brother had brought thugs to his home to rip him off. He had every right to demand justice. But Tuck, who'd trusted him, needed help. He needed direction. Zach remembered how he himself had been derailed as a kid due to vengeful adult agendas.

Feeling torn between his ruthless desire and his personal code of ethics, Zach threw the documents onto the table. Then he glared at Summer fiercely, willing revulsion into his gaze.

But she was wide-eyed, vulnerable. Her perfect face was tight-lipped and pale; her shoulders slumped. She'd said she never wanted to see him again, but she'd come today. With a career like hers, she'd probably been busy as hell, but she'd come because she was genuinely worried about her brother and wanted to help him.

When she'd thanked Zach for getting the right doctors, he'd seen real gratitude in her eyes. And he'd liked pleasing her. Too much. In that white dress, which clung in all the right places, she looked young and innocent—not to mention breathtakingly sexy.

He wanted her in his bed. He wanted revenge for all that she'd done to him.

Do what she's accused you of. Use Tuck. Make your demands.

Yet something held him back.

For years, he'd told himself he hated her, had willed himself to hate her. But when he'd held her and kissed her at her grandmother's house, his hate had been tempered by softer, more dangerous emotions.

He'd once believed that if he had enough money and power, he would never be vulnerable to the pull of love again.

But now here she was, with her golden hair smelling of perfume and shimmering with coppery highlights so bright they dazzled him, with her lips full and moist, with her long-lashed eyes smoldering with repressed need.

Was she lonely, too? He wanted to hold her against his body and find out.

But more than that, fool that he was, he wanted to protect her. And her idiot brother.

He had to get out of here, go somewhere where he could think this through.

To her, he snarled, "This meeting's canceled." Then he punched the intercom and spoke to his lawyer's secretary. "Tell Davis to take over."

"I don't understand," Summer whispered. "What about Tuck?"

"I'll deal with you two later."

She let out a frightened sigh that cut him to the quick. "Zach, please…"

He wanted to turn to make sure she was all right.

Instead, he shrugged his broad shoulders and sucked in a breath.

To hell with her.

Without a backward glance, he strode out of the room.

Three

He was impossible! Arrogant! Rude!

If he'd slapped her, Zach couldn't have hurt Summer more than he had when he'd turned his back on her and walked out.

Fisting her hands, she got up and ran after him. But with his long legs, the elevator doors were closing before she caught up to him.

"Zach, you've got to listen—"

His glare was indifferent and cold as the doors slammed together.

"Well, you've sure got him on the run. You must have scared the hell out of him," Davis said, chuckling behind her. "That's not so easy to do. Usually he shreds his adversaries."

Zach's attorney looked slim and handsome in his tailored Italian suit and prematurely gray hair. He had been a year or two older than she in high school, but she and he had never been close. Davis worked for Zach now, not her.

Her heart swelled with uncertainty. She was afraid to say

anything to Davis because whatever she said would be repeated to Zach. She couldn't risk damaging Tuck's chances.

"Where do you think he went?" she asked.

"We've got a lot of legal work to wrap up, so he's in town for a few days. He spent his morning at the construction site, and he didn't mention having any other meetings this afternoon, so maybe he went home. I'd leave him alone for now, let him settle down. Don't push him into making a rash decision about Tuck. Believe me, he'll call you when he's ready."

But wouldn't it be better to deal with him now, when he wasn't ready? Wouldn't that give her an advantage?

Besides she was under contract to perform in New York, and her calendar was full. She didn't have a second to waste. No way could she stay here indefinitely without major consequences to her career. Directors, producers and other actors were depending on her.

Acting on a mixture of intuition and desperation, she went out to her rental car and followed the winding bayou road to the old Thibodeaux place.

His pale, beige antebellum-style home had a wide front veranda and ten stately columns. Weeds grew in the flower beds, and the grass was overgrown. Wild passion flowers had taken over the edges of the yard. She rang the bell and nobody answered, making her wonder why he didn't have adequate staff.

When she began to pace the veranda, she saw it had a few rotten boards and was in need of a thorough sweeping. She peered through the smudged pane of a front window. Inside, she saw stacks of boxes on the dusty, scarred floors of the palatial rooms.

Apparently, his people hadn't finished moving him in. Was he even here?

When she rang the bell again with no answer, she decided to walk around back by way of a redbrick path that lay in the shade of vast oak trees that needed a good trimming. All the forest-green shutters were peeling, as well.

The mansion had been built a decade before the Civil War and had served as a Yankee headquarters.

Now, the house and yard needed love and lots of money, but with enough of both, it could be a beautiful home for some lucky family. Had Zach bought it because he was thinking of settling down? Marrying and having children? Little dark-haired boys or girls? She imagined them playing out in the yard and hated the way the vision tugged at her heart.

A gleaming silver Mercedes was parked in front of Zach's three-car garage. His car? How many did the man own?

Seeing the low, white-picket fence, also in need of fresh paint, encircling the pool, she opened the gate and stepped gingerly through the high weeds to let herself inside.

Intending to knock on one of the back doors, she headed toward them only to stop when she saw a half-empty bottle of expensive scotch on a nearby table. At the sound of someone bouncing with a vengeance on the diving board, she turned just as a pair of long, tanned, muscular legs disappeared into the water.

"Zach?"

He didn't answer, of course, because he was underwater and speeding like a dark torpedo toward the shallow end. When she heard more splashing, she walked to the edge where the water lapped against the stairs. Centering her white heels precisely on one of the large navy tiles that bordered the pool, she waited for him to come up for air.

He was fast. Obviously, he'd stayed in shape since he'd been on the swim team in high school.

Oh, my God. He was naked!

Suppressing a cry at that realization, she saw his clothes discarded untidily on the far side of the pool. Still, instead of turning and fleeing, she stopped and stood her ground.

Her nervous state was such that she felt it took him forever to surface.

Thankfully, since he was in the water, when he did stand up, she couldn't see much of his lower body, but his perfect, muscular, wetly gleaming, tanned torso stimulated her over-active imagination anyway.

He shook his wet black head, flinging droplets of water all over her.

"Hey!" she cried, stepping even farther back.

He scowled up at her in shock even as his black eyes greedily raked her with male interest. Grinning, he made no effort to sink lower in the water or cover himself. "Why am I even surprised?"

"I knocked," she said defensively as hot color rose in her cheeks. "On your front door."

"Did you really?"

A warm breeze caressed her cheek. She looked anywhere except at his wide, dark chest and muscular arms. Even so, she was aware of his height, of his taut stomach and of that dark strip of hair running down his middle and disappearing into the water.

"You didn't answer," she said.

"A lot of women…women who weren't looking for trouble…would have just left."

"I…I'm not looking for trouble."

"Well, you damn sure found it."

"I have to know what you're going to do about Tuck."

"Since you're obviously determined we're going to have a chat on that subject, maybe you'd be so kind as to get me a towel out of the bathhouse. Since I thought I was alone, I didn't think I'd need one. Or… Do I—need one?"

"Yes!" she cried. "You most certainly do!"

He laughed.

Thankful for something to do other than trying to avoid

looking at his amused and much-too-sexy face, she all but flew to the bathhouse. Returning quickly, she set the fluffy, folded rectangle on the edge of the pool. Patting it primly, she turned her back on him.

Water splashed as his bare feet thudded across concrete. She felt her body warm as she listened to him towel off, visualizing his tall bronzed body behind her without a stitch on.

He was certainly taking his time. Was he trying to tempt her into turning around? She *wanted* to turn. Thankfully, she resisted. Surely he'd had time to secure the towel, but another intolerable minute passed.

Finally, as if sensing her impatience and interest in his physique, he chuckled and said, "It's safe for you to turn around now."

But it wasn't. Not when his fierce black eyes devoured her, obviously reading her wicked desires. Not when he wore only that towel and they both knew he was naked and gorgeous and completely male underneath it.

She wished she didn't feel so keenly alive every time she was anywhere near him. She wished she wasn't drawn by his tanned arms and bare chest, that she didn't remember lying with him as a girl after they'd made love and nuzzling that dark strip that vanished beneath the thick folds of his towel.

Oh, how she'd loved him that night after he'd made love to her. Like a foolish child, she'd thought he belonged to her, that he would always be hers.

Maybe he would have—if she'd fought Thurman and the town. Maybe then she wouldn't feel as she did right now, as if she was starving for love.

"You've got guts to come out here all alone. Aren't you scared of what I might do to you?"

Her heartbeat accelerated. She didn't fully understand her motives. She'd just known that she couldn't let him bully her, and that she couldn't stand by and let Tuck be hurt because of her past sins.

Moving closer to him to prove her bravery, she said, "You ran away. Maybe you're the one who's scared of me."

He flushed darkly. "And then again, sweetheart…maybe not."

Sweetheart. The word ripped her heart. In the past, he'd always said the endearment so tenderly it took her breath away. Today, his voice was harsh with irony.

Before she knew what was happening, his hand snaked toward her, and he yanked her against his body, which was wet and warm and as hard as steel.

Her heart leaped into her throat as she caught the faint scent of scotch on his breath. Too late, she wondered how much he'd drunk.

"I wasn't scared of you, you little fool. I was scared of me. Of what I might be tempted to do if I didn't get away from you. Then you come here…and deliberately invade my privacy. You tempt me…into this, into holding you again. Sweetheart, you're playing with fire."

Again too late, she realized he hadn't had time to swim off any of the liquor he'd drunk.

"Well," she hedged, "I…I see you were right…. And I was wrong. Maybe it would be smarter to set up another meeting tomorrow morning, as you suggested."

Echoing her thoughts, he said, "It's too late for such a sensible decision. You came here because you want something from me, and you want it very badly. You saw I was naked. You knew you were alone with me and you stayed. Since I told you I still wanted you, maybe you thought if you excited me again, I'd be easier to deal with."

"No!"

"Hey, don't back down. You were right. It's good for your

cause that you're here. As it turns out, I know exactly what I want from you. I was just fighting the temptation earlier."

Oh, God.

"I didn't stay because you weren't dressed…and I thought I could manipulate you…or whatever horrible thing you think I was up to."

His swift grin was savage. "You've always been good at pretending. Like back in high school—when your stepfather bullied you into graduating early, you pretended you wanted what he wanted. He wanted you to be a teacher because he thought that was a respectable career for a woman. Did you ever once tell him how important theater was to you before you starred in *Grease* and made him so angry at the end of your senior year? You dated me behind his back, too, because you knew he wouldn't approve. And when he hung me out to dry, you lied to everybody in this town about me. Your whole life was a lie. So, you'd damn sure lie now."

"No…"

"I think you've gone on lying to yourself for years. You know how I know? Because I've been doing the same thing. In my arrogance, I thought you'd taught me such a bitter lesson I was immune to women like you…and to you specifically. Until I kissed you…."

She swallowed, suddenly not liking the way he was holding her, or the way he was looking at her with that big-bad-wolf grin.

"I'd better go."

"You're so damned beautiful." He was staring at her as if she were a puzzle. "How can you look so innocent? I have enough money to buy practically anything, anybody, I want and I usually do. I want you. Why should I deny myself?"

Drawing her closer, he reached up and gently brushed away the lock of blond hair that feathered against her skin.

Her tummy flipped. Tenderness from him was the last

thing she'd expected, and it caused hot, unwanted excitement to course through her.

He smelled of chlorine and sunlight, scotch and of his own clean male scent, which somehow she'd never forgotten. All of it together intoxicated her.

Her reaction frightened her. When she tried to back away, his grip on her wrist tightened.

"I want you to move in with me for a while. I want to figure out this thing that's still between us."

"Impossible!" He wanted sex. He just wasn't going to say it. "There's nothing between us."

Again, she tried to jerk free, but his hand and body were granite hard.

"You're such a liar. Before we kissed, I would have agreed. I wanted to believe that," he said. "But unlike you, I'm uncomfortable lying to myself."

"I'm under contract in New York. I've got an opening night in eight weeks. We're going to be rehearsing, and I have several scenes to shoot for a movie in L.A. My calendar is full. Crammed."

"So reschedule."

"I have commitments, a life…. Other people are involved. Producers, my director, the rest of the cast."

"Odd—you failed to mention your movie-star boyfriend… Hugh, I believe?" His eyes darkened.

"Yes! Of course—*Hugh*. We're in the same film."

Zach's grim smile held no satisfaction. "And you think I don't have someone special or plenty on my plate?"

Someone special.

The thought of him having a girlfriend he truly cared about tugged painfully at her heart—which was ridiculous!

"Even I, who know next to nothing about the theater world, have heard the term *understudy*," he continued. "Reschedule."

"I hate you."

"Good. We're on the same page." His voice was harsh. "You'll live here, with me, weekends only—until your opening night. I don't care how you live the rest of the week. Or with whom. I'll be commuting here from Houston."

"I have to know exactly what you want from me," she whispered.

"I'm a man. You're a woman. Use your imagination."

"This is crazy."

"You forget, I'm a gambler. Ever since you pulled your little stunt and nearly destroyed me, I've gotten to where I am by operating on my gut. If I feel like it's right to go ahead with a deal, I do…whether or not I have all the facts to support my decision. Even if the facts tell me it might be the wrong thing to do—as in your case—I do it. It's worked for me so far."

"This isn't business. I won't have you gambling with my future, with Tuck's future."

"It's the way I operate. Take it or leave it. Since I hold the winning cards where your brother and his band of merry thieves are concerned, I don't think you have a better option."

"Is it sex? Do you want me to sleep with you? If that's it—just say so."

"Sex?" His black gaze raked her. "I won't say that offer doesn't tempt me. Did you mean tonight?"

When she didn't deny it, when she bit her lip and said nothing, he cupped her chin. Again, his hold was gentle, only this time it was more intimate as he studied her, his black eyes lingering on her lips before traveling lower. His hand stroked her throat. When his fingers slid briefly beneath the neckline of her dress, causing her skin to burn and her pulse to race even faster, she gasped in anticipation.

"I want you in bed, but it's not that simple," he finally murmured, removing his hand.

Only after he stopped touching her could she breathe again.

"I want you in bed, but I want you to be willing. So, this isn't just about sex. Not by a long shot."

No, it was about submission, about complete domination and control. She'd read plenty about how ruthless he was. He wanted to humiliate her as thoroughly as he'd humiliated his stepmother.

She shut her eyes because his gaze was too powerful and her own desire was beginning to feel too palpable.

"I loved you," he whispered. "I trusted you, but you betrayed me."

"I…I…loved…you, too."

"Shut up, Summer! You and your stepfather and his cronies nearly sent me to prison. For statutory rape. I was nineteen. Now, any time a reporter shows up here or in Houston to do a new story on me, they dredge up the past. That's not something I'll easily forget. Or forgive—ever."

"But…"

"Even though my uncle got me out of that mess, even though I've made a success of myself, a cloud has hung over my name. For years. No matter how much money I made. Because of you. Do you understand? At the least opportune times, when delicate deals hang in the balance, a belligerent press will hound me about those trumped-up charges, especially because you're so famous now. No matter how high I climb, somebody's always there, wanting to throw me back in the gutter where you put me. So, I came back to this town— to set things straight once and for all. I want to bury the past and silence my accusers. If you move in with me, everybody around here will think you approve of me and always have.

So, yes, this is about more than sex or revenge or whatever the hell else you think."

"You seem to have done okay in Houston."

"No thanks to you! If you'd had your way, I'd be a registered sex offender today. My uncle was at least able to get that part of my record expunged." The rough bitterness that edged his low tone made her shiver.

"Despite what you say, your plan sounds like revenge."

"You owe me," he muttered. "You don't want me to press charges and sic the crazy justice system on your brother, the way you stuck it to me. Because we both know how destructive and long-reaching the consequences for that would be.

If you do what I ask, Tuck gets a free ride. My plane and pilot will be at LaGuardia Airport every Friday at 3:00 p.m. to pick you up and fly you here for as long as your companionship amuses me. Be there, or by damn, I'll forget how beautiful and vulnerable and innocent-looking you are and do as I please with your brother."

"You wouldn't—"

"Are you willing to risk Tuck's future on that assumption? My anger over the way you railroaded me fueled my ambition to achieve all I've achieved. I doubt Tuck will be so lucky if you throw him to the wolves."

She was shuddering violently when he let her go. Still, his burning eyes didn't release her for another long moment.

"And I have one more condition—you're not to tell a soul about our little bargain."

"Don't do this," she pleaded softly.

"If it gives you any pleasure, I feel as trapped as you do," he muttered.

"Then why are you punishing us both?"

"This meeting's adjourned!" he said in a harder tone. "I intend to finish swimming laps. Naked. You can watch me or join me or leave. Your choice."

Grinning darkly with cynical, angry amusement that stung her to the quick, his hands moved to his waist to shed his towel. Even though he took his time, and she had plenty of time to turn away, she stood where she was, daring him.

Like a raptor, his black eyes gleamed diamond hard as he

ripped the white terry cloth loose. With a shocked gasp she watched, mesmerized, as it fell down his long legs and pooled in an untidy heap beside his bare feet.

His tall legs were planted firmly apart as his hard eyes locked on hers. His full, sensuous mouth smiled wickedly in invitation.

Although she willed herself to turn away, he was so uncompromisingly male, so fully aroused, she was too compelled by him not to look.

"Why don't you stay and swim, too? We could start your weekends a week early," he murmured in a low, seductive tone.

Hot color crept into her cheeks. How could just looking at him be so electrifying? If only she could have hidden her admiration. "I…I don't think that would be wise."

"We're way past wisdom," he murmured drily. "You want to. I want you to. We're both adults. You start serving your time, maybe I'll get my fill of you sooner rather than later. I could let you off early…for good behavior."

Tempted, she trembled as she fought the fierce need to move toward him, to touch him. Her hands clenched. Looking at him took her back to the most glorious, sensual night of her life. He was so virile and handsome she couldn't think.

She wasn't that foolish, naive girl any longer. She'd been fiercely independent for years.

But the foolish hopes and dreams of that girl still lurked in her heart, tormenting her. If Summer didn't turn and walk away, or run—yes, run!—she would do something incredibly stupid, something she would regret for the rest of her life.

Just as she regretted their past love.

Only, she didn't feel as if she regretted it anymore.

Why not? What was happening to her?

Did some crazy part of her want to try again? Did she

really want to risk everything she'd achieved for a second chance with him?

He got you pregnant. When you tried to tell him, he wouldn't even talk to you.

But how could she blame him for what he hadn't known?

"I see you're unsure," he murmured with a faint, derisive smile.

"I—I'm not unsure," she said even as the burning desire in his eyes made her feel as if she was melting. "I think you're a monster, so I—I'm leaving. R-right now. Really."

He laughed. "Then check with Davis for my phone numbers. Call me if you decide to take my offer so I can tell my pilot and my caretaker. Since I'm a gambling man, I'll wager that you'll be here next Friday. We can swim together then. Or do whatever else we feel like. We'll have the whole weekend to enjoy each other."

He spoke casually, as if her decision meant little to him. Then he turned and walked away.

Her stomach in knots, she watched him much too hungrily until he vanished behind a wall of shrubbery.

Four

Summer loved Central Park, especially on a sparkling September day when the leaves had begun to turn and a cool front had put a chill in the air.

"Hugh, I'm so sorry I can't fly out to L.A. this weekend."

Hunched over her smartphone on a bench near the fountain at Bethesda Terrace during a rare break, Summer chose her words carefully.

Guiltily, she pushed a blond strand of hair out of her eyes. "My brother's in trouble, so I have to go back to Bonne Terre."

"But…"

"Truly, there's nothing I'd rather do next weekend than be with you at the premiere of *Kill-Hard*."

"My agent swears it's my breakout role."

"I'm so sorry. Truly. I'll be there Sunday…late."

After Zach.

When Hugh hung up, seething, she was a little surprised that her guilt was overwhelmed by relief.

At least Hugh's premiere was one thing she could scratch off her to-do list.

Summer began to flip through her calendar, deleting or canceling other engagements. For the next few weekends she would be doing her own script work, so she could juggle the commute to Louisiana. Later, when rehearsals began in earnest, getting away from New York would be trickier, maybe downright impossible.

She would worry about that later. Zach would probably be tired of her by then anyway.

Daily, hourly, all through the week, she'd resented Zach for causing such immense upheaval in her life. His demand was outrageous, medieval, and she told herself she was furious with him and with herself for going along with him.

And yet, if that were true, why did her breath catch every time she remembered the avid desire in his eyes? Why did she dream of him holding her close every night? Or awaken hot and sweaty from the image of writhing in his arms like a wanton? She would toss her sheets aside, go to the window and stare out at the stars, imagining spending two days and nights with Zach.

Being a man, no matter what he'd said, all he wanted from her was sex.

But what did she want?

She didn't know. And she didn't know what she could tell Gram. Summer didn't want her grandmother to get her hopes up for no reason. Since she couldn't figure that one out and didn't want to lie, she wouldn't call Gram or take her calls until Summer saw her again in Bonne Terre. Until then, Summer would concentrate on her career goals, on developing and playing her roles. It wasn't healthy to obsess over a man whose sole goal was to punish her.

On Friday, at three o'clock sharp, she met Zach's pilot. Once aboard the jet, she pulled out her script, intending to figure out her character for the scenes with Hugh scheduled to be shot in L.A. next week.

Normally, Summer chose roles because she felt affection for the character, but in this case, her reasons had been more pragmatic. When she'd complained that she didn't think she could do a dark, unlikeable sex addict, her agent had pointed out that the money was simply too good to pass up.

So, Summer needed to study her lines and determine how her edgy sex scenes fit into the emotional context of the movie.

But her mind drifted to Zach, making it impossible for her to concentrate on the femme fatale she was to play in Hugh's film.

Staring out the windows of his Houston office as he held his phone, Zach frowned as his pilot brought him up to date. "Yeah. She was right on time. Weather looks good until we hit Louisiana. Looks like you're going to have a nasty drive." He gave Zach the plane's arrival time, and the two men ended the call.

Outside, dark purple clouds hung over the city to the northeast. It was only three, but the freeways were already jammed with cars. Impatient, because he'd wanted to leave the city well before rush hour, especially if there was bad weather, Zach thrust his hands into his pockets and prowled his office like a caged cat.

Leroy McEver, the newly hired contractor on Zach's biggest project downtown, was late as usual. Although Zach was sorely tempted to leave, no way was Zach driving to Bonne Terre without making Leroy understand once and for all that the reason he'd fired Anderson and hired him was that he expected Leroy to stop the constant cost overruns.

But even with pressing business to deal with, Zach was anxious to be on his way to Bonne Terre. To her. As always, his inexplicable need to bed her, even after what she'd put him through, annoyed the hell out of him.

After their love affair had been exposed and made to look ugly in the newspapers, he'd zealously guarded his personal life. He kept his private life private. She was a movie star, who probably courted media attention.

There were multiple reasons not to go through with the bargain he'd made with her. But he wouldn't put a stop to it. He couldn't.

Thus, his impatience to see her again infuriated him. He hated himself for stooping to blackmail.

But he wanted her, and she owed him—big-time.

One minute the road was darkly veiled in mist. In the next the brightly lit Thibodeaux house loomed out of the shadowy cypress and oak grove. Summer got out, grabbed her bag and thanked Zach's pilot, Bob, for the lift.

"I've got orders to wait until I'm sure you're safely inside."

Summer's footsteps sounded hollow as she marched up the path, crossed the porch and rang the doorbell.

Setting her bag and briefcase down, she turned the key Bob had given her in the lock, jiggling it until the door opened.

"Zach?"

Again, as her shy, uncertain voice echoed through the empty rooms, she marveled that a man like him, with a house like this, had no staff. As she felt blindly for the light switches on the wall, she heard a man's heavier tread approaching. When she saw a tall, angular shadow splash across the floor between the stacked boxes, her heart began to pound as unwanted, craven excitement coursed through her. All week, she'd waited for this and had been too ashamed to admit it.

"Zach?"

"It's just me, Summer," Tuck said as he ambled through the door at the far end of the room. He had earbuds in his ears and was bouncing to some soundless beat. His hands were jammed into jeans that rode so low on his skinny hips she marveled that he didn't worry about them falling off.

She couldn't see much of his skinny face for the thick golden hair hanging over his eyes.

"You doing okay...since the hospital?" she asked.

"Ever since Zach told me he's not going to press charges, or even fire me, I've been fine. Can you believe he gave me a second chance?"

"Big of him."

"Course, he locked his liquor up and set some pretty strict ground rules," he muttered more resentfully. "Oh, he said I'm supposed to tell you that you can have the bedroom down the hall on the first floor. He made me stock the fridge and get the room ready for you. And he told me to carry your suitcase inside for you."

Tuck came to an abrupt stop in front of her. When she reached for him, he allowed a quick hug.

"I'm glad you're okay," she whispered, ruffling his hair. "Next time, think."

He leaned down and grabbed her suitcase. "Zach told me to tell you about the security system." He told her the code and asked her if she wanted him to write it down or show her how to set it.

She shook her head.

When he showed her the room, she was pleasantly surprised to find antique furniture, curtains and rugs that went together. A silver mirror and comb and brush set lay on a low, polished bureau.

"It's pretty," she said.

"Because Zach sent a dumb decorator and lots of other people over to boss me around and make sure it was."

"Where is Zach?"

"On the road. His meetings ran a lot later than he expected."

"Oh."

"So, why are you here tonight if you hate him so much?"

"I—I don't hate him. It's…it's complicated."

"You're not here because of what I did, are you?"

"Oh, no. It has nothing to do with you." She felt her cheeks heat. "We just…er…reconnected. That's what happens sometimes…with old flames."

He stared at her as if he didn't quite buy it. "So…okay… everything's cool, then. Can I go? I was gonna play some pool tonight before I found out about you and Zach."

She gritted her teeth, not liking that he'd accepted them as a couple so easily. He'd talk, and everybody would believe him.

He stared at her through the greasy strings of his blond hair. "You sure you're okay about this?"

"I'm great! Never better!" She gave him a bright smile.

"You've sure got the whole town talking."

She winced. "You know how people in Bonne Terre talk."

"Yeah. When I shopped for stuff, people kept asking me questions about you."

"So, who are you playing pool with?" she asked, anxious to change the subject.

"Some guys. *Good* guys."

"Hope so. Hey, did Zach say when he'll get here?"

"Maybe. I don't remember. So—can I go now?"

"Give me another minute."

She had work. Lots of it. Since she was a trained stage actress, movie roles did not come naturally to her. Scenes would be shot out of order, and she wouldn't be able to fall back on the rhythm of the play to carry her character into her scene. Since she needed to study the *before* moments that preceded every scene, she should be happy Zach was running late, but, for some reason, the thought of being alone here in his house with her script depressed her.

Making her way into the kitchen, she opened the fridge and found it full of her favorite cheeses, eggs, fresh vegetables and sparkling water. Zach must have talked to Gram to find out things she liked before sending Tuck to get them.

Closing the fridge door, she realized she wasn't going to work tonight when she felt so empty and strange being in Zach's house without him.

"Can I go now?" her brother repeated.

"If you'll give me a ride to Gram's first."

"If I were you I wouldn't go over there. The local gossips really have her and her friends all stirred up about you. She's been hounding me for details. Says you won't return her calls."

She knew Tuck was right, but she'd rather be at Gram's facing hard questions than stay in this house alone, waiting for Zach. On the drive to Gram's, she switched the conversation back to Tuck. "So, how come you agreed to work for Zach again after you got in trouble? Is it the job you like? Or him?"

"The work's boring, but he's okay. Funny, he's almost like a friend."

Her stomach tightened with alarm. Zach was far from a friend. Tuck should have better sense than to trust that man. But there was no way she could tell Tuck that without giving herself away.

"I wish you'd go back to school and find something that interests you. Then you wouldn't have to do boring work. Or work for Zach."

"School's even more boring. And like I said, I sort of like working for Zach."

"Maybe if you tried to be interested, you'd become interested."

"That's what Zach said the other day when he drove me over to the junior college."

"He what?"

"Drove me to the tech campus. In his Lamborghini. Boy, was everybody impressed."

"I can't believe he took the time.... He's a very busy man." She couldn't hold back now. "You know, Tuck, he's not really your friend."

"Hey, where do you get off criticizing him? You're never here. He is." His tone was low as his sad eyes whipped around to regard her. "You're this big famous actress. Until Zach came back to Bonne Terre, Gram and me didn't interest you much. With your glam job, how could you understand what it's like for someone like me, somebody who's ordinary and stuck here? I can't help if it's hard for me to get excited about my life. It's not much to get excited about."

"Then you've got to do something with your life, Tuck."

"I've heard it before."

"If you don't do something, nobody else is going to do it for you. Life is what you make it."

"Easy for a big shot like you to say. Why don't you stay out of my business, and I'll stay out of yours? Deal?"

"No, it's not a deal!"

Damn. Because of Zach, she was losing precious ground with her brother.

Refusing to come in, Tuck dropped her off at Gram's. As Summer got out of the car, he sped away in an angry whirl of dust and gravel.

Dreading being grilled by Gram, especially after not taking her calls all week, Summer squared her shoulders before marching up to the house.

Summer was barely inside before Gram switched off the television and plopped Silas down on the floor.

"Why didn't you return any of my phone calls?"

Because I was too ashamed of what I was doing.

"That was…unforgiveable of me," Summer whispered. "I did listen to every single message though…if that counts."

"So, when were you going to tell me you've started seeing Zach Torr?" Gram asked excitedly.

"It's not what you think," Summer hedged, feeling acutely uncomfortable that her grandmother was hoping for a true romance.

"What is it, then?"

"Look, it was a long flight. I'm thirsty. Do you have some tea?"

"Why didn't you tell me? Why did I have to hear this from all the gossips?" Gram asked rather gloomily as she and Silas followed Summer into the kitchen.

Summer didn't say anything as Gram splashed tea from a pitcher in the fridge into a tall glass.

"Well, if you won't talk, I'll say my peace. I think it's great that you're reconnecting with Zach."

"We're not…."

"It's high time you two sorted out the past."

"Gram—"

"It will do you both a world of good…to talk it out."

"There's nothing to talk out."

"Oh, no?" After stirring in lemon and mint Gram handed Summer the tall glass of iced tea. "You could talk about New Orleans. And the baby."

Summer's chest felt hollow and tight.

"You looked like death when you came home from New Orleans. I used to wonder if you'd ever get over it. Maybe if you told Zach, let him share that grief with you, maybe then both of you could move on. He's just as stuck in the past as you are."

Summer shook her head. "That was fifteen years ago. It's way too late for us."

Losing his baby after he'd rejected her had hurt so much, Summer had locked her sorrow inside. She'd never wanted to suffer because of it again.

Tears burned behind the back of her eyelids. "I can't talk about it, not even like this, to you, Gram."

Gram's arms slid slowly around her, and Summer, fighting tears, stayed in them for quite a while.

"Spending time with him is the brave thing to do. I think it's a start in finding yourself. I, for one, am going to pray for a miracle."

"You do that," Summer whispered, not wanting to repeat that, for her and Zach, it was hopeless.

"In the meantime, we could play Hearts," Gram said more cheerfully .

"Gram…I…"

"I just love it when Zach stops by to play Hearts…. A man with as much as he has to do taking time for a little old lady… And he's not even my grandson."

Zach again…besting her. Was there no competing with him? No escaping him?

Feeling cornered, Summer sat down with Gram to play Hearts.

Except for the lights she'd left on, the Thibodeaux mansion was still dark several hours later when Summer drove up in Gram's borrowed Ford sedan, after having lost too many games of Hearts. She hadn't bothered to set the security system, so she simply unlocked the door and let herself in.

Feeling restless because Zach still wasn't there, she showered and dressed for bed in a thin T-shirt and a pair of comfortable long cotton pants. Intending to mull over her scenes for a little while, she pulled back her covers and slid into bed with her script.

But just reading through the sex scene made her squirm, so when she saw the remote, she flicked on the television, surfing until she found the weather channel.

There was a big storm over east Texas that Zach would have to drive through. Video of downed trees, traffic signs and power lines made her more apprehensive, so she turned the television off.

Was he okay? If he'd been in an accident, would anyone even think to call her?

He's fine. Just fine. And why should you care if he isn't?

Even more restless now, she got up and padded into the kitchen where she poured herself a glass of sparkling water. She was pacing when her cell phone rang. Hoping it might be Zach, she sprinted back down the hall to answer it.

"What the hell do you think you're doing?" Thurman demanded without bothering to greet her. "How can you move in with that bastard? You should be ashamed of yourself."

She *was* ashamed, and furious at Thurman for punching that hot button.

Headlights flashed across the front of the house as her stepfather lambasted her. Stiffening her spine, she stood up straighter. She wasn't some teenage girl her stepfather could blackmail or control.

"How did you get this number?" Summer said. "I've told you never to call me."

"What are you doing over there? I demand to know."

"It's none of your business. And it hasn't been for a very long time. Mother's dead. I'm an adult. Goodbye."

"You're dragging the family down into the dirt all over again!" He swore viciously.

She turned her phone off just as Zach's key turned in the lock.

Thinking she should give him a piece of her mind for putting her through all this, she stomped toward the front door. Then he stepped wearily across the threshold. She registered the slump of his broad shoulders, which looked soaked in the gray light.

"Hi," she said, feeling an unwanted mixture of relief and sympathy for him.

"Sorry." He seemed as tense and wary as she was. "I hope I didn't wake you up."

"You didn't." No way would she admit she'd been worrying about him. "Thirsty." She waved her glass of water. "Thanks for getting all my favorite stuff. For the fridge, I mean."

"All I did was have Rhonda make a phone call to your grandmother. Rhonda's my secretary." When he smiled crookedly, he was incredibly handsome despite the dark circles of fatigue shadowing his eyes.

"Long day?" she whispered, feeling slightly breathless, already having fallen under the spell of his lean, sculpted beauty.

He nodded. "Even before the drive. Long week, too. When it rains…it pours. Literally."

"Oh, and the storm. Was it bad?"

"It slowed me down."

From the late hour and his tight features, she was almost sure that was an understatement.

"Do you have any more bags? Could I help you carry something inside?"

"You're being awfully nice. Too nice," he accused, his dark eyes flashing dangerously. "Why?"

"Yes—and I don't know why. I don't trust myself, either."

When he smiled and seemed to relax, she felt her own tension ease a little. But just a little. After all, their shared weekend loomed in her imagination. She wasn't sure what he expected of her tonight.

"No," he said. "I don't need help. This is all I brought." He paused. "If you hadn't spent your night here waiting on me, what glamorous place would you have been?"

"In L.A., at Hugh's premiere."

At the mention of Hugh, Zach's eyes darkened.

"I was going out there this weekend because we start shooting together next week."

"Are you two doing a love scene?" His voice was hard now. *More than one.*

Annoyed because he'd nailed her and because, like most people, he so obviously attached undue significance to anything of a sexual nature on film, she ignored his question.

"I don't want to talk about Hugh with you."

"Good. Because neither the hell do I."

She hesitated, wondering why he sounded jealous and not knowing where to go from here. "Are you hungry?"

"Look, there's no need for you to worry about me. It's late…. And I've screwed up your schedule enough today as it is."

Of course he was right, but he looked so bone weary, as if it had taken everything out of him to get here while she'd rested on his plane and had been pampered at Gram's.

"I'll just put some cheese and ham out," she said. "You bought it, after all."

"Not so that you would stay up and wait on me. I can take care of myself."

"It won't take a minute," she insisted, stubbornly refusing to let him boss her around.

"Okay. I'll be back down after I freshen up." He left her and carried his bag and briefcase upstairs.

By the time he strode into the kitchen, she'd opened a bottle of wine and set a single place for him at the kitchen table.

When he sat down, she noted that his black hair was still gleaming wet.

"You're not eating?" he said, sipping wine, when she hovered but didn't sit.

"I ate at Gram's earlier."

"Not those chocolate-chip cookies she baked just for me, I hope?" he teased.

"She bakes them for me, too—even though I tell her not to." Summer grinned back at him. As she pulled out a chair, she couldn't stop staring into his utterly gorgeous eyes. Was there a man alive with longer lashes? A tiny pulse had begun to throb much too fast at the base of her throat, causing her breath to catch.

What was going on? How could she actually be so thrilled he was here, safe and sound, when he'd forced her to come to him, when he intended to deliberately humiliate her? When Thurman and the rest of the town were judging and accusing her? When Hugh was sulking in L.A. and her agent and director were apoplectic? When she'd disappointed poor, darling Gram, who was hoping for a happy ending to this farce?

"I had a few cookies after a chicken sandwich," she replied, striving to sound nonchalant. "Dessert is allowed sometimes, you know."

"Even for an actress who has to keep her perfect figure... so she'll look mouth-wateringly sexy in those love scenes... with Hugh?"

His angry black gaze flicked over her breasts in her thin T-shirt. His male assessment accused her even as it made her blood heat.

"Love scenes in movies aren't the least bit sexy. They're all about creating an illusion for the viewer."

"Is that so? You always were good at creating illusions."

He glanced away abruptly, trying to hide his obvious interest in her body and his fury at the thought of her with Hugh, but it was too late. Suddenly the walls of his kitchen felt as if they were closing in on her, and she couldn't breathe. How could he charge the air between them with a mere question and a hot, proprietary glance?

"You have no right to attack me or to look at me like that. No right at all."

"Then maybe you shouldn't dress the way you do," he muttered in a tone so savage she knew he was as provoked as she.

"I'm wearing an ordinary T-shirt."

His hard eyes burned her breasts again. "Right. I guess it's the fact the material's so thin and you're braless underneath that's getting to me."

"Sorry!"

When she felt her nipples tighten and poke at the cotton fabric, she clenched her hands. He was impossible. Since he'd come back to Bonne Terre, he'd been turning everything into some sort of sex game.

"Why you're determined to put us both through a weekend like this, I can't imagine."

He stared at her for a long time. "You know why. Just as you know you have it coming." He stabbed a piece of cheese.

"I think I'd better go back to bed," she said abruptly, not trusting herself, or him, or the intimacy of their cozy little situation. "We're obviously not a couple who can cohabitate easily and naturally."

At her rejection, his dark face was suddenly blank and cold. "Good idea. Go ahead. I'll clean up—alone."

"You're supposed to be a billionaire. Why don't you have staff to do all that?"

"Because they're people, and I'd have to deal with them and their problems. Because I want to live informally here and not be bothered by too many prying eyes. Because I couldn't be here…like this…with you, if I had a staff. Not that I don't have a cleaning lady. And my secretary just hired a gardener. So, do you have more questions about how I live my life before you leave me in peace?"

He wanted *her* gone! She was getting on *his* nerves! His attitude infuriated her. He'd blackmailed her into coming here, hadn't he? He'd launched the blatant sexual attack.

What had she expected—wine and roses?

Her heart pounding, she turned stiffly. Marching to her bedroom, she locked herself in and threw herself on the bed where she lay wide-awake, tossing and turning and staring up at the ceiling for what felt like an endless time.

Her mood was ridiculous. She should be thrilled he didn't want her tonight.

She heard the savage clink of dishes and silver in the kitchen, of a garbage lid being slammed, of the disposal grinding violently. His heavy tread resounded in the hall outside her door and on the stairs. Then he stomped about in the room above hers. Something crashed to his floor so hard she sprang to a sitting position. Fisting her sheets, she stared at the ceiling listening, but after that bit of violence, he quieted.

When he turned on the water, the sound of it hummed in her blood. She imagined him naked in his shower with hot suds washing over his warm, sleek muscles. And despite what he'd said to anger her, she wanted to go up and join him.

Slowly, she got out of bed and went to her bathroom. Stripping, she turned on her own shower. When the water was warm, she stepped into the steam, threw her head back and let the pulsing flow drench her. She cupped her breasts and imagined him seizing her, thrusting inside her. She imagined her hands circling his hard waist. She imagined pressing herself against him even tighter as she begged for more.

The water ran down her limbs and circled in the drain. Sighing in frustration, she fell back against the tile wall while the spray streamed over her. A strange sensation of loss and a fierce longing to move beyond their past and their present darkness possessed her.

She clenched her fists, beat the tiles, but it did no good.

He disliked her, yet he would force her to stay with him.

Did he intend to hook her on his lovemaking and then laugh at her and leave her? Would he flaunt their relationship to everybody in Bonne Terre and beyond to prove she and her stepfather had wronged him?

She closed her eyes and pushed her wet hair out of her face. Because of her own shameless desire, she was on emotionally unsafe ground.

How would she make it through the weekend without falling more deeply under his spell?

Five

When Summer awoke the next day, she sat up slowly, her heart racing, as she thought about Zach upstairs in his own bed. Except for the birds, the house seemed too quiet and dark. But that was only because she was used to pedestrians on the sidewalks and tenants on the stairs, to sirens and traffic, to garbage trucks making their early rounds as the Upper West Side woke up.

Fearing Zach might not have slept any better than she had, she crept noiselessly from her bed to the bathroom where she brushed her teeth, washed her face and combed her hair.

Rummaging through her suitcase, she put on a T-shirt and a pair of tight-fitting jeans. Okay, so he'd probably comment on how tight they were, but she didn't own any other kind.

Grabbing her script, she headed for the kitchen where she found a bag of coffee. She closed all the doors before she ground the coffee and started a pot. Listening to the birds, she decided it might be more fun to work on the porch.

She went to the door and was taking great pains to open it without making the slightest sound, when the security alarm began to blare.

With a little scream, she clamped her hands over her ears and fought without success to remember the code.

"Blast it!" she muttered as Zach slammed down the stairs.

Wearing nothing but a pair of jeans, and dragging a golf club, he hurled himself into the kitchen.

"My fault. I forgot about the alarm," she said, staring at his chest and finding him heart-throbbingly magnificent. "I was trying so hard not to wake you."

He punched in the code and set the golf club down. "It's okay. Usually I get up way before now. Coffee smells good." He raked his hands through his hair.

"It does, doesn't it?" She broke off, tongue-tied as usual around him, maybe because his gaze left her breathless.

"Did you sleep okay?" he asked in a rough tone.

"I guess."

"I had a tough night, too," he murmured, grinning sheepishly.

His super-hot gaze made her tummy flip. Suddenly, sharing the kitchen with him when he was sexily shirtless, when he kept his eyes welded to hers, seemed too intimate. She felt as awkward as she would have on a first date when she knew something might happen but didn't know what. Quickly, she turned away and poured herself a coffee. Then she scurried outside. Behind her she heard his knowing chuckle.

Not that she could work out here, she mused, not when he was bustling about in the kitchen.

Concentrate on something else! Anything else but him!

The morning air was fresh and cool, and the sky a vivid pink. As her frantic gaze wandered to the fringe of trees that edged the far corner of his property, three doe and a tiny fawn picked their way out of the woods in a swirl of ground fog to nibble a clump of damp grass.

Summer tiptoed back to the kitchen door and pushed it open. Holding a fingertip against her lips, she waved to Zach to come out.

When he joined her, he smiled, as charmed by the scene as she.

"I'll bet you never see anything like that in Manhattan."

"There are all sorts of amazing sights in Manhattan," she murmured in a futile attempt to discount the awe that sharing the dawn with him inspired.

"I'll bet somebody as famous as you could never live anywhere as boring as Louisiana or Texas again. Or be serious about anybody who wasn't a movie star like Jones."

"I didn't say that!"

His hard eyes darkened as they clashed with hers.

An awkward minute passed as she tried to imagine herself living with Zach, here, in Houston, anywhere. Impossible—she was an actress, who lived in Manhattan.

"To change the subject—what do you want to do today?" he asked casually.

"I need to study those scenes I have to shoot next week."

"That's fine. I did make tentative plans for us to meet Tuck and Gram at the new Cajun café on the bayou. Over lunch I thought we could encourage Tuck to enroll in one of the tech programs at the junior college."

"Tuck's not interested in school."

"Really? When I informed him I might press charges if he didn't take some responsible action about his future, he told me he'd like to take some courses that could lead to a career as a utility lineman."

"I can't believe this! You're threatening Tuck, too, now."

"It's way past time he stepped up to the plate. I took him over to the junior college Wednesday and introduced him to Travis Cooper, who's the young, enthusiastic head of that particular program. He was a late bloomer, like your Tuck, which may be why the two of them hit it off immediately."

"Okay—I can do lunch," she replied. "I like your results, even if I don't approve of your tactics. Then I'll need to study my scenes this afternoon…since I procrastinated last night."

"Okay. While you do that, I'll inspect one of my building projects."

He took a long breath, his black eyes assessing her with such frank male boldness her tummy went hollow. "But, I'll want to spend the evening with you. Alone. Here."

"Of course," she whispered, her skin heating even as she fought to look indifferent.

Without warning, he stepped closer and grinned down at her. "I'm glad you agreed so easily. I want you to be eager."

He bent his handsome black head toward hers, and she was so sure he would kiss her, she actually pursed her lips and stood on her tiptoes as if in feverish anticipation.

But he only laughed, as if he was pleased he had her wanting him. "Save it for tonight, sweetheart."

A very colorful curse word popped into her mind, but she bit her lips and made do with a frown.

Lunch with Tuck and Gram was amazing. First, the succulent fried shrimp, which were crunchy and light, were so addictive Summer had to sit on fisted hands to keep from stealing the one Zach left on his plate just to tempt her. As she was staring at that shrimp, Tuck finished his gumbo and astonished her by informing Zach that, yes, he'd decided he was fine with giving Cooper and his dumb program a chance. She was further amazed when she listened to him converse easily and intelligently with Zach, as Tuck rarely did with her. She could tell that Zach really had been devoting a great deal of time to Tuck, and that Tuck was lapping up the attention.

Despite all that was enjoyable about lunch, she didn't like the attention from surrounding diners, who stared and snapped pictures with their phones.

"Did you have an ulterior motive for lunching with all of us so publicly?" Summer asked after they dropped off Tuck and Gram and were driving home.

Zach's mouth was tight as he stared grimly at the road. "Being railroaded on felony charges and then being tried in the court of public opinion wasn't any picnic, either."

"That still doesn't make it right for you to use Tuck and Gram to get even with me."

"Maybe I just want people to see that I have a normal relationship with all of you," Zach said.

"But you don't. You're blackmailing me."

"Right." His dark eyes glittering, he turned toward her. The sudden intimacy between them stunned her. "Well, I want people to know that you're not afraid of me. That you never were. That you liked me, loved me even. That I was not someone who'd take a young, unwilling girl off to the woods to molest her. Is that so wrong?"

His face blurred as she forced herself to focus on the trees streaming past his window instead of him. The realization of how profoundly she'd hurt him hit her anew.

Yes, he'd hurt her, too, and yes, he'd gone on to achieve phenomenal success. But he'd never gotten over the deep injury her betrayal had inflicted—any more than she'd gotten over losing him and the baby.

Because of her, Zach had been accused of kidnapping and worse. All he'd ever tried to do was help her.

When a talent scout had been wowed by her high-school performance in *Grease,* her stepfather had forbidden her to go back to her theater-arts class. He'd sworn he wouldn't pay for her to study theater arts in college, either.

So she'd run away to Zach, who'd forced her to go back

and try to reason *with Thurman*. Only after her stepfather struck her and threatened her with more physical violence if she didn't bend to his will had Zach driven her to Nick's fishing cabin on the bayou in Texas. There they'd hidden out and made love. There they'd been found in each other's arms by Thurman and his men.

She did owe Zach. More than a few weekends. And not just because of Tuck. If Zach wanted to be seen with her and gossiped about—so be it.

"You don't have to drive me home before you go to your site," she said softly. "I'll go with you."

"I thought you needed to work on your love scenes with Hugh."

His voice hardened when he said the other man's name, and she felt vaguely guilty. Which was ridiculous, since she wasn't in a relationship with either man.

"I do, but I'll study on the plane, or later, when I get to L.A."

"Well, if you're coming with me, I've got to take you home anyway. Those sandals won't work at the construction site and neither will that tight, sexy skirt."

"Oh."

"You'll need to wear a long-sleeved shirt, jeans and boots. I'll supply you with a plastic hard hat and a safety vest with reflective tape."

"Sounds like a dangerous place."

Even though it was Saturday, cranes, bulldozers and jack-hammers were operating full force as battalions of work-ers carried out all sorts of tasks, none of which made sense to Summer as she adjusted the inner straps of her hard hat. Zach seemed as happy as a kid showing off as he led her around the site, pointing at blueprints, sketches and plans with a pocket roll-up ruler, introducing her to all of his foremen and contractors. Local men, all of them, who eyed her with open speculation.

Zach was developing hundreds of acres along the bayou, creating a dock for his riverboat casino, as well as restaurants, a hotel, a small amusement park, shops, a theater, a golf course and no telling what else.

"I've never built anything," she said, "so I'm impressed. Look, you don't have to entertain me. I'll explore on my own."

"You be careful and don't go too far."

At first she stayed close to him because the ground was rough and muddy. Then she began walking toward the dock on two-by-fours that men had laid across deep holes as makeshift bridges.

She was standing on such a bridge when Nick drove up in his battered pickup, looking for Zach. The elderly shrimper wore faded jeans, a T-shirt and scuffed boots. Even though he dipped his cowboy hat ever so slightly when he saw Summer, his cold, unsmiling face told her he hadn't forgiven her. Until Zach's uncle had shown up, Nick had been Zach's sole advocate.

"Didn't expect to see the likes of you here, *cher*," he said when he walked up to her. "Dangerous place for a woman."

Nick was thinner than the last time she'd seen him, his tanned skin crisscrossed with lines, his wispy hair steel-gray. But the penetrating blue eyes that pierced her hadn't changed much.

"And you're a dangerous woman for any man, even Zach. I warned the boy to stay away from you, but he won't listen," Nick said, eyeing Zach, who stood a hundred yards to their right, deep in conversation with a contractor. "He never did have a lick of sense where you were concerned. I don't like you settin' your hooks in him again. By coming out here with him you'll have the whole town talkin' and thinkin' you're a couple again."

"Tell him. He invited me for the weekend."

Nick spat in disbelief. "Well, you tell him I stopped by and that I'll catch up with him later. Or, if he'd prefer, he can drop by…after he gets rid of you."

She nodded.

He turned and left.

Her mood dark and remorseful, she headed toward the dock. Because of the deep holes in the ground, she was forced to cross on the makeshift bridge again. She'd nearly reached the dock when Zach called out to her.

Maybe she turned too fast—one of the boards slipped, and she tumbled several feet into the muddy hole filled with rocks and debris. When she tried to stand, her left ankle buckled under her weight.

She looked up in alarm and saw Zach running toward her, his dark eyes grave. Leaping over the boards, he was soon towering over her. "Are you okay?"

"Yes—except for my left ankle."

"I should never have brought you here."

"Nonsense. I fell. It all was my fault."

"Hang on to me, then," he commanded, jumping down into the hole.

Half carrying her, he led her out of the pit and back to his car. As he drove away from the site, he called Gram, who recommended her doctor, a man who generously offered to meet them at the emergency room. Dr. Sands actually beat them to the E.R., and Summer, who'd once fallen off a stage in Manhattan and had waited hours in a New York E.R., was both appreciative and amazed to be treated so quickly and expertly in such a small hospital. Most of all, she was grateful to Zach for staying with her.

When a team of nurses stepped inside the treatment room and asked him to leave, Zach demanded to know what they planned to do.

"Dr. Sands wants her to disrobe for an examination, so we can make sure we don't miss any of her injuries."

"But it's only my ankle that hurts," Summer protested.

"Hopefully you're right. But this is our protocol. We have to be sure."

Summer reached for Zach's hand. "Would you…"

So, he stayed beside her, gallantly turning his back when they handed her a hospital gown and she began to undress. But once, when she moaned, he turned. She saw his quick flush and heard his gasp before he averted his gaze from her body.

Her stomach fluttered. Funny that it hadn't occurred to her to be embarrassed that he should see her almost naked. She simply wanted him beside her.

When the professionals finished checking her body and stooped to examine her ankle, she cried out in pain.

Zach was at her side, pressing her hand to his lips. "Hang in there. We'll be home before you know it."

Home. How sweetly the word buzzed in her heart. She squeezed his fingers and held on tight, feeling illogically re-assured.

He was right. In less than an hour she was back at Zach's house, propped up on his couch by plump pillows, surrounded by his remotes, her script and her favorite snacks.

Strangely, after the hospital, there was a new easiness between them. Gram and Tuck had stopped by to check on her, and after they departed, Zach remained attentive, never leaving her side for long. He said he wanted to be nearby in case she needed anything. She found his hovering oddly sweet and realized it would be much too easy to become dependent on such attentions.

When the sun went down, he cooked two small steaks and roasted two potatoes for their dinner while she watched from her chair at the kitchen table. They had their meal with wine and thick buttered slices of French bread out on the back veranda.

Again she marveled that a man who must be used to servants knew his way around in a kitchen. She didn't mind in the least that he hadn't thought to prepare more sides. The simple meal was perfect even before the three deer reappeared to delight them.

Later, when she was back on the couch again and he'd finished the dinner dishes, he pulled up a chair beside her. Pleased that he hadn't gone up to his room, she declared the steak delicious and thanked him for his trouble.

"I'm not much of a cook," he said. "Eggs, steak and toast. That's about it."

"Don't forget potatoes. Yours were very nice. Crispy."

"Right. Sometimes I can stick a potato or two in the oven and sprinkle them with olive oil and salt. I have a cook in Houston, but I don't like eating at home alone. So, mostly I eat out."

"Me, too. Or I do take-out. Because I don't have time to cook."

"I imagined you in ritzy New York restaurants, dining on meals cooked by the world's best chefs, eating with famous movie stars."

When his expression darkened, she suspected he was thinking of Hugh.

"Not all that often. Fancy meals take time to eat…as well as to cook and serve," she said, avoiding the topic of Hugh. "And fans pester you for autographs. Besides, there's nothing quite like a homemade meal, is there?"

"You used to want to be an actress so badly. What's it like now that you've succeeded?"

"It's nice, but I work almost all the time. Even when I have a job, I'm always auditioning for the next part. When I sign on with a show that isn't in New York, I travel and live out of a suitcase. One minute it's a crazy life, full of parties and friends, then it gets pretty lonely. You can't hold on to anything because it's all so ephemeral. The friends I make within a cast feel closer than family for a while. Then they vanish after each show closes," she admitted.

"But when you sign with a new show or film you have a new set of friends."

"Yes, but as I get older, I see that, despite the bright lights, a life without stability isn't nearly so glamorous as people think."

"It's what you wanted."

She sighed. "Be careful what you wish for. I guess I took my real life for granted. Lately, I've realized how much I miss family…and roots."

"What does that mean?"

"My job is so all-consuming that I…I haven't been good at relationships. I'm Southern, like Gram. She sees my single state as a failure, and lets me know it every chance she gets. Her dream for me was marriage to a handsome husband. I was supposed to have two children, a boy and a girl, and live happily ever after in a cute house surrounded by a white picket fence."

He smiled. "But you, being a modern woman, aren't into such an outdated, traditional formula for happiness. Strange, that it can still exert such a hold over a female as wise as your grandmother."

"You're right, of course. I just wish I could make her understand that I have everything I set my heart on. I'm grateful for what I have, for what I've achieved. So many people would give anything to be me."

She was saying the same truths she'd lived by for years, but, for some reason, the words felt hollow tonight.

Zach didn't say anything.

She'd never imagined having such an ordinary, simple,

companionable evening with him, and she found herself enjoying it more than she'd enjoyed anything in a very long time. When they'd been kids, they'd been friends before they'd been lovers. They hadn't fallen in love until after he'd graduated and she'd been entering her senior year.

Now, as an adult, she spent so much time working on her image and her brand, so much time learning various roles, and never very much time being herself. What would it be like to have a lifetime of such evenings with a man like him? To take them for granted?

She sighed. That wasn't who she was now. She had her career, a bright future—and it was on the stage and screen.

"What about you?" she whispered. "You're successful. Are you happy?"

"Like you, I'm not unhappy," he muttered thickly. "I, too, have everything I always thought I wanted…except maybe for…" He shot her a look that was so intense it burned away her breath.

"For what?"

"It doesn't matter," he growled. "Not even billionaires can have it all. Not that we don't pretend that we can, with our fancy cars and homes and yachts." Frowning, he sprang to his feet and then glanced at his watch. "But you're injured, and it's late. You must be tired. Besides, Sands prescribed that painkiller. I'm afraid I've been very selfish to keep you up so long."

She didn't want him to go. "No. I'm barely injured, and you've waited on me hand and foot…. And I just sat there and let you."

"Well, I won't keep you any longer."

"But I really do want to know…about you," she whispered.

"Let's save that boring tale for later," he said, cutting her off. "Who knows—maybe you'll get lucky and never have to hear it." He picked up her crutches. "Why don't I help you to your room?"

Feeling stunned and a little hurt by how abruptly he'd ended their pleasant evening, she got to her feet. As she stood, her uncertain eyes met his. But he wouldn't hold her gaze.

Suddenly, she again felt awkward at the thought of their sharing the house for another night. Stiffening, he handed her the crutches and then backed away.

"I hate these things," she said as she placed the crutches under her arms.

"It's a minor sprain. The doctor said you might even be off them as soon as Tuesday."

"I hope so. Thanks again for tonight. When you convinced me to come here for the weekend, I never thought…we would have this kind of evening or that I could enjoy simply being with you so much."

"Neither the hell did I," he admitted in a stilted tone, still not looking at her. "Believe me—I had a very different kind of weekend in mind."

"Well, you've been very nice."

"Good night, then," he muttered, his voice sounding so furious she realized he'd had more than enough of her company.

He'd blackmailed her because he'd wanted revenge. He'd wanted sex. Had this evening, with its simple pleasures, bored him?

She felt hurt and rejected, just as she had last night.

Six

Zach knew he wouldn't be able to sleep for a while, so instead of undressing for bed, he poured himself a glass of scotch. Then he strode out onto the balcony where the humid air smelled of honeysuckle, jasmine and pine.

Damn those bewitching blue eyes of hers and her pretty, sweet smile that made him want her so badly he hurt.

Why hadn't he taken Summer as he'd intended? Why hadn't he punished her? Usually he came on strong with women. What the hell was wrong with him this weekend?

Next week she would be with Hugh, making love to him—at least on film. And probably offscreen, too. Not that her relationship with Jones should be any concern of Zach's. Still, he burned every time he thought about her with that egotistical phony.

Their first night here she'd seemed so vulnerable and uneasy. Then today, when she'd fallen, she had taken his hand and begged him to stay with her. Her fingers and wrist had felt so slim and fragile in his much larger hand. What kind of man forced his presence on a woman who seemed so defenseless and in need of his protection?

Still, Zach wasn't so noble that he could forget the glimpses he'd seen of her breasts and her creamy thighs. He wanted to kiss those breasts, tongue all the warm, succulent places between her thighs. He knew what she'd done in the past, how close she'd come to nearly destroying him—but for reasons he didn't understand, he continued to balk at using her sexually.

No longer did he want to expose their relationship to the press for public consumption.

This weekend had backfired. Damn it.

The sensitive male was a new role for him.

She'd beaten him.

To save his own ass, tomorrow he'd tell her their deal was off and send her packing.

Then he'd do the smart thing: return to Houston and forget her.

The next morning, when Summer awoke, her ankle was so much better she could almost walk without limping if she used one crutch. When she went into the kitchen she discovered that Zach had already cooked and eaten breakfast. She looked down at his dishes in the sink and realized he was avoiding her.

Rolling the scrambled egg and bacon he'd left for her into a tortilla, she walked outside and saw him swimming laps in his pool. When she waved, he got out.

As he dried off, it was all she could do not to stare, even though he wore swimming trunks.

His eyes were guarded as he strode up to her. "How's the ankle?"

"Much better," she whispered, lowering her lashes.

"Good. Bob is standing by to fly you to L.A. So, whenever you're ready, just call him. I know you've got work, and so do I, so I won't keep you."

He was so remote and cool that her acute disappointment and hurt felt like withdrawal, which was ridiculous.

"What about next weekend?" she whispered, her voice catching. "Do you still want to see me?"

Zach sucked in a breath. "Like you said, maybe spending the weekends together wasn't such a good idea. So—you won." His voice was cold, revealing nothing.

He slung a towel across his shoulders and turned away, dismissing her as if she were of no importance to him.

"Are you mad at me?"

"Yeah. Mad at myself, too."

"Zach…"

"You have your real life…in the theater. And I have mine. I think we should just cool it."

He was right, of course.

"Or maybe not," she said huskily as she focused on his profile. "I want to know why you blackmailed me and then changed your mind, why you were so nice last night and are so cold today."

"Maybe I started thinking about what happened fifteen years ago and don't see this going anywhere positive."

He wasn't making sense. Last week he'd wanted to punish her. And now… What did he want?

"What if I disagree?" she whispered. On impulse, she leaned forward on her tiptoes and kissed his rough cheek tentatively.

When he jerked away as if burned, she beamed. "I enjoyed last night, you see. Too much. And I thought maybe you did, too…just a little. You were sweet."

"Sweet?" He almost snarled the word.

She smiled gently. "And I thank you for what you're doing

for Tuck, too…taking him out to the tech school and all… especially after what he did to you."

"Forget it," he snapped.

"What if I can't?"

"Soon you'll fly to L.A. to film those love scenes with Jones. Don't waste your charm or blatant come-on sexuality on me. Save it for him."

"I don't care about him."

Not believing her, he scowled.

"I don't."

When she edged closer and held her hand to his face, Zach froze. At the first light touch of her fingertips on his warm throat, he shuddered. When he tried to wrench away, her hands came around his neck so she could hold him close. She had no idea what she was doing or why she was doing it, she only knew she didn't want to part from him so dispassionately, when something new and wonderful was beginning in her heart.

"Can't you at least kiss me goodbye," she whispered, too aware of her taut nipples pressing against his hard, bare chest.

"Not a good idea," he growled.

"You sure about that?" She rubbed her hips against the hard ridge of his erection, sighing as her body melted against his.

On a groan, he reached for her, gripping her with strong, sure arms, pulling her close, like a man who was starving for her.

She was starving, too, starving for the intoxicating sensuality of his mouth claiming hers. He tasted so good, so right. For fifteen years, she'd wanted this and denied it. Why should she fight it now? Moaning, she kissed him back.

His savage grip crushed her. His hungry passion ignited unmet needs. Murmuring his name feverishly, her fingertips ran through his thick, inky hair.

"All weekend I wanted this," she whispered. "Wanted you. Wanted to touch you, to kiss you…to be in your arms…even though I tried to tell myself I didn't. Friday night I lay in bed, wanting this more than I'd ever wanted anything. And last night after we talked, I craved it even more, craved it so much I felt like I was about to burst. Then you went upstairs, and I felt so lost and alone in that bed. I—I couldn't sleep for hours. You told me you'd make me want you, and you were right."

"You shouldn't say these things."

"I don't understand any of it and yet…it's the truth."

"Hell," he muttered. "This isn't some damn role you've got to understand. Life's messy and chaotic and doesn't make a lick of sense most of the time. Like now. Like last night. I decided you're the one woman I should have nothing to do with. And yet here I am…."

"Tell me about it," she whispered. "You're definitely bad for me, too."

When his mouth took hers again, his desperation and urgency made her dizzily excited.

"This is crazy," she whispered as her fingertips glided across the damp hair on his bronzed flesh. "I didn't want to come this weekend, and now I can't bear to go."

"I don't want you to go, either."

"Punish me like you swore you would. Make love to me," she whispered.

The next thing she knew, he was lifting her, kissing her wildly as he carried her up the stairs, into the house and then down the hall to her room. Locking the door, he drew her down to the bed.

In no time, she stripped, but even in her rush, she enjoyed the striptease, for never had she played to a more fascinated audience. He lay on the bed watching as she undid her blouse in the shadows. Button by button, her slim fingers skimmed downward. He held his breath, his eyes burning when she threw her blouse aside and unhooked her bra.

"You are exquisite," he rasped when she slid her lacy panties down her thighs. Vaguely she was aware of him rustling with a foil wrapper. Then, reaching for her, he lay down beside her and buried his face in the curve of her neck.

She let her head fall back, offering him her breasts. "You're pretty okay yourself."

His lips traced the length of her throat. He tasted first one nipple and then the other until they beaded into damp, pink pearls. She trembled with an enjoyment she couldn't hide, which she could see excited him even more.

When his lips found hers again, she fell back against the pillows and opened her mouth so his tongue could slide inside.

"Strip for me," she whispered. "I want to see you naked."

"Wicked girl."

Grinning, he ripped off his swimming trunks. Her breath stopped. He was huge and gorgeous, magnificently virile. While she watched approvingly through the screen of her lowered lashes, he tossed his trunks into a far corner.

Reaching toward him, she slid her hand over his manhood, circling it so that he inhaled sharply. While she touched him, he caressed her most secret, delicate folds with blunt-fingered hands, teasing her sensitive nub of flesh until her breath came hard and fast and she wanted him inside her more than anything.

But he refused for a while longer, teasing her with his mouth and hands while she grew hotter and wilder.

How had she lived without him all these years?

Squeezing him, she rubbed in an urgent, methodic way until he groaned and gathered her close. She heard the sound of a foil wrapper again. Then he slid the condom on and, much to her delight, positioned the head of his shaft against her damp entrance.

Murmuring her name, he hovered there, kissing her hair, her brow. Only when she arched her hips upward in sensual invitation did he slide all the way inside. For a moment, he stopped and simply held her so they could savor the sensation of their joined bodies.

"Zach," she pleaded.

His hips surged. She cried out as he drove himself home.

Their eyes met and held. With her hands, she cupped his face and kissed each of his cheeks and then his nose.

He sighed, as if relieved of some immense weight. Then, all too soon, some primal force took over.

How she loved lying underneath him, staring up at the breadth of his bronzed shoulders, at his black hair that dripped perspiration onto his gorgeous face as he pumped. She felt on fire. With every thrust he claimed her, and she surrendered to him as she had as a girl, completely, irrevocably, giving him every shattered piece of her heart.

Thus did he sweep her away to emotional and sensual peaks she'd never known before. Crying out in the end, she held on to him, feeling lost and yet found again as he exploded inside her. In a blinding flash, she saw that he had always remained at the center of her heart.

For a long time she lay trembling quietly beneath him. Then she kissed his damp eyelashes and eyebrows. *I love you,* she thought. *I always have. This is what has been missing.*

If I have everything else and lack this, I can never be complete.

Only gradually did she grow aware of how wonderfully heavy he was on top of her. When she opened her eyes and looked up at the hard angles of his handsome face, she saw that he was staring down at her with a brooding intensity that frightened her.

"You've got to go soon, so you can cram for those damn scenes with Jones." Frowning, he kissed the tip of her nose.

"Yes," she replied drowsily without the least bit of enthusiasm. "I think you just sapped all my ambition to be a movie star. I just want to stay here with you."

He nipped her upper lip a little firmly…as if to snap her out of her languid mood. "But that's not who you are, is it? You said your career is what completes you, not relationships. And with my uncle not there to help me anymore, I've got a helluva lot to do in Houston. So…"

No sweet words. Nothing. Just those two parting kisses.

A chill swept her. Had she been wrong about their sex being spiritual as well as physical? Had it just been revenge for him after all? Now that he'd had her again, was he done?

"And next weekend?" she murmured, deliberately keeping her voice light. "Do we meet again?"

"I'll call you," he said slowly, but there was no conviction in his voice. Her heart sank as he stroked her neck absently. "Like I said, we both have a lot on our plates."

"Sounds to me like maybe I'm off the hook. For good behavior?"

"Maybe," he admitted.

"Okay, then. I get it."

He stared at her, sucked in a breath, but didn't reply.

She rose, reached for her clothes and began to dress hurriedly.

So what if he wasn't going to call? She'd served her time, so to speak. Now he wouldn't press charges against Tuck.

Logically, she knew that it was probably best if this thing between them ended here. For her, sex with him had been too intense, too all-consuming for her to have a light affair. He would break her heart all over again if she wasn't careful. No smart adult should let herself become involved with a man she'd loved and obsessed over for years.

But she wasn't feeling logical. She was feeling sensually

and emotionally aflame after his lovemaking. The whole world seemed aglow. He seemed a part of her, her other half.

Naturally, she wanted to see him again, to lie in his arms like this again. She felt she'd lose a vital part of herself forever if she couldn't. Which meant he'd completed his mission, by using sex as a weapon to punish her.

He'd won.

Seven

On her flight to L.A., try as she might, Summer found it impossible to concentrate on her script. Hurt simmered inside her because of Zach's coolness at their parting. Thus, the minute the jet's wheels slammed against tarmac, she turned on her phone, desperate to check her messages.

She swallowed when she found only a single text from Hugh.

can't meet u. nominated sexiest man n known universe 2day. jerk leaked information about hot scenes n dangerous man. horde of paparazzi @ my bldg.

No sooner had her plane rolled to a stop in front of a private hangar than a herd of photographers stampeded her jet.

Great. I'm on my own. This is what I deserve for letting the world think even for one minute I was ever serious about Hugh.

Bob stuck his shaggy head out of the cockpit and said, "Not to worry. I've already notified security."

When she finally left the jet, with a security detail, paparazzi on motorcycles chased her limo all the way to her hotel. Apparently, Hugh's premiere had been well-received by critics and the public, so for now he was the hottest talent in La-La Land.

Welcome to Hollywood, she thought as she bolted herself into her hotel room.

When room service arrived with her breakfast the next morning, Summer found a weekly tabloid tucked under her door along with a note from her agent. The tabloid's banner headline read: Sexiest Man In The Universe Teams With Reputed Lover, Broadway Actress Summer Wallace, To Shoot Super Sexy Love Scenes. The article beneath the headline made her feel cheap and tawdry, especially after her weekend with Zach.

Summer Wallace upset legions of fans this weekend when she failed to attend the premiere of *Kill-Hard* on the arm of rumored lover, Hugh Jones, star of the film. Instead, the actress tiptoed into the city late last night. It's no secret their fans can't wait for a sneak peek of their favorite couple out on the town together this week. Or better yet, a sneak peak of those love scenes in *Dangerous Man*. We hear they're going to be sizzling.

Her week got crazier, but what made her *feel* crazier was that Zach never called or texted.

When she was on the set, Summer didn't know if it was the soul-stirring sex she'd shared with Zach or Hugh's sulky attitude toward her after she'd told him she'd reconnected with Zach over the weekend, but filming intimate moments with Hugh was awkward. She was tense, Hugh impatient and their director, Sam, who called for endless takes, apoplectic.

It didn't help her mood that every male employee in production made up some pretext to show up on the set to leer. During the most intimate scenes, she felt as if she was betraying Zach. Even though he'd dismissed her and had shown no inclination to see her again, she worried about what he'd think of the finished film. Not that she or Hugh had to strip for the camera—in fact, she had a clause in her contract that protected her against nudity.

By day two she felt as if she was playing Twister with a sullen, male octopus. Whatever spark had ever existed between Hugh and her was absolutely dead. The only way she endured her scenes with Hugh and managed to respond in character was to remember how she'd felt when Zach had touched her or kissed her.

She wanted Zach, but his silence made her that wonder if her longing was one-sided. At night, when she was alone in her hotel room, hoping Zach would call, she felt lost and lonely and under more pressure than ever.

By Thursday, they were forced to film late into the night. Just when she thought the endless, excruciating takes on that satin bed would never end, Sam yelled it was a wrap. He was thrilled with the rushes.

"You were fantastic, Summer," he said. "Gorgeous in every shot. Every man in America will envy Hugh."

For the first time in her career, she didn't care about that. She just wanted to be with Zach. Even though it was pretty obvious Zach didn't feel as she did, Sam's praise reawakened her concerns about how Zach might react to the movie.

Relieved to be finished, Summer headed back to her hotel. While she was showering, her phone rang. She grabbed for a towel and then her cell. She could see from the number that it was Zach.

"Hi," Zach said as she pulled the towel around her dripping body. "How's the ankle?"

His voice sounded so hard and cold, she wondered why he'd even called.

"Actually, I'm not on crutches anymore. So, it's great...." Her voice died into nothingness.

"Glad to hear it. So—you won't sue me," he murmured drily.

She held her breath, waiting, hoping his mood would lighten, hoping he'd called to say he wanted to see her again.

"I called to say I decided not to let you off for good behavior after all."

"Oh." She stopped, stunned, wondering where this was going and whether his motive stemmed from the need to punish or the desire to be with her.

"There's a ground-breaking ceremony tomorrow—Friday night—at my construction site. My PR people think I need a date, and they think you'd be the perfect one.... You being a celebrity and a hometown girl. Since you still owe me, I decided to call. You'll need to dress up and look beautiful—movie-star beautiful."

So this wasn't about them; this was about his work.

"But you've already broken ground. I mean... I fell in that hole, didn't I?" she said softly, hoping he would admit to feeling more for her.

"Won't happen tomorrow night because I'll be holding on to you all night long. Good for my image."

Her hopes and his tension warred in the silence that hung between them. She was a big girl. She should be used to men wanting her only for publicity.

"The whole town will be there," he said. "So, a fringe benefit of this appearance will be having the gossips around here see that you don't view me as a threat. I know this is late no-tice, but you do owe me."

"Of course, I'll be your date," she whispered.

When he didn't say anything, she realized anew how tense he was. How could he have made love to her so passionately and then have turned so cold? It was as if he'd turned off a switch and now disliked her more than ever. How could she have been so wrong about what they'd shared?

To keep him from hanging up, because some tiny part of her believed she hadn't been wrong, she said, "So—how've you been all week?"

"Fine." Again his voice was too abrupt.

"Work went okay?"

"The usual challenges. And your scenes with Hugh? How did they go?" As always, when discussing the subject of Hugh, his tone hardened. Which was strange—he'd been so aloof since they'd slept together. Why would he care?

Maybe she should explain about how grueling and un-sexy the work had really been. Maybe she should tell Zach that because of him, she'd ended it with Hugh. But she didn't want to discuss Hugh, not when Zach was in his present dark mood. Not over the phone.

"Sam, our director, says he's happy. I'm…I'm just glad the week's over. After Bonne Terre, it felt like the four longest days of my life…because I…I missed you."

She willed him to say he'd missed her, too, to say any-thing…. When he didn't, she chewed at the edge of a fin-gernail.

"Zach…"

"Hmm?"

She took a deep breath. Why was it so impossible to talk to him now when it had been so easy the night after her fall?

"Never mind," she finally said. "I'll see you tomorrow."

"Tomorrow," he repeated sternly. "Bob will call you and

set a time and place to pick you up." He hung up after an impersonal goodbye that left her feeling emotionally dissatisfied.

If only he'd sounded the least bit eager to see her.

He'd called, hadn't he? He'd demanded that she spend another weekend with him.

Maybe she'd given up on them too soon when she'd been younger. She didn't want to make the same mistake a second time.

"There's no such thing as bad publicity." That's what Zach's PR guys said. They loved that somebody had stolen the hot love scenes from Summer's new movie and plastered them all over the internet.

Zach disagreed. Tension fisted around his lungs as he studied the stolen clips of Summer with Jones. She was so gorgeous he couldn't breathe. Even though she was lying beneath another man, just the sight of her sparkling eyes, tremulous lips, breasts and silken hair got his pulse thudding violently. In an instant, he remembered her looking at him exactly that way and how nauseatingly vulnerable he'd felt when he'd realized there was no way he could make love to her again without surrendering his heart. In one stolen weekend, she'd gotten through every careful barrier he'd spent years erecting, which made her too dangerous to fool around with.

Since there was no way he was ever giving her his heart again, he'd sent her packing.

But that hadn't stopped him from wanting her.

Hell. She'd plunged him back into hell. That's what she'd done.

Within minutes of starting the clip, he'd seen more than he'd ever wanted to see of Summer on those satin sheets. Did she have to moan under that egotistical actor just as she had when Zach had made love to her last weekend?

She was just acting.

Or was she?

Maybe she'd been acting in Bonne Terre, in Zach's bed.
It didn't matter.

He damn sure hadn't been acting. He'd been wildly upset that he'd felt so much more than lust for her; furious that he'd experienced the same shattering, soul-deep bond he'd felt for her as a kid.

He knew too well the destructive power of those emotions, so he'd known what he'd had to do. She'd acted hurt when he'd dismissed her, and that had gotten to him, too, but then she was an actress.

He'd lived without her before. He could do it again.

But then, when he'd been missing her the most, his PR guys had come up with the idea to invite her to the ground-breaking, to put a positive spin on an old story by dating her.

His PR guys had handed him an excuse to see her again. So, he'd broken his vow to himself and called her. He'd told himself it was business; it would only be for one night; they'd be in public. He had no intention of sleeping with her again. He'd be safe.

But he'd been lying to himself. He'd called her because he wanted her.

Damn it, he wanted her so badly he couldn't think rationally. Even as he'd willed himself to forget her and move on, he'd spent the week fantasizing about her lips, her wide eyes, her sweet, responsive body. He'd remembered the same soft expression on her face that he'd just seen captured on film.

He'd been suffering serious withdrawal from his weekend with Summer Wallace.

Zach wished to hell he could cancel her flight. But it was too late for that now. She was already in the air.... Probably an hour away. Bob had said they would run into bad weather west of Louisiana. The last thing Zach wanted was to distract Bob when he was flying during a storm.

He knew it would be a mistake to see her again. Even though his PR guys were even more adamant that he court her after the internet clips were released, Zach wanted to make the smart move and avoid her.

He hated the way she tore him in two. Hated the way he'd felt so out of control, during sex and ever since.

He clenched a fist. He knew one thing for sure. Tonight, after the ground-breaking, he would end it for good.

Eight

As soon as Zach's jet landed on the narrow tarmac nestled between tall pines outside of Bonne Terre, Summer bent over her phone and frowned. She saw dozens of texts and voice-mail messages from Sam and several other producers of *Dangerous Man,* but none from Zach. Gram and her agent had left messages, too. What was going on?

First, she called Sam, who began ranting about pirated scenes and a lunatic Brazilian hacker, before she could even say hello. He spit out words so fast she could only catch half of what he said.

"But how could this have happened?" she demanded after she finally understood the gist. "And what are you going to do about it?"

"Somehow the kid hacked into my laptop, that's how, damn it," Sam yelled. "I've got firewalls. She's fifteen! That little hacker gave away everything. For nothing! Just 'cause she's got the hots for Hugh. She's cost us millions. Maybe cost me my job. She's denying it, of course, but we've got her IP address."

After more of the same, Sam finally wound down and hung up.

Oh, God, had Zach seen the video? With grim foreboding, Summer listened to Gram's message.

"Everybody's been telling me about some love scenes you're in.... What's going on? Call me!"

Of course, Zach had seen them. Taken out of context, the scenes might look pornographic and might compromise the integrity of the movie, not to mention her integrity as an actress. Summer felt violated, but her main concern was how Zach would interpret those scenes.

With a heavy heart, she listened to Gram's second message.

"You swore to me you weren't going to take off all your clothes. And what about Zach? Everybody says you're his date tonight. Call me."

She hadn't been nude. A double had been used in the only nude shot.

Press coverage had caused tension at home before. Why couldn't Gram learn not to believe all the lies that were printed about celebrities to sell newspapers?

It would be nice to have understanding and support from those who loved her and really knew her. But, no, those closest to her were as easily manipulated by the press as everybody else.

Feeling very much abused and in no mood to explain herself to anyone—not the town or even Zach—she shut her phone off and buried it in the bottom of her purse.

Thibodeaux House was so dark she could barely see it among the trees when Bob dropped her in the drive.

As she was heading up the walk, he called after her. "Hey!

Zach just sent me a text. He'll be here at six to pick you up for the ceremony."

Fumbling with the keys Bob had handed her, she let herself into Zach's shadowy house and unset his alarm.

Had Zach seen the pirated scenes? Did he think the worst of her?

Of course, he did. And he was furious, no doubt.

Carrying her bag, she went to her room and threw herself on the bed. There she lay, hugging herself, as she listened to the birds and the creaks of the old house as the light went out of the sky. She knew she should get ready, but she felt too weary to move.

Finally, after what seemed an eternity, she heard Zach's car on the gravel drive. She ran to the window and watched him walk grim-faced toward the house.

The front door opened and slammed. He strode briskly into the kitchen. When she heard his heavy tread on the stairs, she sat up warily. He hadn't even bothered to check on her.

As if he read her mind, he stopped. She held her breath during that interim before he headed back down the stairs.

Finally, he rapped his knuckles on the door.

"Come in," she whispered brokenly.

He flung the door open and stared at her across the darkness, his blazing eyes accusing her. When he flipped on the light, she sat up, brushed her fingers through her hair.

"Not ready I see." His voice was hard and clipped.

"I was tired," she whispered.

"I can well imagine." His black eyes glittered coldly.

"I didn't know what to wear…. Or if you'd still want me to go with you…."

"Not go when everybody in Bonne Terre is so anxious to see you?" he said in a low, cutting tone. "Not that you left much of yourself to the imagination."

"I can explain…."

"I'm sure—but why bother? Besides, my PR guys are thrilled. They say all your internet coverage is great for Torr Corporation."

He walked over to the luggage rack and unzipped her suitcase. After rummaging through her clothes, he yanked out a low-cut, ruby-red gown that a personal shopper had bought for her in L.A. before she'd known about the pirated love scenes.

"Wear the red. Perfect choice," he said. "You'll look the part your legions of fans expect you to play. And you'll be gorgeous beside me, which is all my PR people care about."

But what did *he* care about? Whatever it was, it was devouring him alive.

"Zach, I haven't seen the videos, so I don't know exactly what you saw…. But I was acting."

"Save it! I'll be back down in a minute!"

"Please—I can explain…."

"Sorry. I don't have time for one of your offscreen Oscar performances. Although you're good—very good. And you were even better last week—in my bed."

He slammed the door in her face and was gone. As she listened to him stomp up the stairs, her heart constricted so tightly she was afraid it would shatter into a million tiny pieces. So, he didn't care how she felt at all.

"You'll get through this," she whispered to herself. "You've gotten through worse."

But had she? She'd never gotten over him…. Or their precious baby.

Don't think about that. You'll go crazy if you do.

Zach didn't speak to her on the drive over, and he looked so grim and forbidding she decided it was wise to give him time.

She had done nothing wrong. She'd done her job. Actors acted. She hadn't made love to Hugh for the camera. Her character had. She didn't even like Hugh. It wasn't her fault someone had stolen the video.

Something told her Zach's mood went deeper than jealousy.

The glow that hung over the trees ahead of them brightened as they neared the construction site. When they reached their destination, Zach parked and helped her out of the car. She drew in an awed breath.

The construction site looked nothing like it had last weekend. Transformed into an enchanted fairyland, it was lit by a thousand lanterns. White tents covered dance floors and a dining area. Champagne was being served by a dozen bartenders. Warm laughter and music drifted through the happy crowd. A podium had been set up in front of a thousand chairs.

No sooner had he stopped his Mercedes than reporters and photographers surrounded them.

Taking her icy hand, Zach led her into the thick of the paparazzi where they were blinded by flashes.

His expression fierce, Zach gave the screaming horde a brief statement and posed beside her for more pictures. Then he'd had enough. She hardly knew how he managed it, but with a wave of his hand, his own people led them past the press and into a cordoned-off area where the music and laughter died. For a full minute, she clung to Zach's arm, while he braved this fresh crowd gaping at them with stunned expressions.

Before those prying eyes, she began to tremble, feeling the same guilt she'd known fifteen years ago when these same people had thought the worst of her and Zach.

"Easy," Zach whispered against her ear as he placed a protective hand over hers. Then he signaled his contractor and the band, and the music resumed.

We've never done anything wrong, she thought. *We were wronged.*

Slowly, people turned away and began talking once more. Still, even though Summer held her head high, she felt their lingering interest too acutely; just as she felt the steely tension emanating from Zach's hard body beside her.

Never had she been more conscious of having a spellbound audience. During the politicians' speeches and the ceremonial breaking of the ground with shovels, people couldn't stop staring at her and Zach.

She couldn't let their stares matter. All that mattered was Zach.

Maybe he was furious at her. Maybe he felt utterly betrayed. Never once did he leave her side, but perhaps he was putting on a show for the public. Would he make such an immense effort to show his support merely for publicity reasons?

He even danced with her beneath the softly lit lanterns and moonlight, holding her close, swirling her about while all she wanted was to run home and have him to herself so she could explain.

Instead, he forced her to brave the curious, fawning crowd, forced her to stay until all the important guests and photographers had departed. Only then did he whisper in her ear, in a tone that chilled her to the bone, "The crowd has lost their appetite to devour you. Time for us to go home, sweetheart, and start our weekend."

Once they were out of the area that had been cordoned off from the paparazzi, the horde chased them to his Mercedes.

A microphone was shoved in her face. "Is Torr your man now?"

"No comment," snapped Zach as someone snickered.

"When do you plan to make up your mind, Summer?"

Summer felt a jolt as Zach shoved a reporter aside so he could open her door.

A flash went off in her face, blinding her as Zach raced around the hood.

He jumped behind the wheel. "Get your head down. There are cameras everywhere."

"I thought this was what your PR guys wanted."

"Yes, they're probably thrilled."

A moment later, he sped out of the parking lot with the pack tailing them. Inside his Mercedes, which was lit by the headlights of the paparazzi, Zach was fiercely silent behind the wheel. So fierce, she thought his anger had built during the opening ceremonies. She didn't dare say a word during that endless drive through that tunnel of trees to his home.

No sooner were they at his house than the photographers circled them, snapping photographs and yelling questions again.

Zach put his arms tightly around her, shielding her face, and escorted her inside.

"I can see that after this, I'm going to have to build a wall and hire guards to protect my privacy," he muttered once they were in his living room and had drawn the drapes.

"What did you expect, when you asked me to come here as a publicity stunt?"

He double-bolted the front door and turned on her.

"Okay. I got what I deserved—in spades. The PR junket is over. Tomorrow I want you gone. They'll soon forget."

"No, you and I know they never forget."

"Well, I intend to forget. Bob will fly you wherever you want to go. My only request is that you and your bags are on the front porch at 8:00 a.m. That's when I told Bob to pick you up. Do you understand?"

She nodded. "Why won't you even let me explain?"

"I'm sure you could explain your way out of hell itself, but I'm not interested in hearing it."

"What about Tuck?"

"I won't press charges."

"You just want me gone? Out of your life?"

"That about sums it up."

"Zach, please—"

"Save it for your true loves—the stage and the press." He turned on his heel and headed to his room. When his door slammed, she sagged against the wall as he banged about upstairs.

"But they're not my true loves," she whispered. "Not anymore."

In fact, sometimes, such as now, being an actress felt like hell. She was a human being, a woman, whose privacy had been invaded and whose work had been exploited to serve as lurid entertainment for a mass of strangers on the internet. They'd hurt her, but it was Zach, and his refusal to hear her explanation, that ripped her heart out.

An hour later, Summer felt worse than ever as she closed her laptop after having viewed the pirated clips.

The integrity of the film had been compromised by allowing those provocative scenes to be viewed out of context. She felt used and abused as a woman, as well.

She did look wildly enthralled in the videos, but those hadn't been her real emotions.

After the connection they'd shared last weekend, she'd worried about Zach's reaction. Maybe she should have explained what was involved in filming sex on-screen for a major motion picture before she'd left for L.A. She should have made it clear that it was work, hard work…. That it was far from a sensual experience. But Zach had been so cold and forbidding.

Well, she had to talk to him now; had to do whatever was necessary to make him listen…. To make him understand that they had a bond worth fighting for. She wasn't about to leave him again without doing so. That's what she'd done fifteen years ago.

Her heart was beating too fast as she pulled on her robe and headed up the stairs. In her anxious state, it seemed that every stair creaked so that he had plenty of warning to throw the bolt against her.

Much to her surprise, when she twisted the knob and leaned against the door, it opened.

She saw the bottle of whiskey on the table beside the bed. A crystal glass glimmered in his clenched hand as he stood by the window.

"Zach, I'm not going until we talk…."

He whirled. "What do you want now?"

"You. Only you."

"Get out, damn you."

"You'll have to throw me out, because I'm not leaving on my own. Not until you let me explain."

"There's no need."

"You're being unfair…like Thurman and the people of Bonne Terre were to you fifteen years ago."

"And you!" he said. "You were the star of that public farce, too!"

His words felt like blows.

"I was sixteen. Thurman had been running me so long, I didn't know what to do."

"Except stand by him and sell me out."

"I—I never intended to hurt you. The whole thing just got out of control. All I know is that I don't want to lose you again."

She pushed her robe off her shoulders, indifferent as it slid down her arms and pooled on the oak floor. She stood before him in a shimmering, transparent nightgown.

"Last weekend you made me feel so special when you made love to me. I hoped it might be a new start for us," she whispered, feeling fearful because he was so cold and determined to shut her out.

"Did you now? Well, there is no new start for us. There never was, so put your robe back on and get out."

Even as his harsh tone ripped through her, she stepped farther into the room, shut his door and then locked it. She was shaking when she flipped off the light. "You'll have to make me," she said softly, refusing to lose her courage.

"Don't think I won't." Slamming his glass down on the windowsill, he stormed across the room and seized her by the shoulders. "Listen to me—this ends now!"

She put her arms around his waist, lifted her eyes to his, then laid her head against his chest and clung.

He stiffened.

"Please! Don't do this," she begged, even though she felt desperate that he might push her away. "Last weekend…being with you…meant everything…. Don't let the press's distortions destroy us."

"Stop it," he rasped even as he shuddered from her nearness.

Her breath caught. She could tell he wanted her every bit as much as she wanted him, but he was fighting his emotions. Maybe because he didn't trust them, or her.

"I can't. Not until you hear me out. When I saw you at Gram's that first day, all those weeks ago, something started between us again. At least it did for me. Maybe it never died. I didn't want to admit it. I had my career, and that was enough. Then you kissed me… And then we made love. Now none of what I had before you is ever going to be enough. I…want you so much. So very much. Even though I live a crazy life that leaves no time for relationships, I want you."

"What about Hugh?"

"I told you—there's nothing between Hugh and me now except for a little chemistry on the screen and whatever fantasy lingers in fans' minds. We never really dated. I became involved with him after Edward, my boyfriend, walked out on me publicly. I knew the press would focus on Hugh instead of my failure with Edward because Hugh loves media attention and encourages it. It seemed less invasive because it was false. Now I see I shouldn't have used him like that."

"Those love scenes between you two were pretty hot. When I saw you on those satin sheets, looking up at him the same way you looked up at me, something snapped."

His face was closed; his eyes had gone flat and dark. She could tell there was a lot he wasn't telling her.

"I…I can't even begin to imagine what you felt. I only know that if I saw you give another woman that special smile or look, I'd feel betrayed. Foolishly, I thought I'd be able to explain about the love scenes before you saw them…since *Dangerous Man* won't come out for nearly eight months." She paused. "I'm afraid I was thinking about you, when I was with Hugh in front of the camera."

"I don't much like hearing that." His black eyes impaled her from beneath his dark brows.

"I know it was wrong, but I was turned off by Hugh and my selfish, seductive character. It was the only way I could get the work done…. So, in a way, I did use you…use us…. But it's hard for an actress not to use parts of herself to make a role convincing. Our tools are our own emotions."

"Does the acting ever stop?"

"Yes. Now. This is me, and I'm begging you to give me—to give us—another chance."

Terrified, feeling naked to the soul after asking this of him, she inhaled a long breath and waited as he considered what she'd said.

"I don't know," he said finally, but the anger had gone out of his voice. "Since I was nineteen, when everything I read about us was distorted and used to hang me, I've worked hard to keep my private life private. There were, of course, always those reporters who wrote new stories about what I'd supposedly done to you, but mostly my life was a private affair.

"I've never dated a famous actress before. Frankly, I never wanted to. But here you are—a bomb that's gone off in my life. If we date, your career, with all its fuss, is going to take some getting used to."

"I know. I'm sorry about that."

"I thought I had my life under control. It was simple. It was all about building and developing and making more money. Then I lost Uncle Zachery. And I saw your tear-streaked face and kissed you on Viola's porch."

"See—your work is not so different from my roller-coaster career. Until that kiss, I lived for interesting parts and good reviews and felt like death when some critic said I couldn't act."

"I don't like feeling out of control—or in your control."

"That's understandable because I hurt you before," she whispered.

"I don't want this…you…us," he growled. "You're bad for me."

"Not according to your PR guys," she whispered with a smile.

Zach took a deep breath. For a moment, she was terrified that her little joke would backfire, that he was still going to send her away. She wouldn't have blamed him.

But he smiled. "I should never have listened to them."

"Were they really the only reason you called me?"

"Point taken. No… But I wish I could say they were. Then maybe I could resist you."

"That's not the wisest course," she whispered.

Very slowly, his arms gentled upon her shoulders. Wrapping her closely against him, he drew her to his bed and pulled her down onto the mattress beside him. For a long time they just lay together in the darkness growing comfortable in each other's presence.

His nearness calmed her and made her feel safe again.

Then he rolled on his side and began to stroke her lips, her ears, her neck—and lower.

"All night, at the ground-breaking, I was so miserable... because I knew you were going to send me away again." Her words were muttered shatteringly against the base of his throat, her hands clinging to his shoulders.

His hand traced the length of her spine.

"I thought that this second chance was over before we'd even begun to understand what we feel," she continued.

"I damn sure wanted it to be over. You're like a dangerous drug, and I'm an addict."

His hands were smoothing her tumbled hair out of her eyes. His lips kissed her brow lightly. Then he pulled her fully against him, so that she was pressed against his long, hard length. Again—he felt so right.

While he petted her hair, she poured out the details of her past week in a jumble—the male members of the crew jamming the set to ogle her, a dissatisfied Sam shouting commands, the alienation she'd felt every night in her lonely L.A. hotel room when she'd longed for him to call.

"I know people think I have a glamorous life, but sometimes it just feels lonely. One minute I'm onstage admired by thousands. Then I'm home alone—or vilified in the press." She buried her lips against the warm hollow of his neck. "Edward couldn't stand my crazy life, and I don't think you will be able to stand it, either. I'm good at acting, at fantasy onstage. But so far, ever since we parted fifteen years ago, I've never been able to hold on to anything real."

"Just promise me you won't act when you're with me," he said roughly.

She nodded.

"I don't want to look at your face and wonder if you're

using an emotion you felt for someone else to make something work for us."

"I'd never do that."

"Okay, then." His mouth fastened on hers with a passion that soon spiraled out of control. He stripped her, stripped himself and flung their clothes on the floor. Then he mounted her, his knees wide. Straddling her thighs, he cupped her breasts.

She ran her hands down his lean torso. How she loved the way his body was hard and warm; how every part of him was gorgeous.

He breathed in rapid pants, and she was just as hot for him.

He kissed her with such desperate urgency she could only imagine he felt as she did. A foil wrapper rustled. Then, with his condom in place, he thrust inside her, each stroke deeper and harder than the last. She clung, arching her pelvis to meet his. Relentlessly, he took her higher and higher until, at the end, he clutched her close. When he shuddered and ground his hips against hers, she cried his name again and again, her release glorious.

For a long time afterward, their bodies spent, they clung. An hour or so later she awoke to find herself still wrapped in his arms. Never had she felt closer to anyone.

This is where I belong, she thought, refusing to consider the secrets she still hadn't told him.

Some time later he began to kiss her with a feverish need that fueled her own desire into an instant blaze. He licked his way down her slim body, exploring secret feminine places until she felt she was so hot and tremulous even her bones might melt.

Don't stop, she thought. *Don't ever stop....*

After she recovered from the most shattering climax of her life, he made love to her again. Then they napped and made love again, and maybe again. She lost count.

Needs she'd never experienced before made themselves known. Their bodies spoke to each other in a dark, sweet language only they understood. They said things and did things they'd never done before. Things they could only do now because trust was building between them.

They played erotic games, with tied hands and blindfolds. Sometimes their love was rough, but mostly it was gentle. For an endless time, Summer lived in a sensual universe she shared only with Zach. It was nearly dawn when she drifted to sleep in his arms once again.

She felt changed, as if she'd been reborn within the dazzling magic of his love.

At eight o'clock sharp, his phone and doorbell rang at the same time.

They sprang up groggily, laughing when they realized it was morning.

Zach grabbed for his phone, cursing when it wouldn't stop ringing.

"It's Bob! How the hell could I have been so crazy as to ever tell him eight?"

She giggled. "You wanted me gone, remember."

"Strange how that seems a lifetime away."

He spoke much too curtly to Bob then, who said he was surrounded by paparazzi.

"Poor guy," she said after he hung up.

"I'll apologize. But later. He's too busy keeping the screaming horde at bay." Zach's gleaming eyes met hers sheepishly. "Now that we're up, we might as well make the most of it."

"First, I'm going to go downstairs and take a shower, brush my teeth…present a more civilized—"

He laughed and grabbed her hand, preventing her from squirming across the sheets and running downstairs. "I don't want civilized! I want the wicked wanton I had last night all over again, only wilder."

"Not possible."

"I'm going to prove to you that you're wrong. You're going to stay right here where you belong. Under me. In my arms."

Unable to deny him anything in that moment, she lay back and waited for him to again turn their world into a fiery wonderland that was theirs alone.

Nine

Summer Wallace Steps Out With Billionaire Zach Torr!

"What the hell do you think you're doin', boy?"

Nick slapped a newspaper with the two-inch headline onto Zach's desk, covering the blueprint he'd been studying.

When Zach looked up, Nick began to read him the article in a low, sarcastic voice.

"It seems the thirty-one-year-old actress known for her light comedy roles has revamped herself. Shortly after pirated film clips from *Dangerous Man* exploded all over the internet, Wallace was seen on Torr's arm at the ground-breaking ceremony for his new casino. The couple has a scandalous history. She once charged Torr with—"

"What is this? Read-aloud time?"

Zach wadded the paper and pitched it into the trash. "I've seen it already. Read it already."

And he'd been sickened to have the most beautiful thing in his life described in such cheap terms.

"You said you saw her again for the publicity, yes? Was her two-day sleepover a publicity stunt, as well?"

"That's my business, and hers—not yours! And certainly not the damn newspapers'!"

"Then date another woman."

Zach's voice was meticulously polite. "Look, I intend to. In the future. Right now...I'll be seeing more of Summer."

No way in hell could he give her up now.

"Tell me you've got more sense than to start up with her again. You know as well as I do that she's a liar to the core of her rotten soul, yes? You had to sneak around with her in high school because her step-daddy thought you was trash. Then look what they done to you, those high-and-mighty folks, first chance that they got."

Zach remembered too well. He still wasn't sure about what had been real back then between him and Summer. Hell, he wasn't sure what was real now. But he wanted to find out.

"People don't change, boy. She's probably stepped on a lot more folks to get where she is. You gonna end this or not?"

Or not.

Since he couldn't reassure Nick, Zach fixed his gaze on the blueprint. The tension between them built until Martin knocked on the door of the trailer.

"Pete's here," Martin said. "He thinks he sees a way to get what you want done and not go over budget."

"Great." Zach turned on Nick. "I'm busy as hell. I've got things to do here. The costs on a project in Houston are going through the roof, so I've got to fly home ASAP. You and I— we'll catch up later, okay?"

"I'm not finished here, no. That little gal proved what she was fifteen years ago, yes. All that she ever worries about is what's good for her. She don't care about you. She never did. She never will."

Flushing with dark embarrassment to have interrupted his boss's personal conversation, Martin backed out of the trailer.

Zach's face grew stony. "Look, Nick, I've dated a lot of women since Summer. Can't a guy fool around?"

"Not with her, you can't, no. You're not just playing with fire. She's nuclear."

Zach clenched his fist around his pencil, letting go of it right before it snapped. "You're right. You're right."

"Which is why you're madder than hell, yes."

"Stay out of this, Nick."

Grabbing the blueprint, Zach stormed past Nick and out of the trailer.

"No! No! No! Earth to Miss Wallace!" Paulo, Summer's stage director, was bouncing up and down as he bounded toward her, his face purple.

"You still haven't got it! Quit thinking about your personal love triangle and listen to me!"

Summer blinked first. Then she blushed. She was sick of the ceaseless teasing she'd had to endure due to all the news stories.

"Sorry." Rubbing her forehead, she fought to concentrate on what Paulo was saying.

Paolo was actually a very insightful, inspiring director, one of the rare ones who really understood actors. Still, it wasn't easy for her to take direction. She was too worried about her fragile new start with Zach and about how she would tell him about the baby. She was concerned about how all the media attention impacted him, as well. Again, the sex had been glorious. Again, she'd felt she'd shared everything with him in bed. But once they'd separated and the stories about them had hit full force, he'd erected the old walls between them.

So, she was no closer to feeling the time had come for her to confide in him.

He'd called her once, texted her twice. All three times her heart had leaped with joy. Even as his husky, but oh-so-controlled tone had made her remember all the thrilling things they'd done to each other—against the wall, on the floor, in the bed, on the chair—she'd sensed his emotional withdrawal.

In Bonne Terre, after their night together, she'd felt so close to Zach. He'd seemed easy, open. But now he was unreachable. Really, she couldn't blame him. He wasn't used to life in a fishbowl. He'd said he'd hated the stories that had linked them for years.

Rehearsals were difficult during the best of times and trying to give birth to a character could be exhausting. Summer's head, back and feet ached from the effort. Distracted by Zach and the media storm, she'd found the rehearsals this week to be sheer torture.

She would think about him and break character, lose her bearing. Another actor would say a line, and she would just stare at them, lost. The entire cast was out of patience with her, as she was with herself.

She needed to get a grip before she sabotaged the show completely. At night, when she was alone in her apartment eating takeout, her obsession was worse.

She would try to imagine living with Zach as an ordinary couple in a house with a garden and a picket fence, try to envision holidays with Gram and Tuck, dinners with friends, shared vacations, dark-haired children that looked just like Zach.

But, always, her vision would pop like a bubble as an inner voice taunted her.

Zach has his life and you have yours. You're still keeping your secrets. He values his privacy, and you can never have total privacy. So—just enjoy what you have now.

An affair such as theirs couldn't last long, not with her secret eating at her and the world interfering and them living so far apart, not with each of them working at all-consuming careers. Added to those obstacles, there would be no way for her to leave New York on the weekends once her show started.

She thought of Gram, who was always pressuring Summer to marry and have children, who now called constantly to express her pleasure at Zach's renewed visitations and to express her concerns about how their story was playing out in the media and around Bonne Terre.

"You are running out of time for children," she would say. "He isn't."

"Gram, please…don't!"

Gram's advice added unbearable pressure to Summer's already fragile situation.

Until Zach, Summer had focused only on her career. Now when she thought of the possibility of little darlings and a more private life, she felt an eager wistfulness.

What if Zach wanted children but saw her career and all that went with it as obstacles too large to surmount? Since he was a man, he could simply enjoy her for as long as it was convenient and then move on. He could choose a woman young enough to bear his children.

An urge to see him again and to make love to him—to claim him in all the imaginative ways he'd taught her—filled her.

By Thursday night, when he hadn't called her again, she finally weakened and picked up the phone.

"I've missed you," she whispered the minute he answered, fighting to keep the tension out of her voice.

Oh, why did I say that of all things?

"I missed you, too," he admitted, his tone polite.

"I'm sorry about all the press coverage."

He said nothing.

"I saw where you were besieged in your Houston office."

"I didn't realize you were so famous." He didn't sound happy about it.

"Hey, you're the handsome billionaire. I think your money and your looks are as big a draw as I am. It's a huge part of the fantasy reporters are trying to sell."

"Oh, so now it's my fault, too," he mused, but his voice had warmed ever so slightly. "When I couldn't get into my building downtown for all the reporters, I wondered why the hell I'd ever gotten myself into this mess. It seems so cheap... what they write about us. Maybe we should take a break until all the fuss dies down."

When he fell silent after dropping that bomb, her breath caught painfully. For a long second, the wound from his words seemed too hurtful to bear.

"Zach, I...I hope you don't really want that. I know the press is a major hassle right now, and I'm truly sorry. But once my show starts, I'll be too swamped to travel. You'll get busy with other projects, too.... And then we'll...drift apart...." Her voice cracked on a forlorn note.

"I've lived in the spotlight for years. It won't always shine this brightly or be this invasive. I swear."

"That's reassuring," he said in a smart-aleck tone that somehow cheered her.

"My PR people spend a lot of time manipulating my brand. It's all so false. The person you read about in those stories is not me. It's this pubic person, the actress. The real me often feels lost in all the hubbub.

"But there is a difference. Last weekend, after the ground-breaking, was wonderful and true. I've never been happier in my whole life."

"Me, too," he admitted slowly.

"So, will you give us another chance?"

"Sweetheart, who am I kidding? Don't you know by now,

that no matter how much I hate the press, I'd go crazy if I didn't see you again—and very, very soon. I need you, even though I hate needing you. But that doesn't kill the need. It's fierce, unquenchable."

She drew in a long, relieved breath because she felt the same way.

"I'm new to this, too," she whispered. "I haven't dated anyone outside the business before. Maybe we should only worry about how we are together…so that those on the outside don't matter quite so much. What we have shouldn't be about them or what they think. It should be about us. I want this piece of my life to belong to me and to you and to nobody else."

He was silent for a long time. "We do live in the real world, you know, an intrusive world."

A world that would devour them all over again if it learned all their secrets.

"I know. But I want to try to keep our relationship a personal matter. There are things I need to share with you…. Personal things I've been afraid to share…."

"You sound very mysterious all of a sudden."

"I can't talk about it over the phone. So, about tomorrow… Do we still have a date?"

When he hesitated for a heartbeat, he put her in an agony of suspense.

"I can't wait," he admitted in that low, husky tone she loved.

Friday afternoon came at last, and she rushed to LaGuardia in a chauffeured car with a single bag. Hours later, when his jet set her down on a deserted airstrip several miles from the one Bob usually used outside Bonne Terre, she saw him— and no press—waiting beside his Mercedes at the edge of the dark woods. A wild joy pierced her.

Stepping off the plane, she told herself to play it cool. But at the bottom of the stairway, she cried his name and flew into his arms.

"I missed you so much," she admitted ruefully as she flung her arms around his neck.

He pulled her to him, folded her close.

"You smell so good," she whispered.

He slanted a look down at her and smiled. "So do you."

Feeling the fierce need to taste him, she pulled his mouth down to hers. Then he kissed her with a wonderful wild hunger that turned her blood to fire, the ferocity in him matching her own. Suddenly, it didn't matter that he'd barely contacted her last week or that he'd had so many doubts about their very public relationship. Even the unbearable weight of her secret felt a tiny bit lighter on her heart. There was truth in his kiss, in his touch, a truth he couldn't hide.

"I brought you something."

Soft white flashed in the darkness as he handed her a bouquet of daisies.

"They're gorgeous." She jammed her nose into the middle of their petals and inhaled their sweetness. "Simply gorgeous. I love them."

"It's a cliché gift."

"I don't care."

"You've got gold dust all over your nose now."

"Pollen, they call it," she whispered as she dabbed at her nose and giggled. "All gone?"

"Not quite." He dusted the tip of her nose for her.

Then he wrapped his arms around her and held her close in the shadows of the trees. After another kiss, this one brief and undemanding and tender, he said, "Let's go home, sweetheart."

The press corps waiting for them at his pillared mansion were held at bay by a team of security guards, so Zach drove around back where they could run inside without having to face questions.

Locking the door of the little sitting room where they'd entered, he pulled her into his arms and kissed her hard. So urgent were his kisses as they skimmed her lips, her throat, her breasts. She began to tremble violently. Then he lifted her skirt and found that soft place in between her thighs.

"You're not wearing panties, I see."

His tongue made contact and she gasped.

"No…."

She was wet and breathless and dying for more as he peeled off the rest of her clothes.

"Am I bad?" she whispered as he undid his belt and began tearing off his jeans and shirt.

"I like bad."

When they were naked, he shoved her against the wall and held her close. "Wrap your legs around me, sweetheart."

When she complied, he put on a condom and ground himself into her, scraping her back and shoulders against the wall in his eagerness. She didn't mind. She cared only for him as he rode her fast and hard. Arching her pelvis to meet his thrusts, she cried out. Again, he took her to that strange, wild world that was theirs alone. Clinging to him fiercely, her heart pounded in mad unison with his.

Afterward, their bodies drenched in perspiration, they sank to the floor with their arms still wound around each other.

"I don't know if I can ever stand up again," Summer whispered breathlessly.

"Not to worry, sweetheart. You don't have to."

He lifted her and carried her through the house to the bed in the room she'd used that first weekend. Then he lay down beside her and stared at her hot, damp body gleaming in the moonlight.

When she was with him like this, she felt almost sick with

pleasure and terror of losing him. She thought about her secret and how he might react when she confided in him. How, when could she tell him?

The long, lonely years without him had taught her what loss felt like, and she dreaded anything coming between them again. But something would. All it might take was her confession about the baby.

She'd been young when she'd loved him before. People like Thurman, who'd been wrong in all the advice they'd given her, had told her she'd been lucky to have lost their baby girl, lucky a lowlife like Zach was out of her life, lucky that she could start over. They'd said she would meet someone else, someone respectable, have another baby, that all would be just fine.

She'd learned better. Thurman had been wrong about almost everything, but he'd been especially wrong about how she felt about losing Zach's baby and about losing Zach himself. Yes, she had her career, and she'd enjoyed national, even international, acclaim. But never once in all those years had she felt this alive.

Zach was special. When she'd been a foolish, naive girl, he'd lived in a shack. He'd been considered beneath her by the kids at school, and she'd still thought he was the one. Until Thurman and his cohorts had twisted and turned their love into something ugly and sordid and had driven them apart.

Now Zach rolled over, took her hand and interlocked his fingers with hers. When he looked at her, her blood beat with a mixture of desire and fear. When she kissed him, she realized she was going to take the easy way out…at least for now. They could talk in the morning. The happiness she felt was simply too precious to risk.

That night they made love several more times, but early Saturday morning, when they might have talked, Zach had to go to the site because his contractor had encountered a new challenge. Then he wanted to see Nick. He said they'd had a minor quarrel earlier in the week and he wanted to make things right on his way home.

"I hope you didn't quarrel about me."

His eyes narrowed, and she knew that they had.

"I see. Okay, then," she agreed, feeling a little relief at the reprieve, deciding it was probably best for him to handle Nick as he saw fit. "You'd better stop by. Last week I was terrible in rehearsals, so I really need to go over the script."

But no sooner was he gone than her whirling emotions centered on her secret and him and she was unable to concentrate. Her need to confess made her as uncertain as a young girl in the throes of first love, and she could do nothing except worry about what Nick might say against her.

Hours passed. Unable to focus, she stared at the daisies and her script.

Her phone rang. When she saw it was Gram, she answered it, glad of the distraction.

"I've got some news. I was calling to invite you and Zach over to dinner. I could tell you then."

"I'll ask Zach…. See what he says." *If they went out to dinner, it would be more difficult to find the perfect moment to confess.*

"Tell Zach I'm cooking chicken and Andouille gumbo, crawfish étoufée and a shrimp salad. Oh, and those chocolate-chip cookies he loves so much. Maybe after dinner we could play Hearts."

When Gram hung up, Summer remained as unfocused as ever, even as she comforted herself that it was all right not to work, that sometimes procrastination was part of any actress's process.

Finally, Zach's car roared into the drive out back. Jumping up, breathing hard, she ran to a tall window where she stood until she saw a reporter. Only with the greatest effort did she tiptoe back to the table, pick up a pen and sit down before her script. But when Zach walked through the front door and called to her, she answered with her next breath.

"In here! Working!" She giggled at that last.

He strode inside the kitchen and kissed her. "Sorry it took so long. I hope you got something done."

"I tried," she said evasively.

Her frustration must have shown because he ran his knuckles up the curve of her neck. "Sounds like somebody needs a holiday."

"Right.... It's your fault I couldn't work. I *was* thinking about you the whole time you were gone."

"Ditto." He swept her into his arms and devoured her mouth in a dizzying kiss.

As eager as he, she tore off her clothes while watching him do the same. They ended up making love on the kitchen table—but only after she'd removed the precious daisies for safekeeping.

"Oh," she said, while they were dressing afterward. "I almost forgot and Gram would have killed me...."

"What?"

"She said she had something to tell us, and she invited us over for dinner tonight."

"It must be nice, having family to share things with," he said.

She realized it was, even if Gram had her own ideas about how Summer's life should be and never stopped pushing for her own agenda.

"I take it that's a yes," she said.

Zach would never know exactly at what point that night he knew for sure that no matter what she'd done in the past, no matter what the masses believed, Summer was the one woman who was essential to his happiness. Nothing spectacular happened; it was simply a very special evening.

To elude the paparazzi, he had a pair of doubles drive away in his Mercedes so he and Summer could slip out the back to the dock and take his airboat. As they sped along the glassy water, laughing like children, the sun glowed like gold in the cypress trees, turning the bayou into a gilded ribbon of flashing darkness and light.

Summer's hair whipped back from her pale face, and her heavily lashed blue eyes shone every time she glanced at him as if she were as exhilarated by his nearness as he was by hers. She wore a navy dress with tiny white buttons and held the filmy skirt down with hands pressed against her knees.

Why had he thought he couldn't get beyond their past and her fame? Despite the betrayals, when they were together, he forgave her everything and felt as comfortable around her as he had as a kid. Upon reaching Viola's rambling old plantation house, he followed Summer around the yard as she stooped in the tall grasses to pick wild violets for the dinner table while amusing him with tales about her funniest roles. In turn, he talked about all the various disasters that could befall a construction project.

"I can't believe a giant crane costing millions can actually topple over," she said, sounding amazed.

"Yes, we were so lucky nobody was killed, we didn't even care about the money."

They smiled and laughed together. Holding hands, they carried armfuls of violets into the house, which was redolent with the smell of Cajun spices. Together they looked for a vase and finished setting the table while Tuck followed them around like a lost puppy.

"Tuck's very good at looking like he's doing something when he isn't," Summer whispered when steaming dishes needed to be carried to the table and her brother chose that moment to say he had to go to the bathroom.

"He'll grow up. You'll see."

"We keep hoping…."

Zach enjoyed the simple dinner party. When Viola started tapping her crystal goblet filled with ruby-red wine, Zach felt Summer tense beside him.

"Careful, Gram. Mama's crystal," she chided.

Gram shot her a look. "I'm always careful with dear Anna's crystal. I was only trying to get your attention, dear." She took a deep breath. "And now that you're all listening—I have something to tell you, something I couldn't be more thrilled about." Her sharp blue eyes sparkled like a naughty child's.

"Oh, no, now what have you gone and done?" Summer asked.

In the flattering candlelight and in her soft gray dress with those sharp, mischievous eyes dancing, Viola looked years younger than her age.

"Well, your Gram has bought herself a condo in Plantation Alley."

"Without even telling me," Summer said, shocked.

"I told you I was thinking about it, didn't I? It was such a good deal. I had to snap it up. Besides, you're never here, dear. If you lived closer, maybe I'd form the habit of confiding in you."

"Well, I'm here now," Summer said. "I've been here all weekend."

"I wouldn't dream of disturbing you, child," her grandmother replied innocently, slanting a pointed glance at Zach. "And you didn't drop by…not till I invited you."

"Zing," Summer murmured in Zach's ear.

"Stop whispering, you two! I want to hear everything that's said at my table."

He squeezed Summer's hand.

"Do you want to hear about my new condo or not?" Viola asked peevishly.

"We want to hear," Summer soothed.

Viola brought them a folder that contained a colorful brochure spelling out the amenities of the complex as well as a contract and a copy of the deposit she'd put down. Then she described the condo she'd bought in detail. Several of her friends already lived in the complex, so she'd have lots of company for playing Hearts. The clincher was that Silas approved. He simply adored the cozy window with the view of the bayou where he could sit and watch birds.

"The girls and I sort of thought that if we lived in the same complex we could look after each other, call one another every day, you know."

"The girls are her Friday Lunch Bunch," Summer explained. "They eat together every Friday at a restaurant another friend owns. That's where they hatch their mischief, which mainly has to do with thinking up schemes to meddle in my and Tuck's lives."

"We do not!"

Zach picked up the contract and scratched a few things out, added a sentence or two, explaining why he'd made the changes.

"I'm not sure I understand," Gram said.

"Just take this to Davis first thing Monday. Tell him I sent you. He'll take care of you."

Gram nodded. "It has three bedrooms, so there'll be room for you and Tuck to stay anytime."

"Well, that's a relief. I'm glad you're not kicking me out," Tuck said.

"You won't have to move out on your own, until you're ready, dear. And, Zach, you're always welcome. Silas is so fond of playing Hearts with you."

"Gram! I'm sure Zach's had enough of Silas's opinions for one evening," Summer teased.

"Well, who's going to speak for him, since dear Silas won't speak for himself?"

"Exactly," Summer said.

Tuck hadn't said much during dinner, but he'd come to the table with his hair combed and had answered all Zach's questions about his classes. The small changes in him pleased everyone since he was mildly enthusiastic for a change.

The gumbo and spicy étouffée were delicious.

All in all, it was one of those rare, pleasant evenings, a family evening, the kind of evening Zach hadn't experienced since his Uncle Zach's death. He felt like he belonged—with Summer, with all of them. Suddenly, the past and its pain didn't matter quite so much.

Suddenly, he wanted nothing more than to start over with Summer.

Realizing that thanks to Tuck's misbehavior, they had already started over, Zach took Summer's hand, turned it over in his own, drew it to his lips. For a second he caught a haunted expression in her eyes, but when she flashed him a dazzling smile, he forgot where he was. He would have planted a quick kiss on her cheek if he hadn't caught a very pleased Gram watching his every move. Not in the habit of public displays of affection, he let go of Summer's hand in the next instant.

When dinner was over, they retired to the card table where Gram's three guests conspired to let her win more than her fair share of the games.

"It was a perfect evening," Gram said after they'd helped her clear the table. As they stepped out onto the porch, the black, misty darkness was filled with the cloying scent of honeysuckle and the glorious roar of cicadas. They were saying their goodbyes, and Summer's beautiful face was aglow beneath the porch light.

He loved her, Zach realized.

Love. He hated the word. He'd sworn never to fall under its dark power again, but here he was, lost in its grip. After everything she'd put him through, it was stupid of him, terrifying for him, but he wanted to claim her—to marry her.

When her beaming grandmother read the emotion in his eyes, she closed the door and wisely left them alone. Like a fool, the minute they were alone, he wanted to get down on bended knee in the damp St. Augustine grass and propose.

Luckily, he caught himself, opting to proceed with caution. If this new relationship with Summer was to work, he'd need to reorganize his business, his entire life. He'd need an office in Manhattan for starters. That was okay. He'd worked all over the world; he could work anywhere.

He would have his people contact several knowledgeable Realtors in Manhattan. He'd tell them he wanted to shift the focus of Torr Enterprises, that they were to start searching for opportunities in the northeast. He'd buy Summer a penthouse with a view of Central Park.

Not that he would want to live there all year. But surely she'd meet him halfway by living in Houston or even Louisiana for at least part of the year.

As they sped home across the black, glassy waters of the bayou, Zach seemed quieter, more withdrawn, and yet content.

Their speed wasn't as fast as it had been earlier, since it was dark now and there were patches of ground fog, but there was no way she could speak to him over the roar of the airboat.

Arriving home without incident, she watched as Zach secured the boat quickly and efficiently with the easy expertise of a man who knew exactly what he was doing. Nick had taught him all of that, she thought.

Then Zach pulled her close, and they walked across the lawn holding hands in the moonlight with no paparazzi to spoil the exquisite, shared moment.

He paused beneath the long shadows of the live oak trees to kiss her. She thought his kisses were different somehow, sweeter, and they filled her heart with joy.

Everything felt so right, so perfect—the way it had felt when they'd first fallen in love. It was as if they'd reclaimed their lost innocence and faith in one another. For the first time in years, it was easy to imagine them belonging to each other forever. A knot formed in her throat as she thought about the little girl she'd lost. She had to tell him. But when?

For Summer the evening had been magic. It had been nice to bring Zach to Gram's, so nice to share this man she cared about with her family, especially since her controlling stepfather used to force her to sneak out to see him.

Summer had learned not to stand up to Thurman. It had seemed smarter to maneuver around him. Still, she'd felt like a spineless wimp not taking up for Zach. But if she had, Thurman would have gone ballistic. He would have stopped at nothing to destroy her relationship with Zach.

The only reason Zach had stayed in Bonne Terre that year after his graduation was to wait for her.

Her memories merged with her present need to find a way to tell him about the baby. But when he pulled her close and slanted his hard mouth over hers beneath the shadows of the oak, she sighed and wrapped her hands around his neck to better enjoy the kiss.

Time stopped. There was nothing but the two of them. Their bodies locked as they surrendered to each other in the magical pine-scented darkness. There was no Thurman to stop them now.

She could have kissed him forever, but she began to feel him, hard and swollen, pressing against her thighs. She opened her eyes and met the burning urgency of his gaze.

When he spoke, his voice was rough. "Let's get the hell inside."

Quickly, he took her hand and they ran to the back entrance. When they were in the house, and he'd locked the door, he kissed her again even more fiercely than before. Then he lifted her into his arms and carried her up the stairs into the enveloping darkness of his bedroom.

"Now, where were we, sweetheart?" Zach demanded as he set her on his bed. His eyes were intense as he began to undo the tiny white buttons on her dress.

"I can't believe you want to make love to me after a big old dinner like that."

"Well, I do. We played cards for an hour, didn't we? Besides, do you have a better idea?"

"We could sit outside on the upstairs veranda, enjoy the moonlight and talk…maybe about the past." *About our baby….*

"The past…." He frowned. "I'm in much too good a mood to want to go there. Trust me. We're better off making love, enjoying what we have now. We deserve some happiness."

"But aren't we hiding from things we need to think about and resolve?"

"You expect me to care about what's over and done with, when you're so damn beautiful I hurt?"

But she felt so close to him right now, close enough to tell him everything…. Even tell him about the baby. It would take more than a single conversation, she knew. But she felt a profound need to share everything with him. He had to know the worst.

She wanted him to listen, to hold her, to forgive her, to

grieve with her and then to make love to her. Had she been wrong about their special bond tonight?

He grazed her lips with his mouth with such infinite tenderness he soon sparked a wild conflagration.

But he was a man, and he was aroused. So, now wasn't the time to talk after all.

They could not get their clothes off fast enough. Then they took their time exploring each other. He took his turn kissing and touching her, and then she broke away and started kissing him everywhere, her tongue running down his body until she found his manhood, which was thick and engorged.

She took him into her mouth. He was too close to the edge to endure this for long. Soon he moved on top of her and slid inside.

That was all it took for her to explode.

He thrust deeply and then shuddered, too.

Afterward, as they lay in the darkness, while he held her close, she gathered her courage again. "Wouldn't you feel better if you knew exactly what happened to me and why I might have failed you years ago?"

"What?"

Perspiration glistened on his brow as he rolled over to brush his hand through her tangled hair. "I can't believe you're bringing that up again. Now."

"I just think we should talk. It's a perfect time, after our lovely evening."

"No. Let's not tarnish tonight."

He sat up so he could stare down at her. "Look, I'm not blaming you for the past any longer, if that's why you want to talk about it. On Viola's porch that first day we reconnected, I felt this terrible lingering sadness in you. It made it impossible for me to continue blaming you for everything. That's all the explanation I need about the past. I hurt you, too. I know that."

"But…"

"It's over. I'm trying to forget it. I suggest you do the same."

"But there's something I really need to share…."

He ran a finger around the edges of her lips and shushed her. "Don't ruin what we have right now. It's too special. I want to hold on to it. We can talk later. I promise."

When she frowned, he pulled her close and kissed her.

But he was so adamant, and she wanted this time with him so much, she let him have his way. So, when she left on Sunday, she still hadn't told him about what happened in New Orleans.

"Why don't I come see you next weekend, for a change?" he said as he put her on his jet. "It just so happens I have a few things to do in New York."

"That would be wonderful."

"I'll come up on Thursday, rent a suite at the Pierre and take you anywhere you want to go."

"So, you intend to spoil me hopelessly?"

"Absolutely."

"Lucky me."

"No. Lucky me," he said as he kissed her.

Ten

Something was different about Zach, and Summer wasn't sure what it was.

Their first three-day weekend together in New York was not as intimate as their previous weekends in Bonne Terre. But that was to be expected under the circumstances. He had business affairs to attend to and she the theater. Only at night could they make time to be together.

If his purpose in coming to the city had been to impress her with his grand lifestyle, he succeeded. His gilded suite was spectacular. Limos followed by the paparazzi whisked them to fabulous dinners and nightclubs where he knew people, some of them beautiful women.

"Zach has a thing for blondes," Roberto, one of his top executives, whispered in her ear while Zach conversed with a beautiful woman during a business dinner.

"Good thing I'm a blonde, then," she quipped.

For the first time since their reunion, Zach hadn't shared

details about his current project. She wondered exactly what he'd done all day while she'd rehearsed. When they were alone later, she grilled him.

"Where were you all afternoon? What business exactly do you have to do here?"

"I'm tweaking an important project."

"Tweaking?"

"I'll explain everything when it's all in order."

"Does this project concern me?"

"I said I'll explain later."

"You're not bored with me and chasing another woman already? Another blonde?"

"Good Lord, no! Whatever gave you that idea?"

She refrained from throwing Roberto to the wolves for one ill-advised remark. "Oh…nothing. Forget I asked."

"There's no other woman for me, and there never will be."

"You're a billionaire. You could have anybody."

"Strange as this may sound, that's not true. Believe me, I have had plenty of time to discover that there's no substitute for the real thing. You're the real thing."

Something twisted near her heart. "Oh. Am I? Tell me more…."

But that was all she could get out of him other than a quick kiss on the tip of her nose.

He was hiding something. *Just as she was.*

The next weekend as Zach stood in a glamorous penthouse that had seventeen gloriously imagined rooms with high ceilings and tall windows, he thought of Summer's cozy apartment. Was the penthouse too much? Would she like it? Women could be very particular about their homes. Maybe he should show it to her before he bought it, but he was too impatient.

She could call the marble and gold vulgar and rip it out if

she didn't like it, he decided. She was too creative not to find a way to make it hers. The location was too stupendous to pass on, and he needed a place like this to impress the business people he dealt with.

All week Zach had been in a fever to ask her to marry him. Every time they'd talked, the question had been at the forefront of his mind. The pressure to wait until he had the ring selected and the penthouse bought and his new offices acquired and a contractor to remodel Thibodeaux House was making him feel explosive.

She'd looked so haunted when she'd tried to talk to him about the past. Was he rushing into this because he knew he should wait?

What if she said no?

Zach opened a glass door and walked out onto the terrace. The air was cool and crisp. Central Park was ablaze with riotous fall colors forty stories beneath him.

"I told you the penthouse was fabulous and the view lovely," the Realtor gushed behind him. "Now do you believe me?"

"I had to make sure," Zach said. "It's a deal, then." He turned and shook the woman's perfectly manicured hand. "Send me a contract."

She grinned brilliantly. "I like you so much."

"Roberto Gomez will be handling this for me."

"Yes. I've already had several emails from him. Charming man. It's been a pleasure...."

Zach nodded, turned on his heel and strode toward the elevator. He had a long day ahead of him and no time to waste.

He'd arrived in Manhattan a day early this weekend to approve his future office space in Lower Manhattan and the penthouse that his most trusted people had selected. Summer didn't expect him until tomorrow.

He was staying at the Pierre. She'd liked the suite there so much last weekend, he'd rented it again.

In the elevator, he slipped his hand into his pocket and touched the small, black-velvet box.

Tomorrow, at the Pierre, when they were alone, he would offer her a glass of champagne, get down on his knee and hand it to her.

When he got off at the bottom floor, his excitement about the gorgeous penthouse and his new offices and the ring was so great he wanted to share his news with her. Why wait until tomorrow to propose when he felt so sure this afternoon?

Why not go to the theater and propose to her now? He knew she was in rehearsals and that they hadn't been going well. He knew he shouldn't bother her. Still, he wanted to see her. He wanted to hold her. Most of all he felt an urgent need to propose to her. He was afraid if he waited, somehow he'd lose her again.

He pulled out his phone and studied his calendar. Calling Roberto, he told him to cancel the rest of his meetings.

Then he stepped into his limo and ordered his driver to take him to her theater.

Bad idea, he thought. But he couldn't stop himself.

Summer raced to her dressing room during a break in rehearsals to return her agent's calls, of which there were three. She hoped the call wouldn't take long because she wanted so badly to call Zach.

Carl answered on the first ring. "You're an angel for getting back to me so fast."

"What is it?"

"Hugh Jones is in town. Just for the day. The PR people from the studio want to set up a short interview for the two of you."

"When? Where? I'm really busy."

"They had a hard time talking Jones into it as well, but they've got him to agree. So—say in an hour. In your dressing room."

"Impossible. Things for the show aren't going well, and some of the production's big investors are here giving Paolo a hard time. He's pretty insane."

"The studio has already talked to Paolo. He's fine with it."

"What?"

"The interview won't take more than fifteen minutes. There was so much buzz about your scenes with Jones that…"

She shut her eyes. That buzz, as Carl termed it, had nearly destroyed her relationship with Zach. Except for the fact that she hadn't found a way to tell him about the baby, things were going so well for them right now. She didn't want to stir up another round of press interest, and Hugh was a hot button she didn't want punched until Zach truly trusted her and their relationship was on less fragile ground. Until she'd told him about the baby….

"The movie isn't coming out for months. I don't see why I have to do an interview with Hugh this afternoon."

"Well, the PR department makes those calls, not us. Their team thinks it's essential to keep up the momentum."

Translation: they wanted hordes of paparazzi questioning the true nature of her relationship with Jones and continuing to chase her and take pictures of her with Zach. The PR department wanted her face and name out there, so she'd be a draw. They didn't care that by linking her to Jones, they drove Zach crazy. To them, this was just another juicy story.

She had to protect her relationship with Zach at all costs.

"Sorry!" she said and ended the call. But no sooner had she hung up than Sam rang her.

"You signed a contract agreeing to do promotion. Paolo's okay with it, so what's your problem?" Sam read her the clause in her contract. It didn't take a genius to understand his thinly veiled threat. They could sue her if she didn't do as they commanded.

Feeling queasy and a bit shaky, which had been happening a lot lately, especially in the mornings, she hung up and called Zach's cell.

But his phone went to voice mail. She didn't want to leave this kind of news in a message. When she called him repeatedly, and he still didn't answer, she began to feel sick with worry. She had to tell him about this interview before the paparazzi caught up with him and peppered him with questions he was not prepared to answer.

On the way to the theater Zach's limo got caught in traffic beside a flower stall, so Zach whipped out and bought two dozen roses from the elderly flower seller. The perfect buds were so bright in the sunlight they blazed like flames, but they burned no brighter than the towering emotion in his heart.

Inside the limo, their scent was so overpowering he set them aside. When the driver braked, Zach leaned forward, staring at the sea of vehicles surrounding them, cursing vividly when a truck cut in front of them.

Damn it. He sat back against soft leather and forced himself to try to relax. But he couldn't. He was out of control, which he hated. He was impatient to see Summer, to take her in his arms and beg her to love him. To ask her to make a life with him.

He could walk iron without breaking a sweat. So what was so terrifying about baring his soul and asking the woman he loved to marry him?

When his cell phone rang, Zach answered it automatically.

"You bastard!"

"Hello, Thurman."

Zach hadn't heard the other man's voice in years. Funny, that he recognized the cold, dead tone instantly.

"You think you're so smart, that you know everything, but you don't. You're a gambler. I'd bet money Summer hasn't told you what she did in New Orleans...."

The hair at the back his nape rose. "What the hell are you talking about?"

"Why don't you ask Summer?"

Thurman laughed nastily and hung up.

When Zach jumped out of the limo at the theater with a conflicted heart, a dozen reporters leaped toward him, hammering him about Summer as their flashes blinded him.

His expression turned to stone as he stormed past them into the auditorium, slamming the door on their idiotic clamor.

Zach was remembering how vulnerable Summer had looked every time she'd tried to talk to him about the past. What hadn't she told him? What did Thurman know that Zach didn't?

He knew exactly where Summer's dressing room was since she'd given him a personal tour last weekend, so he wasted no time on his way through the crowded corridors. Backstage was like a maze, but he didn't stop, not even when actors, who were milling about, tried to greet him.

He wondered why everyone was on break. Maybe this meant Summer would be free to talk to him. He wouldn't have to wait.

When he found the door with her name on it, it was closed. He banged on it impatiently.

What he wanted was beautiful golden Summer with her long-lashed eyes to open the door and blush charmingly when she saw him. He wanted to take her in his arms and then set a time for a private talk. This time he would listen to whatever she had to tell him. Then he would tell her how much he loved her and ask her to be his wife.

What he got was Hugh Jones and a photographer.

The reporter didn't miss a beat when he saw the chance for a shot of the two men together.

When the flash went off twice, Zach turned on his heel. No way could he face the press when he felt so conflicted privately. Then Summer was behind him, her voice nervous and high-pitched.

Instead of smiling, her blue eyes were wide with panic and guilt. "Zach, what are you doing here?"

Logically, he knew he shouldn't have interrupted her on such short notice, but he wasn't feeling logical.

"Making a damn fool of myself. Again."

"Zach, no.... Wait! Listen!"

She'd gone pale, and her hand shook as it tugged at his sleeve. He felt sorry for her, so he let her pull him into the dressing room beside hers and listened impatiently as she whispered to the young actress inside it. "Can we please talk here for a few minutes?"

"Sure. Anytime." Moving like a dancer, the girl, who was thin as a rail, got up languidly, picked up the magazine she'd been flipping through and left in a swirl of silken yellow skirts as she winked at Zach.

"We were just doing an interview for *Dangerous Man.* That's all. My agent called me less than an hour ago or I would have told you.... I had to do it. Because I signed a contract saying I would. I tried to call you, but you didn't answer."

"I understand. I was on the phone." *With Thurman,* he thought, frowning.

"No, you don't understand. I can see that. You look furious...."

"I said I believe you're doing an interview, and I do. But before the press is through with this story, nobody else will. I can't help wondering if this will always be the way we have to live—with the press playing up your nonexistent relationships with other men and making me look the fool."

He knew he wasn't being totally honest. He felt too raw to be completely open with her. He'd come here to propose, and then Thurman had called and stirred up all his old doubts about her.

"Zach, I want you in my life. I do…. What are you doing here a day early?"

He shouldn't have surprised her like this. He felt vulnerable, as if his heart was on his sleeve, and suddenly he didn't want her to know about all the plans he'd made. Now wasn't the time to ask her about New Orleans or to propose.

"It doesn't matter. I'm leaving."

"I wish you'd stay."

"Well, I'm not sure I want idiots second-guessing every stage of our relationship when I feel…" He stopped, torn.

"When you feel…what?"

"Nothing."

"Zach, what's wrong?"

"Maybe I'm not in the mood to share you with everyone in the known universe. So, I'd better go, so you can finish the damn interview. The entire crew and cast is waiting on you, right?"

She swallowed. "Talk to me, Zach. Please talk to me."

Her eyes were so earnest maybe he would have, if a red-faced Paolo hadn't burst into the room, shattering the moment.

"Sorry to interrupt, but Sandy said you were in here. You did say fifteen minutes. How much longer is this damn interview going to take?"

"Sorry. We haven't started yet."

"Why the hell not?"

"It's my fault, but I'm going," Zach said.

"No!" she cried, grabbing him.

Paolo shot him a look of disgust before he turned and left.

"I'm beginning to realize how demanding I am," Zach said. "You see, I'm the kind of guy who expects his wife to put him first sometimes…like now, even when I know it's a very bad time for you."

"Your wife…. Did you say *your wife?*"

"I came over here because I had something very personal to say to you…. Something very important, to me at least. Now I see that you have a lot more to deal with than my concerns."

"Zach, did you come over here to ask me to marry you? Because I will."

He didn't want to ask her now, like this. He was beginning to think he shouldn't ask her at all. Instead of answering her, he said, "On the way over here I got a phone call. From Thurman."

"Thurman?" She went very white.

"He told me to ask you about New Orleans. He insinuated that you've been keeping something important from me. Is that true?"

"Oh, Zach…." Her eyes misted with guilt-stricken anguish. Her hands were shaking. "I…I tried to tell you in Louisiana. I want to talk about it. Truly I do, but not now. I have rehearsals, the interview…and you're too upset."

"It doesn't matter," he said.

He saw now that he'd been a stupid, emotional fool to be in such a rush to marry her. They both had huge, time-consuming careers; their past had haunted them for years; the press wouldn't leave them alone. Was there room for love and marriage with so many distractions, responsibilities and conflicts?

"Maybe neither of us has time for a marriage," he said.

"That's not fair. This is just a very bad time for me. What if I happened to drop in on you, when you were in the middle of a negotiation and forty people were waiting on your decision?"

"That's the point, isn't it? I've just realized there's not room in a marriage for two huge egos and two big careers…along with everything else that's between us. I don't like goodbyes, Summer, so I'll just make a quick exit."

"You're not telling me everything," she said, grabbing his arm to keep him in the room.

"I could say the same thing to you, couldn't I, sweetheart?"

The last thing he saw was her ashen face as she staggered backward, knocking a wig stand over as she sank down onto her friend's couch. Her big blue eyes glimmered with unshed tears, and she looked white and shaken. It tore him up to realize he'd hurt her again.

But maybe there had always been too much between them for a relationship to ever work. Maybe he'd let their chemistry blind him. Had he been rushing into marriage because he hadn't wanted to stop to think about the realities?

On his way out of the theater, he pitched the perfect red roses in the first stinking trash barrel he saw. Then he stepped through the throng of reporters and into the hushed silence of his luxurious limo.

"Take me to LaGuardia Airport," he said.

Eleven

Summer Wallace Dumps Billionaire For Movie Star.

Summer felt sick to her stomach as she sat up straighter in her bed to turn the page of the newspaper.

She'd tried to phone Zach, but he wouldn't take her calls. She had to tell him about their lost little girl even if the timing was awful and the news killed whatever remaining tenderness he felt for her.

"When will the thirty-one-year-old actress make up her mind...."

There was an awful picture of Zach and Hugh together. Two more shots showed Zach entering the theater with roses, and there was one of him looking furious as he dumped the gorgeous bouquet on his way out.

Why did the headlines always have to mention her age and remind her that her biological clock was ticking? Why did every headline have to remind her that Zach would never marry her? That she would never have his darling black-haired children.

She felt a rivulet of perspiration trickle down her back. Then a hot sensation of dizziness flooded her. Cupping her hands over her mouth, she lurched to her feet and ran to her toilet where she was violently ill.

When she was able to lift her head, she opened the window and gulped in mouthfuls of sweet, fresh air. Then she put the toilet lid down and sat, holding her head in her hands.

The episode of nausea was the third she'd had this week. Since her stomach was often queasy during rehearsals and she'd been so busy, she hadn't really thought about it. Until now.

"Oh, no," she whispered as comprehension dawned.

Slowly she arose and stared critically at the reflection of her white face in the mirror.

She was pregnant. Since she'd been pregnant before, she should have recognized the signs. Her breasts were swollen, and her period was late. She had the oddest cravings at the strangest times. Like that other night when she had to have a corn dog and a tomato and a pickle and nothing else would do. She felt lethargic, different.

Great timing. Just like last time.

Zach had left her. And she hadn't even told him about their little girl yet. He wouldn't be happy to learn the truth about their past, nor would he be overjoyed that they were going to have another child.

Then there was the not-insignificant detail that she was starring in a play that was going to open in less than three weeks. One where her character was not pregnant and the director and cast were on the verge of a collective nervous breakdown if things didn't start coming together soon.

Zach had been swimming laps in his pool behind Thibodeaux House for an hour, so it was time to get out.

He wanted to forget Summer, to go on with his life. So, he'd ignored her calls; ignored the pain he felt at her loss.

He would get through this. He would. Not that it would be easy.

As he toweled off, he heard furious shouts and scuffling out front.

At first he thought it was the press and paid no attention. They'd been stalking him all week, ever since they'd caught him with Jones the day of the interview. Then he recognized the hateful voice.

"Let me through, damn it," Thurman Wallace yelled at Zach's security team. "I've got something to say to Torr, and I won't go until I say it."

Pulling on a shirt without bothering to button it, Zach strode to the front of the house. "Let him in," he said.

When Wallace stepped through the gate, Zach smelled the hot stench of liquor on the man's breath.

"Say your piece and leave, Wallace."

"You think you're something, don't you, you arrogant you-know-what, coming back here, to my town, getting everyone on your side because you're rich…. Taking up with Summer again…. Using her like a…"

"Watch your language. Say your piece. Then get the hell off my property."

"It wasn't all me, wanting to bring those charges. You think she wanted you back then, but she didn't. She thought you were trash, same as I did."

"Shut up about her."

"If she'd cared for you, why did she kill your baby?"

"What the hell did you say?"

"You got her pregnant. I had to send her to New Orleans before she started to show so nobody around here would know about her and ruin my good name."

"I don't believe you! Get out of here before I throw you out!"

When Wallace didn't move, Zach started toward him. "Get out of here now, or you'll be sorry!"

Wallace took one look at Zach and ran for his life.

Zach sank to his knees and thought about a younger Summer, pregnant and alone in New Orleans. Whatever she'd done, he'd never believe she'd deliberately killed their baby. But she hadn't told him about it, had she? So, how could he trust her?

All doubt that he had made the right decision in leaving her vanished.

The sudden certainty hurt.

God, how it hurt.

Billionaire And Actress Had Secret Baby!

The ugly headline screamed at Summer, shattering her heart into a million tiny pieces.

Gram had warned her about the awful story that Thurman had sold to the tabloids. In spite of the warning, Summer was still shaking as she laid down a wad of cash for all the newspapers on the rack at the tiny grocery store a block from her apartment.

Folding them, she plunged them into her bag, put her sunglasses back on and ran outside where she dumped them in the first trash bin she saw. It was a hollow gesture since there were hundreds of thousands on similar racks all over the country. Everybody would see them when they were in the check-out lines.

How could Thurman be so filled with hate? How could he have sold such a personally heartbreaking story? She felt brokenhearted, betrayed and mortified at the same time. But most of all she hurt for Zach. This was no way for him to discover the truth.

Until now, she'd held on to a fragile hope that Zach might be missing her as much as she missed him, and that given time, he would change his mind and come back to her.

Thurman's story extinguished all such hope.

She felt like weeping, not just for herself, but for the baby she was carrying.

Then a reporter sprang out of nowhere and called her name. When she turned, he took her picture.

"Gram, I've got to talk to Zach."

A week had passed since Thurman's story had hit the stands. Zach was still refusing to take her calls. His secretary was impatient whenever Summer called his office and left a message. So she'd called Gram, hoping for her help.

"But I thought that he and you…that it was…over," Gram said.

"It is," Summer said softly. "I've called him so many times, and he won't talk to me. But that's not the worst. Gram, I'm pregnant. I don't know how it happened…because we were always careful."

"It was meant to be," Gram said in her know-it-all way.

"No," Summer replied, knowing Gram couldn't be right. "What this means is that in spite of everything that's wrong between us, I've got to talk to him."

"Nick told Moxie Brown, who told Sammy, who told me that Zach has fired the contractor he'd hired to remodel that old Thibodeaux place and has put it up for sale. Nick said that big gambling boat of his is arriving at the end of the week. So, Zach's coming to town to inspect it."

Summer let out a breath. Finally, she'd caught a break. Once the play opened, she'd be doing eight shows a week. It would be very difficult for her to take time off. Paolo would pitch a fit, but maybe she could sneak in an overnight trip home.

She couldn't make the same mistake she'd made the first time they'd broken up, when he'd put up roadblocks and she'd given up on telling Zach the truth about their little girl.

She had to see him one last time—to tell him face-to-face about the baby they'd lost and this precious baby that she was carrying.

Their baby.

Summer barely glanced at the chain-link fence covered with No Trespassing notices meant to keep out the press. And her. Nor did she take note of the large sign over the gate that blared in big red letters, No Admittance. Employees Only.

Hunched over, with a pink pashmina covering her hair, Summer rushed past a uniformed man.

"Ma'am, you can't go in there. Ma'am…"

Running now on her ice-pick heels, Summer ignored the burly individual in the hard hat and brown uniform as she sped toward the dock where Zach's magnificent floating gambling palace was now secured.

"Ma'am!"

What luck! There he was.

Every muscle in her body tensed. Then she forced herself to let out a breath.

Holding a clipboard and pen, Zach stood in the middle of a dozen men. His stance, with long legs spread slightly apart, reminded her of a large cat who looked relaxed but was coiled to spring. His face was hard, and he was talking fast. The other men, their heads cocked toward him, held clipboards and pens, too. Those standing beside him were frowning in frustration as they wrote furiously in an effort to keep up.

"Zach," she cried, pink heels clattering as she ran farther out onto the dock.

She wore a soft pink dress. The bodice clung and its skirt swirled around her hips. Once he'd accused her of dressing to be desirable. Well, today she'd given it her best shot. She'd gone shopping and had deliberately picked a sexy dress for this confrontation.

All the men stopped talking at once. She let her pashmina slide to her shoulders.

Jaws fell. Zach spun, then hissed in a breath at the sight of her. Even though his eyes went icy and hard, she'd seen the split-second spark of attraction her appearance had caused. She'd caught him off guard in front of his men, exposed his vulnerability, and she knew he hated that.

Grief that he was hers no longer, that she couldn't run into his arms, slashed through her like a knife.

He didn't look as sure or confident as he had the last time she'd seen him. His face was thinner; his eyes shadowed.

"Get her out of here," he ordered, his frigid voice radiating antagonism.

"Sorry, Mr. Torr. Ma'am, I'm gonna have to ask you to leave," the burly man said behind her.

She had only seconds before she'd be forced to go.

"Zach," she cried. "I've got to talk to you."

"Too bad. I'm in a meeting." Slamming on a pair of dark glasses, he turned away.

The burly man grabbed her arm and began to tug her gently in the direction of the exit. "Please, ma'am…"

Frantic, she struggled to free herself. "Zach… You've got to listen to me."

The man's grip hardened. "Come on, ma'am."

"Zach! Please!"

His face tight and determined, Zach tapped his pen against his clipboard and continued to ignore her.

She didn't want to tell him like this—not when he was

surrounded by other people. She didn't. But what were her choices?

"Zach, I'm pregnant!"

Zach had selected the elegant office onboard his ship as a place where they could be alone, but the space felt cramped and airless to Summer as Zach subjected her to a thorough, intimate appraisal. Never had she found his arresting face more handsome, but when she searched its hard, angular planes for a trace of sympathy, she found none.

His eyes were so intense and cold, they made her feel almost faint with grief.

"Zach…" For a second, everything in her vision darkened except his face, which blurred in swirling pinpricks of light.

His hard arms reached for her, steadied her, led her to a chair, where she gulped in a sweet breath of air.

"Are you okay?" he demanded.

"I—I'm fine."

He stood over her, watching her carefully to make sure.

"Zach, I didn't want to tell you the news like that…in front of your men…when you were so furious. But I had to tell you face-to-face. I didn't want to leave a message with your secretary, or for some reporter to accost you with questions because I was having our child."

"Oh, really? You didn't bother to tell me the last time you were pregnant. Are you eager to share this child with me since I've got money now? And when do you intend to tell the press, so as to heighten your box-office draw? Frankly, I'm surprised you didn't bring the hounds with you today."

Again Zach's eyes had become emotionless. She felt as if her heart were freezing and dying. It was as if, instead of her, he saw some cruel, cunning stranger.

She took a deep breath. "No… Why would I… You can't, you can't believe I'm that low."

"You're wrong."

"I want to protect our baby. And I have my own income, I'll have you know. So, money is the last thing I need from you."

"I'll set up an account and do what's necessary. But the less I see or hear from you, the better. In the future, my lawyers will talk to your lawyers. I'll want to see our child rather frequently, I'm afraid. As you know, I'm sorely lacking in close family. And as I distrust the mother, I'll need to be as big an influence in his life as possible if he's to have a fighting chance. And I repeat, I will see to it that these matters are arranged so that we meet as infrequently as possible."

"I—I know how you must feel…finding out the way you did…about our first baby. You must think me truly awful…."

"No! You don't know how I feel! You couldn't possibly imagine."

For a moment his hard face was expressionless. Then he shook his head. "You don't understand me at all."

"I know I didn't stand up for you the way you wanted me to when my stepfather brought charges against you. You thought I went along with him, but I didn't. I loved you. I still do."

"Don't use that four-letter word. You say it too easily. All it's ever been for me is a one-way ticket to hell."

"Zach, I was sixteen…pregnant…terrified…of him and of the accusations, of all the ugliness. I was so confused. Hysterical, really."

"It doesn't matter anymore," he said in a weary, defeated tone.

But it did matter to her, fiercely. She'd thought she'd learned to live with her regrets, then he'd come back into her life and made her love him again. Being with him right now, when he was so distant, knowing that he was shutting her out forever, made her want to confess everything, to finally share all the regrets she'd carried alone for so long.

She'd organized a funeral for their first baby, had attended it by herself in the rain. Her mother, who would have come, had been too ill to leave Bonne Terre. Gram had been caring for Summer's mother, and Tuck had been too young to be of any comfort. Summer had stayed in the cemetery until she'd been drenched, until the last clod of dirt had been thrown, until a compassionate grave digger had plucked a single white rose from the funeral wreath she'd bought and handed the dripping blossom to her.

"Press this in that Bible you be carrin', *cher*. And go home. You can't do any good here. The little one, she's in heaven now."

Summer had placed angels on the grave.

Somehow she swallowed her tears when she came back to the present. "I went to Houston when I was nearly five months along. I tried to talk to you, to find you, but you wouldn't see me."

"Because I knew you were manipulating me."

"But I tried to tell you about the baby. I really tried."

"Not hard enough apparently. You could have told somebody else…. My uncle, maybe. He would have gotten the message to me. But you didn't."

"I was out of money. I wasn't feeling so well. I—I thought it was no use, so I went back to New Orleans. I—I lost the baby the next week. I was all alone. I wanted you so desperately. I never wanted you with me more."

A muscle in his carved cheek jerked savagely, but when he spoke, his voice was low, contemptuous.

"You didn't do anything deliberate to bring about that unhappy event, did you?"

"What?" His words hit her like a blow. Once again his face swirled in blackness. If she'd been standing, she would have fallen. Only with the greatest effort did she manage to catch her breath.

"No." The single word was a prayer asking him to believe her. The single tear that traced down her cheek spoke the truth.

Not that he could see the truth, blinded as he was by his own fury and sense of betrayal.

"You damn sure know how to deliver a line." His low voice was hoarse. "I'll give you that. You need to remember that little trick for the stage, sweetheart. It was very effective."

"Okay. I understand," she whispered. "You'll never trust me again. Or forgive me."

"You've got that right. The sooner we finish this conversation, the sooner we can get on with our separate lives. I said I'd help you with the baby, and I will. You don't look well. I want you to take better care of yourself this time. Cut back on your schedule. You can't possibly do eight shows a week. I'll pay for the best doctors...anything you need. And I want to be there when you deliver. Not for your sake, but for the baby's."

She nodded, feeling crushed at his efficient tone.

"I love you," she murmured. "I'll always love you."

"Then I'm sorry for you because it's over between us. I consider myself a stupid fool for getting involved with you again. Usually I'm smart enough to learn from my mistakes. Nick tried to warn me you were nuclear. He was right."

"I'm so sorry I've caused you so much pain...."

"Sorry never cuts it, does it?"

Ravaged, she stood up. Then turning from him, she fled.

Outside, the sunlight in the trees was as dull as old pewter, and she was deaf to her favorite song playing on her car radio.

She didn't want to go back to New York and work onstage, work with people. She wanted to curl up somewhere in a dark room and cry.

Then she remembered Gram's tin of chocolate-chip cookies on the shelf above her fridge. She would go back to Gram's and confide in her. Her grandmother would take Summer in her arms as she had after Summer had lost Zach, her mother and her little baby girl, and, for a brief spell, she'd feel better. Then she'd stuff herself on her grandmother's cookies until she fell asleep.

Slowly, she'd gather enough courage to go through the motions of living. She'd pack her suitcase and set her alarm. Tomorrow she'd dress and drive to the airport. Then she'd return to her lonely apartment and get back in her old routine and try to forget Zach all over again.

It wouldn't be possible, but she'd try just the same.

The memory of her soft, pale face with those unshed tears tore at him.

"I can't do this. Take over for me," Zach growled as he slammed his clipboard down on a table inside the casino.

Roberto and his men watched silently as Zach stalked past them, the rows of slot machines and then the gaming tables. Outside, the air was thick and oppressive with the scent of rain. He looked up and saw threatening black clouds moving in fast. A fierce gust ripped across the bayou.

Perfect weather, he thought, as the first raindrop pelted him.

No sooner had he slammed the door of his Mercedes, started the engine and roared out of the parking lot, than it started pouring. Not that the rain kept him from whipping violently across the narrow bridge and skidding onto the main road. A truck honked wildly. Brakes squealed as it surrendered right-of-way.

Zach took his foot off the accelerator. No use killing some innocent motorist. Summer damn sure wasn't worth it.

It was going to take a long time for his love, or rather the illusion of who he'd believed she was, to die again.

Maybe forever.

She'd looked so damn pretty in that soft pink dress that

had clung to her slim body, and so desperately forlorn with those damp blue eyes that had shed that single spectacular tear at exactly the right moment. She'd shredded his heart all over again. It would probably thrill her to know she'd nearly had him believing what he saw and felt instead of what he knew to be true.

His gut had clenched, and his heart had thudded violently. He'd wanted to grab her, pull her close, soothe and console her, kiss that tearstained cheek and those beautiful, pouting lips…just one last time. He'd wanted it so much he'd almost lost control.

Then he'd remembered she was an actress, who'd dressed to entice him, who'd played her role perfectly despite her vows never to act when she was with him.

He remembered all her lies of omission about the baby. What part of their relationship had ever been true? What was he to her? Another circus act in the three-ring show she put on for her adoring fans? Did she need a man in her life to complete the picture of her as America's number-one sweetheart? Acting was a highly competitive career. What sin wouldn't she commit to stay on top?

He thought of all the magazine-cover stories he'd seen about actresses with their adoring babies and husbands. Were any of those heartwarming stories truthful? Weren't they all just fodder for fools like him, who, deep down, wanted to believe the dream?

Had anything she'd said today been real?

Whether it was or not, she'd damn sure shattered his heart and sent him to hell and back all over again.

Twelve

Zach moved silently through the long shadows of the tall spreading oaks near Viola's house, stepping past Silas, who looked like a black-and-white fur ball as he napped under the pink blossoms of his favorite crape myrtle bush.

The dazzling pink flowers blurred, and suddenly Zach saw Summer instead of the worthless feline: Summer with her heart in her eyes, Summer looking lovely and too sexy for words in that ridiculous pink confection of a dress.

Damn her. As the image dissolved, he experienced burning, agonizing loss.

Frowning, he approached Viola's screen door warily.

Why was he even here? He had a plane to catch. It wasn't as if he had to show up at her request. Hell, these days he ignored most invitations, and he had every reason to ignore Viola's. Why was he putting himself through this?

Because she'd sounded so fragile when she'd summoned him. Because he genuinely liked her. Because she was family now, in spite of everything Summer had done. Viola would be his son's great-grandmother. Because she was hurting nearly as much as he was that the dream wouldn't come true.

Viola's bossy cat trotted toward the screen door and rubbed his tail arrogantly against Zach's jeans. Then he sank a claw into the screen as he waited to be let in.

Viola welcomed them both. Silas, who sprang inside first, she gave a can of tuna. Zach, she gave a plate of chocolate-chip cookies and a glass of iced tea that she'd flavored with mint from her garden.

He didn't have time for tea or cookies, but he was loath to say so. Viola had a strange power over him.

When he saw the empty shelves and all the boxes stacked against the walls in every room, in an effort to make polite conversation, he asked when she planned to move to her new condo.

"I'm taking my time. I can only do an hour or so of packing each day before my back starts howling. Tuck's not much help, bless his lazy soul, not even when I pay him. Slow as molasses. Drops things, he does. And Summer's not going to rent out this old place after all. Because of the baby...." She said that last with reverence as she lifted her sharp gaze to his.

When she didn't avert those piercing eyes that saw too much, his heart sped up to a tortured pace.

"She's feeling quite sentimental about the old place. Said she's going to keep it for herself and the baby, so the baby will grow up loving it as much as past generations have before her. That's nice, don't you think?"

Her? Funny how Zach always thought of their kid as a boy. A little boy with golden hair and bright blue eyes. But it could be girl, couldn't it? A beautiful little girl who looked like Summer, who'd break his heart because he loved her so.

Viola noted his empty plate. Usually, she hopped up to re-fill such a plate. But not today.

"I'm afraid there aren't any more cookies. You see, Sum-mer ate practically all of them the other day...stuffed herself on them, the poor dear. Not a good thing really, in her condi-tion. She has to get into all those costumes, too, you know. But she was so down before she left. Kept eating one after another, couldn't stop herself. Until I took the plate away and froze the remaining cookies for future guests. And here you are."

"Why did you ask me to come over here today, Viola? I have a plane to catch, meetings in Houston...."

"You poor dear, with your big, important life. You know, you don't look any better than she does. I can see that, despite your tough exterior, this is just as hard on you as it is on her."

Zach froze. "Did *she* put you up to this?"

"Who?" Viola's eyes were suspiciously guileless. "Put me up to what?"

Those innocent eyes, so compelling in her wrinkled face, seemed to search his soul in the exact way that Summer's sometimes did. But unlike Summer, Viola's deep compas-sion for him was genuine.

"Zach, is this really what you want? You two are going to have a child. Summer's brokenhearted, and I think you love her, too. I think you always have and always will."

He felt the ice that encased his heart melting beneath the brightness of her sweet, determined gaze, but his face re-mained a mask.

"Zach, you have the baby to think of. When parents don't live together, it's the child who suffers most. The family's bro-ken. That's what happened to Summer when her father walked out on Anna. Look at poor Tuck, how he's still struggling. A baby needs to be part of a close, loving family."

"Unfortunately, we can't all have the ideal family," he mut-tered. "I was on my own after my mother left my father, and then my father remarried a younger woman, who threw me out after he died."

"So, then you know how it feels. Do you want your baby to suffer the way you did, when you could so easily prevent it?"

Easily?

Again, he asked himself why he'd come here. It was hard enough to let Summer go without this fragile old lady, whom he liked, trying to pry his innermost secrets from him. Summer was wrong for him. Period.

He'd believed in the dream, but it had all been a lie. Summer was the ultimate liar. And even if it weren't for that calamity, even if she were the lovely illusion he'd believed in, he couldn't live with the press pouncing on them every time one of them had so much as a conversation with another attractive person. He didn't want his marriage to be a feast for public consumption. He wanted a real marriage—a private, personal bonding of two souls—not some mirage of perfect love that would heighten Summer's popularity.

"I don't need this," he growled as he stood up.

"Sit back down," Viola commanded in her bossy way.

Strange that, in his hopeless mood, he found her firm manner oddly comforting.

Slowly, he sank back into the chair, Summer's favorite chair, which happened to be his favorite, too.

"I may be a pushy old lady, who doesn't know half as much as she should, but I know you two belong together."

"Not anymore. Too many things have happened. The past...our first baby...all the lies. I don't want everything we do to be magnified by the media."

"Summer is a wonderful girl, and you know it! Thurman was a real stinker. Hasn't he cost us all enough? As for the press—why do you care so much about what other people think?"

"It's not that simple."

"I say it is. I say maybe you're too proud, too arrogant. And maybe, despite your bluster, you're something of a coward."

He scowled at her.

"I know this because I've been guilty of the same thing at times. When anything bad is written about Summer, my friends all tease me. I don't like it. I feel put down and ashamed. But they're jealous, you see, of her success. Not that any of them will admit it. But don't they just love it when unkind words are written about Summer or an unflattering picture of her is taken? I fall for their bluster every time and blame Summer. Either she sets me straight or I get my bearings back on my own. All the negative stuff is backward praise in a way. People see how wonderful she is and want a part of her. It's up to me to stay centered and put her first and everybody else last—where they belong."

"We've got an ugly past to live down, as well."

"When you've lived as long as I have, you learn you can live anything down."

"Look, our lifestyles just aren't compatible."

"Then modify them. Maybe it won't take as much give on your part as you think. When two people who are right for each other come together, the most insurmountable obstacles can be conquered."

"I've gotta go."

"My, but you're stubborn. It's probably one of the reasons you're so successful. You stick to what you decide to do, and do it. But in this case, you're wrong. You're making the biggest mistake of your life."

"Usually, I go with my gut. This time, though, I made an intelligent decision, based on past and present experience—that's all."

"Maybe you should stick with your gut."

"Not smart. She's too good of an actress. She throws off my instincts."

"Has this all been about revenge, then—about you wanting to get even with her for what happened fifteen years ago?"

"Hell, no."

"Well, too bad, 'cause you'd sure be even with her if it was. You really hurt her this time. I haven't seen her like this since she failed to carry your first child. It seems so unfair that here she is pregnant again, you both have a glorious second chance, but you're walking out on her like before. You just about killed her last time."

"I don't need this."

"I say you do. When you were in jail, Thurman found out she was pregnant and sent her away to New Orleans to have your baby. He didn't want you or anybody else to know about the baby because he was afraid it might sway public opinion in your favor. There were people, even back then, who sided with you and didn't like the way Thurman was using his pull to rush the due process of law.

"Did you know Summer tried to contact you shortly before she miscarried?"

"You're not telling me anything I don't already know."

Viola ignored his protest. "Summer was inconsolable when she couldn't find you. Finally, she felt that she had nowhere to go but back to New Orleans, and that's where she lost the baby. Summer had the saddest little funeral for that child. Not that I could go. I was too busy tending to my dying daughter. When Summer finally came home to stay, she was different, changed.

"Then Anna, her mother, died. Summer blamed Thurman for everything that had happened, for the end of her mother's remission, for losing you, for the death of the baby. She said she couldn't live in this town with her memories, so she broke away from all of us and went to New York. That's where she took bit parts while going to college in her spare time. I sent money. She worked herself to the bone in an effort to forget you. But she never could."

"I had my own problems back then."

The ancients and the wise say a man can learn the greatest truths of the universe in an instant. Suddenly, that was true for Zach. No sooner had he said those bitter words than his perspective shifted dramatically. All the pieces of the story he had imagined to be the truth about his love affair with Summer arranged themselves in a new and different order with a new and different meaning.

Had he been hurt and too bitter to consider what Summer had gone through? He had. And he hadn't known the half of it. When she'd sought him out in Houston, how coldly he'd rejected her.

Just as he was rejecting her now.

All that had ever mattered was their love for each other. If they'd kept their focus on that, no one could have touched them.

The pain he felt was staggering. He'd hurt Summer terribly, more than Thurman ever had. Because he'd been stubbornly focused on his own grievances. And blind to hers.

The image of that single tear trickling down her beautiful face tugged at his heart. Why hadn't he listened to his instinct and drawn her close and kissed her tears away?

"I've said my piece, so you can go now," Viola said as she laid a gnarled hand on Silas, who purred in her lap.

For a long moment, Zach sat where he was, stunned. Without Summer beside him, he faced nothing but long years of emptiness. He would fill up his days with work, but the nights would be long and lonely. There would be no one to hold him in the darkness. No one to care about his failures or share his successes. He would be forever diminished without her love.

And he was throwing it all away.

"You have a plane to catch, don't you?"

"Thank you for the cookies and tea," he muttered mechanically, like someone in a dream.

He stared at the spot on the porch where he'd kissed Summer as a girl. She'd been so blushingly shy and lovely. When he'd kissed the woman in that same spot fifteen years later, she'd been hurt and defiant and in denial, but he'd seen into her heart and had fallen in love with her all over again.

He loved her.

He wasn't going to stop loving her just because he willed himself to do so. His love for her was the truest and strongest part of him. By sending her and his child away, he faced the death of everything that would ever matter to him.

He had to make this right.

He needed Summer and their child.

Damn the press. Why hadn't he seen that he should put her first, instead of his own damn ego? She'd carried his child and lost it while her mother had been gravely ill. The thought of her alone and pregnant again was excruciatingly unbearable. If anything happened to her or the baby because of his horrible cruelty, he would never forgive himself.

He had to take care of them. He had to find a way to protect them from the press instead of blaming Summer for the made-up headlines. And when he couldn't protect them, he'd endure the media coverage…. If only Summer would forgive him and take him back.

Thirteen

It was raining outside the theater, pouring. Not that Summer cared.

Opening nights were all about families and friends. Thus, her dressing room and bathroom overflowed with vivid bouquets of flowers, embossed cards from the greats and the near-greats and telegrams, as well. Everybody she remotely cared about was packed inside these two tiny rooms with her. Everybody except Zach, the one person who mattered most.

As she waited for her place to be called, her grandmother and brother sat to her left on her long couch, while her dresser, hairdresser and agent sat to the right. It was a tight squeeze, but Summer needed their support desperately because Zach wasn't here.

She still felt raw and shaken from their breakup, and she'd kept people with her constantly so she wouldn't break down when the press asked their prying questions.

She kept telling herself she needed to accept that he was

gone so she could move on from this profound pain, but some part of her refused to believe he was out of her life forever. She kept hoping against hope for a miracle. He would relent and forgive her.... And love her. She wanted this miracle more than ever, and not solely because she was carrying his child.

That's why she was barely listening to the buzz around her, why she couldn't stop staring past Gram toward the door, why she couldn't stop hoping the door would open and she'd find him standing there. If only he'd walk in, take her in his arms and say everything was all right.

Then, only then, would she be whole and happy again. She didn't want to get over him. She simply wanted him in her life, in her baby's life, every day for the rest of her days. She wanted to wake up to his face on the pillow and go to sleep with the same vision, and she couldn't seem to get past that heartfelt desire. So for days—or was it weeks, she'd lost count—she'd lingered in a dreadful suspended state of suffering.

She was an actress, so she hid her pain with brilliant smiles and quick laughter, but those who knew her weren't fooled.

Suddenly, there was a roar in her ears, and she felt faint.

Summer closed her eyes and wished them all gone. She needed some alone time before the places were called to get her mind off Zach and onto her character, but everybody else was drinking champagne and having way too good a time to leave the couches.

Suddenly Paolo stormed into the dressing room. His expression was so serious when he yelled for everybody to be quiet that the uproar died instantly. He motioned for them all to leave, and because of his imperious manner, Paolo got what he wanted. They fled.

Normally, she would have thought his actions meant her reviews were bad and he'd come to tell her this bitter truth, but tonight she couldn't stop thinking about Zach long enough to care.

Paolo took her hand, squeezed it fiercely. "*Bella!* I came to tell you your reviews are sensational! The critics loved you in the previews! They adore you! We've got a hit!"

"You're sure?"

"I'm sure."

"Oh."

"Is that all you can say?" he thundered, quite put out at her lack of enthusiasm.

"I'm thrilled. Of course, I'm thrilled," she whispered dully as the overture began and places were called.

She was hardly aware of the music or of Paolo as she rose.

Paolo kissed her cheek and shoved her toward the door. "Go out there and break a leg."

She was on her way out the door when she remembered her secret ritual on opening nights. Walking swiftly to her dressing table, she flung open a drawer and removed the white-leather volume with fading gilt letters on its covers. She opened it and pressed her lips gently against the withered, yellowed rose.

Then she replaced the cherished volume and ran.

Lightning lit the sky. Thunder reverberated almost instantly.

Then all was dark again as torrents of rain slashed the jet.

Inside, Zach jammed his cell phone into his pocket impatiently and began to pace the length of the plane. He should have been in Manhattan hours ago, before Summer's play even started. He'd taken a box seat. He'd planned to be in it when she came onstage. He'd never make curtain call now.

He went to the liquor cabinet and grabbed a bottle of scotch. Splashing it into a glass, he drank deeply. Then he fumbled in his other pocket to make sure the tiny, black-velvet box was still there. He'd told himself to get rid of the ring, but he hadn't. Had he known even then that he couldn't live without her?

Pulling the ring out, he lifted the lid. The enormous engagement diamond shot sparks at him as he imagined himself slipping it onto her beautiful hand. If only, she'd have him after he'd pushed her away.

He hated this feeling of being in limbo, on edge, vulnerable. Only his need for her could reduce him to this.

What if Summer said no?

"Stop!" Zach said when he saw Summer's name blazing in red neon atop a brightly lit marquee.

Grabbing the dozens of red roses he'd bought her, he got out of the limo in the middle of traffic and made a dash across the street for the theater.

Brakes squealed. Horns honked. Cabbies cursed him. A reporter yelled his name and took his picture. But he didn't care.

Maybe he could still catch her grand finale.

When he opened the doors of the theater, he heard the roar of applause and a thousand bravos.

They loved her!

His heart swelled with joy and admiration. He loved her, too, and he was nearly bursting with pride at all she'd accomplished. No wonder so many people craved the details of her life. They saw her as a princess in a fairy tale, and they wanted a place in the dream.

He remembered when she'd wowed everybody in Bonne Terre in her high-school production of *Grease*. Zach had believed in her dream then. He had wanted her to succeed, and now she had.

He was running down the center aisle of the orchestra section when she walked onto the stage in a glittering gold gown to take her final curtain call. At the sight of her, so slim and stunningly lovely, the crowd went even wilder, yelling her name along with more bravos.

There must have been two thousand people in that theater, and they were packed to the rafters.

She bowed gracefully as people stood cheering.

Zach waved and called her name, but she couldn't hear him over the roar of her audience.

Everyone began to throw roses at the stage.

This was her moment. He stopped and waited, allowing her to shine.

There would be time later to take her in his arms, to tell her how sorry he was he'd hurt her, to swear to her he'd never do it again, to beg for her forgiveness. He'd tell her he wanted to marry her so he could spend the rest of his life making it up to her.

The past didn't matter. Her fame didn't matter. Only she and their baby and the life they would make together was important to him.

Blinded by the stage lights and feeling a little faint, Summer took another deep bow. When she straightened, she raised her hands and blew kisses as the audience continued to clap.

They stomped and screamed louder, so she bowed a final time.

This time when she straightened she heard a man on stage right call her name.

His voice shuddered through her, or did she only imagine him there?

Hoping, she turned and was overjoyed to see a tall man in a dark suit holding the biggest bouquet of roses she'd ever seen.

"Zach," she whispered, not really believing what she saw, as she took a faltering step toward him. She sucked in a breath. "Is it really you? Or am I dreaming? Oh, please, God, don't let me be dreaming!"

Then he came nearer, and his dear face with all those hard angles came into focus, and she saw that his eyes were warm and filled with love. He smiled sheepishly, but he dazzled her just the same.

"Oh, Zach. You came. You really came. I wanted you here so much. You'll never know…how much."

Handing her the huge bouquet of red roses, he swept her into his arms and kissed her.

Dozens of flashes exploded. The crowd roared, loving him, loving her, loving them together because their fairy tale had come true.

She couldn't believe he'd come tonight, that maybe he still loved her. But then she could believe it because his kisses took her breath away as did the tears shining in his beautiful, dark eyes.

"Forgive me," he whispered. "Love me…. Please love me again or I'll die."

"Oh, Zach…. With all my heart," she replied. "Always. And forever."

Although the corridor outside Summer's dressing room was noisy, Summer was aware of nothing except Zach, who was on bended knee, looking up at her, his expression fierce, almost desperate, as he clutched her hand.

"Tell me you weren't playing a part for the crowd when you promised to love me out there, sweetheart."

"I wasn't."

"I wouldn't blame you if you were. I deserve that…and worse."

"I've loved you since I was thirteen. I never stopped loving you. I never will."

"I never stopped loving you, either. I'm sorry I was so brutal when you came to Louisiana to tell me about our baby. You were so beautiful in pink, so damned beautiful, so sad…."

And I deliberately hurt you. Maybe because I felt so much and was determined to ignore those feelings. Gram called me a fool for not listening to my gut and a coward for pushing you and your love away, and she was right."

"It's okay. It's okay." Gently Summer cupped his rugged face in her hands. "It's okay. I understand. I do."

"To ever think you weren't worth whatever it costs to make our life together was the second biggest mistake of my life. The first was that I should have stood by you fifteen years ago instead of blaming you for not standing by me. I've always been a selfish, egotistical bastard."

"I should have done better by you, too."

"We can't go back," he said. "Or control the events of the past. We can only control how we view them."

"And the press? You really think you'll be able to stand all the fuss?"

"I don't care what the world thinks about me or you. Whatever we have together is true. It is the strongest force in my life…. Stronger even than my ambition, stronger than any lie the vicious press can write or say. I haven't given a damn about work since we've been apart. Nothing matters to me as much as you and our child. Nothing. I can't change the past, but together we can change our future."

She'd waited so long to hear such words from him, to feel loved by him so completely. Happiness overflowed in her heart.

"Will you marry me, then, Summer Wallace? Will you honor me by becoming Mrs. Zach Torr?"

"What? And give up my stage name?" she teased.

He pulled a black-velvet box out of his hand and opened it.

The diamond sparkled with a vengeance.

But her eyes shone even brighter as she stared down at him. "Oh, my! You could persuade a lot of girls with a rock that size."

"You're the only one I want, and you didn't answer the question."

"That's because I'm still in shock. But, yes. Yes!" she cried as he slid the ring onto her finger. "Yes!"

"Then kiss me, Summer. This time I won't complain about an Oscar performance."

She laughed as she pulled his face up to hers and pressed her lips to his and did just as he commanded, for a very long time. Only it wasn't a performance, it was true and real.

She'd always been true and real. He would never doubt her again.

"Mrs. Zach Torr," she breathed in an awed tone when he finally released her.

A single tear traced down her cheek. Only this time it was a tear of joy.

Summer had never had more fun at a cast party than she was having tonight with Zach beside her and his ring glimmering on her left hand. At the same time she couldn't wait to steal away from the lavish affair, so she could spend the rest of the night with her fiancé.

But they had forever, didn't they? Or at least as long as they both should live.

Because they'd known the reviews would be good, the producers were out to impress. They'd rented a fabulous ballroom at the top of one of New York's most prestigious hotels. The food was excellent; the champagne vintage. She had to stay awhile because she was the star.

When Hugh crashed the party unexpectedly and began garnering more press than anybody else, she tensed, whispering to Zach that she'd tell the show's producers to make him leave.

Zach pressed a fingertip to her lips. "Let him stay, sweetheart. I don't care. The press can write whatever they want about the three of us."

"You really don't care?"

"I swear it. Don't worry about me. Introduce me to the bastard. I'll even pose with him. Go do what you have to do. Work the crowd. Let the photographers take the appropriate pictures of you with your cast and producers. Because the sooner you do, the sooner we can leave and have the rest of the night for each other."

She listened to his sure, calm voice, which didn't hold the faintest trace of jealousy, and felt as if she'd come home. At last.

Happiness filled her. So much happiness, she couldn't speak.

"Oh, Zach."

He pulled her into his arms. For a long moment, as he held her close, she realized that this was her new life, their shared life. He was part of all she was, just as she would be part of all he was. No more scandals stood between them.

They would be together forever.

Epilogue

The stairs creaked as Summer carried Terri, who was bundled in pink blankets and asleep, up to the nursery. But she couldn't put her beautiful, dark-haired little girl in the crib. The baby was too soft and warm and cuddly, and every minute Summer held her was too precious.

The joy-filled days passed so fast. Summer had given herself a year off for maternity leave, and already four months of it were gone. So she sat in the rocker and began to sing to her little girl while she stared out at the pines that fringed the house that had belonged to her family for more than a hundred years.

Summer loved the time she and Zach spent in this old house, the time when they left their nannies and servants in their larger residences in Houston and New York, and they could be together with Gram and Tuck.

Downstairs Gram was cooking a dinner for all of them, so the house was fragrant with the rich aroma of Cajun spices.

Nick had supplied Gram with shrimp, and she'd promised them all, including Nick, a big pot of gumbo.

Nick, who adored Terri so much he'd even made a place in his heart for Summer, would be joining them.

Summer heard Zach's Mercedes in the drive. Then the screen door banged behind him. Would that man ever learn to shut a door quietly when it was nap time?

"Summer!" Zach hollered.

"Up here," she called down to him softly and was relieved when he didn't yell again. Much as she adored Terri, like any other new mother, she counted on having a breather when her little darling snoozed.

Zach strode silently into the room and knelt beside them. Reaching out his hand he touched Terri's cheek. In her sleep, the baby smiled. Then she grabbed on to his little finger, and he gasped.

The baby's pale fingers with their little fingernails were so tiny and perfect; his tanned ones so large and blunt.

"Can I hold her?" he whispered.

Summer nodded, lifting their daughter into his arms. She got up so he could have the rocker.

"She's got me. I'm afraid I'll never be able to be stern and say no to her," he whispered. "I'll spoil her rotten."

"Well, we won't have to discipline her for a while."

Summer's eyes pooled with tears of happiness as she watched her two raven-haired darlings—her rugged husband and their trusting and innocent baby daughter.

She wished she could hold on to this moment.

The past would always be a part of them, especially the loss of their first daughter. But love filled Summer's days now with all its richly rewarding experiences. Marriage. Motherhood.

Life was so wonderful, she was determined to savor every sparkling moment of her shared happiness with Zach.

"Come here," he whispered as he got up to put their baby in her crib.

Turning to Summer, he took her in his arms and pressed her tightly against him.

"I love you," he said.

He told her that every day, and she never tired of hearing it.

She was glad that love was no longer a four-letter word he equated with hell. She was glad their love had become the guiding force in his life.

As it was in hers.

* * * * *

THE THINGS SHE SAYS

BY
KAT CANTRELL

Kat Cantrell read her first Mills & Boon novel in third grade and has been scribbling in notebooks since she learned to spell. What else would she write but romance? She majored in literature, officially with the intent to teach, but somehow ended up buried in middle management at Corporate America, until she became a stay-at-home mum and full-time writer.

Kat, her husband and their two boys live in north Texas. When she's not writing about characters on the journey to happily-ever-after, she can be found at a soccer game, watching the TV show *Friends* or listening to '80s music.

Kat was the 2011 Mills & Boon *So You Think You Can Write* winner and a 2012 RWA Golden Heart finalist for Best Unpublished Series Contemporary Manuscript.

To Cynthia Justlin, the sister of my heart.
You wouldn't let me give up on this book
and I'll never forget it. Thank you for all the years of
cheerleading, support, gentle critiques, encouragement
and friendship. I'm so happy we're sharing this journey.

One

The only thing worse than being lost was being lost in Texas. In August.

Kris Demetrious slumped against the back end of his borrowed, screaming-yellow Ferrari, peeled the shirt from his damp chest and flipped his phone vertical. With the new orientation, the lines on the map still didn't resemble the concrete stretching out under the tires. Lesson for the day—internet maps only worked if they were accurate.

The Ferrari was no help with its MP3 player docking station but no internal GPS. Italian automotive engineers either never got lost or didn't care where they were going.

Mountains enclosed the landscape in every direction, but unlike L.A., none of them were marked. No mansions, no Hollywood sign and no clues to use to correct his wrong turn.

He never got lost on the set. Give him a controlled, detached position behind the camera, and if the scene refused to come together, starting over was as simple as yelling, "Cut."

So what had possessed him to drive to Dallas instead of fly?

A stall tactic, that's what.

Dying in the desert wasn't on his to-do list, but avoiding his destination was. If he could find food and water, he'd prefer to stay lost. Because as soon as he got to Dallas, he'd have to announce his engagement to America's Sweetheart Kyla Monroe. And even though he'd agreed to her scheme, he'd rather trash six weeks' worth of dailies than go through with it.

He pocketed the phone as bright afternoon sunshine beat down, a thousand times hotter than it might have been if he'd been wearing a color other than black. Heat shimmered across the road, blurring the horizon.

Just then, churning dust billowed up, the only movement he'd seen in at least fifteen minutes. A dull orange pickup truck, coated with rust, drove through the center of the dirt cloud and pulled off the highway, braking on the shoulder behind the Ferrari. Sand whipped against Kris in a gritty whirlwind. He swept his hair out of his face and went to greet his rescuer.

Really, once he ran out of gas, he could have been stuck here for days, fending off the vultures with nothing more than a smartphone and polarized sunglasses. He'd already spun the car around twice to head in the opposite direction and now he'd lost his bearings. The truck driver's timing was awesome and, with any luck, he would be able to give Kris directions to the main highway.

After a beat, the truck's door creaked open and light hit the faded logo stenciled on the orange paint. Big Bobby's Garage Serving You Since 1956. Dusty, cracked boots appeared below the opened door and *whoomped* to the ground. Out of the settling dust, a small figure emerged. A girl. Barely of driving age and, odds are, not Big Bobby.

"Car problems, chief?" she drawled as she approached. Her Texas accent was as thick as the dust, but her voice rolled out musically. She slipped off her sunglasses, and the world skipped a beat. The unforgiving heat, lack of road signs and the problems waiting for him in Dallas slid away.

Clear blue eyes peered up at him out of a heart-shaped face and a riot of cinnamon-colored hair curled against porcelain cheeks. Not a glimmer of makeup graced her skin, unusual enough in itself to earn a second glance. The sun bathed her in its glow, a perfect key light. He wouldn't even need a fill light to get the shot. She was fresh, innocent and breathtakingly beautiful. Like a living sunflower. He wanted to film her.

She eyed him. *"Problema con el coche, señor?"*

Kris closed his mouth and cleared his throat. "I'm Greek, not Hispanic."

What a snappy response, and not entirely true—he'd renounced his Greek citizenship at sixteen and considered himself American through and through. How had such a small person shut down his brain in less than thirty seconds?

"Wow. Yes, you are, with a sexy accent and everything. Say something else," she commanded and circled a finger. The blue of her eyes turned sultry. "Tell me your life is meaningless without me, and you'd give a thousand fortunes to make me yours."

Somehow his mouth was open again. "Seriously?"

She laughed, a pure sound that trilled through his abdomen. A potent addition to the come-hither she radiated like perfume.

"Only if you mean it," she said.

There was too much confidence in the set of her shoulders for her to be a teenager. Mid-twenties at least. But then, how worldly could a girl from Nowhere, Texas, be? Especially given her obvious fondness for romantic melodrama and her distinct lack of self-preservation. For all she knew, he might be the next Charles Manson instead of the next Scorsese.

With a grin, she jerked her chin. "I'll cut you a break, Tonto. You can talk about whatever you want. We don't see many fancy foreigners in these parts, but I'd be happy to check you out. I mean check *it* out." She shook her head and shut her eyes for a blink. "The car. I'll look at it for you. Might be an easy fix."

The car? She must work as a mechanic at Big Bobby's. Intriguing. Most women needed help finding the gas tank.

"It's not broken down. I'm just lost," he clarified while his imagination galloped back to the idea of her checking him out, doctor-style, with lots of hands-on analysis. Clawing hunger stabbed through him, as unexpected as it was powerful.

Maybe he should remember his own age, which wasn't seventeen. Women propositioned him all the time, but with the subtlety of a 747 at takeoff, which he'd never liked and never thought twice about refusing. He had little use for any sort of liaison unless it was fictional and part of his vision for bringing a story to the screen.

This woman had managed to pull him out from behind the lens with a couple of sentences. It was unnerving.

"Lost, huh?" Her gaze raked over him from top to toe. "Lucky for me I found you, then. Does that put you in my debt?"

Everything spilled out of her mouth with veiled insinuation. When combined with her guileless demeanor and fresh face, the punch was forceful. "Well, you haven't done anything for me. Yet."

Slim eyebrows jerked up in fascination. "What would you like for me to do?"

He leaned in close enough to catch a whiff of her hair. Coconut and grease, a combination he would have sworn wasn't the least bit arousing before now. Same for the big T-shirt with the cracked Texas Christian University Horned Frogs emblem and cheap jeans. On her, haute couture.

He crooked a finger and she crowded into his space, which felt mysteriously natural, as if they'd often conspired together.

"Right now, there's only one thing I'd like for you to do," he said.

His gaze slid to her lips and what had started as a flirtatious game veered into dangerous territory as he anticipated kissing this nameless desert mirage, sliding against those pink lips, delving into her hot mouth. Her laugh pulsing against his skin.

Kissing strangers was so not his style, and he was suddenly sad it wasn't.

"Yeah? What would you like me to do?" She wet her lips with the very tip of her tongue, heating his blood all the way to his toes.

"Tell me where I am."

Her musical laugh poleaxed him again. "Little Crooked Creek Road. Also known as the middle of nowhere."

"There's a creek somewhere in all this sand?" Water—wet, cool and perfect for skinny dipping.

No. No naked strangers. What was wrong with him?

"Nah." Her nose wrinkled, screwing up her features in a charming way. "It dried up in the 1800s. We lack the imagination to rename the road."

"So tell me, since you're local. Is it always this hot?" Truthfully, he'd long stopped caring about his sticky, damp clothes, but the urge to keep her talking wouldn't go away.

"No, not at all. Usually it's hotter. That's why we don't wear all black when it's a hundred and ten," she said, scrutinizing him with a gaze as sizzling as the concrete. "Though I like it on you. What brought you so far off the beaten path, anyway?"

"I wish the story was more interesting than a wrong turn. But it's not." He grinned and tried to be sorry he'd veered from the interstate but couldn't conjure up a shred of regret. Surprisingly, being in the middle of this scene wasn't so bad. "I left El Paso pretty sure I was headed in the right direction, but I haven't seen a sign for Dallas in a long time."

"Yeah. You're lost. This road winds south to the Rio Grande. It's really not grand or even much of a *rio*. Can't recommend it as a sightseeing venture, so I'd head back to Van Horn and take the 10 east."

"Van Horn. I vaguely remember passing through it."

"Not much to remember. I was just in town, and it hasn't changed since the last time I came in March. Speaking of which, I need to get a move on. The part I picked up isn't going to magically install itself in Gus's truck." She sighed and stuck a thumb over her shoulder. "Van Horn's that way. Good luck and watch for state troopers. They live to pull over fast cars.

"Or," she continued brightly, "you can go thataway and take your first right. That'll put you on the road to the center of Little Crooked Creek and the best fried chicken in the county."

He wasn't nearly sated enough on the harmony of her voice. Or the charming way she rambled about nothing but piqued his interest anyway. Real life loomed on the horizon, and even if it took him a month to arrive to Dallas, he'd still be unhappy with the creative financing deal for *Visions of Black.* Kyla would still be Kyla—unfaithful, selfish and artificial—and he'd have to expend way too much energy not caring.

But, he reminded himself again, it was worth it. If he wanted to make *Visions,* he had to generate plenty of free publicity with an engagement to his beloved-by-the-masses, Oscar-winning ex-girlfriend. A fake engagement.

"Fried chicken is my favorite." And he was starving. What could a couple of hours hurt? After all, he'd driven on purpose so it would take as long as possible to reach Dallas. "What's Little Crooked Creek?"

"The poorest excuse for a small town you'll ever have the misfortune to visit in your life," she said with a wry twist of her lips. "It's where I live."

The Greek god was following her. VJ sneaked another glance in the rearview mirror. Yup. The *muy amarilla* Ferrari kept pace with Daddy's truck. God had dropped off a fantasy on the side of the road in a place where nothing had happened for a millennium and he was *following her.*

Giddy. That was the word for the jumpy crickets in her stomach. She'd been waiting a long time for a knight in shining armor of her very own and never in a million years would she have expected to find one until she escaped Little Crooked Creek forever, amen. Yet, here he was, six feet of gorgeousness in the flesh and following her to Pearl's. Shiver and a half.

She pulled into a parking place at the diner and curled her lip at the white flatbed in the next spot. Great. Lenny and Billy were here. Must be later than she thought. Her brothers never crawled out of bed until three o'clock and usually only then because she booted them awake, threatening them with no breakfast if they didn't move their lazy butts.

Hopefully they weren't on their second cup of coffee yet and wouldn't notice the stranger strolling through Pearl's. The last thing she wanted was to expose her precious knight to the two stupidest good ol' boys in West Texas.

The Ferrari rolled into the spot on the other side of Daddy's truck, and the Greek god flowed out of it like warm molasses. He was the most delicious thing in four states, and he was all hers. For now. She wasn't deluded enough to think such an urbane, sophisticated specimen of a man would stick around, but it was no crime to bask in his gloriousness until he flowed back out of her life. Sigh. She grabbed her backpack and met him on the sidewalk.

Pearl's was almost empty. Her stranger was as out of place as a June bug in January, and it only took fourteen seconds for all eight pairs of eyes in the place to focus on them as she led him past the scarred tables to the booth in the shadow of the kitchen—the one everyone understood was reserved for couples who wanted privacy. She plopped onto the bench, opting to take the side sloppily repaired with silver duct tape and giving him the mostly okay seat.

He slid onto the opposite bench and folded his pianist's fingers into a neat crosshatch pattern right over the heart carved into the Formica tabletop, with the initials LT & SR in the center. Laurie and Steve had been married nearly twenty years now, a small-town staple completely in contrast to this man, who doubtlessly frequented chic sushi bars and classy night-clubs.

What had she been thinking when she invited him here?

"Interesting place," he said.

Dilapidated, dark and smelling of rancid grease maybe, but *interesting* wasn't a descriptor of Pearl's. "Best cooking you'll find for miles. And the only cooking."

He laughed and she scoured her memory for something else funny to say so she could hear that deep rumble again. Then she abandoned that idea as he pierced her with those incredible melty-brown eyes. She settled for drinking him in. He was finely sculpted, as if carved from marble and deemed so perfect that his creator had breathed life into his statue and set it free to live amongst mere mortals.

"My name's Kris." He held out a hand and raised his eyebrows expectantly. "From Los Angeles."

Surreptitiously, she wiped the grime and sweat off her palm and clasped his smooth hand. Energy leaped between them, shocking her with a funny little zap.

"Sorry, static electricity. It's dry this time of year." She folded her hand into her lap, cradling it with the other. Was it too melodramatic to vow never to wash it again? "I'm VJ. From nowhere. And I'll keep being from nowhere if I don't get to work. I'm saving every dime to get out of here."

She jumped up, hating to desert him, but it was almost four o'clock.

"You're leaving me?" Kris cocked his head and a silky strand of his shoulder-length hair fell into his face. She knotted her fingers behind her back so she couldn't indulge the urge to sweep it from his cheekbone. Touching the artwork was a no-no, even when it wasn't behind glass.

"Not a chance," she said. "I have to put my uniform on, then I'll take your order."

He glanced at the other customers, who weren't ashamed

to be caught in open inspection of the foreigner in their midst. "You work here?"

His accent was amazing. The words were English, a language she'd used her entire life, but every syllable sounded exotic and special. It was the difference between Detroit and Italy—both produced cars, but the end result had little in common other than tires and a steering wheel.

And it was way past time to stop rubbernecking. "Uh, yeah. Five days a week."

Her brothers lumbered off their stools at the counter. Out of the corner of her eye, she watched them hulk over to the booth.

"Who's the pansy?" Lenny sneered. VJ butted him in the chest with her shoulder until he glanced down.

"Back off," she demanded. "He's just passing through and no threat to you. Let him be."

Lenny flicked her out of the way as if she weighed no more than a feather.

Before she'd fully regained her balance, Kris exploded from the booth and descended by her side, staring down Lenny and Billy without flinching. Okay, so maybe he didn't actually need defending. Her heart tumbled to her knees as he angled his body, shielding her, unconcerned about the five hundred pounds of Lewis boys glaring at him. Nobody in Little Crooked Creek stood up to even one of her brothers, let alone two. He really *was* heroic.

"Kristian Demetrious. You are?" His face had gone hard and imperious—warrior-like, about to charge into battle, sword drawn and shield high. As if she needed another push to imagine him as her fantasy knight, come to rescue her from Small Town, USA.

Then his full name registered.

She blinked rapidly, but the image in black didn't waver. Kristian Demetrious was standing in the middle of Pearl's. No one would believe it. Pictures. Should she take pictures? He looked totally different in person. Gak, he probably thought she was a complete hick for not recognizing him. She had to call Pamela Sue this very minute.

Right after she made sure Lenny and Billy weren't about to wipe the floor with Kyla Monroe's fiancé.

"These are two of my brothers. They like to play rough but they're mostly harmless," she said to Kris. "I apologize. They don't get day passes from the mental institution very often."

With a hard push to each of her brothers' chests, she said, "Go sit down and drink another cup of coffee on me. Cool off. Mr. Demetrious isn't here to pick a fight with you."

And just by saying his name, Kris turned into someone remote and inaccessible. A stone rolled onto her chest. He was Kyla Monroe's fiancé. Of course he was. Men like him were always with women like Kyla—gorgeous, elegant and famous, with a shelf full of awards. Well, she'd known her Greek knight was out of her league but she hadn't known he was *that* far out. Actually, she'd thought maybe he was flirting with her a little—but he couldn't have been. She'd misinterpreted his innocent comments, twisting them into something out of a romance novel.

Lenny and Billy skulked away, shooting spiteful glances over their shoulders, and hefted themselves onto their stools, where they eyed Kris over their earthenware mugs. Cretins.

"I'm afraid you've discovered my secret superpower. I'm a moron magnet." She met Kris's eyes. "Thanks. For standing up for me."

How inadequate. But what could she say to encapsulate the magic of that defense from someone like Kristian Demetrious? Small to him, huge to her.

He shrugged and flipped hair out of his face, looking uncomfortable. "One of my hot buttons. So, it's Mr. Demetrious now?" He slid onto the bench. All the hard edges melted and he smiled wryly when she opted to remain standing. She couldn't sit at the same table like they were even remotely in the same stratosphere. "I'm not a fan of formality. I introduced myself as Kris for a reason. Can't we go back to being friendly?"

His smile was so infectious, so stunning as it spread over his straight, white teeth, she returned it before catching herself. "No, we can't. My mama raised me to be respectful."

"I liked it better when you were being disrespectful." He sighed. "Obviously you know who I am. I'm going to guess it's because of Kyla and not because you've seen my films."

"Sorry. I read *People* magazine, of course, but we're lucky to get a couple of wide releases at the theater in Van Horn. For this corner of the world, the films you direct are entirely too… what's the word?" She snapped her fingers. *"Cosmopolitan."*

"Obscure," he said at the same time, and something passed across his features. Determination. Passion. "That's going to change. Soon."

"I have to clock in." And put some distance between them before she asked him how and when. What his work was like, his plans. His dreams. She could listen to him talk all night. Sophisticated conversation, the likes of which she'd never had the opportunity to participate in.

She turned to go. His fingers grazed her arm, and tightened with a luscious pressure, holding her in place. What a thrill it would be to have that golden hand—both hands—wandering all over, undressing, caressing—and enough of that, now.

"Change fast. I'm starving," he said, his eyes went liquid and a brow quirked up. Before realizing he was taken, that was the kind of comment she would have misread, mistaking his smoldering expression as invitation.

"You're the boss. I'll be back in a jiffy."

She edged away, terrified if she shifted her eyes, he'd disappear.

So what if he did? He belonged to Kyla Monroe, the blonde goddess of the screen.

Her stomach flipped. They were from different worlds. He

was only here by an accident of navigation, not some divine plan to make all her wildest dreams come true.

Kristian Demetrious was another woman's man who'd landed in the middle of Little Crooked Creek for a heartbeat and then would be gone.

Two

Kris leaned against the hard booth and watched his desert mirage do a dozen mundane things. Punching her time card in the antiquated machine mounted to the wall of the open kitchen. Making a phone call at the honest-to-God pay phone nestled between the upright video game and the bathrooms.

She moved with vibrancy, like the progression of a blooming flower caught in time-release photographs. Suddenly bursting with color and life. Magnificence where a moment before had been nothing special. Where was his camera when he really needed it? Anything that visceral should be captured through the lens for all posterity.

No. Not for anyone else. Only for his private-viewing pleasure. A selfish secret celebrating artistry instead of capitalism. Maybe that was the key to unlocking the yet-to-be-conceptualized theme for *Visions of Black,* a frustration he'd carried for weeks.

The light in this dive was sallow and dim. All wrong. He'd position her outside, with the late-afternoon sun in her face and mountains rising behind in an uncultivated backdrop. Maybe an interview, so he could capture that mellifluous drawl and the unapologetic raw honesty. With VJ, everything was on the surface, in her eyes and on her tongue, and he was greedy for transparency after drowning in Hollywood games.

He'd left his condo in L.A. before dawn this morning, intending to drive straight through to Dallas, where he'd meet up with Kyla to start the engagement publicity and get rolling on preproduction work for *Visions*.

But one more Kyla-free night now felt less like a reprieve and more like a requirement.

He just wanted to make films, not deal with financing and publicity and endless Hollywood bureaucracy. *Visions of Black* was the right vehicle to propel his career to the next level, with the perfect blend of accessible characters, high-stakes drama and a tension-filled plot. Audiences would love Kyla in the starring role, and her charisma on the screen was unparalleled. She was a necessary part of the package, first and foremost because executive producer Jack Abrams insisted, but Kris couldn't disagree with the dual benefit of box-office draw and high-profile PR.

The need to commit this story to film flared strongly enough that he was willing to deal with his ex and any other obstacles thrown in his path.

Tomorrow.

VJ skirted the tables and rejoined him, smiling expectantly. "Fried chicken?"

"Absolutely." Nobody in L.A. ate fried chicken and the hearty smell of it had been teasing him since he walked through the door. "And a beer."

"Excellent choice. Except you're in the middle of the Bible Belt. Coke instead?" she offered.

"You don't serve alcohol?" A glance around the diner answered that question. Every glass was filled with deep brown liquid. Five bucks said it was outrageously sweet tea.

"Sorry. I'm afraid it's dry as a bone here." She leaned in close and waggled her eyebrows. "We're all good Baptists. Except behind closed doors, you know."

He knew. Where he came from, everyone was Greek Orthodox except behind closed doors. Different label, same hypocrisy. "Coke is fine."

"I'll have it right out for you, sir."

He almost groaned. "You can stop with the sir nonsense. Come right back. Keep me company," he said.

Keep the locals at bay. A convenient excuse, but a poor one. He liked VJ, and he'd have to leave soon enough. Was it terrible to record as much of her as possible through the camera in his head until then?

"I can't. I'm working."

"Doing what?" He waved at the dining room. "This place is practically empty."

Her probing gaze roamed over his face, as if searching for something, and the pursuit was so affecting, he felt oddly compelled to give it to her, no matter what it was.

"Okay," she said. "But only for a few minutes."

She glided through the haphazard maze of tables and bent over her order pad, then handed it to the middle-aged woman in the kitchen. Pearl, if he had to guess.

The brutish brothers, clearly adopted, continued to shoot malevolent grimaces over their shoulders, but hadn't left their stools again.

Only a couple of things were guaranteed to rile Kris's temper—challenging his artistic vision and picking on someone weaker. Otherwise, he stayed out of it. Drama belonged on the screen, not in real life.

A slender young woman with a wholesome face whirled into the diner and flew to VJ's side. Amused, he crossed his arms as they whispered furiously to each other while shooting him fascinated glances under their lashes. Benign gawking, especially by someone who intrigued him as much as VJ did, was sort of flattering. After a couple of minutes, the other woman flounced to the bar, her sidelong gaping at him so exaggerated she almost tripped over her sandals.

"Friend of yours?" he asked as VJ approached his table.

VJ was giving him a wide berth, something he normally appreciated, but not today and not with her. There'd been an easiness between them earlier, as if they'd been friends for a long time, before she got uptight about his connection to Kyla. Friends were hard to come by in Hollywood, especially for someone who cultivated a reputation for being driven and moody. He lost little sleep over it. Different story with VJ, who made the idea of being so disconnected unappealing.

"Yeah, practically since birth. That's Pamela Sue. She's only here to ogle you."

He laughed. "I'm not used to such honesty. I like it. What does VJ stand for?" he asked and propped his chin on a palm, letting his gaze roam over her expressive face. Women were manipulative and scheming where he came from. This one was different.

"Victoria Jane. It's too fancy for these parts, so folks mostly call me VJ."

VJ fit her—it was short, sassy and unusual. "Most? But not all?"

"Perceptive, aren't you? My mom didn't. But she's been gone now almost a year."

Ouch. The pain flickering through her eyes drilled right through him, leaving a gaping hole. Before thinking it through, he reached out and gently enfolded her hand in his.

"I'm sorry," he said. After the ill-fated exchange of harsh words with his father sixteen years ago, Kris had walked away from a guaranteed position at Demetrious Shipping, the Demetrious fortune and Greece entirely. His relationship with his mom had been one of the casualties, and phone calls weren't the same. But he couldn't imagine a world where even a call wasn't possible. "That must've been tough. Must still be."

"Are you trying to make me cry?" She swallowed hard.

Dishes clinked and clacked from the kitchen and the noise split the air.

"Pearl's subtle way of telling me to get my butt to work." VJ rolled wet, shiny eyes. "Honestly, she should pick up your check. This place hasn't seen such a big crowd since Old Man Smith's funeral."

While he'd been distracted, locals had packed the place. Most of the tables were now full of nuclear families, worn-out men in crusty boots or acne-faced teenagers.

"So you're saying I'm at least as popular as a dead man?" It shouldn't have been funny, but the corners of his mouth twitched none the less.

Soberly, she pulled her hand from his and stood. Her natural friendliness had returned and then vanished. He missed it.

"Well, I have to work." She eased away, her expression blank. "Nice to meet you, Mr. Demetrious. I wish you and Ms. Monroe all the happiness in the world with your upcoming marriage."

He scowled. "Kyla and I aren't engaged."

Yet. It didn't improve his mood to hear rumors of the impending engagement had already surfaced, courtesy of Kyla, no doubt.

Why was this still bothering him? He'd agreed to give Kyla a ring. The deal was done if he wanted to make *Visions of Black*. He entertained no romantic illusions about love or marriage. Marriage based on a business agreement had a better chance of succeeding than one based on anything else. Of course, he was never going to marry anyone, least of all Kyla, whom he hadn't even seen in a couple of months, not since she'd called off their relationship in a fit of tears and theatrical moaning. At which point she'd likely jumped right back into bed with Guy Hansen.

"Oh. Well, then, have a nice life instead." VJ smiled and bounced to the kitchen.

At least he'd been able to improve her mood.

Later that night, VJ grinned as she walked up the listing steps to the house, jumped the broken one and cracked the screen door silently.

Kris and Kyla Monroe weren't engaged.

Oh, it made no difference in the grand scheme of things, but she couldn't stop smiling regardless. He was compassionate, sinfully hot and a little more available than she'd assumed.

Was there *anything* wrong with him? If so, she didn't want to know. For now, he was her fantasy, with no faults and no bad habits.

It was fun to imagine Kris returning for her someday, top down on the Ferrari and a handful of red roses. And it was slightly depressing since it would never happen in a million years. He was on his way to Dallas and that would be that.

She tiptoed into the hallway and froze when a board creaked. Dang it, she never missed that one.

"Girl, is that you?" Daddy's slurred voice shot out from the living room.

She winced. Angry drunk tonight. What had happened this time to set him off?

Her stomach plummeted. The part. She'd forgotten all about the part for Gus's truck, and it was still sitting in the cab of Daddy's truck. Her head had been full of Kristian Demetrious, with no room for anything else.

She put some starch in her spine and walked into the living room. Her father slumped in the same armchair where he had taken residence earlier in the afternoon. His eyes were bloodshot, swollen.

"Lookee here." Daddy took a swig of beer and backhanded his mouth with his knuckles. "Finally decided to prance your butt home, didja?"

He looked bad. They'd all dealt with Mama's death in their own way, but Daddy wasn't dealing with it at all, falling farther into a downward, drunken spiral every day.

"I'm sorry about the part, Daddy. I got to town late," she hedged. "I had to go straight to work."

"Gus needs his truck. You get over there and fix it now," he commanded, then downed the rest of his beer and belched. He set the empty can on the closest table without looking.

It teetered on the edge, and then fell to the floor with a clank. Beer dribbled onto the hardwood floor, creating another mess to clean up.

"It's late. Bobby Junior can fix it in the morning." Along with everything else since he was running the garage in their father's stead.

Guilt panged her breastbone. Bobby Junior had a wife and three kids he never saw. What else did she have to do? Lie in bed and dream about a Greek god who was speeding away toward a life that did not, and never would, include her?

Daddy bobbled the TV remote into his paw. "I told you to do it. Ungrateful hussy. Bring me another beer, would ya?"

Her head snapped up and anger swept the guilt aside. "Daddy, you're drunk and you need to go to bed, so I'll forgive you for calling me that."

"Don't you raise your voice to me, missy!" He weaved to his feet and shook the remote. "And don't you pass judgment down your prissy little nose, either. I ain't drunk. I'm hungry because you ran off and forgot about cooking me dinner. Your job is here."

"Sorry, Daddy. I don't mean to be disrespectful." She bit her lip and pushed on. "But I'm moving to Dallas soon, like I've been telling you for months. You and the boys have to figure out how to do things for yourselves."

Jenny Porter's cousin was buying a condo and had offered to rent the extra bedroom to VJ, but it wasn't built yet and wouldn't be until September. Fall couldn't get here fast enough.

Daddy shook his head. "The Good Lord put women on this earth to cook, clean and have a man's babies. You can do that right here in Little Crooked Creek."

"I'm not staying here to enable you to drink yourself into the grave." Her dry eyes burned. "I'm tired. I'm sorry about Gus's truck and for forgetting your dinner. But I'm done here." She turned and took a step toward her room.

Daddy's fingernails bit into her upper arm as he spun her and yanked until her face was inches from his. "Don't you turn your back on me, girl." Alcohol-laced breath gushed from his mouth and turned her stomach with its stench. "You'll quit your job and forget about running off to live in that devil's den."

He emphasized each word with a shake that rattled her entire body. Tears sprang up as he squeezed the forming bruises. For the first time since her mother's death, she was genuinely afraid of her father and what he might do. Mama had always been the referee. Her lone defender and supporter in a household of males. VJ didn't have her mother's patience or her saintly ability to overlook Daddy's faults.

If she could escape to her room, she could grab some clothes and dash over to Pamela Sue's house.

"Thought you were pretty smart hiding all that money under the bed in your unmentionables box," he said.

It took her a second. "You were snooping in my room?"

She jerked her arm free as panic flitted up her back. Surely he hadn't looked inside the tampon box. Her brothers wouldn't have touched it with a ten-foot pole, and she'd been smugly certain it was the perfect hiding place.

"This is my house and so's everything in it. Needed me a new truck. Tackle got it in El Paso today." Her father smirked and nodded toward the rear of the house.

The room tilted as she looked out the back window. In the driveway of the detached garage sat a brand-new truck with paper plates.

"You stole my money? All of it?" Her lungs collapsed and breath whooshed out, strangling her.

"My house, so it's my money."

Her money was gone.

She could have opened an account at Sweetwater Bank where Aunt Mary worked after all. Then Daddy might have found out about the money but wouldn't have been able to touch it. Hindsight.

What was she going to do? Most of the money had been Mama's, slipped to VJ on the sly when her prognosis had turned bad. It would take at least a week to earn enough at Pearl's to buy a bus ticket. Never mind eating or any other basic necessities. Like rent.

Numb to the bone, she blurted, "My money, so it's my truck. Give me the keys." She held out a palm and tried to remember what Daddy had been like before Mama died, but that man was long gone.

He guffawed. "The keys are hid good, and it's got anti-theft, so don't even think about hot-wiring it. Now that you see how things are gonna go, getcher butt in the kitchen and fix me something to eat."

"No, Daddy. You've gone too far. Do it yourself."

A blow knocked her to the side, almost off her feet. Tiny needles of pain swept the surface of her cheek. She'd never seen the cuff coming.

"I'm tired of your mouth, girl. While you're in the kitchen, clean up a little, too, why don't ya? The boys left dishes in the sink." He fell into the recliner as if nothing had changed.

Her cheekbone began to throb, overshadowing the painful bruising on her arm by quadruple. She had to get away. Now was her chance.

She sprinted to her room, ignoring her father's bellowing. Her body felt heavy, almost too heavy to move. Once inside her room, she threw her weight against the door. After two tries, she wedged a chair under the knob good enough to stay upright, but not good enough to hold off a drunken rage if her father had a mind to follow her.

Numb, she stumbled around the room throwing things into a bag. Lots of things, as many as it would hold, because she wasn't coming back. She couldn't spend a couple of nights at Pamela Sue's house and wait until Daddy sobered up like usual.

She tore out of her waitress uniform, ripping a sleeve in the process, but it hardly mattered since she'd never wear it again. Her father had been right—she would quit her job, but not because he said so. Because she was leaving. Without glancing at them, she pulled on a T-shirt and jeans, blinking hard so the tears would stay inside.

Abandoning Mama's collection of romance novels almost killed her, but five hundred paperbacks lined the bookshelf. Maybe someday she could come back for them or ask Bobby Junior to ship them to her, but they'd likely be thrown out before she had the money for something that expensive. She couldn't leave behind *Embrace the Rogue* and slipped it into the overstuffed bag. It had been Mama's favorite.

A crash reverberated from the other side of the door.

Quickly, she yanked the curtain aside and threw up the window. With the heel of her hand, she popped off the screen and flung a leg over the windowsill, careful not to look back at the sanctuary she'd called hers since the day she was born. Her courage was only as strong as the sting across her face and when it faded, she feared reason would return.

She had nowhere to go, no money and a broken heart.

VJ started walking toward Main and got about halfway to Pearl's before the tears threatened again. Two deep, shuddery breaths, then another two, socked the tears away. She didn't have the luxury of grief. Other folks made a career out of drama and hardship, but none of that nonsense paid the bills. Only firm resolve got things done.

Twenty-six dollars in tips lay folded in her pocket, a windfall on most days. The crowd had been thick, thanks to lightning-quick word of mouth about the fancy foreign car in Pearl's parking lot.

Twenty-six dollars would barely cover a day's worth of meals at the cheapest fast-food restaurant, if by some miracle she could hitch a ride to Van Horn anonymously. Everyone for fifty miles knew her and would tattle to Daddy before breakfast. He'd come after her for sure if that happened.

The school she'd attended for twelve years loomed ahead, ghosts of those years dancing in the weak moonlight illuminating the playground. The next building on the block was the garage, and the sight of it almost changed her mind. Lenny and Billy would only miss her at meal time, but Bobby Junior and Tackle depended on her to pitch in around the shop.

Then again, Tackle had bought the truck for Daddy. Surely he'd asked where the money had come from. Daddy could have lied, but her brother's probable betrayal hollowed out her insides.

She passed MacIntyre's Drugstore. No more hanging out there with Pamela Sue at the lunch counter.

The end of things would have come soon enough once the condo in Dallas was built, but that was later. This was now, and it was harder than she'd expected.

Mercifully, there were no buildings on Main past the drugstore for a quarter of a mile. She finally reached the one and only motel in Little Crooked Creek and rehearsed some lines designed to talk her way into a free room.

A flash of yellow drove everything out of her mind.

Moonlight glinted off the *muy amarilla* Ferrari parked under the lone streetlight. Her pulse hammered in her throat. Kris was still here. Not driving toward Dallas and Kyla, to whom he wasn't engaged.

It was fate.

Maybe he'd give her a ride in exchange for directions. He'd defended her against her brothers. He would help her, she knew he would.

But then she'd have to explain what happened to her money and why the big hurry to get out of town. She ground her teeth. Kris didn't need to be burdened with her soap opera. Neither did she want to lie.

What if she made it seem like she was helping him? What if something was mysteriously wrong with the car?

Oh, it won't start? Let me look at it. Ah, here's the problem. No, I couldn't accept anything in return. Except maybe a ride to Dallas.

Stupid plan. *It's a Ferrari, dummy, not a Ford.* What if the engine was different than the domestic ones she knew?

There was only one way to find out and what else did she have? Not money. Not choices. Here was a golden opportunity to escape Little Crooked Creek forever and start over in Dallas. Her future roommate would surely take her in a little early, allowing VJ to crash on her couch. Once she got on her feet, she'd pay Beverly back, with interest.

Holy cow, the trip to Dallas was like nine hours. Nine hours in the company of Kristian Demetrious. Five hundred and forty minutes. More, if she could stretch it out.

She peered into the interior of the car, careful not to touch the glass in case the alarm was supersonic. The dash was devoid of blinking red lights, which hopefully meant no alarm at all. She fished a metal nail file from her purse and frowned. Not nearly long enough to pop the lock from the outside. Maybe she could peel the convertible top back a little and stick the file in that way.

On a hunch, she tried the handle. The door swung open easily. Unlocked. Only the rich.

Quickly, she released the deck lid and beelined it to the rear of the car. At least she knew the engine was in the back instead of for the front. But it was downright foreign, an engine for a space ship instead of for a car, but one mechanism was the same. She reached in and wiggled the ignition coil wire loose.

Now nothing would start this car without her help. She

closed the deck lid with a quiet click and retrieved her bag. Now, where to wait for Kris?

Wrinkling her nose at the space next to the Dumpster, she settled onto the concrete by the ice machine and tried to relax enough to fall asleep. Not likely with the knowledge this was probably the first of many nights sleeping on the street.

This plan had to work. Had to. Heavy, humid air pressed down on her in the dark silence. Crickets chirped in the field beside the motel, but the music did nothing to take her mind off the panic rolling around in her stomach.

What if Kris wasn't meant to be her knight in shining armor?

Three

Kris examined the engine of Kyla's car. Nothing seemed out of place, but how would he know if it was? The Ferrari had started fine every time he'd driven it. Why had it picked now, and here, to flake out?

Penance, for the delay. That's why. Kyla had undoubtedly cursed it, then texted him to bring it to her in Dallas, pretty please. He should have shipped the car instead of driving it. She wouldn't have cared either way, but no. He'd driven to allow time to obsess over the inflexible Hollywood machine. Muttering slurs on Italian engineers, he yanked his phone out of his back pocket.

"Car problems, chief?" VJ's honeyed drawl rang out from behind him.

He grinned, strangely elated, and twisted to greet her. Whatever he'd been about to say died in his throat.

With a succinct curse, he ran a thumb over the welt on her upper cheek. "What happened to your face?"

She flinched and turned away, but he hooked a finger under

her chin and guided her face into the sunlight. The injury wasn't bad enough to need medical attention but quick-burning rage flared up behind his rib cage nonetheless.

"Who did that to you?" he demanded. "One of your brothers?"

She better start naming names really fast before he tore this town apart, redneck by redneck, until someone else spilled. VJ was small, so small. How could anyone strike her with force hard enough to bruise?

"Nobody. I tripped." She shifted her gaze to the ground and pulled her chin from his fingers. "It was dark."

"Right."

The maids rearranged the furniture again, my darling, his mother used to say. Regardless of the continent, the excuses were equally as ineffective, as if he was both blind and stupid. This time, he wasn't a scared kid, hiding in his room, creating stories in his head where he controlled what the characters did and it all turned out happy in the end.

Fury curled his hands into fists. He'd never been able to help his mother, distancing himself further and further from a powerless situation. Distancing himself from the rage, the only defense he had against turning into his father.

His parents had been madly, passionately in love once upon a time and their relationship had degenerated into ugliness Kris refused to duplicate. So now he employed strict compensation mechanisms: avoiding confrontation, avoiding serious relationships and staying detached. Women got sick of it fast, which he accepted. Maybe even encouraged. Kyla had been no exception.

Now, it was too late to disengage and even he wasn't good enough to pretend indifference. VJ needed his help. Like it or not, his role in this had a second act.

"Really," she said, refusing to meet his eyes. "It was an accident. Can I help you with the car?"

"An accident." He crossed his arms and stared down at her. "What did you trip over?"

"Uh, the couch."

He nodded to the ugly blotch on her arm, which wrapped around her biceps in the shape of a hand, with half-moon cuts at the top of the purple fingers. "Did the couch have hands with fingernails?"

Her face crumpled, and he spit out a curse. Panicked, he enfolded her into his arms, determined to do something, anything to help.

Then he remembered VJ barely knew him. She'd smack him with her bag for being so familiar.

But she didn't. Instead she snuggled into his chest, sobbing. Her head fit into the hollow of his breastbone as if it had been shaped for her, and VJ's slight frame kick-started a fiercely possessive, protective instinct. He tightened his arms and inhaled the coconut scent of her warm cinnamon-colored hair.

After a minute, the bawling stopped. She wiggled away and took a deep breath. Her face was mottled and wet. She swiped at it with the hem of her giant T-shirt, this one with a cracked emblem for Tres Hombres Automotive Distributing, and looked up. "I'm sorry. I don't know where that came from."

"I do," he said grimly. "You've had a rough night, which wasn't helped by sleeping outside. Let me take you somewhere, as long as it's not back to whoever hit you."

"I didn't sleep outside," she protested. "I'm on my way to work. That's the only reason I'm out this early."

"You have a concrete-patterned print down the side of your face. The other side," he clarified as she tentatively touched the bruises. She obviously had no clue how much practice he had in seeing through a woman's lies. Normally, he'd be infuriated with her attempt at deception, but instead, the urge to take action, to fix things for her, unfolded.

"Get in the car." He swore, colorfully, but mindful enough of the offensive content to do it in Greek. "I forgot. Something's wrong with the car. Can you give me the number to your garage?"

Out of nowhere, she burst into tears again.

He rubbed her shoulder and said the first thing that came to mind, "I'm sorry. That wasn't a dig at your mechanical skills. I'd love it if you'd look at my car. Please."

"Don't apologize," she grumbled, sniffling. "That only makes it worse."

"Um, this seems to be the sole situation where it's wrong for a guy to apologize. Can you possibly explain what wouldn't be wrong to say?"

Without a word, she skirted him and leaned into the engine bay. With a couple of skillful twists, she reattached a loose wire he hadn't noticed and she mumbled, "I disconnected it last night. Try it now."

Speechless, he slid into the driver's seat and pushed the start button. With a meaty roar, the engine sprang to life. The RPM needle flicked back and forth with each nudge of the accelerator.

He vaulted out of the seat and rounded the back end before she fled.

"*Now* get in the car."

"I can't." Misery pulled at her expression. "This is all wrong. I'm sorry. I had a stupid plan to trade fixing your car for a ride, but it wouldn't have needed fixing if I hadn't sabotaged it. Then you had to be all nice and wonderful and understanding about my…" She waved a flustered hand at her bruises. "Problems. I'm a terrible person, and I can't take advantage of you."

Kris bit his lip so the bubble of laughter wouldn't burst out. "Let me get this straight. You can't accept a ride because you don't want to take advantage of me."

"Your hospitality," she amended quickly. "I don't want to take advantage of your hospitality. Or take advantage in any other way. Not that you're repulsive or anything. I mean, I would take advantage if I had the opportunity. You're totally hot." She hissed out a little moan, and he yearned to hear it again. "That didn't come out right. Can I crawl in a hole now?"

"No." He crossed his arms and leaned a hip on the side panel. Was it terrible to be charmed by how negotiating a simple ride tore her up? "It's too late. You've already admitted you can't be trusted with my virtue. Whatever will I do?"

She glared at him but then her expression wavered. "I do have a reputation in the greater Little Crooked Creek area. Mothers have been known to lock up their sons when they see me coming."

Her humor and winsome self-deprecation was back, loosening the bands around his lungs. "Well, my mother is six thousand miles away so I guess I'll have to risk it. Let's try this. I'll forgive you for sabotaging the car if you'll forgive me for not believing you tripped." Smoothly, he captured her hand and led her to the passenger side. He opened the door. "Shall we?"

She didn't climb in. Staring at their joined hands, she said, "Yesterday morning you were blissfully unaware I existed. Why do you want to get mixed up in this?"

A fair question, but the wrong one. His involvement had begun the moment she pulled off the highway and ensnared him, forcing him into the action.

A better question was how long he'd stay involved.

"Is someone going to come after me with a shotgun?"

"I doubt it." She snorted out a laugh. "Bobby Junior and Tackle might consider it, but they're too busy. The cretins... sorry. My other brothers would have to notice I was gone first."

"What about your father?"

Shadows sprang into her eyes and her grip tightened. He had his name.

"I honestly can't say what Daddy would do. That's the best reason of all for you to forget about me and drive away as fast as you can."

"You've obviously mistaken me for someone without a conscience. I couldn't sleep at night if I did that. Get in the car, VJ."

"How can you be real?" She studied his face, the same as she had last night, as if looking for the answers to her deepest questions. "It's like I dreamed up the perfect man and poof, here you are."

It should be a crime to be that naive. He dropped her hand. "I'm far from perfect. If you get in the car, you'll doubtlessly find out I'm not always a fun date. Don't turn me into some altruistic saint because I'm offering you a ride."

She hesitated, then nodded once. "Okay. I'll take the ride, but I'm allowed to worship you in secret or no deal."

The bruising on her face stood out in sharp relief against her fragile skin yet when the corners of her mouth flipped up in a small smile, he couldn't help but smile, too. "How could I turn that down?"

He helped her into the passenger seat and slammed the door. She slumped against the leather, and even through the tinted glass, she radiated an aura that pinged around inside him, seeking a place to land.

Dangerous, that's what she was. When was the last time he'd willingly tossed away his stay-detached rule?

Once settled behind the wheel, he slipped on his sunglasses and said, "I've already checked out, so where would you like me to take you? Your girlfriend's house, the one from last night?"

She stared out the window, pointedly not looking at him. "I'm afraid it's a little more complicated than that."

VJ flat-handed sunglasses against her face and debated how to explain she was going to Dallas without coming across as a freeloader, or worse, a stalker.

Her only plan had died the second Kris held her and let her cry on his fifty-dollar T-shirt. How was she going to convince him to let her tag along when she had nothing to give him in return? Well, nothing other than an annoying set of calf eyes, cowardice disguised as automotive expertise and twenty-six dollars, twenty of which Kris had tipped her in the first place.

"Complicated is my specialty," he commented mildly and

drove to the motel lot exit. His graceful fingers draped over the wheel casually, as if he was so in tune with the car, it anticipated his bidding instead of relying on mere mechanical direction. "Right or left?"

She inhaled sharply and the scent of new car and fresh leather hit her like a freight train. A fitting combination for a new start.

Might as well go for broke.

"Left and then another right at the Feed and Seed. Go about five hundred miles and then another right. That'll put me pretty close to where I want to go."

"Ah." He nodded sagely and slapped a palm to his chest, Pledge of Allegiance style. "A woman after my own heart. You're running away. Why didn't you say so?"

Because running away sounded so juvenile, especially out of his mouth.

"Am I that transparent?"

"Yeah." That slow, sexy smile spread across his face. "Don't worry, I like it."

"Hmmpf. I'd rather be a woman of mystery and secrets."

"No, you wouldn't." His gaze shifted to the highway and stayed there. "You just think you would. Secretive women are irritating."

He meant someone specific. Her curiosity spiked, but the firm set of his mouth said *don't ask*. So she bit her tongue and mirrored his feigned fascination with the road stretched ahead through the windshield. Little Crooked Creek fell away at a rapid pace. Good riddance.

After a while, she might miss someone or something other than Pamela Sue, Bobby Junior and Tackle. Mama's grave. Pearl probably. The sunset against a mountain backdrop.

For now, the call of adventure and a new life drowned out whispers of the past.

Kris nodded toward the floorboard, where a broken-in black

leather bag was wedged under the dash. "Find my MP3 player and pick out some music. It's a long drive to Dallas."

"You're going to take me?" She'd been studiously avoiding the subject, hoping to segue back into it later. Like after it was too late to turn around.

"You're in the car, and I'm driving to Dallas. Seems like that's going to be the end result."

Relief lessened the weight on her shoulders. Nine hours in the company of Kris. Nine hours in an amazing car with her Greek god in shining armor. It wasn't nearly long enough, but far more than she deserved. "You aren't mad?"

With a half laugh, he said, "About what? Didn't we go through this already?"

Sinking low in the seat, she tried to make herself as small as possible. "Because I wasn't honest with you. I practically forced you into taking on an unwanted passenger."

After a beat of silence, he tapped the steering wheel in a staccato rhythm. "I drink coffee black, I refuse to screw the lid on the toothpaste when I'll have to take it back off again, and no one—*no one*—can force me to do something I don't want to do." A wealth of pain and untold history underpinned the sentiments, darkening his tone. She hated being responsible for bringing back bad memories. "Now you know the three most important things about me. Next time, ask instead of making assumptions."

Her fantasy gained dimensions and layers. And she craved more depth, more knowledge, more understanding of this extraordinary person in the next seat.

"Oh, no. You busted my deal all to pieces. I can't worship someone who doesn't screw the lid back on the toothpaste." She shook her head and tsked. "That's wrong. What if it gets lost?"

His million-dollar smile burst into place, and she intended to keep it there. It was the one repayment she could give him. Of course, it was a win-win in her book.

"Lost? I throw it away. Waste of plastic."

"Figures."

The craving intensified. What kind of music did he listen to? She hooked the bag and pulled it into her lap, then rifled through it, absorbing, touching. These were Kris's personal belongings. A green toothbrush. A stick of deodorant. A brush with a black stretchy band twisted around the handle. She'd never seen him with his hair tied back and hoped she never did. His loose, shoulder-length style was nothing short of mouthwatering.

"Having trouble finding it?" he asked a touch sarcastically, as if he knew she was a heartbeat from inhaling the citrusy scent of his deodorant.

"I confess. I'm actually a reporter for a celebrity magazine doing an expose on independent film directors. And their luggage." She was rambling. Spitting out whatever came to her mind because her fingers had closed around a small, square box with a hinged lid that every woman on the planet could identify. Blindfolded. "You caught me."

She dropped the ring box, but her hand still stung. Why did an engagement ring in the bag of a man she'd just met put a lump in her throat? So he wasn't engaged to Kyla yet, but obviously it was only a matter of time. Better all the way around to accept that he was completely unavailable. Much, much better. Then she could make a clean break. Wipe him from her mind once he left her in Dallas.

He glanced at her over the top of his sunglasses. "What's wrong?"

"Nothing's wrong." She yanked the only electronic device from the bottom of the bag and waved it, hoping it wasn't a newfangled garage-door opener. "Got it. Let's see what we have here. How do I turn it on?"

"You've never used an MP3 player?" Amusement colored his question. "Touch the screen to wake it up."

"It's asleep?" Fascinated, she flipped the gizmo over and right-side up again. "Does it snore and hog all the covers, too?"

His rich laughter washed over her and she wallowed in it. He reached over, slid a fingertip across the device and colors illuminated the screen. Colors she barely registered because his arm pressed against her shoulder, sparking like a firecracker in a Coke bottle as he deftly tapped the MP3 player.

The brush of body parts was totally innocent but the pang low in her belly unleashed a flood of longing more akin to original sin.

"There's the song list," he offered nonchalantly. "Pick one."

She glanced down at the screen, contracting her diaphragm until she could speak again. "I don't know any of these artists." Was that her voice? She cleared her throat and prayed it eliminated the huskiness. "Any Kenny Chesney or Miranda Lambert?"

Nope, still croaking like a late-night ad for a 1-900 number.

"There's no country music on this and there's not going to be." He took the player from her and stuck it in the holder on the dash. Two taps later, a stringed instrument wailed through the speakers, the melody so instantly heartbreaking, it stole her breath. She'd never imagined such passion could be poured into music.

"The musician is Johannes Linstead," he said. "Do you like it?"

"It's so beautiful, it hurts my chest. Is it weird that it makes me feel like weeping?"

With two fingers, he slid off his sunglasses and impaled her with stormy, liquid eyes, searching her face with an immeasurable intensity. "The music makes me feel like that, too."

She couldn't break their locked gazes. Didn't want to. A whole other world lived inside his eyes, a world she wanted to fall into.

"It'll be our secret," he whispered and snapped his attention back to the road as he obscured his eyes with the sunglasses again.

Her heart beat so fast, she was shocked it wasn't audible.

She stared at his profile. What had just happened? It had been A Charged Moment. Thrilling—for her, at least. But what did it mean?

She might be from Nowheresville but she could follow instructions. "Instead of assuming again, I'm going to ask. Why does it seem like you're flirting with me sometimes?"

"I am."

"Why?" Additional words, phrases, ideas escaped her. In fact, it had been a surprise her tongue worked at all.

"Why not?" He lifted a shoulder. "I like you. You're fun. Beautiful."

He thought she was beautiful? The jumpy crickets stampeded through her stomach.

Stuff like this didn't happen to her. Oh, she'd had her share of boyfriends—small-town, small-minded boys who wouldn't know romance if it bit them in their unimaginative butts.

The difference between them and this enthralling, charming man beside her was the difference between Ford and Ferrari.

But he wasn't finished. "What does it hurt? It's harmless and has zero calories. Besides, you're flirting back."

Harmless. Nothing more than sport for the beautiful people. Yes, Kristian Demetrious was exactly like his car. Smooth, exotic and his engine was equally unfathomable.

The crickets died a quick death. "Of course I'm flirting back. You're driving. I'd hate to be dumped on the side of the road."

He paused for a beat and didn't laugh. "Women don't flirt with me. They slip me room keys and follow me into the bathroom. Flirting with you is the polar opposite of that. I enjoy it. There aren't any expectations. It's safe."

Now she was safe. How appealing.

She needed to throw it in reverse, distance herself, or eventually he'd drive right over her heart, flattening it like an unfortunate armadillo too transfixed by the bright lights of the freeway to see the splat coming. "Tell me about Kyla. Where did you meet her?"

He glowered, tightening the lines of his cheeks and mouth, and the expression looked wrong on him. "I don't want to talk about Kyla."

The reference to his glamorous soon-to-be fiancée was like a shock of icy water. The atmosphere in the car cooled and grew icicles. Fantastic. Exactly as she'd intended. Now she wasn't thinking about that seething, charged moment. Or the sparkling weight of his arm against hers.

"Well, I don't want to talk about Kyla, either. Tell me about your next movie." That should be an innocuous enough subject, and she'd been dying to revisit it after seeing his entire demeanor transform upon mentioning it at Pearl's.

"I'd rather not talk for a while."

She flinched at the bite in his tone. "Sure. No problem."

The less they talked, the better, because then his beyond-sexy accent wouldn't skim down her spine and take up residence inside, heating every pore of her skin as if she'd crawled into the sun.

They barely knew each other. They were strangers soon to part ways and only thrown together because she lacked the fortitude to leave Little Crooked Creek on her own. What else could they possibly be to each other?

Road signs for Van Horn flashed by twice before Kris sighed. "Sorry. I can be a jerk."

She waved dismissively. "Don't apologize for not wanting me to pry into your life. I'm sure people do that all the time, and you'd like to keep some things private."

"That's true, but it's not the reason I'm a jerk. It's complicated."

"Complicated is my specialty."

He grinned and shot her another of those enigmatic glances over the top of his sunglasses. "Have I mentioned how much I like you?"

"Yes, but you should definitely tell me again." Maybe she was getting better at the sport of flirting. The trick was not to let on how that kind of statement thrummed straight to the place between her thighs.

He bit his lip, contemplating. She had to avert her eyes from the sight of his white teeth sinking into flesh.

"The problem is," he said, "Kyla's starring in my next film, *Visions of Black*. I guess I'm kind of touchy about it because of the unconventional demands around the financing. Without the right backing, the project's dead. The downside of not being affiliated with a studio."

"Contract negotiations are shaky. I get it. Is it worth whatever your investor is demanding?"

He froze, and her hand flew to his arm before she'd realized it. She wanted to comfort him but had no idea why.

She did know one thing—Kris wasn't and never would be a stranger. There was something between them. A recognition. A mystical draw she couldn't ignore or pretend to have imagined.

"Is it worth it?" He exhaled and nodded slowly. "To have a chance to direct this film, which will solidify my career and put me on the A-list? Yes, it is. I've been busting my back for years to get this shot."

The raw longing and aspiration carved into his expression hit her in a wave way hotter than the music. She swallowed, hard. Her fantasy imploded and shrank down to one crystalline shard of desire—that he'd look at her like that. She tucked it away before it grew too sharp.

"That's a lot of mileage for one film." No doubt he'd be successful, as soon as his investor was happy. "Out of curiosity, what is he asking you to do?"

A tiny muscle in his forehead jumped. "Announce that Kyla and I are engaged."

Four

Kris could have gone at least another hundred miles without mentioning that. Next he'd be telling VJ it was all a publicity stunt, one he strongly suspected Kyla had talked Abrams into as a method to either push her way into Kris's bed again or drive him insane. Maybe both. Kris assumed she'd split with Guy Hansen and was on the hunt for another warm, male body, but, knowing Kyla, she could have other ulterior motives. Until he figured out her agenda, it was better to stay off the subject.

Regardless of who had devised the fake engagement, he recognized the value of Kyla's attachment to *Visions* and had to suck it up. Without her in the starring role and without the publicity, Abrams would pull out. Without Abrams's experience making blockbusters, Kris's career couldn't move to the next level. Period.

"Oh." As if fascinated, VJ stared out the window at the landscape dotted with lumpy cactus and heat shimmers, which she'd doubtlessly seen a million times.

VJ was at a loss for words. That was unfortunate, but the less said about Kyla and engagements, the better.

"Hungry?" he asked.

She shook her head. "No. Thanks."

"Is that your wallet talking or your stomach?" He glanced at her, certain it was the former. He'd never met someone so determined not to accept nice gestures.

Her forehead scrunched. "Are you practicing your ESP?"

"Yeah." He turned back to the road. "For my next trick, I'm going to levitate."

The joke went over like his last film, with zero reaction and a lot of white knuckles. Where had all the fun and flirting gone? From the moment VJ appeared out of a swirl of dust, the awful temper he'd been in since leaving L.A. had fled and he didn't want it to come back.

After a few minutes of silence so loud his eardrums hurt, she said, "So. Kyla's a lucky woman. I'm sure you'll be really happy together. How are you going to propose to her? Put the ring in a champagne glass?" Her tone was bright and saccharine-fake.

Kyla had her spooked. Inexplicably, he opened his mouth to tell her that he and Kyla had split up a while ago. But, he closed it. He valued his relationship with Jack Abrams and hoped to partner on many more films with the man. VJ probably wouldn't tell but accidents happened and his job was to drive positive press. Not put the smile back on the face of his desert mirage. "I haven't thought about it. I'll probably give her the ring and ask."

VJ gaped. "You can't do that. It's a *proposal,* not asking her to dinner at a dress-up place. She's dreamed of it her entire life. It has to be perfect. Something she can tell your kids and grandkids over and over because it's so outrageously romantic. You have to do better."

"Are you kidding? You've never met Kyla, I realize. But come on." He downshifted to go around a slow-moving cattle truck.

She flipped a spiral of cinnamon hair over her shoulder. "You don't think she's dreamed about her one and only proposal her whole life?"

One and only? Huge disparity in world views there. Kyla had already been married once to an Australian actor, a fact VJ's celebrity magazines had clearly omitted. Before he could mention it, he suddenly envisioned stepping on puppies. Treading lightly might be a better idea than squashing her idealism. "Have you?"

"Of course! Like a million times."

Her face took on the glow he'd been missing and his gut clenched. His reaction to her was so pure and elemental, with no expectations. Which was why he enjoyed it—no danger of it going anywhere. So she was the romantic sort, envisioning her new last name and assigning genders to her unborn children. Delusions which led to heartbreak when the passion faded. Figured.

While nothing about relationships made for his favorite topic of discussion, if he got to bask in VJ's fresh smile, he could buck up. "Tell me."

"About my dream proposal?"

"You've imagined it a million times. Should be easy."

Leather squealed as she sank down into the seat. If he didn't know better, he'd think she was trying to disappear into it. "You'll think it's stupid."

"No, I won't." His curiosity flared. Ever since he'd mentioned the engagement stunt, she'd withdrawn. He wanted her in-your-face honesty back. "I want to know. Everything about you interests me."

She shot him a sidelong glance behind her sunglasses. "You're not allowed to laugh, okay?"

"No chance."

She took a deep breath. "I want to get my engagement ring as a present in a huge box, so I don't guess what's in it. When I open it, the little box will be inside. Then I'd realize."

That was the proposal she'd imagined a million times? "Sounds very nice."

And boring. A hundred scenarios sprang to mind, all of which eclipsed that in terms of romantic proposals. In seconds, the entire scene unfolded in his head and he started dropping in thematic elements like roses and soft lighting. Maybe that was the key to the theme for *Visions of Black*—lighting.

"Beats the one I got."

She'd done it again. Pulled him out from behind the lens with an intriguing statement. "Someone proposed to you?"

"Walt Phillips." Her lip curled. "It wasn't really a proposal. More of a statement. Like it was foregone we'd get married because we'd been dating since high school. How long have you and Kyla been together?"

Back to that again. "I don't know." He tapped the steering wheel with restless fingers. "I don't pay attention to stuff like that."

"You don't celebrate anniversaries?"

"There's more than one?"

"Anniversary of your first date, anniversary of your first kiss. The first time you made love, the first time you…" She trailed off as he raised an eyebrow. "What?"

Nobody kept track of those milestones. "Nothing. Are you sure you don't want breakfast?"

"Are you sure you want to marry someone you aren't in love with?"

The car veered toward the center line and he overcorrected, shooting the passenger-side tires past the white line of the shoulder, jouncing them both until he got the wheel under control. Precisely the reason he stayed behind the camera—so he couldn't be caught off guard. "Seems like you're the one practicing ESP. What makes you think I'm not in love with Kyla?"

"Please." She snorted. "I don't need ESP to know you're not in love with her. Even if you are from Hollywood, you wouldn't be flirting with me if you were. You'd remember the first time you kissed her. The first time you held her all night. You wouldn't be able to stand being separated from her, yet this car's got a V-8 and you're barely driving the speed limit. Doesn't take a rocket scientist to do the math."

He bit back a nervous laugh. He'd been angling to get her smart mouth back. Just not with that much punch. "Would you like to drive since I'm doing such a poor job?"

"Deflection. Yet another obvious factor. You don't even like to talk about Kyla."

While he might prefer to stay behind the camera, VJ never let him retreat. Women usually gave up trying to engage him after several unsuccessful rounds. VJ didn't have to try—she was naturally engaging. With renewed respect, he eyed her. "Maybe because my relationship with her is private."

"Or because you don't have much of a relationship. Marriage is forever. You should only marry someone you're desperately in love with. Someone you can't live without."

Actually, he'd be ecstatic to be desperately in *like* with Kyla. They were going to be spending a lot of time together, after all, filming the movie and doing public appearances. At some point, he should probably tell Kyla he didn't hold the affair with Guy against her. He still stewed about it occasionally, but only because Hansen was an idiot.

"That's not love, that's passion. Which is all hormones anyway and I can't think of a worse reason to marry someone. Passion dies."

And when it died, it ruined everything.

"Are you looped?" she asked. "Love and passion are tied together and the *only* reason to marry someone. Clearly, your education is lacking in the romance department."

She stroked his arm and it wasn't accidental. His eyes unfocused as heat radiated from the contact of her fingers. His groin tightened. Again.

Not only did VJ keep him engaged, she poked at something

elemental inside. In the past, attraction had led to satisfaction, not this raw yearning for…more.

"Oh, I see," he said when his mouth stopped being too dry to talk. "You're an expert on romance."

"I am, actually." She seemed pleased with his insight. "We have hours to kill until we reach Dallas. I'll be happy to give you some instruction."

Romance instruction at the hands of Victoria Jane. The idea should have been hilarious. It wasn't. "How did you get to be an expert on romance? Walt Phillips?"

"As if. Romance novels."

"Books?"

"Books are a perfectly legitimate method for learning. That is why they use textbooks in school."

Now he had that image stuck in his head. VJ in a classroom wearing a school uniform and clutching a tattered paperback with a half-naked Viking on the cover. Naturally, that progressed to imagining VJ half-naked. The camera would love the color of her skin and capture the perfect lines of her body with a reverence he'd seldom experienced behind the lens.

"Go for it, then," he said. "I can't wait to learn about romance according to VJ."

"Well." She sat up in the seat, instantly animated. "Romance has stages. A progression. You can't dive right into bed."

Really. Who says? VJ might need an education of her own.

With that thought, he forgot about the camera. This was his scene, and he'd maim anyone who tried to take him out of it. He was having fun. What was the harm in playing along? "Stage one. No diving into bed. Got it."

She shook her head. "That's not stage one. Be quiet and listen. The goal isn't to learn the stages. It's to understand them. Believe them. Recognize them as truth. So then it'll be obvious you're not in love with Kyla."

His eyebrows flew up. "That's the goal?"

Fantastic. He was already ahead. Never once had he mistaken what he felt for Kyla as love. Her talents were legendary and he appreciated them—both on the screen and between the sheets. But then, they'd drifted apart so long ago, he barely even remembered the latter. Maybe it hadn't been all that spectacular.

"Yeah," she said. "When we're through with all the stages, you'll admit you're not in love with Kyla."

VJ's wholesomeness pricked at his sense of honor. How fair was it to play this game when he had no illusions about his relationship with Kyla?

Love and marriage had little to do with each other and neither had anything to do with him. This desert mirage had about a point zero-zero-one percent chance of convincing him differently.

"So, what if I admitted that right now?"

VJ off took her sunglasses and stared at him openly. "Clearly you didn't understand the rules. I'm supposed to go through the stages and *then* you admit it. Why in the world would you marry Kyla if you're not in love with her?"

"I never said I was marrying her. I said I was announcing our engagement. Let's not get ahead of ourselves."

"Oh, pardon me for assuming an engagement leads to a wedding." She made a disgusted little noise. "That's your problem in a nutshell. You think these things are all separate and they're not. You need romance instruction worse than anyone I've ever met."

He couldn't stop the grin. "Then educate me."

"I'm not sure it'll help. You might be too far gone." She licked her lips and faced forward. "Are you going to marry her or not?"

"It's…" *Complicated.* When had that become the norm for his life? "Look, I know I said to ask instead of assuming, but this is the sole exception. I'm announcing our engagement, and she's well aware that I'm not in love with her. Leave it at that, okay?"

"Okay." She drawled out the syllables, overloading them with meaning.

Great. She'd taken him at his word and created all sorts of assumptions. Well, if he hadn't wanted that, he should have kept his mouth shut. But he hadn't. She deserved as much honesty as he could give her, and now it was time to drop it.

"So, what's stage one?"

For a beat, she didn't respond, like she'd changed her mind about educating him.

"Attraction." Her legs slid together and crossed, slowly, snagging his attention from the road. "A sense of awareness that wasn't there a minute ago. Maybe you've known each other for years and one day, something happens. Pop! You notice how nice her eyes are or how sexy she looks in that shirt. Maybe you're strangers, but eyes meet across a smoky room at a party and it's a lightning bolt to the spine."

Or an orange pickup pulls off the road and out spills a provocative sunflower with coconut-scented hair. "Hormones. Like I said."

"If you want to be clinical." She frowned and the shadow of a road sign threw her into murkiness, then rushed away. "Reality is much more complex. Why do your hormones react to this woman and not that woman? For example."

Interesting point. She wasn't spouting text from the pages of a bodice-ripper. Some analysis had gone into this. "Maybe that woman is a pain in the butt."

"We're still in the attraction stage. You wouldn't know anything about the woman's personality in a relationship at this point. That's the next stage. Once you recognize some primal, fundamental reaction to her, then comes stage two."

"Which is?"

"Attention."

Subtly, she shifted closer, and below his sleeve, a firm breast brushed his biceps. A breast only covered by a thin shirt and definitely not encased in a bra.

"You pay attention to her," she said. "Not like giving her lame flowers from Piggly Wiggly. But paying attention to stuff she likes. Music. Books she's read. You notice little variations in the color of her skin. You give her a nickname. Remember details, like the things she says." Her breast nudged his arm muscle with little licks of heat. "Stage one and two. You're hot for her, and you pay attention."

Hot. Yeah. His lungs were on fire with the effort it took not to gulp oxygen. He was swamped in the sensation of a rough cotton T-shirt against his arm, the only barrier between his skin and hers, and it was a miracle the zipper on his jeans hadn't busted a few teeth.

"How many stages are there?" he asked, his voice involuntarily husky.

"Six," she said and her voice had dipped a couple of notches, too, causing her answer to sound like *sex.* Or maybe that was due to his hormone-laced senses. "Romance isn't simple."

What was simple? Not this blazing stage one between them, which had to be leaving scorch marks on her, too, as perceptive as she was. Besides, she might have been serious enough with a guy to be talking marriage, but that didn't make her experienced.

Then there was the engagement, which had to be real to the public in order to work. He wasn't sure of Kyla's angle yet, but if the engagement was designed to throw them back together like he suspected, she'd perceive VJ as competition. No one deserved to be in those crosshairs.

He sighed. The reasons for nipping this thing with VJ in the bud were legion.

Because this situation didn't suck enough, he'd just transformed VJ into ripe, delicious, forbidden fruit. Cursing, he yanked on the wheel and swerved to avoid a dead armadillo.

Half-blind, he struggled to keep his attention on the road and off VJ.

Stop. Detach. Immediately.

He hated to step on any of her puppies, let alone her fanciful ideas about romance. Unfortunately, it might be the only solution capable of getting his mind out of the gutter.

"This is all fascinating. But I don't believe in fairy tales."

"Who said anything about fairy tales?" VJ countered and wiped damp palms on her jeans stealthily, so Kris remained unaware of how nerves were kicking her butt. "Romance instruction" had grown from a ploy to prove he wasn't in love with Kyla, which he'd readily admitted, into a death match of wills over something far worse. He didn't believe in romance. And she was going to change his mind.

"Romance novels are not fairy tales. I'm talking about real life."

"Whose real life? Yours?"

"Sure. One day." She shrugged. "That's why I said no to the proposal. Walt Phillips and romance don't even speak the same language. It might as well be Greek."

She winced. Freudian slip. Or something. This conversation was going to kill her one way or another.

With a hint of a smile, Kris peeked over the rim of his sunglasses and said something foreign and sexy. "I'll translate that for you some other time."

Her breast still tingled where it had touched his arm and that voice did nothing but heighten it. What was she doing? Was this really about changing his views toward romance or a thinly veiled excuse to get close to him now that she knew his relationship with Kyla was not what it seemed?

The car passed the Van Horn city limit. "Okay, now I'm hungry," she said, even though she wasn't. She needed time to regroup. "We can stop here for breakfast."

Kris pulled into a crowded fast-food place without comment.

He parked the Ferrari among rusted flatbeds, semis and beat-up four-doors, then sped around to her side to help her out of the low seat. Always a gentleman, and jumping jellybeans was that ever attractive. She took his hand, and the contact sparked. "Would you mind ordering? I want to freshen up."

He nodded and followed her inside, where she fled to the filthy bathroom. The crust on the sink lost her attention when she caught sight of the dark welt under her eye. No wonder he'd freaked. She looked horrific.

Kris didn't believe in fairy tales because his entire life already was one. She had to believe in them. Otherwise, how could she possibly hold out hope that life might be different than the tragedy she'd escaped?

They ate breakfast in silence, or rather, he ate and she picked at her sausage. The longer they didn't talk, the tighter the tension stretched, and it wasn't helped by the fact that watching him do anything with his hands set off a throb low in her belly.

"Can I borrow your phone?" she asked when he stood to collect trash from the table.

"Sure. It's in the car."

"Do you mind giving me some privacy?" She jerked her head in the direction of the Ferrari. "I have to let someone know I'm okay. I'll just be a minute."

Without a word, he slid his gorgeous body back into the molded chair with grace, which made *not* imagining those long, golden limbs wrapped around hers impossible.

"Let me know when it's safe," he said.

She bit back a snort. "You haven't figured it out yet? You'll never be safe from me." Then she spun on a toe and flounced to the car, heart pounding in her throat as she elbowed through the throng of testosterone checking out Kris's Ferrari.

She should be committed. Romance instruction. Where did she come up with these ideas? The best plan was to focus on getting to Dallas and then, the rest of her life. Kris had no place in the middle of that, even without the nebulous engagement. He was from Hollywood. She wasn't.

His phone lay in the hollow between their seats. *The* seats.

Nothing in the car belonged to her except her bag. She had to remember that.

After three fumbles with the confusing little pictures crowding the screen of Kris's phone, she figured out how to play a fishing game, use the timer and search for a restaurant on Santa Monica Boulevard. Then she found the section that looked like numbers to dial an honest phone call. Rich people.

She shook her head as Pamela Sue said hello on her end.

"It's me."

"VJ. Thank God." Pamela Sue heaved out a long sigh. "Your daddy's been here twice, saying you've been gone since last night."

The hot leather burned into her thighs as she shifted to find a more comfortable spot. "I'm okay. I'm on my way to Dallas."

"Dallas? How'd you get to the bus station? No one's been near Van Horn—"

"I'm with Kris."

"*Kris?* Kristian Demetrious? That Kris? Wait. Are you with Kris, or *with* Kris? Hold on, let me sit down." Bedsprings squeaked in the background. "In case it's better than I'm imagining."

"Don't be ridiculous," VJ hissed and darted a glance through the tinted window to make sure that Kris wasn't strolling across the concrete toward the car. "It's not like that. He's surrounded by beautiful women all the time. He doesn't have to pick up waitresses along the road."

"Hey, you were Miss Little Crooked Creek a couple of times. You're every bit as beautiful as they are," Pamela Sue insisted. "Don't sell yourself short."

She smiled a little at the blind loyalty. Pamela Sue hadn't seen her face and therefore didn't realize VJ resembled a raccoon. "I love you, even when you're lying."

"Well, I hate you. A lot. How dare you ride off into the sunset with a sexy guy in a sexy car? I'll never forgive you unless you have a smoking hot affair and spill every last detail."

"Deal." She sobered. "Don't tell anyone, okay? It's a secret. The media, you know."

She didn't think Daddy would come after her all the way to Dallas, but it couldn't hurt to take precautions.

"Oh, yeah. I do know. The media chases me around all the time." Pamela Sue cleared her throat. "What happened, VJ? I know you didn't hop on the first set of testicles to wheel through town. This isn't like you."

"Nothing happened. It was time." She injected a note of levity. "I ran into Kris this morning, and he offered me a ride. How could I refuse? Long way to Dallas. Lots of opportunity to help him forget about those beautiful women he used to know."

Pamela Sue laughed and a tear slipped down VJ's cheek. They'd never lied to each other. Never. But neither would she let anyone think of her as a victim, besides Kris, but only because it was too late. Pamela Sue might run straight to Bobby Junior or Tackle, tattling about how VJ had been hit. There was a part of her that wondered if they'd let Daddy slide or take his side out of loyalty. If she lost that battle, what then? She'd rather take the real rescue from her knight in a shining Ferrari.

"You gonna stay with Jenny Porter's cousin?" Pamela Sue asked.

"Yeah." Beverly Porter wouldn't mind if VJ asked to stay on her couch until the condo was finished. The worst thing that could happen is she'd have to pay rent early. Or at least that's what she kept telling herself.

"Call me when you get to Dallas. Be careful."

"Yes, ma'am. No talking to strangers."

"I meant buy a box of condoms."

A diluted laugh slipped out and was ragged enough to communicate to her best friend what she couldn't say aloud. "Good bye, Pamela Sue."

She hung up—or at least she thought she did after punching random pictures on the slick screen—and went to retrieve her Greek god.

When she rushed back into the main dining room, Kris was staring at the flaking wall, chiseled lips pursed and troubled, fingers drumming the table.

"Ready?" he said, and unfolded his frame from the chair-table combination bolted to the floor.

Something was off in his rigid stance. An invisible layer drenched with stress. "What's wrong?"

"I'm ready to go. After you." His granite expression didn't waver, reminding her of inaccessible Kristian Demetrious from the diner when he'd faced down her brothers.

This time, that look was directed at her. Their interaction was a lot of things, most of it too difficult to pin down, but she couldn't stand for *strained* to be on the list. The foreign engine in his mind had begun to reveal its secrets, and she wanted to take it apart to see what made it tick.

She let it drop until they'd both slid into their seats and he hit the button to start the engine. Over the hefty roar, she said, "If you want to talk, I'd be happy to listen."

"I said there's nothing wrong."

"No," she said. "You said you were ready to go, as if to imply you were impatiently waiting for me. You're restless, not impatient."

His expression relaxed. "I've got a lot of things on my mind."

"Of course you do." Impulsively, she threaded his golden fingers through hers. After a not-so-quick squeeze, she let go. "Being responsible for an entire movie must be a heavy burden."

His forehead scrunched. "It is. Most people don't get that. But I don't think of it that way."

"How do you think about it?"

As they sat in the parked car, the air conditioner blasted to life, jetting dark strands of hair off his cheekbones. "Blank canvas. I have this story in my head and a million frames to capture it. Until the final cut, it can turn into anything I choose. There's a lot of power in committing my vision to permanency.

And a lot of nail-biting because I'm opening it to be interpreted through someone else's lens."

The tension had almost totally drained away. "What's the first step when you start a film? Wait." Before her burst of daring fled, she reached over and slipped off his sunglasses. "Now talk. Your eyes do this thing when you're passionate about the subject, and I want to see it."

He swiveled his head to capture her gaze, and her diaphragm seized so hard, she went light-headed. A baptism of liquid fire washed over her skin as his hard brown eyes roamed across her face.

"What do they do?" he asked and she would have sworn he didn't move, but suddenly, they were a breath apart. About to kiss.

"What does what do?" she whispered, afraid to shift, afraid to exhale, afraid to think.

"My eyes. When I'm talking about a film. What happens?"

"Oh. Um." Simple language escaped her. All she could concentrate on was the fiery, clamping need twisting through her abdomen. She ached to lean into the space between them, to lose all sense of time in the raw pressure of his lips on hers.

That mystical connection beckoned, laden with promise.

A car horn startled her and she jerked. Backward, not forward, breaking her gaze. She scrambled to pick up the threads of conversation. "Um, they light up. Your skin holds everything inside but the passion builds and builds and the only place it can escape is through your eyes."

He shifted smoothly, drove out of the parking lot and merged onto the freeway. Obviously unaffected. She'd overreacted to the almost kiss. That, or he spent his day fending off forward women and took it in stride.

His face implacable now, he said, "You have an active imagination. I approach film as an art, but it's also critical to stay detached. Too much emotional investment leads to sloppy structure."

"Nice try. But you can't will it away, Lord Ravenwood."

"I'm sorry, what?"

"Lord Ravenwood," she said with an airy wave. "He's the duke in *Embrace the Rogue,* the finest book about romance ever written. He hides from his emotions, too."

"Really." Sarcasm oozed from his clipped response. "That's what you think I do? Hide?"

"Yeah. I bought your line about not believing in fairy tales, but I see now that it's not true. That's not your actual problem." The angel on her shoulder screamed at her to shut up. This couldn't lead to anything other than disappointment and grief when he went back to Hollywood. But he was lying to himself. She couldn't sit idly by while he coasted through life, completely isolated, when it was obvious he yearned to cross that chasm with the gas pedal to the floorboard.

"Since you've got me all figured out, what's my actual problem?"

This amazingly sensual man seemed content with a bloodless Hollywood-style engagement to someone he didn't love, and, if she'd correctly interpreted his careful response, had no intention of marrying—all to secure the right backers for his film.

He needed to be shown what a mistake he was about to make. He needed VJ to set him free from his self-imposed prison. If he'd given any indication of having a real relationship with Kyla, she'd have backed off. But he'd done the exact opposite. Deliberately, she was convinced.

"You want desperately to believe. You're just too afraid."

The devil on her other shoulder whispered, *Time for stage three.*

Five

Perfect. Instead of carefully steering around VJ's fanciful ideas, he'd driven her to psychoanalyze him. Incorrectly.

Kris laughed, but it sounded hollow. "I'm not afraid of fiction. That's why I'm a filmmaker, to create fictional worlds. But fiction is not reality. Real life's tough. You get knocked down a lot and each time, it's harder to pick yourself up."

The dark shadow across VJ's cheek taunted him from his peripheral vision. Of course she knew the realities of life and didn't need to be preached to about them.

VJ was a rare woman, determined to reach for her destiny instead of waiting around for it to find her. He admired that.

And, she'd easily pulled him out of his bout of brooding. Some of Kyla's best off-screen performances included temper tantrums about his moods. VJ was a force to be reckoned with.

"You're absolutely right," she said. "Do you think we'll reach Dallas by dinnertime?"

"Why? You got a hot date?"

She meticulously inspected the rocky terrain out the passenger window. "You asking?"

"No," he said in a rush. He cleared his throat. "Maybe we'll grab dinner."

The truth was he liked her company. He liked the spike through the gut when her sizzling gaze caught him just right. She saw things, stuff no one else saw. Dangerous, all the way around, and he liked that, too.

It was a miracle he'd kept his hands off her this long, but he had to. And they still had a long, long way to go.

"Drive slower and we'll be having dinner together by default," she suggested, then threw in, "Maybe breakfast, too." Since his blood pressure hadn't climbed high enough already.

Visions of a cozy, roadside motel spun through his head, where a convenient convention had booked all the rooms but one and they had no choice but to take the room with the solitary bed. Then… He groaned. Well, he'd been accused of a lot of things, but lack of imagination wasn't one of them. Lack of interest, yeah. Lack of attachment, definitely. Lack of emotion, without fail.

Before registering the impulse to do so, he'd backed off the accelerator. "I'm not in that big of a hurry."

"At that rate, you'll be driving backward before too long. I have a better idea. Take the next exit." She nodded at the green sign for a town called Lively.

Curious now, he gunned the Ferrari down the ramp and followed her directions to the center of town. Such as it was. The rustic buildings, peeling paint and layer of dust were markedly similar to the rut in the desert VJ called home.

At the end of Main Street, she pointed left and he turned into the middle of a traveling carnival set up in the parking lot of the local grocery store. Flashing lights on the large Ferris wheel winked in the midmorning sun and music piped from hidden speakers. Cheerfully painted booths promising big prizes lined the parking lot.

A carnival. Really.

"It'll be fun, I promise." VJ grinned mischievously. "And, it's the ideal place for you to learn about stage three."

"Romance instruction at a carnival?" He slid out of the car and went around.

He'd been praying romance instruction had been forgotten because he had a sneaking suspicion about the direction it was headed, and stomping caution flat seemed like the opposite of a good idea.

"Yes, definitely," she said as he took her hand to help her out of the car.

He followed her to the nearest blood-red ticket booth and fished out his wallet to hand over enough cash to last for hours. Or at least long enough to find out what stage three was. Whichever came first.

Kris ushered VJ into the den of iniquity she'd chosen as the means to educate him on the fine points of romance. Or was it love? With VJ, it seemed they were one and the same.

"We've beaten the crowd," Kris commented as they strolled the deserted midway. VJ's gaze flitted everywhere at once and he smiled, oddly charmed. The awe on her face was worth the price of admission. "Are you in the mood for rides or games?"

"The Scrambler."

This obviously wasn't her first carnival. "Which one is that?"

She pointed. At the other end of the midway, the ride spun drunkenly, a smudge of red, green and yellow against the backdrop of mountains and sky. Wonderful. One of those toss-your-cookies-at-the-end rides. She sauntered off and he hurried to catch up.

She was being unusually closemouthed. His curiosity was killing him. What was stage three?

In anticipation of her explanation, his senses honed in on the smallest detail. The swish of her jeans as she walked, thigh against thigh. The precise point at which the T-shirt dipped

against the creamy hollow of her throat. He was getting a head-
ache from sidelong glances at the riot of colors corkscrewing
through her curls from crown to tip. Some auburn, thin blond
streaks and that warm cinnamon. He wanted to slide a strand
against his palm—to test the temperature.

His fingers clenched into a fist against his leg.

Her hand accidentally bumped his and the spot on his
knuckle where they'd touched turned immediately sensitive.
Her heat was blatant, easy to sort from the radiating concrete,
but not easy to dismiss.

He was obsessing over the way VJ walked. What was wrong
with him? He'd spent less time setting up a camera to shoot
a Dutch angle.

An agonizingly silent eternity later, he followed her into
the Scrambler's empty queue. They threaded through the turns
and at the bend of one, he misjudged her speed. The collision
of his chest with her back triggered a shock. He got a whiff
of coconut from her hair and blood shot straight to his groin.

Torture. That must be stage three. There was no other explanation.

A grizzled ride operator took the tickets from Kris's hand
and lifted the bar on the closest car. Kris climbed in. VJ wedged
in next to him, ignoring the four feet of seat on her other side.
The operator slammed the bar into place, and as they were
the only thrill-seekers around, shuffled off to the control box.

"Put your arm around me," VJ said, and nudged him when
he didn't immediately comply. "I mean it. The centrifugal force
on this thing is going to hurt if you don't."

Physics. That was a new angle. He secured his sunglasses,
slung an arm around her shoulders, and she snuggled up against
him, curving into his body naturally. Of course, because it
fit well with the torture theme playing out under the guise of
teaching him about romance.

Gears ground, tinny, harpsichord music bleated through
the air, and the ride started spinning. As it gained momentum,

VJ pressed closer and closer until he couldn't have shoved her away with both hands, mostly because one was occupied with hanging on and the other had snaked into place against VJ's stomach, which filled his palm nicely. He thoroughly enjoyed it.

As he guessed was the intent.

Most of his blood kept his jeans uncomfortably tight, but some of it still circulated in his brain. Enough to be suspicious of the convenient ride choice.

Eventually, the ride slowed but his head kept going. The ride operator unlocked the safety bar, and Kris tried to stand, but his legs buckled. VJ was having trouble with watery legs, too, so he left his arm around her—to keep them both off the ground, no other reason. They staggered for the exit.

She led him to a couple of other rides in the same vein but he couldn't have named them at gunpoint. He was too busy inventing ways to continue innocently touching her. Taking her hand to help her into a ride. Brushing hair off her shoulder so it wouldn't get in her eyes when the speed increased. Buying a tub of buttery popcorn and reaching into it at the same moment she did.

It was challenging to keep rationalizing it as carnival fun, but she'd started it and he ached to finish it.

"Next up?" he asked. "Funnel cakes maybe?"

"Ferris wheel," she said decisively.

Abandoning pretense, he laced his fingers with hers and they ambled toward the Ferris wheel. She pretended not to notice they were holding hands, as if they'd done this a thousand times, but there was no way she could ignore the sizzle of awareness melding with the sun's heat. Thirst lashed the back of his throat, and the crevice between his shoulder blades beaded with sweat and frustration.

He was human and a guy. He needed water and VJ naked. Not necessarily in that order. Or separately. And he couldn't have the one he really wanted. Which sucked.

The Ferris wheel car swung dizzily as they settled into it,

or maybe his head was spinning with images of undressing VJ, slowly revealing those perfect breasts. Once the bar was secured, she turned and searched his face. Her eyes matched the summer sky, and it was the perfect shot. When was the last time he'd even thought about filming her? Forever ago, before the torture began. Before she'd dragged him under the hot spotlight of her gaze.

"So stage three." Her tongue darted out to moisten her lips. "Touching."

She trailed fingers along his arm, igniting landmines. The tips of her nails disappeared under his sleeve, just the tips, but it was so much sexier than if she'd gone straight for his zipper. The wheel turned, and he couldn't tear his eyes from hers.

"Touching," she repeated, her voice low. "Accidentally at first. Then you do it deliberately, because you can't unring that bell. Once you've got the imprint of her on your fingertips, it's like an addiction. You can't stop. You're thinking about the next hit before the current one's even faded."

Yeah, like imagining her forbidden fruit bared before him, his mouth open and all but salivating to taste her. He shut his eyes until the throb in his gut lessened enough to hopefully avoid an embarrassing accident.

"That's stage three. How'm I doing?"

His lids flew open. "Not bad. I wasn't expecting a demonstration along with the commentary."

Not bad? VJ was an evil genius.

"Demonstration?" she questioned primly. "I'm just having fun. Aren't you?"

"Oh, yeah, loads. This is the most fun I've had in ages." Actually, he was having fun in a perverse way. Nothing was going to happen with VJ—nothing he couldn't handle anyway.

They stopped at the zenith of the Ferris wheel. The vista was stunning—mountains, heat shimmers, vast blue…and VJ. Without thinking, he said, "Here's a romantic proposal spot."

She glared at him. "Are you making fun of me?"

"Not at all." Since their earlier conversation, the perfect proposal had been brewing in the back of his mind. He'd directed one in his third movie, and the scene had been flat. Faulty acting, he'd assumed. "But seriously. No guy spends more than five minutes on how to propose. She's going to say yes or no regardless of how you ask, right?"

"Do you practice being that cynical or does it come naturally?"

"Both. Come on." He nudged her with his elbow. "You know I'm right. If you were really, really in love with a guy and he got down on one knee in your living room after dinner, would you refuse because he asked without fanfare?"

"I don't know. I've never been really, really in love. Have you?" she asked, arms crossed and a defiant sparkle flushing her cheeks. God, she was beautiful.

"Hold on. You've never been in love but you're presuming to teach me about it?"

"Wow. The master of deflection, that's you. I'm not presuming to teach you anything. I *am* teaching you." She nodded to his hand, which rested unobtrusively, comfortably, on her knee. "Wasn't your last movie called *Twilight Murders?*"

"So?"

"How many murders have you committed, Mr. Big Shot Director?"

The grin cracked before he could check it. "You're amazing. Will you have my children?"

Frozen, she stared at him. "Do you take any of this seriously or am I wasting my time?"

"I don't know." He shrugged and set the car in motion. "What are you trying to accomplish? We blew past simple education a long time ago. What's the real goal here?"

She inspected the chipped paint on the safety bar, flicking off a small bit before answering. "To prove you suppress your passionate side."

He laughed. "You're going to fail miserably at that before

you even start. You've got me cast in your head as the real-world equivalent of your Duke Whoeverwood, but I'm just Kris. A guy who wants to make movies."

The catch in his throat shouldn't be there. He shouldn't have the urge to tell her she was right, or how so much of his soul ended up on the screen because it was the only place he could express himself without fear of turning into something monstrous. Like his father. "What you see is what you get. I'm not hiding or suppressing anything."

"You've got so much pent-up, seething passion inside, you can barely sit still."

"That's the sway of gravity against this monstrous Ferris wheel, babe." He crossed his arms to keep his hands where they belonged—off her.

Her teeth gleamed when she bared them. "And I disagree. Strongly."

Man, she pushed his buttons. Every single one. What was he supposed to do with her? What *could* he do?

Nothing.

The film was too important to jeopardize over an alluring mirage, no matter how concrete she became.

Her eyelids drifted closed and then opened in a slow blink. Instantly, the atmosphere turned sensual. She studied him, an allover perusal loaded with hot appreciation. "This shirt is soaked."

She bunched the cotton up between her breasts, baring her midriff, and with the other hand, fanned her face. That swatch of glistening skin below her shirt drew his eye magnetically. The tiniest sliver of the underside of her breast peeked out from the cotton.

He hardened in an instant. Did she have a clue what she was doing?

"Seems like we've been stuck here for an hour," he said hoarsely in an attempt to dial down the heat. "Wonder why we're not moving?"

"I paid the operator to take a break once we got to the top," she said. "You didn't notice. It'll be a while till we're on the ground. So here we are, me and you. And no prying eyes."

"Why'd you do that?"

She pierced him again with her know-all, see-all gaze. "The view."

"You're not even looking at it."

"Yeah, Kristian, I am."

His name rolled off her tongue like molasses-coated barbed wire. Except for the media, nobody called him Kristian. And nobody ever would again, not like that. He yearned to sink into her and never come up for air.

With one finger, she swept a thatch of hair behind his ear, and the light touch curled his toes. She threaded strands through her fingers, letting it waterfall away, and exhaled in a raspy moan that speared his hard-on. That had to be the sexiest sound ever.

Deep in her throat, she moaned again. "I want you to kiss me. Do you know how bad I want it?"

At least as badly as he wanted to. He tried to think about something unsexy. Not happening.

"I have a pretty good idea," he muttered.

One hot hand wandered over his chest, delving into the dips of his muscles and tracing the line of his collarbone. Pushing him toward insanity. He wished she'd find the hem, slide underneath the T-shirt. Touch his bare skin and say his name again.

"I'm dying for you to kiss me," she said. "But you can't. We can't."

Can't? Says who?

He shook his head, hard. No, it was true. They couldn't.

Then she leaned in with the smallest incline of her head, offering up lips puckered in a superb *O*. Just before she hit the point of no return, she whispered, "Kristian."

Her breath brushed his jaw, swirled down his throat and spread through his body, heating it, warming corners he'd have insisted weren't cold. The space between them slowly disappeared. Too slowly.

His control vanished. He shoved fingers through her hair, cupped the back of her head and kissed her. Hard. Open-mouthed. Tongue seeking, sliding along hers in a fiery path. Tasting every crevice of her smart mouth. Unleashing the frustration he couldn't ease any other way.

At last.

He dragged her half into his lap and worked a hand under her shirt to thumb one of those taut nipples. Perfection. One should be in his mouth. Right now. He growled.

More.

He changed the angle and drew her tongue deeper into his mouth, sucking on it with quick little pulls then broke away to bite his way down her neck, back up to her earlobe. He took it in his mouth and nibbled on the sweet flesh.

He needed more.

Her hot lips locked onto his. Hot, so hot. He guided her hand to his groin and dragged her palm across the rock-hard bulge, nearly exploding right then and there from her blistering touch.

With a lurch, the Ferris wheel started up again and jolted them apart. Bleary-eyed, he fought through the lust-induced haze, taking in VJ's mussed hair and swollen lips both screaming *take me fast*. He barely resisted yanking her back.

"Good thing you're so, um, reserved," she said without a trace of irony, her irises molten and seductive. "That was so tame, I invited the Baptist Knitting Club over to watch."

A good, honest laugh burst out in spite of it all, and he winced as vibrations traveled through his throbbing erection. He'd never had a chance. Hadn't wanted one. "Okay. You made your point."

And how.

It was disturbing how easily she'd snapped his control and how much he'd liked letting go into that dark free fall of passion. Disturbing how accurately she'd gauged the truth. Disturbing and unprecedented.

"Kissing is stage four," she said. "By the way."

Of course it was. A sin and a shame he liked her so much because only the worst kind of slime could pretend to be engaged to Kyla while having an extremely satisfying side-thing with VJ. That wasn't fair or respectful to either woman.

No, VJ was the marrying sort of woman. He knew that. Now that his brain was functioning—the real one, not the one he'd been using five seconds ago—he had to face that he'd crossed so far over the line, it was but a distant slash.

It couldn't happen again. He probably wouldn't be able to look in the mirror as it was. No matter how much he burned to dive into the pleasure VJ promised, he had to stay in control from now on. It was totally not cool to lose it like that. He kept himself in check for a reason, usually without any trouble. VJ was exceptionally unique in more ways than one.

And he was still so hard, he couldn't walk.

While Kris took a moment in the portable bathroom, VJ slumped on a bench with a great view of the Ferris wheel and fingered her chafed lips.

The vilest word she'd ever said aloud slipped out. She clapped a hand over her mouth. Mama was surely rolling over in her grave. Her daughter was nothing but a cursing harlot. The only thing VJ had proven at the top of the Ferris wheel was that a small-town girl like her couldn't handle the highly specialized, foreign engine beneath the hood of Kristian Demetrious.

Kissing him had been like licking a nine-volt battery. A stun to the tongue and ill-advised.

A man who could kiss like that, and likely had many other talents, chewed up women and spit them out on a regular basis. She'd set him free, all right. Naively, she'd assumed her vast

understanding of men in books would transition to men in real
life and the truth put a huge chink in her delusions.

She was so out of her league.

Kris came into view, his gait easy and loose and sexy.
Ebony, glossy hair brushed his shoulders. Good night, the man
was hot. There'd been a possibility the chemistry between them
would disappear after her stage-four experiment. The exact opposite was what had happened. And now she knew what his
golden hands felt like when they touched her. Just watching
him move made her squirm.

She was in so much trouble. People in Hollywood played
at relationships, played at things she held dear, like long-term
commitment. Kris had flat-out admitted as much, then she
practically handed the man an engraved invitation for a one-
night stand.

Was that really what she wanted?

"Ready?" she said and gave him an everything's-cool smile.
Ferris wheel music crashed through the midway, loud and rau-
cous.

He paused in front of her, crossed his arms and peered over
the rim of his sunglasses. "Were you the slightest bit affected
by that kiss or was it strictly designed to prove me wrong?"

Her mouth fell open. "I'm not quite that blasé about having
the inside of my skin set on fire. But I'll take it as a compliment that you have to ask."

"Is that a yes?"

"Does it matter?"

"Yeah." He frowned. "Well, no. Not really. You and I both
know the score here. Right?"

Nodding, she stifled the urge to scream at him to shut up
and let her have her fantasy for a while longer. "Of course.
I proved you suppress your passions, just like Lord Ravenwood, so I win."

He grinned, and her heart grew a little heavier. All the

inconvenience of her misinterpreting that kiss as something meaningful was alleviated.

She couldn't be too upset. This was her fault, after all, for leaping into deep water without a floaty.

But provoking Kris into boiling over had been too easy to resist. A man more in denial didn't exist.

"So," he said. "Does that mean I get to move on to stage five?"

"If you want to," she said nonchalantly, though this whole game of romance instruction had become a lot less fun now that she'd unlocked him. Every sinfully delicious bit of that stormy passion called to her, and she wanted badly to answer.

But not badly enough to let him love her and leave her. "I figured we were done since I proved my point."

Something sizzled through his expression, but with the dark shield of his sunglasses in place, she couldn't interpret it. She'd rather he hadn't put them back on.

"Not by half," he said.

Pain stabbed at the backs of her eyes. So he wanted to play, as long as she didn't read too much into it. Was she completely crazy to consider it?

Yes. She *was* crazy. Except she *knew* he'd been trying to tell her something without telling her when he hinted the engagement wasn't exactly typical. He'd deflected the question about whether he'd ever been in love far too fast. His heart was buried underneath layers of cynicism and Hollywood.

What if she could uncover it?

Oh, how she wanted to, wanted all of him. The taste of that untamed kiss still blasted the roof of her mouth. If she had any hope of moving past flirtation, any hope of guiding him away from the weird engagement, any hope of claiming all that passion for her very own, stage five was the key.

"Then we better get started." She grasped his proffered hand. "Stage five is very tricky."

Six

The interior of the Ferrari was the perfect temperature to bake a cobbler in less than ten minutes, and the heat smacked VJ the moment she slid into the passenger seat. "Hurry with the air conditioner."

Kris dropped into his seat and hit the ignition. The sun wasn't the only thing heating up the interior. But it was the one she could reasonably handle at the moment. Cool air washed over her as he drove out of Lively and onto the freeway toward Dallas.

"Music?" he asked.

"Not the sexy stuff. Something else." She couldn't take the thrum of Spanish guitars right now. Here in this exotic, European car, surrounded by unimaginable luxury and privilege intrinsic to people in Kris's stratosphere, her resolve didn't feel so…resolved.

An upbeat tune sailed out of the speakers, and he immediately turned it down so it was atmospheric background noise.

"So, stage five," she said. "It's emotion."

"I was hoping it was sex."

Of course he was. No surprise after she threw herself at him on the Ferris wheel.

Sex echoed in her mind and triggered visions of what might have happened if the Ferris wheel hadn't rotated at the very worst time.

Best time. *Best time.*

"That's because you're thinking like a guy."

"Yeah. I'm sort of bound by the equipment God gave me."

"That's why I'm here. To help you think with something other than your equipment."

His laugh crossed her eyes. There was something really powerful about making a man like Kris laugh. Especially because it was all she had to keep her warm at night, when it came down to it.

She could pretend all day long that stage five was the key, but in reality, unsophisticated VJ Lewis might need a million stages to crack Kristian Demetrious. She had about the same ability to decipher his instruction manual as she did the one for his car. Zero.

"I'll keep that in mind. So, emotion?"

The mere word hadn't scared him off the subject. But he wasn't most men, despite her intimate knowledge of his similar equipment. Her cheeks heated and she looked out the window so Kris didn't notice.

"Yep," she said to the glass, and her fingers curled into thin air of their own accord. She'd touched him. *There.* Her tummy flipped. He'd been harder than Texas soil in a drought. For her. No instruction manual needed to understand that. "Stage five. Figuring out her emotional needs and granting them."

"Just hers? Guys don't have emotional needs?"

"You're the one with the equipment. You tell me."

"Sure. We have a really emotional need to have as much sex as possible before we die. Survival of the species, you know."

"Yeah. Survival." She rolled her eyes because it seemed

like an appropriate reaction when two people shared a dangerous, seductive attraction and one of them felt totally out of her depth. "So that's why this is about her needs, because guys are easy."

"It might be easy to get us willing, but that's not what we're talking about, is it? This is all about romance. I'd love to know a woman's secret for romancing a guy."

So would she. Especially the one in the next seat. Then maybe stage five wouldn't feel so insurmountable.

She shook her head. "No way, Jose. Women everywhere would throw rotten tomatoes at me as I passed by on the street if I told you."

He snapped his fingers in mock disappointment. "Fine, then. Tell me what I'm supposed to be doing to figure out her emotional needs."

"That was the paying attention stage. You should already know. Now you have to do it."

For a minute, he was quiet, as if processing, and the steady hum of tires on concrete filled the car. "So I've figured out what her greatest emotional need is and I've done it. What do I get out of the deal?"

His sidelong glance caught her in the abdomen. A lock of hair fell against his cheekbone. His hair was unbelievably glossy and soft and now that she knew what it felt like, it was so much harder not to touch.

She sat on her hands. "You're hopeless. I thought we'd made more progress. You get the realization you're in love and it's going to last forever. Stage five means you're thinking about someone else instead of your own selfish needs. That's the definition of love. Sacrificing what you want to make someone else happy."

"And in your mind, romance and love are the same."

"They're not in yours?"

Instantly, his expression iced over, and the chill infused her skin. "Not at all," he said. "Love is elusive. Fleeting. It doesn't last, and therefore it's too difficult to pin down with a simple definition. Romance is all about action. A back and forth. Doing something to get somewhere."

"Nice." She tsked to clear the tremor in her throat. He was speaking from the rock bottom of his shriveled heart, and nothing she'd said was getting through. "So, it's all a necessary evil to get a girl naked."

"That's not what I meant." His frustrated growl coaxed a smile from her. "Romance is a verb. There's a physical aspect you can point to and say there's the romance in this scenario. Like flowers. The right lighting, the setting."

"Flower is a noun, Kris. And love is more of a verb than romance. You can't say 'I romance you.' Well, I guess you can, but you'll sound like English is your second language."

"English *is* my second language."

He glared at her, and she started giggling uncontrollably. "I'm sorry. I'm picturing you swooning at my feet as you declare, 'I romance you.'"

She laughed so hard, she couldn't stop, and had to wipe tears from her eyes, ignoring the couple extra that squeezed out. That was stupid, to cry over the fact that such a passionate, expressive man had been hurt badly enough to believe love didn't last. Yet she presumed to heal all that in a couple of hours. How big *was* her ego?

Kris's lips were twitching. "Glad you could find some amusement at my expense."

More giggles slipped out, and the tears threatened to spill over. "Sleepless night catching up to me. Sorry."

He captured her hand and kissed the back of it. Casually, like they were an old married couple—except the way his lips grazed her skin should come with a hazard warning. "Sleep, then," he said. "I'll let you argue with me about this later, since you're not going to win anyway."

She folded her still-sparking hand into her lap, all traces of humor dried up. "Okay. I am exhausted."

She faked a yawn, pillowed her arm against the door, then lay on it. When she closed her eyes, she swore she'd only think about football and what kind of job she'd get in Dallas. But the Ferris-wheel kiss drove all that out of her mind. Instead, she replayed it over and over and over, extending it in a torturous parade of images where Kris swept her away in a sensual haze and made love to her until dawn.

With a start, she woke and only then realized she'd fallen asleep. "What time is it?"

Kris glanced at the dash clock. "Almost two. Are you ready for lunch?"

"Yeah. I'd like to get out of the car for a while."

And prolong the inevitable. Dallas loomed at the edge of the horizon and she'd slept away a good bit of her precious few hours with Kris. In no time, they'd go their separate ways. Nothing had changed that, and nothing likely would—unless she came up with a heck of a Hail Mary.

They ate more fast food and talked. Kris told fascinating stories of growing up in Greece and spending his youth on his father's boats. She entertained him with anecdotes of redneck politics, of which she had an endless supply.

How in the world had Kris ended up so down-to-earth instead of obnoxious and stuck-up like all the rich people on TV? He'd grown up Trump wealthy, and after a painful fallout with his father, turned his back on the money and left Greece forever to follow his dreams of being a filmmaker, on his terms. She couldn't even find a way out of her pathetic life on her own.

No wonder she'd been thus far unable to pile-drive through the brick wall in his chest. She'd invented a crazy notion about saving him from a bloodless engagement to Kyla Monroe, one of the most successful and accomplished actresses in Hollywood.

But they were made for each other. Even if they weren't in love or getting married, at some point, they'd found a mutual appreciation and likely enjoyed common interests. A woman like Kyla didn't have to resort to flirting and stupid games like romance instruction to get Kris's attention. She already had it.

Somehow, VJ had convinced herself Kyla would be thrilled to get out of an engagement with someone who was only doing it for the sake of a film and it never occurred to her that the star of Kris's movie might be in it for the same reason.

Until now.

It was way past time to stop fantasizing about what could be and get some traction on the rest of her actual life.

"I need to borrow your phone again," she told him. "I'm sorry I have to be such a freeloader."

"VJ, I have an unlimited usage plan. You're not going to bankrupt me with two five-minute phone calls." He motioned to the Ferrari parked outside. "Help yourself."

"You're the only person on the planet who doesn't keep their phone on them." Even in Little Crooked Creek, ranchers dropped cell phones into the pockets of their jeans and teenagers texted each other as they walked to school.

He shrugged. "No one is so important they can't leave a message. Find me when you're done."

She slid into the Ferrari and dialed Beverly Porter on the first try. No one could say she didn't learn from her missteps.

Her only hope of shelter answered. "Beverly, it's VJ Lewis."

"Oh, hi. Just a minute." Beverly said something but it was muffled as if she'd put her hand over the speaker. "You're not calling to cancel on me are you? The condo's almost done."

Relief sang through VJ's veins. "The opposite, in fact. I'm on my way to Dallas and was hoping you wouldn't mind a roommate a little early."

She was pathetic, mooching off Beverly and barging into the one-person home of a girl she'd last seen over Fourth of July weekend last month. Friendship had its limits, and she was pushing them.

"Oh." Beverly's pause did not put VJ at ease. "You're on your way now? As in today?"

"I should be there by nine at the latest," VJ chirped, and winced at the fake brightness. "That's not too late, is it?"

"I'm really sorry, VJ. I'm in St. Louis at my grandparents' house. I had to let my old apartment go. They wanted me to sign another six-month lease or get out, and the condo won't be move-in ready for at least three weeks. My grandparents had an extra room and my boss is letting me work remotely. I had no idea you'd be moving so soon."

"No problem. I totally understand." There were bound to be loads of fifty-cent-a-night hotel rooms in Dallas.

"Do you have another place to stay?" Beverly's clear concern was almost her breaking point. "I know a few people who wouldn't mind."

Depending on the kindness of strangers. Even more pathetic. "That's okay. Thanks anyway. I'll find something else. I'll call you soon to give you my new phone number."

And that was that. Now she was homeless for the next three weeks.

VJ was eerily still for so long, Kris considered taking her temperature.

Each time the car passed another exit, he anticipated instructions to turn off so they could visit the world's largest ball of twine or the Petrified Wagon Wheel Museum, which VJ would artfully turn into a way to make him crazy. Or make him think. Or thaw him out a little more.

Each time she didn't speak, he grew more frustrated. He recognized the wisdom of taking big, giant steps back from that line. He did. He just didn't like it.

During the stage-five discussion, he'd had a hard time keeping his attention on the road and off her mouth. It wasn't only the things she said, but the way her lips formed the words, and how she never hesitated to spit out what was on her mind.

Twice, he'd had to physically restrain himself from pulling onto the shoulder in order to put that smart mouth to better use.

"You know what?" VJ said after several miles and several provocative images later of what those perfectly formed lips could do.

"What?"

"I turn twenty-five in two days, and I've never been outside of the state of Texas."

They'd have parted ways by then. He frowned at the sudden compulsion to stick around until her birthday and shower her with presents and champagne. "Do you want to go somewhere in particular or just over the state line?"

"I don't know. I haven't had the luxury of thinking about much more than the next dime in the bank. Mama was sick for so long and everything I planned to do..." She trailed off, and he had to swallow at the despondent note in her voice.

"Where would you go, right now, if money was no object?"

"Greece," she said instantly. "To see boats bobbing in crystal-blue water and watch the fishermen pull up nets. Like you talked about at lunch."

"Greece is nothing special. I couldn't leave fast enough." He'd walked out the door at sixteen and never looked back. Every once in a while, he missed odd things, like the strong tang of homemade *tsipouro,* which he used to drink with the help in the kitchen while Cook pretended not to notice. Strange—he'd lived in America now for the same length of time he'd lived in Greece. Sixteen years. Each place claimed half of his life, shaping him in different ways.

"Kris. I watched you talk about it. You can't pretend you don't miss it."

He downshifted, then couldn't figure out why he'd automatically gone for the gear shift when there was nobody in front of him.

No, that was a lie.

VJ unsettled him, and his response was to do something with his hands. Something other than touch her.

"I don't know what you think you see when I'm having a

regular, old conversation. My eyes are not the window to my soul," he said lightly.

"What is?"

"My films," he blurted out and then regretted it.

He opened his mouth to change the subject and suddenly didn't want to. Soon, he and VJ would arrive in Dallas and he'd never see her again. A margin of safety existed inside the car where real life didn't—couldn't—intrude. Her presence sharpened and clarified his thought process. His emotions. Why fight it? "No one else knows that."

"Because you hang out with all blind and deaf people?"

In spite of the somberness coating the back of his throat, he laughed. How did she do that? He had the capacity to fall into moodiness for days—had, many times—but she blew right through it as if it didn't exist. "Yeah. I guess so. But I don't sit around having heart-to-heart talks with anyone about why I love being a director, either."

"It'll be our secret, then." She smiled, and it dove right into his stomach. He forced his attention back to the road and tried to forget how her breast felt like velvet, which was impossible with the scent of coconut wafting in his direction as she leaned forward and said, "Tell me another one."

"I can't figure out the theme for *Visions of Black*." Wow, that had not been what he'd meant to say at all. "It's bothering me. Normally, I'd have all that down by now."

"What's the movie about?" Her hand inched closer to his but didn't touch it.

"It's a drama about a woman who wakes up in the hospital blind and suffering from amnesia, but she can see visions in her head of disjointed scenes. A persistence of vision she can't stop." He glanced at her, and she was watching him closely. No doubt picking apart his brain with her odd insight. "Persistence of vision is a theory that an image stays on the eye after that image has actually disappeared, which is how some scientists think people process the individual frames of film. So it all ties together. I'm boring you."

"Not at all," she said softly. "I love listening to you talk. Your voice does something to me. And it's kind of delicious."

The atmosphere in the car grew thick with thrumming anticipation again. He had to shift it, get a barrier up fast, or he was going to fall headlong into her and this time, he wouldn't stop. He cleared his throat. "The backing and publicity for *Visions of Black* are really important. My career is at stake. I've been trying for years to find the right combination of art and commercial success with no luck. In Hollywood, it's all about the numbers. A bigger budget and the right names attached to the movie are the only things I haven't tried." He fiddled with the air conditioner until it was blowing at exactly the same rate and temperature as before he'd started. "I have to do this, and Kyla's a big part of it. Film is important to me. It's my only outlet."

"Oh. I see."

He had a really distinct feeling she did. "No jokes about how repressed I am? You're not going to offer to be my other outlet? I handed that to you, gift-wrapped. With a bow."

She shrugged. "Trust me, I had a scintillating response on the tip of my tongue, but I'm going to apologize instead. I'm sorry I pushed you so hard. About love and romance. It's none of my business. I understand the engagement is important to the film. I'll back off."

The barrier thumped into place. Quiet filled the car and pressed down on his shoulders. "You don't have to apologize for having an opinion. A really strong opinion." She didn't smile. His shoulders got heavier. "Truthfully, I was looking forward to more stage five."

She sighed. "It's kind of pointless. You don't even believe in love."

Ouch. That pained expression on her face had him stumbling to speak. "What people think is love fades more easily than anyone will admit. Love is best confined to the screen, where it can last. So why not have a marriage based on a business agreement? At least then everyone's on the same page."

Even the idea of marriage nauseated him. Passion died, without a doubt, and when it did, a wife was on the front line for what it turned into. He couldn't allow that to happen to anyone, least of all to a person unfortunate enough to fall in love with him.

Passion didn't last. Love didn't last. His career had been built on capturing both the only possible way. The safest way.

"You're challenging me to prove love can last forever," she said. "Which is impossible since I haven't lived forever yet. Hook up with a vampire if you want better data."

"Until I find one, you're the only expert I've got. Why are you so sold on this whole idea of hearts and cupids? Read too many books?"

That was the wrong thing to say. Stiffly, she rested the side of her head on the glass, and he had the impression it wasn't far enough away for her. "I just am."

Something sharp clogged his windpipe. She had shut down, thanks to his stupid barriers, and he couldn't stand it. "You can't cop out. I'm being brutally honest. Now it's your turn."

She sank down in the seat. Way down. "I promised Mama. On her death bed."

The last word was cut off as she buried her face in the T-shirt's hem. Crying. Did his stupidity know no bounds?

Without hesitation, he took the next exit and rolled to a stop as soon as the car cleared the white line. Some things required his full attention. He stroked her back until she peered up from the pile of shirt. "Better now?" he asked.

"I'm not usually such a crybaby."

"I'm not usually such an idiot."

She choked out a laugh, and he finally took a deep enough breath to clear his head. One tear ran down her cheek and she seemed too drained to notice, so he wiped it away with the palm of his hand.

"I sat by Mama's bed and read to her," she said. His hand rested against her collarbone because he was unable to stop touching her while she hurt. "For two years. Romance novels because she liked knowing it was going to end happily. Mama had a tough life. She made me promise to find my own happiness outside of Little Crooked Creek, because she knew I'd end up like her if I stayed."

VJ's gaze sought and held his, begging him to understand. He did. The bruise under her eye said it all. Her hand slid up to cover his.

"I have to believe," she said. "Those stories aren't some author's imagination. The magic between a man and a woman is out there. All I have to do is find it."

"Magic?"

"Yeah, you know. The perfect blend of love, passion and friendship."

Agape, eros and *philia*. Magic was indeed the only way they'd ever come together in one person. He yanked his hand away. That was a whole boatload of puppies to step on and the poignancy behind her single-minded perseverance added a few kittens.

The fairy tale she sought wasn't some adolescent, misguided dream, it was a death-bed vow she intended to keep. She deserved a man who believed in the possibility of forever.

All the more reason to stay far, far removed from VJ. Emotionally and physically. Good thing they'd be parting ways soon.

"I hope you find it," he said sincerely. He liked the thought of her out there in the world, happy and fulfilled.

She searched his face, looking for something, and this time he wished he had it to give, but knew he didn't. The moment passed and he shrugged it off.

"Me, too," she said. "Though I need to find a place to stay

first. The condo I'm moving into won't be ready for three weeks and my roommate is out of town until then." She made a face. "So I'm homeless. Great plan on my part to escape Little Crooked Creek with no backup and no money."

"You don't have any money?" How did she intend to support herself? He'd assumed she had a place to go or they would have had this conversation before now.

Guarded tension hardened her expression. "I'll be okay."

"VJ." She wouldn't look at him. "You told me at the diner that you've been saving every dime. What happened to your money?"

"We have a long way to go. Get back on the freeway and drive."

"Like hell I will." This situation had him so angry he was cursing in English. "Answer the question."

She wrapped her arms around her chest like a shield. "I'm not your responsibility. I'll figure it out."

"In the dark? In a strange city? You have a screw loose if you think I'm going to let you fend for yourself. Keep your secrets about the money or don't. I don't care. But you're staying with me until you find other arrangements. Period."

Mouth tight, he stomped on the clutch, threw the car into gear and turned up the music so she couldn't argue. And so he couldn't hear his subconscious laughing at his pathetic effort to sound noble when he'd greedily latched on to this perfect excuse to keep her around.

"I'm not sharing a hotel room with you," VJ shouted over the music.

With a stab of his finger, he cut off the music. "I have a suite. Two bedrooms. So humor me," he said, keeping his eyes trained straight ahead. "And separate bathrooms before you start on that."

Like the insubstantial impediment of a wall mattered, when

VJ was on the other side of it, all gorgeous and amazing and alone.

How much of a glutton for punishment was he, really?

Seven

A modest square sign of carved ebony wood marked the entrance to Hotel Dragonfly, visually separating it from the short-circuiting neon signs of every motel in VJ's neck of the woods. Dallas really was in another realm.

Kris downshifted to turn into the drive and steered around a tour bus splashed with the name of a rap artist even VJ had heard of.

"Don't worry. He's one of the quieter ones." Kris nodded toward the bus resembling a giant bumblebee as he parked.

"I guess you know a lot of famous people." It wasn't a surprise, but she'd been enjoying her Ferrari bubble where no one existed except for her and Kris. "Have you stayed here before?"

"Several times. The Dallas Film Festival is where I won my first award and the Studios at Mustang Park are a Mecca for those of us in independent film." He helped her out of the car, and they walked to the lobby. "I'm going to use the studio for my new film, even though I'll have a larger budget. Kyla and I are supposed to meet with a couple of other people there on Tuesday."

That douse of cold water woke her up. She'd known he was driving to Dallas to meet Kyla, but it had always been later. Now it was now. "Is Kyla staying at this hotel, too?"

Lord have mercy, was she that daft? Of course Kyla was staying here. Probably in Kris's room. Just because they weren't getting married didn't mean they weren't sleeping together. She should have asked more questions a long, long time ago. She should have said no to the offer of a room.

As she weighed the mortification of sharing a hotel suite with the lovers versus another night on the street, he shook his head. "She's from Dallas. She's staying with her mom."

Breath she hadn't realized was trapped in her lungs hissed out. Kris and Kyla weren't involved. She'd stake her life on it. Regardless, he wasn't like that, looking for opportunities to humiliate her, and she was ashamed for even thinking it. He wanted to rescue her. Again. But without expecting anything in return. He was an all-around decent guy with hands skilled enough to make a girl lose her religion. A guy whom she did not have to say goodbye to for at least another night.

It didn't matter. *The Rescue of VJ Lewis* wasn't the title of a romance novel, and the extra room didn't mean anything other than a place to sleep. Space he thought nothing of offering because Kris was generous to a fault—as long as it didn't require him to give up anything emotionally important.

The chic clerk at the front desk greeted Kris by name, drew attention to her cleavage and dismissed VJ in one shot. VJ was too busy trying to hide the bruising on her face to have much energy left over to care. Kris slid a black credit card across the marble desk and smiled back at the tramp.

"How many keys, Mr. Demetrious?" Tramp asked.

"Two," he said and nodded to VJ. "Ms. Lewis is helping me with preproduction on my new film, and we have a lot of work to do."

"Of course," she said with a fake smile and tapped on the keyboard in front of her. She handed Kris a small envelope, carefully touching her fingers to his before releasing it. "Enjoy your stay."

VJ followed Kris to the elevator. Once inside, she glanced at him. "Smooth. Do you often squirrel away women in your hotel room under the guise of 'helping' with your movies?"

God on High, did she *really* want to know the answer?

Kris just laughed. "First time. Usually the hotel staff is pretty discrete. Have to be with so many headline-grabbers under one roof. But why invite someone to create a story where none exists?"

And didn't that bit of truth hit the barn broadside? Yep, no story here. He needed Kyla to make his movie, and VJ couldn't stand in the way. It meant too much to him. And she owed him an immeasurable debt. A step back from romance instruction and flirting and trying to claim his buried heart was the least she could do. Even if it made her eye sockets burn and her throat scratchy.

The top-floor suite defied description. She didn't want to touch anything lest the magic wear off. Espresso-stained modern furniture dotted the living area and splashes of sage green, beige and dark purple accented the uptown theme. There was a cozy dining-room table on a raised dais with a half circle of windows beyond it offering an unbroken view of downtown Dallas skyscrapers, all lit for the night in winking splendor. A small area with a sink, microwave and refrigerator occupied the space next to the table.

Small being relative. Her kitchen at home was half that size.

The last time she'd stayed in a hotel was the after-prom party, of which the remarkable highlights were Walt throwing up eight wine coolers on her dress and Pamela Sue helping clean it up in the tiny bathroom. This was…not even close.

As promised, two doors, one on each side of the room, led

to the bedrooms. "I'm going to sleep for about ten hours," she said.

"This one's yours." Kris guided her to the room on the left and opened the door. "Do you want dinner?"

"Not really. You've done enough for me already. I can't ever repay you."

She turned to enter the room so she could collapse but he stopped her with a solid grip on her arm. "VJ."

She kept her back to him.

Not now.

She might break into a million pieces if he said something sexy. Or nice. Or in Greek...

Actually, it didn't matter what he said, her fragileness was due to being at the threshold of the rest of her life and scared to death. Scared she couldn't hack life outside of Little Crooked Creek. Scared she'd made a mistake in getting into the Ferrari this morning. Scared she'd never find anyone else who lit her up inside like Kris did.

"Sleep well," he said and released her arm. She had the impression it wasn't what he'd intended to say but she didn't dare press it.

"Good night," she whispered and shut the door behind her.

The bedroom was done in the same style as the main area of the suite, but she hardly noticed it. She trudged to the giant, elegant bathroom and took off all her clothes. Her small bag looked forlorn and out of place against the richly tiled floor. Guests in a hotel like this probably had servants with more luggage. As if she'd needed some additional clues she didn't belong here.

A hot shower went a long way toward improving her mood. The boiler at home never gave up more than about ten minutes of hot water, and she loved every second of the half an hour she stood under the multiple jets and streams. Beautiful little bottles lining an indention in the shower wall contained exotically scented shampoo, conditioner and shower gel, which she gratefully used. Finally, she felt clean and stepped out, kicking her clothes under the vanity at the same time.

She dripped water all over the bathroom floor and spent longer mopping it up than she had energy for, but couldn't bear the idea of overworked maids cleaning up after her. In the drawer of the vanity, she found toothpaste, lotion and a brush and used them all.

Naked, she fell into the giant bed and wiggled under the covers.

When she woke, it was still dark. The clock on the chunky bedside table read 2:20 a.m.

Her stomach rumbled. It had been twelve hours since she'd eaten. She debated. Check the refrigerator in the other room for food or order room service? Either one would be charged to Kris's slick credit card.

She bit her lip. None of this was what she'd intended or expected. The lure of escaping with the gorgeous stranger in the *muy amarilla* Ferrari had been irresistible. An adventure with endless possibilities.

Well, here she was, smack in the middle of the only possible outcome. Gorgeous stranger was about to be engaged to Kyla, she had nowhere else to go and she was starving.

Morosely, she stabbed her arms into the fluffy bathrobe from the peg in the bathroom and placed the sign hanging from the pocket on the vanity, which read, *Help yourself to this complimentary robe. We will gladly charge your room for it.*

Everything cost something. That was the lesson here. So she'd wear it for now, and put it back neatly the way she found it. At least wearing the robe, she felt more like she belonged in this luxurious suite.

She eased the door open and tiptoed out into the main living area. The year of living quietly with Daddy's drunken rages had honed her ability to creep through any room with the finesse of a jewel thief.

"Can't sleep?"

Kris's voice cut through the black, and VJ yelped. An exhale of breath, low and even, came from the direction of one of the trim couches, indiscernible in the dark.

"Hungry," she said, and cleared her throat. "I was hoping the refrigerator had something in it."

"It does. Champagne." His voice snaked around her, burrowing under the robe to kiss her bare skin. "What are you hungry for? I'll order room service."

Before she told him exactly what she hungered for, she asked, "Why are you awake? I was expecting you to be in your room." *Or I never would have left mine.*

"Blocking scenes in my head. I have a whacked out creative process, which works best in pitch-black with no distractions. Bed is for sleeping."

Full dark did something sinful to his accent. It was more pronounced and breaking at odd intervals. Fatigue, no doubt, and not due to the same heavy awareness messing with *her* voice.

"Sorry I intruded, then." She started to back away and tripped, almost swan-diving into the unfamiliar low-pile carpet. Thankfully, the lack of light hid her graceless recovery.

"You didn't. Stay. This is your room, too. I don't want you to feel like a guest who can't be hungry."

His disembodied voice was disturbing as it spiraled around inside her, heating places it couldn't be allowed to affect. He needed to be with Kyla, and she needed more than one night. Melancholy lodged behind her breastbone. "Can you at least turn on a light? I'm not part cat."

Some shuffling and muted light spilled into the room from the half circle of windows as he drew back the drapes. He'd changed into a pair of soft pants which clung to every line of his hips and thighs. And he was shirtless.

Her tummy tumbled to Mexico. The glow of skyscrapers rippled along his shoulders and his lean torso as he tucked the heavy curtains aside. His arms were as sculpted as his face, bulging slightly with muscle, tendons wrapping to his wrist in a trail she'd follow any day.

"Um, maybe dark was better," she blurted and smacked her forehead. *Shut up.*

"I disagree. I like that tousled look on you."

He disappeared into his room and returned covered up by a shirt and she stifled a sigh. Well, the image of his bare back was emblazoned across her retinas like lightning forking through the sky, shirt or no shirt. In what world did someone so charismatic and finely built end up behind the camera?

"I'll order us something. I haven't eaten, either," he said as he settled back onto the couch as if nothing had happened. Nothing *had* happened, but she was still frozen four feet from her door.

It was just dinner. She'd eaten two other meals with Kris. But neither of those meals had taken place behind closed doors while she wore nothing other than a big towel.

"Sit down." He nodded to the empty cushion a quarter inch from his thigh and picked up the phone from the end table. "You're not bothering me. Really."

You're bothering me.

Cautiously, she edged onto the couch—the other couch—and tugged the robe up around her neck as a flimsy barrier.

The tranquil sage and deep purples artfully strewn about the suite invited her to relax, to enjoy the rare reprieve from taking care of Daddy and her brothers, but the oasis had no effect on her goose bumps. Or the grasshoppers in her stomach. This was entirely too intimate, and she had no business being here with an almost-engaged man.

Even if he wasn't going to marry Kyla. Especially if he wasn't.

Nothing good ever happened after midnight. This was the time of night when Cinderella was still hobbling home, minus a shoe and toting a fourteen-pound pumpkin. Good Baptists were in bed. Asleep.

They sat in edgy silence for an eternity.

"I've been wondering," he said, startling her out of a fantasy where she'd stripped him of all his clothes and straddled him, still wearing the robe, but loosening the sash enough for it to slip off one shoulder.

"Hmm?"

"What's stage six?"

Her heart stumbled over a beat. "I'll tell you tomorrow."

"What's wrong with now?"

Where should she start counting all the reasons why not now? "It's late, and you're working."

"I'm done. Why are you sitting way over there?"

"I like this couch. It's comfortable. That one is too small for two people. With your long legs and all." God, she was babbling.

"My legs aren't on the couch."

He sounded amused, and why wouldn't he be? She was laughably inexperienced at sitting around in the half-light of a bustling urban city with a sophisticated man almost engaged to someone else.

"What's stage six?" he asked again, and merciful heaven, a knock at the door signaled the arrival of dinner. She sprang for the door before he could move.

A white-coated waiter stood in the hall with a rolling cart, staring at her expectantly. Kris materialized behind her, pressing the length of his taut frame against hers, leaning into it. Her breath rattled in her throat as the shock of awareness, the heat of his body, thrummed through her.

Then Kris gently guided her from the doorway to allow the waiter to roll the cart inside. Her breath rushed out in a sigh. She'd been in the way. That's all. This roller coaster of hope and dashed hope was getting ridiculous.

Ridiculous because she shouldn't have any hopes except to get her life settled and move on.

Kris tipped the waiter and moved the dishes from the dining area to the low coffee table shared by the couches. "Is this okay? I hate eating formally. Reminds me too much of when I lived with my parents."

"Sure." She wasn't going to be able to swallow anything anyway. Then he lifted the metal cover from one of the plates. Fried chicken. She almost laughed, until the meaty smell of it weakened her knees. Okay, so she'd eat a little something.

Five pieces later, she couldn't shove anything else in her mouth with a pitchfork.

Kris reclined on the floor opposite her, licking his fingers, and she avoided another stray glance at his tongue. Too late. Heat gathered in her core as she recalled the way he'd devoured her at the top of the Ferris wheel. He'd done something wicked with his mouth, drawing her tongue into it and sucking, but she'd felt it between her legs simultaneously.

"Is it tomorrow yet?" he asked, and she glanced at him.

He was watching her, his eyelids low and sexy as if well sated after a good, hard roll in silk sheets. Why did he have to be so hot?

"It'll be dawn soon. I guess that makes it tomorrow."

"Then what's stage six?"

"What's the fascination with stage six?"

What was her fascination with his mouth? She couldn't stop staring at it. She wanted to keep him talking but this was the wrong subject.

"The best way to get me interested in something is to withhold it. Curiosity isn't only hazardous to felines."

Bingo. The secret to romancing Kris was to withhold. And keep withholding until he was exploding with need. She sighed. Useless information now. "Of course. You don't really care what stage six is. You just care that I know something you don't."

He grinned and leaned back against the couch, legs spread underneath the coffee table. "Exactly."

Lights from the window threw his body into relief. Hair fell into his face against the fine planes of his cheekbones, and she sat on her hands before she did something really ill-advised. Only a dimwit licked a battery twice. "Well, you know lots of things I don't. How is that fair?"

"Trade you, then. Tell me about stage six, and I'll tell you something you don't know."

Suspicious, she planted her elbows on the low table and leaned forward. "No deal. It's late, and I'm tired."

She wasn't. She'd never been more awake—aware—in her life. There was a coffee table between them but it provided no barricade against the spark of his presence.

Gracefully, he edged across the carpet and tipped her head up with the finger that, seconds ago, had been in his mouth. His heat branded her chin and she wasn't so sure she had it in her to withhold anything from him.

He peered into her eyes. "What's going on in there? Are you afraid of something?"

"Kris. Please don't touch me."

"You are afraid. Of me." His shoulders slumped as he dropped his hand to the floor. "I don't want you to be afraid. Would you prefer a separate room?"

"No!" Had she shouted? "I mean, I'm not scared of you. This whole middle-of-the-night scenario just isn't proper. You're about to be engaged, and we've already…done things. Things we shouldn't have. I know I gave you the wrong impression, but I'm not some wild woman out for a good time with the first man I find."

"I don't think that." He reclined into a different position. Closer. He extended his long legs behind her and propped up his head on his palm as if they were having a slumber party instead of a Come To Jesus about this electric attraction boiling the atmosphere.

She rolled her eyes. "Why wouldn't you? I attacked you. On the Ferris wheel."

"Well, I was warned you'd take advantage of me at the first

opportunity." He was fighting a smile. "It's my own fault I allowed myself to fall into your clutches. Would you feel better if I told you I knew what you were up to at the carnival?"

No, she would have preferred to continue deluding herself about how clever she was. But obviously that ship had sailed.

"Kris." She couldn't keep up this back-and-forth dance. "You have to do the engagement, and I can't be your dirty secret, hiding in the extra room and pretending to be your assistant or whatever. There can't be anything between us. That's why we can't talk about stage six."

His entire body stiffened, and she was ashamed to have noticed.

"I never intended to make you feel like a dirty secret when I offered the extra room. I'm sorry," he said. Sincerity deepened the hollows along his cheekbones. "We could have avoided all this if you'd taken my trade."

"What trade? Oh, where I tell you about stage six and you tell me something?" She exhaled. Well, she'd laid it all out there, and he'd apologized instead of laughing. What's the worst that could happen now? "Fine. Dazzle me."

Eyes dark and unfathomable, he stared at her. Slowly, he reached out to take her hand. He laced their fingers together and with a lift of his chin, he said, "You first. Stop being so cagey about stage six. Tell me what it is."

His thumb traced her knuckles in a crazy, sensual pattern, and her brain shut down. At least that was her excuse for being so stupid as to continue this dangerous game of romance instruction. Being struck brainless had to be the reason she opened her mouth and whispered, "Consummation."

His hand tightened and an elemental shock blistered up her arm as his expression heated. "I like stage six."

She was trapped in his gaze, trapped by his touch. He lifted her hand to his mouth and watched her with clear intent as his lips molded around the tips of her fingers in a kiss.

"That wasn't a suggestion. It's only a word. We're just talking." She yanked her hand from his and desperation set in. He had to stop crawling inside her with that hooded expression, as if he'd been stranded on a desert island and she was water. "I'm not trying to convince you of anything anymore. You can get engaged to Kyla with a clear conscience. I give you my blessing. Now I told you about stage six. It's your turn."

He sat up and his presence spread, creeping into all the molecules around her until she was overwhelmed. "The engagement," he said and waited until she met his eyes, quite against her will, before continuing. "Isn't happening. I'm calling it off."

The room snapped out of focus. "What?"

"It's nothing more than a publicity stunt. A stupid one, at that. I won't go through with it."

Okay, she'd kind of already pieced together the publicity thing. But suddenly *bloodless* seemed too tame to describe such a cold business proposition, especially when applied to the institution of marriage.

"Wait." Her head spun. "Is this because of all the things I said about romance and being in love? Am I *that* convincing?"

"You're very convincing. But I never wanted to do it in the first place even though I saw the potential benefit." He shrugged. "I decided it wasn't worth it after all."

"Just now you decided?" His nod answered that question. "But your career. Kris, you can't give up your movie."

"I'm not. There has to be another way. And I'll find it." He wouldn't let her look away. "Please keep this between us. I can't stop you from telling the media. But I'm asking you not to."

"I'm not going to say anything." What would she say when none of this revelation made a lick of sense? "Why are you telling me this?"

Please let him say he wanted to remove all the obstacles, in true heroic fashion, before sweeping her into his arms, professing his feelings and making love to her all night.

This was it, where fantasy became reality. Her pulse leaped like a gazelle. She was so underdressed.

"Because. I don't want you to be upset about kissing me or about being here with me in a hotel room. The whole day was a blast. The most fun I've had in a long time. Let's keep going."

Fun.

The fried chicken churned greasily through her stomach. He was calling off the engagement because he didn't want to do it. Not because she'd unlocked him and he couldn't live without a fulfilling relationship a second longer.

"So," he continued, oblivious to the crushing anvil pressing on her chest. "Door's wide-open while I'm in Dallas. You've still got me in your clutches. Feel free to take advantage of me anytime."

How romantic. Not only had nothing she'd said penetrated, he expected her to make the first move while he kept his heart nice and safe behind the wall marked No Trespassing. He was testing the waters to see if she might be up for a little no-strings-attached fling while he was in town.

"I have to get some sleep," she whispered. "Two sleepless nights in a row might kill me." If the poisoned arrows in her heart didn't do the job first.

"Sure," he said as she stumbled to her feet and fled for the bedroom.

With a quiet click, she closed the door. Spine against oak, she slid to the floor in a heap of terry-cloth robe and bit her lip, but the pain didn't eclipse the hurt stinging through her heart.

Really, what had she expected?

Wait a minute.

She sat bolt upright. Kris might pretend to be a casual sex kind of guy, but if he really thought she was an easy target for a fling, tonight had been the perfect opportunity for seduction, with close quarters and various states of undress. Why hadn't he gone ahead?

She crawled to the bed and climbed into it. He hadn't because he'd wanted to put the power in her hands.

The power to what? Agree to a blistering liaison and then kiss him goodbye in a few days? What exactly *did* he want?

Chewing on her lip, she stared at the shut door, but her X-ray vision hadn't improved. Yet she knew what was on the other side. Furniture. Carpet. Kris. Just like she knew what lay beyond the wall protecting Kris's heart.

He lied to himself about not believing in love. Insisted he'd enter into a loveless business-arrangement engagement when he obviously couldn't. Expended an enormous amount of energy suppressing his passionate nature. He piled all of it on top of that wall, keeping everyone out and himself in.

His greatest emotional need was to embrace the passion he kept buried, and he wanted—needed—her to shove him past that point of no return. It was the only way he'd crack, and his relationship with Kyla had been in the way. So he'd removed it from the equation. Expecting her to do the math.

But what if Greek math wasn't the same as West Texas math, and she'd misread the situation? She thumped the pillow with a fist. She couldn't be wrong. No way. His engine might be wired a little differently than most men, but she'd bet everything she had exactly the right key to start it.

It was a dare.

Subtly, he was asking if she was woman enough to rise to the challenge of winning his heart.

The answer was yes. Yes, she was.

Eight

After an excellent night of sleep, Kris flipped on the water in the shower and experienced a moment of pure shock when he realized the buoyancy to his step was happiness.

VJ was so unlike other women. Challenging. Provoking. Exciting. He loved being around her. He hadn't consciously planned to ditch the engagement, but she'd been so broken up about kissing him, the words had fallen out of his mouth. And the weight lifted instantly.

He hated the idea of manipulating the public with a fictitious engagement between the star and the director of a movie. How had it taken this long to realize it? There had to be a different publicity angle because he wasn't doing the fake engagement. Now or ever. A desert mirage in an orange pickup truck had knocked some sense into his head.

What was wrong with selling tickets by promoting *Visions of Black* as a good film? He'd gladly work eighteen hours a day to generate that kind of publicity. Talk shows, viral campaigns via the internet, free early screenings. He'd find something Abrams and Kyla could agree to, even if he had to walk Ventura Boulevard with a bullhorn.

Kyla was going to be royally pissed but he'd deal with it. *Visions* would be good for her career, and she'd see that. He'd help her see that.

With all the complications out of the way, he could focus on VJ. He wanted to pick up where that Ferris-wheel kiss had ended. Right now.

Given her serious romantic fantasies, five bucks said *temporary* wasn't in her vocabulary. *Permanent* wasn't in his. Couldn't be in his. Which meant he had to back off. Way off. He'd laid out his availability for whatever she could cook up. Now it was up to her to decide if she'd jump into a short-term affair. She had to make the move. Period.

He got out of the shower, ran a brush through his hair and dressed quickly, eager to see VJ and not about to apologize for it. When he emerged from his room, she was sitting at the table, staring out the window at the downtown vista. Rush-hour haze still smudged the tops of the skyscrapers, though it was nearing noon.

"Good morning," he said.

Her hair was damp, as if she'd recently emerged from the shower, as well. Where she'd been naked and wet. Not a good image to fixate on before coffee and after deciding to back off.

"Hey." She didn't even glance at him.

Okay. Calling off the engagement should have eliminated tension, not added it.

He tried again. "What's on your agenda for the day?"

"Job hunting. I guess." Her posture put steel to shame, and her hands were clenched into a tight ball in her lap.

The day had started off with such promise—at least on his part. Where had all the easy intimacy between them gone? Out the window, apparently, now that he'd drawn the short-term-only line.

He'd known it would likely go this way, but, selfishly, he

wanted the spark without having to promise her more. As brightly as the attraction burned between them, he'd have a hard enough time keeping himself under control in the short-term.

"Didn't you mention in the car earlier that tomorrow is your birthday?" At her hesitant nod, he pulled out his phone and checked his schedule. "That calls for a celebration. Let me take you to dinner tonight."

"Thanks. Maybe some other time."

Some other time. He'd expected a resounding *no*. He hadn't expected it to suck so much. "Come on. It'll be fun."

"Kris." She shut her eyes for a beat. "I don't have anything to wear."

Of course she didn't. Instantly, he scrapped all his plans for the day, including the two hours he'd blocked to check out casting videos his assistant had sent. Some sacrifices were worth it. VJ deserved more than just dinner. She deserved a fairy tale, and he was going to give her one, whether she agreed to short-term or not. "I'll take you shopping. Consider it part of your birthday present."

Finally, she swiveled. "Don't guys hate shopping?"

He shrugged. "Yeah. I hate traffic, too, but it's unavoidable if I want to get somewhere."

"So shopping is a means to an end?"

Her tone prickled the back of his neck. "An unfortunate analogy. I'm fully prepared for you to shut your door at the end of the night." There was nothing wrong, however, with hoping they'd be on the same side of the door. "I want to do something nice for you. Is that really so awful?"

"No. It's not." Suddenly, she smiled, and the light returned to her face, thumping him right between the eyes. That alone was worth getting behind on his long task list.

"Then let's go. We can get lunch on the way."

He took her to a boutique close to the hotel and turned VJ over to a sales clerk. They disappeared into another section of the store and returned quickly, just as he'd settled into a plush chair to wait. The sales clerk had several garments draped over her arm so either VJ made up her mind really fast—and if so, he'd nominate her for woman of the year—or the clerk had selected them.

Eventually, VJ emerged from behind the divided panel, flustered and adorable, with nothing in her hands. "Are you sure about this?"

"Very sure. Pick out a dress. Pick two." Kris scouted around for the clerk. "Miss? She needs shoes and everything else a woman requires for a night out. *Everything.* Also, can you write down the name of a good spa?"

A blush spread over VJ's cheeks. "For what?"

"So you can spend the day being spoiled. Don't even think about saying no." He guided her in the direction of the clerk and crossed his arms so he couldn't yank her to him and kiss her senseless.

His hands tightened into fists. Backing off was harder than he'd anticipated.

Playing chauffeur for the rest of the afternoon gave him plenty of downtime to make reservations and get directions. The spa took a couple of hours, so he squeezed in the casting videos, not at all annoyed to view them on the small screen of his phone instead of his laptop.

"Dinner's at eight," he told VJ when she slid into the Ferrari after the spa session. "Will that work?"

"Sure." She put a hand over his on the gear shift. "Thanks. I'm having a great day. Four people worked on me at the same time, like I was royalty. The experience was truly wonderful."

They'd put some kind of lotion on her hands, softening her skin.

"Yeah? I'm glad." That creamy expanse of throat above the neckline of her T-shirt caught his attention. Now he was wondering if her skin was that same kind of soft all over and what it smelled like.

"I know you don't expect anything in return. But I got you a little something anyway." She smiled mischievously.

"What is it?"

"It's a surprise, for later. Your favorite color is red, right?" The pad of her finger slid up a tendon in his hand, following the corded line up his arm. His pulse tripped.

"How did you know?"

"I guessed. Wasn't hard. Red's the color of passion. Take me back to the hotel now?"

Take me echoed in his head, and the close atmosphere in the car stirred along his skin. Her eyes were luminous, and her fingers still played with his arm, feeling the crease at the bend of his elbow, swirling along his muscles. Then she lightly skimmed his shoulder and slid fingers into his hair, setting his nerve endings on fire.

He sucked in a hot breath and eased closer, into her space. "If you want to kiss me again, all you have to do is say so."

The blue around her pupils swam with flecks of yellow and glinted when she licked her lips in a slow glide. "Same goes."

Her thumb cruised along his jaw, then rested on his bottom lip with feather-light contact and the tip of her nail grazed it. The impact tightened the base of his spine and spread with tendrils of warmth.

"You have an amazing mouth, Kristian." Her own mouth was slack, forming that *O* he longed to fill.

With an encouraging nibble of his lips, her thumb slid deep in his mouth. As he sucked on it, her eyelids fluttered closed and that awesome moan vibrated in her throat. His groin flooded, tight and hot.

That was it.

He plucked her thumb away and caught her mouth in a kiss. Her hands clutched his shoulders, pulling him closer. Her tongue met his in a hot rush and they twined. He needed her, needed more, and reached for it.

His elbow hit the steering wheel. They were in the car. Kyla's Ferrari, for God's sake.

This was the exact opposite of backing off.

He started to break away and couldn't. One more second against her mouth was all he needed. He slanted his lips at the opposite angle, tilted her head back and relentlessly drank from her.

More.

No. Not more.

He jerked away. He had more control than this. He had to find it. Problem was, he'd never needed to find it. It had never failed before.

"Italian for dinner?" he rasped, his vocal cords dry with need. He shifted into first and tried, unsuccessfully, to ignore the ache in his gut.

"Sure," she said with a small smile.

When they got back to the hotel, she sauntered to her room, hands full of bags, leaving him at loose ends. Aimlessly, he wandered to the couch and flipped on the TV, trying to will away the semi-hard-on he'd had since the car.

Time stood still as he relived the Ferris-wheel kiss. Then the car kiss. And back again, until his almost hard-on turned into a raging one.

The images, the ache. VJ. The swirl became a continual persistence of vision he couldn't control, couldn't dissolve from his mind's eye. He had an incredible amount of work to do and yet, here he sat like a horny seventeen-year-old.

"Kris," VJ called from the bedroom. "Can you help me with something?"

Of course. Because what better way to settle his hormones than to be in VJ's bedroom? Where there was a bed. With sheets smelling of coconut.

"Down, boy," he muttered.

VJ was going to have a romantic evening if it killed him. Her future did not include telling some other guy about how

Kris Demetrious didn't speak the same language as romance. His Greek was more than passable if he did say so himself.

He stalked into her room. She stood in the middle of it wearing that virginal white robe, loosely belted, falling off one shoulder.

So it *was* going to kill him.

One breast swelled above the neckline, practically inviting him to delve into the V created by the folds of fabric. Miles of legs extended beyond the hem and led to bare feet. Red toe-nails dug into the carpet, all but begging to be licked. Begging him to keep going, licking up her smooth legs, straight to what was under that sexy robe.

"What do you need me for?" he asked. Since she was dressed, clearly it wasn't the same thing he needed her for.

She rattled her arms and the robe's sash slipped, exposing a pale swatch of skin. Was she naked under there? He couldn't tear his eyes off that tantalizing glimpse of VJ's flesh.

"Which one should I wear tonight?" she said. "I don't know where we're going."

Out of the corner of his eye, he noticed she had a dress in each hand.

"That one." He pointed without looking away from the gap under the robe's sash.

"I like that one, too." She threw both dresses on the bed and grasped the knot holding the slim belt's ends together.

His legs went numb as she worked to untie it. *Untie. It.* So he could greedily drink in the sight of her uncovered body. Naked before him, ripe and gorgeous.

Anticipation burned through his midsection. Could she labor over that tangle of sash any more leisurely?

Finally, it was loose. With agonizing slowness, she opened the robe. A flash of nipple seared his vision. Immediately, she drew the robe closed, tightening it around her waist, then tying the sash into a firm knot with quick-fingered precision. She turned away. "Thanks for your help. I'll be ready by eight."

He'd been dismissed. Soundly. And it was at least an hour until eight.

Time for a really, really cold shower. Which did not cool his blood. Or slow his pulse. Or reduce the burn of his erection. As he stood under the icy spray, he reshot that scene with an entirely different story line, where he laid her back against the carpet and untied that knot with his teeth. Then he'd spread her legs wide to drink from that well he'd been denied for far too long. He'd slide into her easily because she was so hot and slick for him, and she'd be quaking with that sexy little moan.

Yeah, like that. Again and again, until they exploded. Backhanding hair out of his eyes, he sagged against the frigid glass tiles and suffered.

Why didn't he blast into her room and take her, right there on the floor? Up against the wall. Bent over the dresser. All of the above. A consummation to end all consummations.

Moron. Not only would his creativity in the bedroom scare her blind, he was backing off. She'd get her a special evening, the kind she could remember reverently forever. There were no fairy tales where the prince subjected the princess to a rutting sexual offensive. No real women liked that, either.

It had just never been as difficult to remain detached as it was with VJ.

This was why he stayed behind the camera. Once uncorked, his passions ran over without restraint. He had to find a way to flip that switch back into the off position. He was not his father, who was so ruled by his passions that he allowed them to turn ugly.

Intelligent, funny, in-your-face Victoria Jane Lewis, who'd never left Texas because she'd unselfishly committed to caring for her sick mother, deserved better.

The stages of romance meant something to her. VJ's greatest emotional need was to star in her own fairy tale. So he'd keep his hands off of her until he could take her to dinner and treat her like a princess. Period.

* * *

After stressing over her makeup until it adequately covered the not-quite-faded bruise, VJ slithered into the black dress and blocked out the rushing sound of Mama turning over in her grave. Again.

The dress was designed for sin. Backless and form fitting, it dipped into a low heart shape over her cleavage. Under it, see-through crimson lace cradled her breasts and smooshed them skyward. The clerk at the boutique had spent Kris's money easy-peasy.

How could she have predicted it would put her on edge? Surely Kris had a little less respect for her because she couldn't have purchased any of this on her own. She couldn't ask him to come back later, when she was stable. Then she wouldn't have needed rescue. They probably wouldn't have ever met.

Fate had intervened, pushing them together. She and Kris were kindred souls. Romantics in a world designed to bleed it out of them. Instead of embracing it, he hid his true passionate nature from everyone, apparently clueless that it leaked out all over his films. His choice of music. His heroic defense against her brothers. The way he kissed with his whole body.

If she could convince him to accept that passion, all the obstacles to his heart would be gone. He had to be the one to make the move, to be so overcome, he gave in.

Unfortunately, Kris wasn't any closer to cracking than he'd been all along. For a moment, in the car, she'd thought she'd had him, but no. Then after the nerve-racking robe retying debacle—maybe she wasn't cut out for this.

"Amateur," she whispered to her reflection. He needed a huge push. Bigger than the Ferris wheel, but more effective, with longer lasting results.

Her tummy fluttered. She wanted to be with him something fierce, to see straight into his soul through those limitless eyes because she was the only one he let in. She wanted to fall the rest of the way in love, and if she did her job, he'd be right behind her. When that happened, everything would merge. The future, last names, hearts. That was the real dream come true.

One push coming up.

The black stilettos took fifteen minutes of practice before she could walk in them without stumbling. She wobbled out of her bedroom. Kris sat at the table, tapping at his laptop, and glanced up when she called his name.

His expression darkened as his molten brown eyes did a once-over all the way to her toes, devouring her with his heated gaze. Her thighs pressed together involuntarily against the throb under her brand-new thong.

Without speaking, he shoved the chair back with his thighs and crossed the room. Grasping her hand, he spun her in a slow pirouette. Heat crept up her spine as he took in the backless dress.

"That," he said, "was worth waiting for. I'm almost speechless. You're stunning."

"Thanks." She ducked her head, suddenly embarrassed at the raw desire on his face. Since that had been the whole point of the dress, her reaction made no sense, but he'd been around lots of beautiful women. Surely she paled in comparison.

"Do you have your lipstick in your bag?" he asked.

He drew her closer so he could slide a hand around her neck, resting his fingers lightly on her flesh. She shuddered. "Am I supposed to?"

"Yeah. You're going to need it."

He lowered his head and kissed her. Her eyes shut as he flooded her with the beauty of his skill. When Kristian Demetrious kissed her, it killed her equilibrium.

His clever hands explored her bare back, warming it, sensitizing it. He pressed her against his frame, tight. The tiny pulls of his lips were slow, sensual, with simmering potential. But the kiss lacked abandon, winding down instead of ramping up.

Not so fast.

She shimmied her hips against his with an upward tilt, finding that perfect hard niche where they fit together, and rubbed against his solid chest as she angled her head to let him take her deeper.

Instead, he broke away, taking an unsteady step back and a ragged breath at the same time. "Remind me later to buy you several more pairs of those shoes. I really, really like you at that height."

With her stomach twisting like a tornado, she motioned him over. "Come back. See what I got you."

Warily, he edged closer. With one finger, she hooked the neckline of the dress and pulled it down, revealing the tiny, red butterfly tattoo a centimeter from her nipple.

His eyes went black as he zeroed in on her exposed breast, and he strangled on whatever he was trying to say. Now he was completely speechless.

She was going to hell. With bells on.

After smoothing the dress back into place, she said, "I'm starving. Ready? Where are we going?"

"I don't remember. Give me a minute," he said shortly and stared at the ceiling, running a trembling hand through his hair. "Get your lipstick."

His accent was frayed, and it tingled her spine. She wanted to hear him say something really provocative with that voice, preferably while touching her.

She gathered her things and brushed the bulge in his pants as she walked past him through the door. He sucked in a shuddery breath but didn't say anything. The butterfly had clearly produced results, but not the one she'd envisioned.

She needed to up her game even more. But how?

Casa di Luigi was the height of fine dining, with white-on-black tablecloths, more silverware at each place than she set for a family of four and endless numbers of servers who waited on them. Kris ordered red wine, and when it came, he watched her over the wineglass rim with a shadowy, hooded expression as he drank.

Muted clinks and murmurs of conversation floated around them, but they weren't talking. Instead, a nonverbal swirl of innuendo crackled between them.

He set his glass on the table without breaking eye contact and picked up her hand. "Are you having a good time?"

"The best. This is a great restaurant."

"Tell me more about your book," he said out of nowhere. "What was it called?"

"Which one? *Embrace the Rogue?*"

"The one with Lord Raven. What's it about?"

"Lord Ravenwood." She narrowed her eyes. "Why do you want to know what it's about?"

"I want to talk about something that interests you."

She shrugged. "It's about a duke who rescues a lady from a runaway carriage and it's love at first sight. Except he's... what?"

"That's what it's about?"

"What did you think it was? A more explicit, unillustrated version of the *Kama Sutra?*"

Kris choked on a sip of wine and took his time recovering. "What do you know about the *Kama Sutra?*"

"It's a book, isn't it?" She stared at him with a ghost of a smile. He'd started tracing her knuckles restlessly, but his eyes were fixed on her face. "Why, have you read it?"

"I have."

The expectation sizzling through the air heightened. He brought her hand to his lips and lightly grazed the tips of her fingers. The shock traveled up her arm like a deluge swelling over the banks of the Rio Grande.

Then he said, "I can't figure you out."

"At last, my dastardly plan to be a woman of mystery has been fulfilled." She could hardly keep her attention on the conversation as he nibbled her index finger. "Why does it seem like my fingers are always in your mouth?"

"Because I like the taste of you, and we're in public. This is the best I can do."

She closed her eyes against the rush of need spiraling through her abdomen. If he kept that up, she wouldn't be doing a whole lot of withholding much longer.

Time to go on the offensive. He needed to make a move and do it soon or she would be forced to end this evening in a chaste kiss good-night at nine o'clock.

"So, about the *Kama Sutra,*" she said and leaned forward. The edge of the table shoved her bra down a centimeter. What little it had covered originally had already been pornographic. "Which one is your favorite?"

"Position?" His hand trembled and he pointedly kept his eyes on her face.

She gave him a look. "Yes, Sherlock. Position."

A strangled sound launched from his throat. "Seriously? It's not enough that I can't erase the vivid picture in my head of what's underneath that dress?"

"You started it with the tasting me in public," she whispered in deference to the elderly couple at the next table.

Kris waved the beleaguered waiter away and tightened his grip on her hand. "Fine. You go first. What's yours?"

"I don't know. I haven't tried them all yet." She lifted a brow. "I'm in the market for a guinea pig actually."

His breath hissed out and he let go of her hand. "This is not working."

Then he made a show of examining his flatware. She folded her hands into her lap. Obviously she shouldn't assume she could handle Kristian Demetrious.

"VJ," he said, eyes still on the tines of the fork flipping between his first two fingers. "Help me out. This is your birthday present. A nice dinner. Dancing later. I'm following the stages. And I'm asking you nicely to stop talking about sex so we can have the romantic evening I've planned. Would you like to order dinner now?"

Following the stages? Her heart squeezed. So that's why he'd asked about *Embrace the Rogue*. "No. I really don't want dinner."

"What would you like to do, then? I'm taking you dancing at a place that plays country music. We can go there now if you want and eat later."

Warmth spread through her chest. He remembered what kind of music she liked and was willing to endure it for a few hours. For her. Kris had been trying to show her she'd infiltrated his disbelief in romance. It was a huge move, and she'd almost missed it because it hadn't taken the form she'd expected.

"I'd be happy to help you out," she said decisively. "Take me back to the hotel right now, or I'm never going to speak to you again."

His intense gaze lasered in on hers, evaluating. "Then it's okay to skip all the stages and dive right into bed?"

She swallowed a laugh. Did he really not realize? Or was romance so much a part of his nature, he'd done it unwittingly? "You didn't skip any stages. You hit them all. I'm yours."

More evaluating. "I'll take you back to the hotel if that's what you want. But, VJ, be sure. I'm still leaving to go back to L.A. in a few days."

Not if I have anything to say about it.

She crossed her fingers under the table. If he wanted to keep pretending this was some casual encounter, she could, too. Whatever worked to shove him closer to embracing all the beautiful things he deserved. All the things they could have together.

"I'm clear. We're just having fun, right?"

His mouth twitched. "Where do I volunteer to be a guinea pig?"

His wicked grin kick-started her lungs again.

He met her eyes and a shock of lust uncurled deep in her core as he skewered her with probing intensity. Kris always had a slight sensual edge but it was fundamental to the way he moved and spoke. A fluke of his DNA. This was different. Lashing desire radiated from him, and she couldn't look away.

"I can't wait to find out what your butterfly tastes like," he said. "Last chance to back out."

She went hot and cold simultaneously, and squirmed against the heat licking through her. "Give the waiter your credit card."

"I have cash." He yanked his wallet out of his pocket and tossed a hundred on the table. "How fast can you walk in those heels?"

"Bet you can't keep up," she said and sprang to her feet at the same instant he did.

Nine

The atmosphere during the drive to the hotel was thick with impatience. Kris skidded into a parking place and materialized at her door to help her out, then pulled her through the lobby to the elevator. He stabbed the button, and the doors slid open.

It was empty. As the doors closed, Kris whirled her against the back of the elevator and crushed his mouth to hers. An edge of violent desperation flavored his kiss, thrilling her. His hands were everywhere as he consumed her. He tongued his way down the curve of her neck, yanked her dress down and licked a nipple into his mouth.

Her head lolled back and hit the wall, but she barely noticed as he sucked her nipple hard with the same pulling sensation he always used with her tongue. Heat raged through her, between her legs and down her thighs, and she moaned.

His fingers snaked up the back of her leg, then burned across her bare bottom. He dipped under the straps holding her thong in place.

One finger eased along her crease, parting and thrusting

against the wetness there. Consciousness nearly dissolved with the heightened sensation. His hands were magic, driving deep, filling her, fulfilling her. She thrust against the pressure, and the spiral inside tightened as his mouth switched to her other breast, treating it to the same perfect suction as the other. Then he nibbled on her nipple.

She bucked against his hand.

"Kris… Kris. Stop," she choked out with gasping little breaths, nearly weeping as his mouth left her flesh.

"Why in God's name should I do that?" he snapped.

She yanked on his shoulders until he straightened. "Because we're at our floor. Let's go inside."

His eyelids slammed shut. "Sorry," he mumbled. "I got carried away."

The elevator doors slid open. His obvious chagrin was endearing, but she couldn't for the life of her figure out why getting carried away was bad.

Without a word, he tucked her breasts away and led her out of the elevator. Smoothly, he slid the card key into the reader, pushed the door open and swept her up in his arms to carry her over the threshold and into his bedroom.

Elephants stampeded through her stomach. Rose petals were strewn all over the bed in a wholly romantic gesture. Her heart was lost. Probably had been since the first time he smiled at her on Little Crooked Creek Road.

Oh, God, what if she hadn't recognized the stages? She'd never have known about the rose petals.

He set her down carefully, and without warning, hooked the shoulder straps of her dress and peeled it off, trapping her arms with the fabric.

"That is more like it," he said with appreciation.

He looked his fill, studying her breasts—clearly visible through the transparent bra—with marked intensity, eyes hot and his gaze never wavering, until her cheeks were on fire. The butterfly had him mesmerized.

"I'm not a Monet," she squawked, which was not the sexy voice she'd been going for.

"You are. You're exquisite. And you have on too many clothes." The dress was around her ankles instantly. "Red's not actually my favorite color, by the way."

"It's not?" Dang it. She *knew* she shouldn't have gone with the permanent tattoo. "What is?"

He placed one finger on the edge of the thong and pushed it down. Way down, and then grazed her nub with a knuckle. "That is. I want to see it."

Wet heat pooled around his finger as he rubbed it back and forth. A long wave of desire crested and broke at his touch. He worked the finger inside her folds and then withdrew, pulling a hiss from her. She grabbed at his shoulders when her knees buckled.

"You can see it all you want," she said breathlessly. "But you have to do something for me."

"What's that?"

"Talk to me with that incredible voice." He went deep, and her inner walls clenched tight, and she moaned. "Kristian."

His eyes darkened. "I cannot tell you what it does to me when you say that."

"Try."

He smiled and pulled her close. He nuzzled her ear and whispered a long string of Greek as he unhooked her bra, which he threw over his shoulder. Still murmuring, he backed her up until her thighs hit the bed. He sat her down. Somehow her thong was gone, too.

He knelt between her legs and watched her as he put his mouth where his finger had been. He did that sucking thing, like with her tongue, but against her nub and mouthed some more Greek intermittently, lips brushing her as he enunciated.

Part of her tried to pull away from the intimacy. She'd never be able to look him in the eye again, but oh, it was amazing, and she started to splinter, scooting her hips forward, involuntarily seeking his miraculous mouth.

Her head thrashed back and forth as he sucked and licked and murmured foreign words and drove her off the edge. Her spine curved as she erupted, and heat rippled from the epicenter of her climax.

He kissed her thigh, and she fell back onto the comforter, so sated her bones were like melted chocolate. He crawled up to lie next to her, and she was ashamed to note he still wore all his clothes.

"Talk to you like that?" His hands wandered into her hair, tangling it through his fingers as he stroked her jawline tenderly with a thumb.

How in the world had she gotten so incredibly lucky as to be lying naked on a bed with Kristian Demetrious?

"Exactly like that." Her breath came in spurts. "And may I say you are extremely talented at…um, talking. But there's this other thing I need you to do, too."

In a daring move, she rolled and crawled on top of him, straddling him in that niche where they fit together, hip to hip. The man was hard all over, and she was dying to feel every golden millimeter.

His breath caught. "How talented do you think I am?"

"Let's put it to the test." She crushed a rose petal between her fingers and trailed it over his chiseled lips. "Next time I come, I want you inside me."

Eyes closed, he wound up great bunches of comforter in his tight fists. "You're making this very hard."

She wiggled against his still-covered erection. "Isn't that the idea?"

"Stop." He stilled her hips with a firm hand on each one. "You're driving me insane. I'm trying to do this right, and you're not playing your part."

"Oh? Maybe you should give me a script, Mr. Director. What should I be doing instead?"

"This is supposed to be *your* romantic fantasy evening, not mine." His voice rumbled against her pleasantly. "So far, we haven't eaten dinner, we didn't go dancing and I nearly nailed you in the elevator. You should kick me out, and make me sleep in the car."

He'd almost nailed her in the elevator? "Because why?"

His eyes closed for a beat. Obviously he was struggling with something. Maybe he didn't find her all that attractive now that she was undressed. But then he raised his lids and her breath stuttered at his visible anguish. "You're right. About what's really going on inside me, how I suppress passion, and I'm this close to losing control. You're so small. I don't want to hurt you. Scare you."

"Don't be ridiculous. You could never hurt me."

"Not intentionally." With a swallow, he said, "This should be like one of your fairy tales. I'm trying. I really am."

Her heart contracted, and she fell a little more. Somewhere in his whacked out creative mind, he'd come to the conclusion that romance equaled a chaste, *boring* encounter. He had missed the point.

She slid a hand under his shirt and placed it over his heart. With erratic beats pounding against her fingertips, she said, "Once upon a time, there was this prince who felt things so deeply, he was scared to let anyone else know, so he pretended he didn't feel anything at all. Then he met this princess who really got that. And she wishes he would get over it already and screw her brains out. The end."

He went still. Really still, and she nearly died. Kris being still was bad, especially now, at the watershed moment.

Come on, do it.

"I can't, VJ," he whispered. "You don't understand."

Her pulse leaped as she gave him the final push. "No. You don't understand. I want all of you. No holds barred. I can take whatever you've got. Really. Let go, Kristian."

Hunger whipped through his expression. Without warning,

he sat up, grinding against the naked flesh between her thighs as he captured her mouth possessively with his. Stars exploded in her head, at their joined lips.

She'd given him permission to let go. But she'd vastly underestimated what that meant.

It wasn't a kiss, but a primal mating call that swept through her veins like lava, demanding not only her body, but her soul. Long before the next beat of her heart, she surrendered.

Kris dropped the tight reins VJ had yanked from his fist.

Just for now. Just this once.

His body howled, yearning to feel, snarling to charge ahead. The world ceased to exist.

He wrapped her hair, that seductive riot of curls, in his hand and tilted her head back to expose her neck, sucking and laving until she moaned, vibrating against his length. He throbbed in response.

"Yes," she whispered and rolled her hips against him, hot and fluid. "More. I'm so ready for you. What are you waiting for?"

He set her on her feet and stripped, ripping fabric and then fingering a condom into place. Impatiently, he hustled her backward until her back hit the wall. He crowded against her scorching body, skin on skin, a thigh between her legs and her slick center calling to him. The scent, sharp and feminine, saturated his senses.

Now. It had to be now. He lifted her leg and flung it around his waist. With both hands on her bottom, he boosted her higher on the wall and pierced her in one swift stroke.

Yes, finally.

He sucked in a breath, fighting to keep the explosion at bay as he filled her to the hilt. She stretched to accept him perfectly.

In her ear, he murmured in Greek and suddenly had the strangest urge to switch to English. "This is my favorite position," he said and withdrew so slowly, he thought he'd come apart. His voice was ragged. Raw. "You're so open. So deep."

English. Because he wanted her to understand him like no one else did.

As he pushed into her again, she stared him in the eye and said, "So are you."

Yeah. He was. She'd split him open with her beautiful honesty, and it wasn't terrible. There'd be a struggle to cram the lid back on, but that was later. Much later.

He slid out slowly to savor the feel of her. Too slow. He needed her, needed more, and she gave it instantly. *More.* And still more. She met him in the middle every time. So good. So amazing to just feel. To be lost in it. To give in to all the extremes, whatever they might be.

Harder and faster now, over and over, he pushed and she squirmed, as he wound them both higher with hard, insistent thrusts. She begged for more with that sexy moan. The wall kept her in place, steady, and the heat was intense, enveloping and surrounding him.

"I'm inside you," he said with his teeth on her earlobe. Her fingernails bit into his back in an unearthly mix of pain and pleasure. "Come for me."

With his name on her lips in a soul-shattering whisper, she did, clamping down on him so hard it triggered his own release. He poured himself out, eyes closed, muscles tensed, until he was so empty, he couldn't feel his bones. She'd taken everything and more, even parts he'd intended to keep.

Sweat-slicked chests heaving against each other, he let her slide down the length of his body until she'd gained her balance, then disposed of the condom and drew her over to the bed.

Drained, he lay next to her, face-to-face. Wincing, he fingered the side of her neck. When had he done that? "There's a bruise. I'm sorry. I didn't—"

"I'm not," she said. "Shut up and save your breath for round two, please. There are at least another hundred pages of the *Kama Sutra* left."

He laughed and enfolded her hand with his. All the shadowy guilt drained away. She was something else, with an inner strength he'd almost missed amid all her talk of romantic fantasies. "You're really amazing, you know that?"

"You, too." Her eyes were closed but the small smile on her face warmed him. "Let me know when you're rested up. The wall was hot and all, but I was pretty busy hanging on. I'd like to touch you. Here."

Before he could open his mouth to decline the tempting round-two offer, her fingers trailed down his abdomen and circled his length.

"Mmm," she purred. "You feel nice."

He swore as blood rushed from his head and half filled the flesh under her fingers. He should get out of the bed. Retreat before what little control he'd regained snapped for good. "So soon? Now I know you're overestimating my talents."

"Or you're underestimating mine." Both hands engulfed him and she rotated them in opposite directions, almost yanking another release from him.

This time the curse didn't make it out of his mouth. "Where did you learn that?"

"Auto-mechanic training." She smirked and with a sensuous slide of her body down his, was at his waist and taking him between her lips.

Too late. He couldn't leave now.

He didn't want to leave now.

Lost in the hot suction of her mouth, he shut his eyes. She moaned with him deep in her throat. Vibrations rocked him, his butt tightened and he came. Hard. Twice in one night.

Victoria Jane was going to renew his faith.

"I'm in awe," he murmured when she settled up against him. "You do have talent."

"I've never done it before. Did I do it right?" She buried her face in his shoulder.

She was such a hot mix of seductress and innocent. Everything about her was arousing. He bit back a smile. "Maybe you should try again. Practice makes perfect."

She smacked him, and he did laugh then. "I told you this would be fun," he said. "I can't remember it ever being this good."

"That's because you've always been so focused on pretending you're unaffected. It takes a lot of energy to hold back." She flipped onto her stomach and spread one of those gorgeous hands on his chest. She rested her chin on her fingers and sought his gaze. "Don't do that anymore. Not with me."

"But it's okay with other women?"

She screwed up her face adorably. "Yep. Definitely hold back with other women. Actually, I'd recommend not having sex with anyone besides me ever again."

Adorable and dangerous. Dangerously addicting. She was upfront about everything, including her predictable desire for monogamy, and transparency turned him on. "I'll stick with you for now. Hungry yet?"

"I could eat. You gonna buy me dinner after I've already put out?" She sighed lustily. "Now I know I'm not in Texas anymore."

He pulled her up and kissed her sexy swollen lips. "Get dressed. But not in that." He flipped a hand at his favorite dress in the whole world. "Something that covers you or you'll starve before I let you out of this bedroom."

"Um, don't they have room service?" She arched a brow suggestively. "I remember this guy with a cart."

"Beauty and brains. Have I told you lately how much I like you?"

She grinned and straddled him. "Give me five minutes. Then you can tell me again," she said, and rubbed her slick, naked sex all over his, eliciting a groan from deep in his chest as his groin sprang to life.

"I'll be drowning in you in five minutes."

She took him in her blistering hands, fumbled endearingly with a condom and guided him to her entrance. Just before she impaled herself, she whispered, "I know mouth-to-mouth," and kissed him, tongue hot against his. She slid up and down with slow, tight strokes. His eyes nearly rolled back in his head and garbled words caught in his throat.

"I'm not hurting you, am I?" she asked and paused, concern plastered across her expression. "Or scaring you?"

"No way. Don't stop. Please," he slurred and then saw the furtive smile she couldn't hide. "Oh, you're hilarious. I'm over it, okay? You win by a landslide. Hope that compensates for not getting your fairy tale."

"Kris." She leaned back to peer at him, driving him deeper and nearly killing him. "You're here. That's the fairy tale. Not the setting or the words or the rose petals. All it takes for this to be magic is you."

And then she pushed down even harder, nipped his chest with her fingernails and turned herself into a complete liar because the magic was in her touch. A spell was the only explanation for why he was still engaged, still desperate for her.

It did take a lot of energy to hold back. He'd just never been able to let go before. Never wanted to.

An eternity later, she finally admitted to being too sore to do anything other than eat. They ordered something to be delivered to the room, and whatever it was, he ate it while watching VJ as she entertained him with stories about small town life. She had a glow so strong and beautiful, the camera would pick it up easily, and he had a possessive sense of pride for being responsible.

He also had a responsibility to end this thing quickly. Passion this strong would fade faster than normal, and he was terrified of what would happen when it did. He had no intention of sticking around to find out.

After both plates were clear, she yawned. "Thank you for the wonderful birthday. It was the best present ever. I'm afraid I'm about to crash. Is this the part where we say good-night?"

"Absolutely not." The force of his denial surprised him since he'd been about to send her off to her room. Where had that come from? Sleeping alone was habitual. Necessary. Lonely. "Forget about the other bedroom. Get your things. Move them. That door is off-limits." He thrust a finger at the offending door. "I want to watch you fall asleep in my arms."

Yeah. He did. Just until he went back to L.A. This whatever-it-was with VJ had blossomed into more than he'd been prepared for but with the promise of escape at the end of the week, he could handle it for a few days. It wasn't like moving in together, which he'd never tried with anyone.

"Okay. If you insist." She smiled, and it was treacherous. "I did want to try one other position. In the morning. You know, spoon style. Unless you want to try it now?"

On cue, the shoulder of the bathrobe fell to her elbow.

Ten

At dawn, Kris drew the drapes from the bedroom window and settled back in bed to watch the colors of the sunrise bleed into the indigo above the Dallas skyline. VJ woke long enough to snuggle up and then fell back asleep with her tousled head in the hollow of his shoulder. It was disconcerting how easily she fit and how easily he suspected he could get used to it.

He couldn't remember the last time he'd watched the night disappear into day. Small, restive pleasures were a luxury he'd forgotten in the rush of everyday life. Normally, he was out of bed and doing stuff by now. Restlessness VJ called it, and somehow, she'd tamed it. With a warm and willing woman in his bed, it hadn't seemed so important to bolt into the chaos yet.

Plus, he was stalling.

At 8:03 a.m., Kris eased out from under VJ's head and placed it carefully on the pillow. She sighed and flipped over onto her back, pulling the sheet down to her stomach and exposing that gorgeous butterfly. Small bruises dotted her neck and discolored the fragile tissue of her breasts. Guilt ate at him.

Then he remembered. She could take it. Wanted it. Begged for it. He nearly crawled back in to indulge in sleepy, morning sex. Spoon style.

But he didn't.

Out in the living area, he found his phone on the coffee table and flipped to the *M's*, then hit Call. It rang eight times. On the ninth ring, Kyla finally answered.

"Hey," she said and barely sounded hung over at all. World-class acting even without the camera in front of her.

"Hey." He paused, weighing how to approach the subject of VJ. With Kyla, nothing was simple. "Sorry. It's important or I would have waited."

"I'm still in bed, babe. Nothing's that important. Unless you're coming over to join me?" The hopefulness in her voice crawled on his last nerve and raked it raw.

"I met someone."

And that's what happened when he let Kyla rile him. He blurted out stuff he shouldn't. A loud clatter greeted the announcement, which was better than the cursing he'd expected.

"Okay," she said. "I'm sitting up. So that's why it took you so long to call. Can you give me a minute to find some coffee before you throw something like that on me?"

A few simple words and suddenly, the situation teetered on the edge of becoming a huge problem. Kyla did not like that he'd met "someone." "Listen, Kyla. I'm not going to do the fake engagement. I can't. I never liked the idea."

She was quiet for a minute and then exhaled in a long stream, likely smoking the first cigarette of her two packs a day. "Have you told Jack Abrams yet?"

Of course that was her first question. Digging, to find out how far he'd taken it. "Don't worry. You still have a job."

"I'm not worried about me. I'm worried about you, darling. Have you thought this through?"

"Yes, I have." He gritted his teeth before he called her a liar. She never worried about anyone other than herself.

"Then what's the plan? The contracts are signed. Did you bring in someone else to deal with the publicity and advertising?"

His back teeth scraped together. No. But he should have thought of it. Should have secured an additional investor before bringing this up with someone as savvy as Kyla.

He hadn't because VJ deserved to have these ties severed before he slept with her again. Really, it should have happened before last night, but then he'd been sure last night would end in separate bedrooms. When it hadn't, he'd been a little too busy to pick up the phone.

"I'm still working on the alternative plan. Do you want your car? I'll drop it off to you today."

"Guy's having a thing tonight at Club 47. Bring the car by." He did not like the crafty note creeping into her tone. "And your new friend. I'd like to meet her."

Yeah. That was going to happen. He sank down on the couch, unsure if he'd get through this without breaking something. VJ had uncorked the fire and reclosing the lid on his soul sucked. But he had to find a balance. "We're busy. I'll bring the car to your mother's around three."

"Now you've got me curious. Who is she?"

"No one you'd know."

"She must be dog ugly."

"For Christ—" He was up and pacing before he realized it. "You're unbelievable."

"And you can't still be upset about Guy. We're just friends now."

As he'd suspected. She and Guy had split up, and she'd had her sights set on Kris again.

"I'm not upset about Guy."

"Come to the club. It'll be fun. Show your new friend a good time."

He could think of a hundred things he and VJ could do for

fun besides spending the evening in a pit of vipers. "She's not my friend."

"Oh, my God. It's that serious? Is *she* the reason you don't want to do the engagement? You made it sound like—"

"Kyla. Stop." Now he had to go to the party. If nothing else, to prove to Kyla he wasn't serious about VJ. "We'll be there to drop off the car and kill your curiosity. We won't stay."

His and VJ's relationship had a short life—very short—and that wasn't going to change regardless of what Kyla said to bait him. The engagement was incidental to his feelings about VJ. He liked her, and they had fun. It wasn't as if he'd subconsciously sought to remove the Kyla obstacle in case this thing with VJ progressed.

This thing with VJ *couldn't* progress.

He needed to back off again. The more he practiced reattaching that lid, the easier it would be to do it permanently.

He ended the call and got lost in work instead of VJ, but wondered the whole time why it bothered him. Why the ache in his chest wouldn't ease no matter what he did.

When VJ woke—alone—she cocked an ear for the sound of the shower, but the bathroom door stood ajar and the interior was dark. She sat up and was immediately sorry. Everything hurt. But deliciously, rightly so. Last night had bordered on mythical.

She flopped back on the pillow and grinned at the ceiling. This bed still belonged to Kris even if he wasn't in it. She'd slept sinfully late and he was a busy man, who had spent the entire day with her yesterday. He probably needed to catch up on work and if she left him alone, maybe she'd get some of his time later.

She limped into the bathroom, beamed at the marks Kris had trailed down her throat and threw on a robe. She wandered out of the bedroom. Kris sat at the table chained to his laptop. Morning light spilled through the bay window, cloaking him in an ethereal spotlight. He glanced up, hair falling in his face and that slow smile knocked her knees loose. How had he picked her out of all the other mortals available?

"Come here," he said.

As she crossed to him, he slapped the computer closed, shoved the chair back a foot and pulled her into his lap. Then kissed her. Thoroughly.

If he did that every morning for the rest of her life, it wouldn't be enough. "Um, wow. Good morning to you, too," she said when his lips lifted.

Instead of responding, he slid his hands up her arms and hooked the robe's lapels, drawing them off her shoulders to bare her breasts. He traced a lazy pattern down her neck and circled both nipples until she was nearly panting with need.

He sighed, kissed the butterfly and covered her up again. "I have to do some things today. But I'm taking you out tonight. Will you be okay on your own until about five?"

"Sure." She swallowed and pressed her legs together until the heat subsided through sheer will alone. "I assumed you'd be working anyway. What are we doing tonight?"

"I'll tell you later. Happy birthday."

Her heart skipped. Mama had been the only one who'd ever remembered at home. "Thanks."

"Okay, now go away so I can concentrate." He grinned and pushed her lightly. She left him to his work, with only one backward glance at his pursed lips. The things that mouth could do. Shudder and a half.

She went to the pool and started rereading *Embrace the Rogue* for the four hundredth time. Even her favorite book couldn't hold her interest, so she put it down and closed her eyes, drifting in the hot sun amidst the shrieks of kids splashing in the shallow end. She ate lunch by herself and missed Kris so badly she ached. At four o'clock, hot and sweaty, she went back to the room.

Empty. Kris's laptop was on the table, closed, but he was gone and his phone wasn't on the coffee table.

Well, he didn't answer to her. He'd be back eventually.

Kris had been clear about not using her bedroom so she flipped on the water in his shower and tossed her swimsuit into the corner. As she swung open the shower door to step into the tepid spray, Kris strolled into the bathroom, his grin extremely decadent.

"Exactly where I hoped I'd find you," he said and started undressing as if it was perfectly natural to be in the bathroom with her—naked—at the same time. Her cheeks heated, inexplicably. She couldn't possibly still be shy after last night. Could she?

Her tongue was suddenly too big for her mouth, and she couldn't speak as his shirt came off, then his pants. His boxer briefs clung to his thighs—and why was he taking so long to get them off?

Then he was naked, and he was beautiful. Every smooth, golden limb and whorl of hair on his chest was exquisite. Gorgeous.

He enfolded her in his arms and held her for a moment, hands curved around her back, warm against her skin. Held her, as if cradling something precious and treasured. Embracing her intimately, instead of diving right into hot sex. His touch carried sweet nuances of all his unexpressed feelings. *Yes, yes, yes.* Last night had fundamentally changed their relationship.

Her stomach, then her heart flipped. Holy macaroni, she was so far gone over him.

"Where were we?" he murmured and nuzzled her neck.

"Um, Dallas?"

He laughed and pulled the handle on the glass shower door. "Get wet. I want to make you scream as I'm soaping you up."

Hot waves skewered her, and she almost came right then. How did he do that with just his voice?

He swept her into the shower and spun her, pushing her up

against the tiles, then pressed her flat with his hard body while whispering in her ear. The freezing tiles against her breasts and stomach combined with the heat of him on her back sent a barb through her womb. She'd unleashed a monster, and the power of it nearly finished the orgasm his voice had started.

His lathered hands slid along her sides, scandalously dipping into the crevice of her bottom, but it was luscious and she arched, seeking him, wanting him. His fingers twisted into her center with lovely friction, and she moaned.

"That's right," he murmured. "Tell me how much you like it."

He was checking in. Even after everything she'd done last night, he wanted to be sure she was still okay with no-holds-barred. Subtly asking her for reassurance before he did something irreversible. How could she do anything but fall for him?

"You make me so hot. Feels so good," she said hoarsely, and moaned his name as he teased her with sensuous circles. Sparks gathered and the tightness grew. "I need you now."

He drew her leg up, and positioned her foot on the low shelf, guided her forward and plowed into her. Yes, so good.

"More," she cried. "Faster."

And he did both. She writhed as he touched her everywhere. Then he did something indescribable against her sex as he slid deep, scraping his hard teeth against the hollow of her collarbone. She came in a whirlpool of thick sensation with a half scream.

"Yes. Beautiful," he said fiercely, and held her firm against his chest as she climaxed again and again, lost in a delirium of pleasure. Her vision blurred.

When she could see again, she was still locked in his embrace, water sluicing over her, and he was stroking wet hair out of her face.

"You're so gorgeous when you come," he said, his lips grazing her ear. "So uninhibited. I want you again just thinking about it."

She turned in his arms and took his mouth in a hard, desperate kiss, then shoved him backward until he collapsed on the shelf. She mounted him. "You can see me better from this angle."

His expression turned feral. "You're insatiable. I can't tell you how much I like that."

Circling his hips against hers, rubbing their bodies together carnally, he sparked a mad fire, enflaming her deep at the core. She needed him, craved him. Never had she felt this kind of drive to be with someone. Only Kris.

The monster *had* been unleashed but it was inside her. All her feelings for this man had exploded from their bonds, seeking to claim even as she was claimed. She barely understood the ways he made her whole, made her more than what she'd been. Barely understood the drive to reach completion again and again.

She'd been waiting for this, for him, her entire life.

As he drove her higher, faster, fiercer and longer than the first time, as she was about to drop off that ledge and free fall into climax, she found his gaze and stared into his open eyes as she shattered.

He shuddered with his own release but didn't break their locked gazes, and the emotion in his melty eyes—affection, pleasure, affinity—squeezed her heart. Squeezed so hard, tears formed. One slid down her face, and in the aftermath, still joined and totally overcome, she mouthed *I love you.*

Shock darted through his expression. She cursed. She hadn't meant for him to hear her.

She stood and backed away, taking measured breaths to calm her racing pulse. "Sorry, heat of the moment. Don't worry, it's not contagious."

His eyes turned flat and unreadable. Inaccessible Kristian Demetrious had returned.

"Come back and let me finish washing you," he said.

Eyes narrowed, she did, but when he touched her, it was

impersonal. Great. How in the world would she counteract this disaster?

The atmosphere was strained for the remainder of their shower and as they got dressed. He talked to her. She talked back, but couldn't find the groove where they were intimate with each other. They shared the bathroom sink and mirror, accidentally touched, did a hundred other things that a real couple might but it wasn't right. Panic erupted like a swarm of angry monarchs flying down her windpipe and she couldn't get her eyeliner straight.

They went to dinner at a different place than last night and she had no illusions about whether they would eat this time. Halfway through the salad course, she put her fork down. "Can we talk about it?"

"Talk about what?" He twirled the fork in his fingers and caught it, then stabbed some lettuce as if it had tried to get up and walk off his plate.

"You know what. The shower."

"I'm partial to showers, myself. Aren't you?"

Resorting to deflection. Why was she not surprised? "I say that to all the guys I'm sleeping with. Don't read into it."

His face froze. He picked up his wineglass and sat back in the chair, all pretense of eating gone. "Well, I feel special."

What kind of response was that? Suddenly she was tired of trying to burrow through, under or around that wall. Tired of waiting for that moment when it would all come together.

She buried her face in her hands and willed back the sudden urge to stand and run. "What do you expect me to say? That you're nothing to me, and I can't wait to ditch you? That I don't have any feelings for you? I can't. Both would be as much a lie as telling you I say that to all the guys. Guy. There's only been one other."

"Look at me."

She raised her head. With a small smile, he held out a hand, palm up. Cautiously, she placed her hand in his and he squeezed it tight. She braced.

Here it comes. It's not you, it's me.

"You're the most fascinating and exciting woman I've ever met," he said. "The most attractive part is your honesty. I have to accept that sometimes it might lead to a little more honesty than expected. If that's how you feel, I appreciate that you trust me enough to say so. I'm sorry I didn't handle it well. You took me by surprise. That's all."

"Did you just apologize to me?" Her throat wasn't working right, and it was going to be a close call whether or not she cried. Kris thought she was fascinating and exciting. Instead of continuing to freak out over her slip, he'd apologized. This was way better than a romance novel.

"I did, because I was acting badly. So I'll do it again. I'm sorry. I don't want to spend the rest of our time together being at odds. We've only got a few days before I go back to L.A."

A few days? Back to L.A.?

When had English become *her* second language?

"Can we put it behind us and have a good time tonight?" he asked and stroked her knuckle.

"Sure." Somewhere she'd lost the thread of the conversation and desperately, she cast about, trying to grasp it again. "What's on the agenda for the evening?"

"A get-together with some people I know."

"Sounds fun. Oh, look, here's dinner."

Gratefully, she released his hand and sat back to give the waiter access. She picked up her fork and dug into the main course, with no idea what it was.

Kris was still planning to end it with her and leave in a few days. Instead of breaking down his barriers, she'd screwed up and added one more. Whatever progress she'd made had been thoroughly erased the moment she dropped the *L* word.

Grief pulled at her mouth. She was waiting in vain for the moment when things would come together because her math

skills clearly left a lot to be desired. None of this was working. He'd opened up and all that amazing passion discharged
like a crackle of lightning, just as she'd known it would. But
it was strictly one-way. A release of energy, not a significant
encounter that caused him to reevaluate.

As soon as the waiter was out of earshot, she fell back on the
tried-and-true method to regain her equilibrium. If he wanted
fun, fun he'd get, at least until she figured out how to turn
one and one into two. "What's the wildest place you've ever
had sex?"

He grinned and the tension was gone, at least as far as he
knew. It was still there, across the back of her neck and racing
through her mind as she tried to reconcile the very different
agendas playing out on the field of their relationship.

"You mean someplace other than in the shower with you
earlier?" His fork disappeared into his mouth.

She had bricks in her chest and he was eating.

"Yeah, that doesn't count."

"Sorry, that was so good, it erased my memory. Can I tell
you how unbelievably hot it is that you're ready to go again
within minutes?"

"It's all in the wrist."

He was being purposely evasive, too much the gentleman
to flaunt his experience with other women. Of course it made
her love him that much more. How could they be on such different pages?

"What about you?" he asked with a lifted chin. "Other than
the shower. Wildest place."

"The couch."

He toasted her with his wineglass. "We'll have to remedy
that. Pick a place. Any place. I find myself fond of being your
guinea pig."

"Hood of the car." Really, she couldn't even think about
this now.

He winced. "You mean the Ferrari?"

She raised an eyebrow. "You got another one?"

"The Ferrari belongs to Kyla. I'm dropping it off to her tonight, so maybe you should pick another place. Why are you grinning like that?"

The Ferrari wasn't Kris's. The thought thrilled her. The final piece of the puzzle clicked into place—the engine inside his head wasn't complex and foreign after all. She *knew* Kristian Demetrious, and therefore, she knew better than to believe the lies he told himself. He was falling back on old habits of denying his feelings because…well, she didn't know exactly why he did it but that didn't change the facts. She hadn't misread him or tripped up by confessing her feelings.

He thought he was leaving in a few days. And she was going to change his mind.

One more big push, and he'd never leave her because he would realize they were meant to be together forever.

Eleven

The driving beat, audible even outside the club, thumped against VJ's ribs as Kris led her past the crowd lined up between red ropes and to an unmarked door around the side.

"Secret VIP entrance?" she asked.

"Something like that."

Kris nodded to the doorman, who pushed open the door, and Kris took her hand as she crossed the threshold into another world of thick smoke and strafing lights. People were everywhere, three deep at the bar, crushed together on the dance floor. All of them reeked of money.

"Am I allowed to be a little starstruck?" she shouted over the music and tightened her grip on Kris's hand so she couldn't fiddle with her hair or dress again. No one was going to notice her anyway, not with a Greek god casting her into shadow.

"No. They're just people," he said shortly.

All his answers had been short since they'd gotten into the car after dinner, including when he told her Kyla would be at the club and yes, it would be awkward. Unfortunately, so far, he'd been the one making it awkward with his odd aloofness. Inaccessible Kristian Demetrious was not her favorite companion.

Thankfully she'd worn the black dress last night so she could wear the red one tonight. It was calf-length with a Jezebel slit up the center. All the way up. Any higher and she'd be arrested for indecency. Dozens of glittery straps zigzagged across her bust and torso, then around to her back, allowing a lot of bare skin to peek through. All she needed now was the devil's pitchfork and some horns, but at least she looked her best and it bolstered her confidence.

Another hulking bouncer guarded the ropes leading to some steps and nodded to Kris when they approached. He unhooked the catch and stepped aside. The result of Kris being famous or because he'd been here before? Maybe it was because he radiated a sense of authority wherever he went.

At the top of the stairs, another room overlooked the main dance floor. This was clearly the place to be. The people below didn't reek of money. She'd been mistaken. They reeked of pretense, and there was no comparison. *These* people had wealth, class and prestige that poured off of them in waves. Just like Kris.

Her eyes darted everywhere, taking in the diamonds and European cigarettes along with the faces of celebrities often seen in magazines and on TV. The music was quieter here as if fame had a dampening effect on acoustics.

"Is that a Jonas brother?" she couldn't help but ask and then bit her tongue. She was going to embarrass herself and Kris if she didn't shut up, but she was still off balance from dinner.

Kris smiled without humor and pulled her into the sea of superstars.

Kyla Monroe was ringed by a throng of admirers, a modern-day Scarlett O'Hara in Scarlett Johansson's body. In person, she looked the same as she did on the screen. Perfect. Every platinum hair in place, flawless makeup, unblemished skin. She must carry a salon in her clutch that beautified by osmosis.

VJ's stomach clenched. They'd both slept with the same man. Kris had touched Kyla the same way he'd touched her and probably a lot more times. He'd learned how to do that sucking thing with his mouth from somewhere. Scorpions scuttling along her spine—that's what it felt like to step into the same room as his ex-girlfriend. His beautiful, poised, glamorous ex-girlfriend.

How did people in Hollywood do this?

Like this.

With confidence drawn from who-knew-where, she pasted on a smile and strode forward to take Kyla's manicured hand. These were the people Kris interacted with every day, and she'd fit in or be crucified. If it was the latter, at least she'd be dead.

"So this is your new friend." Kyla's eyes cut over VJ smoothly. "Kris forgot to mention how striking you are. Catch me before you leave, and I'll give you my agent's number. You should call him. I'll put in a good word for you."

"She's not interested," Kris answered for her, fortunately, since she was speechless.

"I'm interested." A breathtakingly stunning male of the blond Nordic variety had materialized at Kyla's side. "Introduce us, why don't you?"

VJ almost fainted when she recognized him.

"VJ Lewis," Kris said icily. "This is Guy Hansen."

"I've seen all your movies," VJ gushed as she shook his hand. "I loved the last one about the runaway train. Very edge-of-your-seat."

"Ah, the magic of editing." Guy hadn't released her hand yet, and he didn't until Kris pulled her away and tucked her underneath his arm.

The glower on Kris's face could have cooked bacon. VJ did a double take. Jealousy. Because she'd seen Guy's movies but not Kris's? Well, it wasn't her fault the Cineplex in Van Horn played blow-'em-up action movies starring actors with six-pack abs and didn't show independent films.

Lacing fingers with Kris, she leaned in so only he could hear. "It's too bad he's so ugly. Think how successful he could be with a little plastic surgery. Although, he doesn't speak Greek, so he'll never be perfect."

Kris kissed her temple and his lips lingered for an intimate beat. Kyla didn't miss it. As she glanced back and forth between VJ and Kris, her eyes glittered against the colored strobe lights behind her.

"Babe, run get us some drinks. I'd like to talk to VJ." Kyla ran a proprietary hand down Kris's arm and smiled at VJ like the lead in a toothpaste commercial. "He knows what I drink. What would you like?"

VJ smiled at Kyla like the lead in a vampire movie and said, "He knows what I drink, too. And how I take my eggs in the morning."

Guy whistled. "Look out."

Kyla laughed and pushed both men aside. "Go. Both of you. Girl talk will only make you vomit."

VJ shooed Kris off. "It's okay. I'll be fine," she whispered.

Kris backed away, his aura full of sharp angles and his mouth hard. He didn't take his eyes off either woman as he flagged down a harried cocktail waitress.

"You're not at all what I expected," Kyla said, once Kris was out of earshot. "But I can see why Kris likes you."

Kris liked her because she understood him better than anyone on Earth and enabled him be the real person he was inside.

But, a glimpse into the psyche of the man VJ loved via his ex was too tempting to pass up.

"Really? Why?"

"You don't take any crap. He likes strong women who take care of themselves. What do you do?"

Kris liked strong women. Who took care of themselves.

So far, she hadn't been racking up too many points on either count. "What do I do about what?"

"For your career." Kyla sat gracefully on one of the leather couches lining the wall of the club and crossed her legs in a way too posed to be comfortable, but which showed off her toned thighs. It was astonishing how she'd done that without falling to the floor.

"I'm between engagements. Considering my options."

The last thing she'd admit to this accomplished woman was how bleak prospects were for eating next week, never mind the luxury of choosing a career.

"Good for you. Very smart to consider all the options." Kyla swept her with another full-length glance as VJ joined her on the couch. "I love that dress. Roberto Cavalli is one of my favorite designers."

"Thanks." There was no way she could reciprocate. She had no idea who'd designed the stunning sequined dress Kyla was wearing and probably wouldn't know how to pronounce it if she did. And she had a feeling Kyla was leading up to something. Nerves kicked at her, and she wedged her hands under her skirt.

"Can I ask you something?" Kyla went on without pausing. "Did Kris tell you about the financing for his next movie?"

"Of course. He doesn't keep secrets from me."

A cigarette appeared between Kyla's fingers and she waved off Guy who'd returned and jumped over with a light. "Then you must know the film's budget is tied to the publicity campaign Kris just threw in the trash. He must care about you a great deal to give up that film."

The flame from Kyla's lighter mesmerized VJ for a moment, and she didn't immediately register what the other woman had said. "What?"

"Oops." Kyla flinched and with a laugh, shook her head. "I assumed you knew the deal with Jack Abrams fell through since you don't have any secrets."

"Fell through? No, Kris is working on alternatives. He told me."

Though she and Kyla were almost the same age, the sudden shrewd light in the other woman's eyes said VJ was young and naive.

"Making movies is about money and ego, and when money and ego are involved, so are contracts. Directors don't have the luxury of alternatives, no matter what Kris told you. Oh, I hope I didn't cause problems between the two of you. He deserves to be happy. Speak of the devil." Kyla nodded with a raised brow as Kris crossed the room with two drinks in hand. The VIP section wasn't nearly dim enough to hide his back-off vibe, which she suspected he radiated reflexively when around other people.

"Enough girl talk." Kris handed Kyla her drink. He extended the same hand to VJ, pulled her off the couch and positioned a stiff arm around her waist. "VJ and I will finish our drinks elsewhere and then we're leaving. Hansen has the valet claim ticket for your car. I'll call you later about meeting with the studio."

"I was doing all right," VJ said as he guided her across the room. "I would have rescued myself if I wasn't."

"I shouldn't have left you with her, but you insisted. I should have said no." Kris downed his drink in one shot, lights bouncing off the shiny glass as he tilted it back. She'd never seen him drink so much. She wouldn't have noticed except for his weird mood, which was getting harder to blame on being in public instead of the more likely cause—he might be okay with honesty, but not with her loving him.

"Kyla was nice."

Kris snorted. "Nice for a cobra. At least once she poisons you, death is quick. What did she say?"

"She complimented my dress and said you deserve to be happy. Which is true."

She should mention the film. She should ask him what was going to happen now that he'd called off the engagement. Naively, she'd assumed it would all work out, and Kris would still get to make his movie in spite of having met her.

Her drink disappeared in a few gulps, but it didn't loosen her tongue.

Kris glanced at his phone and motioned toward the door. "Ready?"

Now was her chance to ask if he was really giving up the film for her. If he was sacrificing something he couldn't afford to lose this time, instead of giving up something he wasn't using anyway. Then maybe he'd admit he was in love with her, sweep her into his arms and announce that no mere movie could compare with the depths of completion VJ brought him. He would confess he'd been acting weird because he didn't know how to handle his emotions.

It could happen.

A tremor stopped her words cold. Music pounded through the sudden hollowness of her chest. He'd spent the last four days telling her how important this movie was and how his entire career hinged on it. Every second he wasn't with her or sleeping, he clacked away on his laptop, dealing with Important Director Matters. Kyla mentioned contracts, which meant legal entanglements she'd never even considered.

She couldn't let him give up the movie. For any reason.

So, either Kris was going back to L.A. in a few days to make his movie like he'd said at dinner, and she'd not only have to accept it, she'd have to encourage him to do the engagement after all. Or it was already too late and she'd ruined everything.

The last option, the one where Kris ended up with her *and* the movie, fell into a distant, highly implausible third place.

Suddenly, she didn't want to know which one it was. Not tonight. Tomorrow was soon enough to ask.

They'd left the club hours ago and Kris still couldn't banish the edgy scrabbling at the back of his neck. Awake and restless, he stared through the open drapes at the dark skyline and pulled VJ's sleeping form a little closer, though she was already almost on top of him. It was never close enough, especially not after exposing her to Kyla and the person he always became around her. VJ cleansed all that from his system.

His plan to take her to the club to solidify the temporary nature of his relationship with VJ hadn't worked. The part where he'd tried to back off again hadn't worked, either. All night, he'd carried a sharp, underlying awareness that VJ was in love with him.

Clearly, they defined the words *fun* and *temporary* differently, or she'd never been on board with either from the beginning, which was the most likely. He'd known better than to get involved, but hadn't been able to resist. Then, when she did exactly as he'd come to expect—said what was in her heart— he acted surprised. His bone-headedness in the shower had been driven purely by the ache in his throat from not being able to say it back.

He'd never said that to anyone, never even come close. Never thought for a moment what he felt might be love. Until now.

VJ made it easy to feel. Necessary to feel. She was in love with him, and the knowledge settled inside with a heavy, unique relevance. Honestly, he'd been eager to leave the club and be alone with her. He'd never cared about that before. Hollywood parties were endless and he usually left unaccompanied. How had this whatever-it-was with VJ progressed this far?

VJ sighed softly and burrowed her head into his shoulder a little deeper. He breathed in the wave of sweetness from her hair, hair he'd washed with his own hands.

The emotionally heavy tang of her on his skin, with that cinnamon hair splayed across his chest as she slept naked in his bed, unearthed a fierce longing in his gut to grab on to her and never let go. To maintain this cocoon she created around the two of them. When he was inside it, anything and everything was possible. *That's* how it had progressed this far.

If anyone could make him believe in fairy tales, she could.

He threaded that amazing hair through his fingers and cupped her face, gently kissing her awake because he had to. She was a persistence of vision he couldn't erase. She stirred and rolled with a tiny wiggle until they were snugged tight with her rounded bottom against his hips. Drowsily, she steered his palm to her breast and murmured, "Need you, Kristian. Love me."

In an instant, he sank into her. Tight inside her, inside that dreamlike state that was somehow reality and he fell into it closefisted. Prolonged it as long as he could. VJ arched against his chest in a beautiful bow and tangled her legs with his, thrusting him deep and tunneling under his skin with her soft sigh.

At the moment he fractured, the theme for *Visions of Black* came to him on a spur of inspiration. It was so brilliant and obvious. How had he missed it?

VJ collapsed into the pillow and fell asleep wrapped firmly in his arms. His brain clicked into high gear with lighting angles, set pieces, script changes. But he couldn't give up holding VJ just yet. Soon, he wouldn't have a choice but to give her up. His life didn't have a fairy-tale ending and he'd be selfish to continue down this spiral when he couldn't promise her anything past the next few days.

The longer he spent with her, the wider she'd crack him open and the harder it would be to keep the lid in place. The harder it would be to control the darkness he knew lived inside, lurking, waiting to turn something beautiful into ugliness.

At dawn he crawled out of bed. Work beckoned. And he needed some time away from VJ or he'd never regain his balance.

As soon as his laptop booted up, he typed a ton of notes. *Visions of Black* had two elements: the full-color, disjointed visions and the black-and-white hospital scenes, which represented the main character's reality of blindness and amnesia. He'd been stumbling over it, but in his moment of clarity, he'd realized the visions were her reality and the hospital the altered state. That's why it hadn't been working. Once he flipped them, everything came together. The theme was altered reality.

After a couple of hours, he'd finished pouring the contents of his brain onto the page. Next, he opened the Creative Financing file and added the idea he'd come up with a few minutes ago. *Borrow against future gross.* Which was not great, because it granted rights to profit on a film he hadn't even conceptualized yet, but it beat the fake engagement.

The other ideas weren't stellar, either. He rubbed his eyes and blinked at the screen. None of this would net the backing he needed to make a blockbuster of *Visions of Black*. Guys starting out did this kind of scrambling, stuff he'd done ten years ago to put enough money in his hands to commit brilliance to film and impress the deep pockets into taking a chance on him.

And finally, after years of bleeding his emotional center onto the screen, one of those deep pockets stepped forward. Jack Abrams signed on the dotted line, but to compensate for Kyla's exorbitant salary, Kris had agreed to cut advertising dollars and stir up publicity with the engagement. It had seemed like a fair trade at the time.

Studios were evil. But they had connections, distribution channels, promotional departments. Things an independent film director only dreamed of.

Kris made coffee and waited until the brewer trickled the final drop into the pot before pulling out his phone to call Jack Abrams. He'd put off the call, hoping a genius idea for promoting *Visions of Black* would fall from the sky.

The hour was still early on the west coast but Jack was a morning person, too. Kris hoped their good working relationship would smooth out the issues from the bomb he was about to drop.

"Mr. Abrams," he said when the other man answered. "It's Kris Demetrious. Sorry to bother you, but I need to tell you I've decided not to announce my engagement to Kyla Monroe."

"Not announcing it?" Jack paused. "Or not going through with it at all?"

"Not going through with it at all," Kris said. "It's not the right path. I'd like to discuss other options."

"I'm a little taken aback," Jack said gruffly. "We all agreed on this publicity angle."

"Yes, sir. I changed my mind. I'd like to renegotiate funds for advertising instead."

"That's not possible. The numbers are the numbers and our contract is solid." Jack Abrams was a powerful man and the nuances of his statement weren't lost on Kris.

"I understand. I intend to honor the contract. I'm asking you to be open to other possibilities."

"I wouldn't be opposed to reallocating."

Which meant Kris would have to cut somewhere else, but the budget was too tight for that. Kyla's salary was the major sticking point. She was a huge draw, and she'd already approved the script. Above all, the role needed her particular spin. No other actress would be right. He couldn't shoot the movie without her. "Thank you, sir. I don't think that will work."

"Then it doesn't sound as if you have a choice but to stick with the original plan."

"No, sir. It doesn't."

Kris ended the call and contemplated smashing his phone through the laptop screen. But he needed it to call Kyla and talk her into taking less money. That conversation didn't go any better. She refused to listen and instead issued a thinly veiled threat to speak to her lawyer if he didn't get with the program. So much for hoping their history might sway her toward a peaceable solution.

His temples throbbed. Years of work, about to go down the drain because he couldn't pretend to be engaged to Kyla. Yes, he'd agreed to it. But that had been before VJ put his cynicism through the shredder and spliced his psyche back together into something he didn't fully understand yet. But he did know people should see *Visions* because he'd created something brilliant, not because of a fictitious engagement.

He had no choice but to find another way. He would not be forced to cool things off with VJ to make an engagement to Kyla believable, all because Abrams and Kyla refused to budge. The cool-off would happen when and how he decided. Hollywood did not control his life.

Disgusted, he stabbed the power button on the TV remote. He hated TV. The chances of finding a decent enough distraction were about zero but he flipped through the channels anyway, hoping to stumble over an old Hitchcock or Kubrick flick.

Photos of him and VJ leaving the club last night, as well as ones from the restaurant the night they didn't eat, crowded the screen of a national morning talk show.

"Wow. That dress photographs well." VJ plopped down on the couch next to him and kissed his shoulder.

His black mood lightened as she tucked her legs up under the robe and leaned against him. He turned up the sound, curious how the two of them were news, just as the still shot dissolved into one of Kyla.

"…statement from her publicist, box-office sweetheart Kyla Monroe confirms her relationship with director Kristian Demetrious has ended," the reporter said. "Unconfirmed speculation names the unidentified woman in these photos as the cause."

"What is she talking about?" VJ glanced at Kris.

"I have no idea." He shrugged.

"Well, your relationship with Kyla is over. At least they got that part right. But it was over a while ago." Her tongue came out to lick her lips. "Right?"

Not this on top of the conversations with Abrams and Kyla and *you have no choice* still ringing in his ears. His temper veered back to bad. "Kyla and I broke up a few months ago, but she asked me not to issue a statement and I didn't. Thanks for the trust."

"I'm sorry. We've never actually talked about it." She

rubbed his shoulder and cleared her throat. "Speaking of which. There's something else we really need to get straight. The promotion for your movie. Kyla said a few things last night that didn't make sense."

Great. First VJ accused him of playing two women at once, and now she wanted to hash out wisdom from the mouth of Kyla. "Kyla says lots of stuff, especially if she thinks it'll get her what she wants. What did she say?"

"Well, she made it sound like the engagement and the movie go hand in hand. Without one, you won't have the other. Is that true?"

"I'm making *Visions* no matter what."

"Good." With a sexy growl, she swung a leg over his lap and straddled him, wiggling against his ever-present erection.

And that was the end of it. Dropped, like it had never happened, and minus any drama. VJ might be the perfect woman. And he might have to face that his resistance to the engagement had more to do with VJ than he'd been willing to admit.

He stared into her gorgeous eyes sparking with that wealth of acceptance and understanding and suddenly couldn't speak.

Passion faded. Then all that simmering emotion had to go somewhere. What would he do then? He refused to give in to the black side of passion—the rage, the anger. The way his father did once his parents' forbidden love affair fizzled.

The right move was to disengage and shove everything back into the box. Save VJ the heartache. He never should have gotten involved with a victim of abuse. Never should have gotten involved with someone so singularly qualified to break that seal on his emotions. Maybe if they'd met later, at a point when he'd practiced balancing a whole lot more, things would be different.

Regardless, they'd met now, and he couldn't keep his hands off of her. She called to him and every cell answered, reaching out, seeking to unify at a level so deep, he hadn't realized it existed. He trusted her like he'd never trusted anyone.

If only he could trust himself as much.

As she lifted his T-shirt over his head and her soft hands sparked across his chest with sweet, intense heat, her scent drifted into the space between them, clenching his gut. He should push her away.

But he couldn't. Not yet.

He had no illusions about what VJ wanted. Expected. A happily ever after. VJ deserved that, deserved someone's whole heart forever. But what did that mean? What if he wanted to be that person but couldn't figure out how to keep his balance? Then it would be too late.

It was better to disappoint her than to take a chance.

This passion between them was going to end in a world of hurt and not all of it was going to be hers. The sooner he let her go, the sooner they could both move on.

By noon, VJ had sent Kris off to a meeting with Some Important Movie People, with strict orders to come back in a good mood, and then parked herself in front of the TV, intending to call Pamela Sue and giggle over how she'd made the news. She owed her friend some juicy details about Kris, too.

She raced through the channels to an entertainment news network. It was noon, so they'd probably lead in with more important stories. Except they were already showing pictures of her in that lovely, obscene red dress, which was currently balled up in the comforter from Kris's bed.

"…unidentified source claims Oscar-winning actress Kyla Monroe was dumped by Kristian Demetrius via phone yesterday. The source, a close friend of Ms. Monroe's, describes her as heartbroken and confused about why her longtime boyfriend would end their relationship over a women he met a few days ago."

The reporter paused as the photo of Kyla next to VJ's head morphed into one of VJ and Kris at Casa di Luigi when the sexual tension had been so high, the sparks between them were practically visible.

VJ flinched. Her fingers were in Kris's mouth in the photo—but when weren't they? She and Kris should have had more discretion. Mama would be so ashamed, especially to hear her daughter had been carrying on with a man she'd just met.

The reporter's face grew grave. "Social media is frenzied over the alleged betrayal of an actress beloved in the films *Sweet as Snow* and *Long Way Home*."

Text appeared on the screen and with a roiling stomach, VJ read the vicious slurs people had posted to various websites. Calling her a home wrecker. A boyfriend stealer, though that was ridiculous since Kyla and Kris hadn't been together. Calling her a nobody. Well, that one was true.

Who went to that much effort to say things about someone they'd never met? And over a situation they knew nothing about? Hilarious how all this was her fault. Apparently the man in a cheating and heartbreak scandal had no culpability.

Breakfast almost reappeared when the author of one of the slurs identified herself as a technician at the spa VJ had gone to. She went so far as to say she'd seen VJ's breasts and they were nothing special. As if that made it obvious Kris had chosen the wrong woman.

VJ had to get out of this room and away from the TV.

She stretched out at the pool and tried to empty her mind through sheer will. She didn't even pick up *Embrace the Rogue*. Her runaway carriage had already crashed and burned and the hero wasn't around to save her anyway.

A commotion by the pool's gate interrupted her misery. Two women in Hotel Dragonfly uniforms were blocking the pool entrance. Another woman clutching a microphone and a man with a camera tried to get past them. Even at a hundred yards, the news channel logo and the raised voices were painfully clear. It was a reporter looking for VJ.

Well, what better way to handle this than to make a statement? According to Kyla, Kris liked strong women who could take care of themselves. So she'd take care of it.

Twelve

VJ wove through the loungers and other hotel guests to the exit. "I'll talk to them," she said to the uniformed women.

"If you're sure, Ms. Lewis." The two hotel employees nodded and melted away.

The camera lens was much bigger than it had looked from the other side of the pool. The cameraman zeroed in on her bikini. She should have scheduled time later, when she was dressed. Too late now.

"I'm Rebecca Rogers from KTVN." The reporter was a sleek blonde woman in heels, with flawless makeup and a tan dark enough to draw the attention of every skin-cancer specialist in Dallas. "Ms. Lewis? Is that your name?"

"VJ Lewis. I didn't steal Kris from Kyla. Can you tell everyone?"

The reporter's expression didn't change. "Is this on the record?"

"You can quote me if that's the question. I heard what people are saying about me and it's not true. None of it is. I'm not that kind of person, who deliberately goes after a man who's unavailable."

She flinched at the lie as soon as it came out of her mouth. No, the engagement was never real and Kris wasn't actually with Kyla, but at the top of the Ferris wheel, she'd kissed a man carrying an engagement ring intended for another woman. They'd had an agreement and VJ had plunked herself down in the middle of it.

"You deny that you're intimately involved with Kristian Demetrious?" The reporter almost shoved the microphone into VJ's mouth in her eagerness.

"I'm denying that he was involved with Kyla Monroe. They weren't engaged. They're not going to be engaged. It was supposed to be a publicity stunt to promote their new movie."

That got the reporter's attention. She fired off a series of questions, and VJ answered them as best she could. She was a good girl from West Texas, not the vixen home wrecker people thought she was, and this reporter could clarify that.

"You work fast," Rebecca concluded with a smarmy grin. "This is quite a cozy arrangement you have going on with Kristian." The microphone was in her face again. The reporter asked, "What's next for you two?"

Wasn't that the million-dollar question? "That's private."

Rebecca's eyebrows rose. "But the rest of your relationship isn't?"

"It should be. But thanks to people like you, it's not. I can't sit by and let everyone believe bad things about me."

"So, you just want people to believe bad things about Kyla Monroe and Kristian Demetrious. Right? You said they were planning to pretend to be engaged as a publicity stunt."

"No." VJ shook her head and frowned. She shouldn't have said that. No one had even mentioned anything about an engagement. Except VJ. "I didn't mean for any of this to come across as bad."

"Comes with the territory. Don't shack up with celebrities

if you can't take the heat," Rebecca advised with a conde-
scending head tilt.

"This interview is over." VJ whirled and scurried to her
lounger, but the pool wasn't a sanctuary any longer. All of
this because she was chasing a happily-ever-after with Kris
that was still a happily-right-now. She snatched her bag from
the adjacent lounger and blew past Rebecca's prying eyes to
go back to the room.

By the time Kris got back from his meeting, she'd curled
up in a ball on the couch and cried all the tears her body could
produce.

He dashed into the room, tossed his phone on the coffee
table and gathered her up in his arms. "I'm sorry."

Which left no doubt he'd either seen or heard about her new-
found notoriety. This was so not what she signed up for. Casual
sex, trading off men with celebrities. Media scandals. None
of that had been on her mind when she got into the Ferrari.

"They think I'm evil," she said.

Kris's phone buzzed against the coffee table but he ignored
it.

"What can I do?" he asked softly and stroked the back of
her head.

"I don't know. None of this is your fault. I feel like the vil-
lainess in a soap opera."

The phone buzzed again.

"Answer it. Please," VJ said and jumped up. "I'll be fine.
I'm taking a shower. By myself."

His eyes tracked her as she stepped away from the couch,
but he didn't try to stop her. "Okay."

She stood under the spray for what seemed like hours and
still couldn't eliminate the oily feel to her skin. If it had been
a sleazy tabloid, *that* she could have shrugged off. Maybe. But
Rebecca the Reporter was from a local TV station and had gotten a stellar scoop by locating VJ at the Dragonfly.

When she trudged back into the main living area of the suite she slammed into the wall of Kris's mood. The atmosphere had changed like a squall line tumbling over the mountains, about to let loose a toad-strangler of a storm.

"What's wrong?" she asked.

He paced a mad trail along the carpet behind the couch, turning sharply before he hit the wall. A black band held his hair in place at his collar but it was a jumbled mess and Kris was never a mess.

"Why is your hair tied up?"

"It was irritating me." And back to pacing. "I'm trying to calm down. That's what's wrong."

Instinct told her she shouldn't press him when he was this upset, but what should she do? She couldn't sit quietly when agitation hung in the air so thick she almost needed snorkeling gear. But neither could she hide in the bedroom, away from the force of his distress on a day when so much had already gone wrong. "Is there another news story circulating about how I'm the love child of Satan and used a voodoo spell to make you break up with Kyla?"

"Not quite." He whirled and faced her, arms stiff at his sides. Unapproachable, like he'd been at the club. "There is this one circulating where you informed the media the engagement was a publicity stunt. You know. The one thing I asked you not to tell anyone."

Her eyelids flew shut, and she struggled to breathe. He *had* asked her not to say anything but she'd forgotten that.

"I'm sorry. So sorry. It slipped out. I was so upset about all the horrible things people were saying. Are you mad?"

"Mad." Wearily, he weaved to the carpet and rested his forehead on the tips of his fingers. "Mad. At you? No, I'm not."

"What are you, then?"

"One more statement to the press shy of losing my career," he said with a short laugh and it crawled across her chest with sharp needles.

Losing his *career?* Not the film and only the film? "What does that mean?"

"What it sounds like. My executive producer called, and he's a little unhappy about news coverage, which is the exact opposite of the agreed direction for *Visions of Black*'s publicity. He's threatening breach of contract. No one will work with me if that happens."

"But you're not mad?" she asked cautiously.

"I'm not happy. The engagement wasn't going to happen regardless, but I haven't had a chance to figure out an alternative. I needed that time. Kyla is beyond furious. It took me fifteen minutes to calm her down long enough to coherently explain to me what you'd done."

"That's who was calling. Before I got in the shower."

"Yeah. It should be funny. She won't admit it, but I have no doubt she's the one who told the press about you and me, trying to upset you and make you look bad. She didn't expect you to return the favor. Good job. It's rare to beat Kyla at her own game." He stared at the floor instead of at her. "I'm going to lose everything without some serious damage control. I have to go back to L.A. and start salvaging. If I'm really lucky and invest a gallon of blood, sweat and tears, I'll still be able to show my face in Hollywood."

The option where Kris ended up with her and the movie dissipated into thin air. She'd fooled herself into believing his greatest emotional need was to embrace his passionate side when in reality, he'd already embraced his passions through his career.

Film was his release, his outlet. Not her.

Even if he threw himself at her feet, vowed undying love and swore to give it all up for her—the film, his career, Hollywood, his soul, all of it—she'd tell him to get up and stop being ridiculous. That wasn't happily ever after, to gut a vibrant, brilliant man, leaving only a cavity behind. But hey, he loved her. Wasn't that all that mattered?

Not even close.

She swallowed to keep the bile down and knelt on the carpet to take his hand and squeeze it. "You can be mad at me. I deserve it. I—" Another swallow. "I screwed up, and I don't know how to fix it."

"That's not on you. I have to put my career back together. I shouldn't have even agreed to such a stupid stunt. Actually it's a relief I'll never have to do it now." Pain planted deep lines around his gorgeous mouth. "Though I wish it hadn't been ripped off the table with such final and devastating consequences."

That made two of them. "When are you leaving?"

"An hour."

"Is this it, then?"

He didn't pretend to misunderstand. "It has to be. For now. I'd like to come back and see you again, but I have no idea when. The only reason I came to Dallas is to start work on *Visions of Black*."

And there it was.

She'd also fooled herself into believing love conquered all—and that Kris sought it, too, she just had to push him into admitting it. This was a fairy tale, all right. Absolute fiction. He wasn't looking for love, not with her, or with anyone.

She wasn't special or gifted with some miraculous ability to understand him. She was nothing more than a fun diversion, which he'd been chillingly honest about.

"I understand."

"Stay in the suite as long as you want. I'll give you my number. Let me know when your condo is ready, so I can settle the bill. Don't be weird about it. Please," he said as if he'd rehearsed the lines ahead of time. Because he'd known for a while he'd be leaving, and nothing had changed except the day. "I like being your knight in shining armor charging to the rescue. That's right up your alley, isn't it?"

If only he'd said that yesterday. This morning. With a vulnerable smile as he said he loved her. At any point when she could still pretend she was woman enough to bulldoze through that wall he kept around his heart. The wall that still had a giant No Trespassing sign, despite her best efforts.

She swallowed against the hot shower of grief in her throat. "Thanks. That's very generous."

She sat frozen, staring at the wall, fighting to hold on to the belief that love could be enough to bridge the chasm between them.

"Generous," she repeated, because it was. "But I can't accept. In fact, I've already accepted too much. I'll take your address and mail you a check for everything as soon as I can."

She couldn't ask him to come back and fall in love with her when she was stable, because that dream was over, but it didn't remove her responsibility to be a strong woman who could take care of herself.

Perhaps if she had been that woman in the first place, they'd be having an entirely different conversation. He deserved someone like Kyla, a natural part of his world and an asset to his career instead of a disaster. Someone who understood him a whole lot better than she did.

"Don't go there. Please. I don't want your money. I want you to stay. I would feel better." He tilted her chin up to force her to look at him. "I'm sorry. The timing sucks. All of this sucks. I can't ask you to come to L.A. with me."

"Of course you can't. You have a reputation to recover. You can't do that with me around. I'd be in the way." She waved it off and fought back a sob. Strong women didn't fall apart when a casual relationship ended. When the man they loved didn't love them back. "You don't owe me anything. We had some fun, and I'm grateful for everything you've done. We would have parted ways eventually, right? Now's as good a time as any."

Confusion clouded his expression. "This isn't how I expected this conversation to go."

"Why? Because I fell for you a little?" She shrugged, feign-ing a nonchalance she could never, ever feel. He was going to lose his career over her unless she let him go, and she loved him too much to be that selfish. "Who wouldn't? This has been the most amazing fairy tale. But fairy tales aren't real. Our clock just struck midnight. I understand that, Kris. Ball's over. It's time to get back to reality."

The confusion melted from Kris's eyes and twisted the knife a little farther into her heart. He was a sucker for honesty, and she'd spoken nothing but cold hard truth. But now she had to lie to him about the most important thing.

"Reality is, I've got a bruise or two but I feel the same way when the Cowboys lose to the Redskins in overtime. I'll get over it. We've only known each other a few days."

Her voice broke. They weren't and never could be strangers.

"If that's how you feel," he said.

Maybe she *should* call Kyla's agent if he believed that. His expression was marble hard and unapproachable and she couldn't look at him anymore. "Pack, or you'll miss your plane. Check out when you leave, and I'll be right behind you."

"Where will you go?"

"Don't worry, I'll be fine. It's time I figured out how to rescue myself."

He stood and helped her up, but didn't release her hand. He hauled her into a fierce embrace, and she almost lost her flimsy grip on sanity as his familiar arms came around her, sliding her into the groove of his body no other woman could possibly fit as well. Greek whispered through her hair, and he kissed the spot where his words had branded her scalp.

"What did you say?" She pulled back and searched his ex-pression.

"Maybe in another life." There was a glimmer in his eye, and it looked like sorrow. But it was probably only a reflection of what he saw in hers.

She fled into her room, the one she hadn't used since the

first night, and lay on the bed, hating the scratchy comforter against her raw skin. She stared at the clock with dry eyes until an hour and four minutes had passed. Then she picked up the phone on the bedside table and called Pamela Sue to wire her some money because she had no pride and no choices left.

"Thank God," Pamela Sue said when VJ identified herself. "I've been calling every hotel in Dallas for hours. Beverly Porter said you're not staying with her and no one had any idea where you went. I'm so sorry to have to tell you this, but your daddy had a heart attack."

Kris couldn't sleep. His condo was too hushed. Too cold. Too L.A. and impersonal with its mix of dark natural stone surfaces, concrete floor stained black and masculine furnishings he'd never thought twice about. It was all too…not where he wanted to be.

He plunked onto the leather sofa near the rush of a river rock waterfall in the living room and ran through scenes in his head, the same place he'd sat a thousand times. It was not working.

It was 2:00 a.m. That was pretty standard. He wore lounging pants and no shirt. Also typical. The leather chilled his back, keeping him alert and honest, and the peaceful shush of the waterfall washed street noise from the atmosphere. Totally normal.

He kept listening for VJ to tiptoe into the room, wearing that virginal white robe with the loose collar. The one so easy to slip off her soft shoulders and bare her beautiful body, allowing him access to that butterfly she'd inked—permanently—into her skin.

Not at all normal.

Why couldn't he shake her out of his system? She lingered in his mind in a persistence of memory tattooed across his consciousness. Impossible to eliminate. Impossible to embrace. He couldn't think. Couldn't eat. Couldn't feel. Never in his life had he been unable to create, to escape into the imaginary as a method to deal with reality.

That refuge was gone.

He should be storyboarding *Visions of Black,* if nothing else, but definitely working up proposals to bring in additional investors. Instead, he was obsessing over the pain and resignation on VJ's face when he'd told her he was leaving.

There'd been a moment, back in the hotel room, when he thought she was going to fall in his arms and beg him to stay. Demand that he love her like she loved him. Verbalize on his behalf what was in his heart because she saw inside him so much more clearly than he did. He'd braced for it, uncertain how he'd respond. The moment passed, and it became painfully obvious the scene wasn't going to end that way.

Instead, he'd thoroughly killed her belief in happily ever after because he couldn't find the courage to reach for it. He'd hurt her, irreparably damaging something precious.

Now he'd live in the purgatory he deserved. Recreating that scene a hundred ways but in the endings he created, he always figured out what had gone wrong before walking out the door.

He had a meeting with Jack Abrams in seven hours. In seven hours, either he'd have a plan to salvage *Visions of Black* or he'd have a front-row seat to the final demise of his career. This movie should have been the springboard, catapulting him to the next level. Not his swan song.

How had it come to this?

The intercom at the entrance to his condo buzzed, startling him out of his morose contemplation. A visitor. In the middle of the night. A short burst of hope that it might be VJ dissolved into the more likely scenario. Five bucks said it was Kyla. Blitzed.

He activated the two-way speaker, pretty sure he was going to be sorry.

"Hey, babe." The cultured feminine voice floated from the box. "In the mood for some company?"

He grimaced. At least Kyla was a happy drunk and therefore less likely to cause a scene. "No. Go home and sleep it off."

"Oh, honey, you don't have to be that way. I just want to talk. Nothing else."

Right. They hadn't spoken since her hysterical call the afternoon everything had fallen apart with VJ, but yet, here she was in L.A., itching for yet another confrontation. "Call me in the morning. It's after two."

Even so, the rush of cars and boisterous pedestrians filtered in along with Kyla's words. "Let me in. This button is hard to push, and I'm wearing five-inch heels."

"Whose fault is that?" Nothing good was going to come of this late-night visit. Nothing. "I was asleep. I'd like to go back to bed."

"Kris." She snuffled. "We were lovers for a long time. I know you weren't asleep. Unless you want a picture of me at your door on the front page of every tabloid in the morning, let me in."

That was the last thing he wanted. A conversation with Kyla was second to last. He buzzed open the lock on the entrance and dashed into the bedroom to put on a shirt. No reason to give her any further ideas since she undoubtedly had plenty of ideas already.

He opened the door and let her totter in to collapse on the couch after she'd miraculously missed tripping over the lamb's wool throw rug. Crossing his arms, he leaned on the shut door. "What's so important?"

She smoothed the microscopic lines of her fuchsia skirt and smiled demurely with flawlessly painted lips. "I wanted to see you. I miss you. Is that so bad?"

With a silent groan, he went to the kitchen and poured a glass of water. "Drink this. I'll call you a cab." He handed her the glass, and when she took it, a long wave of her perfume settled over him. The scent was cloying and sweet. He'd forgotten how much he hated its artificial quality.

"Sit down." She patted the couch and fluttered her surgically enhanced lashes. "I'm sorry about what happened in Dallas. Is your friend okay?"

He shook his head. "Not having this conversation."

Slyly, she tapped a nail on her lips and peered up at him. "Since she's not here, I assume it didn't work out. Too bad. She wasn't right for you anyway."

That explained the timing. Kyla was scoping out his residence for signs of competition.

"Who was? You?" Cursing, he went back into the kitchen so the island would be between them. Small comfort. He'd already given her far too much of an opening.

Her fake interview laugh trilled through the air. "You like to pretend things are over, but there are still feelings between us or you never would have agreed to the engagement."

He wasn't taking the bait. She could talk until laryngitis set in, and he wasn't going to let her goad him into another endless conversation about their relationship.

Except now he was thinking about it, as she'd intended.

Why had he agreed to the engagement? When the deal came together with Abrams, Kris immediately recommended Kyla for the lead role. Film was an industry, not a school yard. He couldn't let personal feelings get in the way, and after she'd read the script, her agent had contacted his assistant to say she was in.

Things had snowballed from there. His palms gripped the hard, granite edges of the island countertop, grounding him. He'd agreed—at the time—because *Visions of Black* was more important than anything else. *Was.* Now it wasn't.

"It could have been a new start for us, Kris," Kyla said and came into the kitchen. She wasn't nearly as drunk as he'd assumed. Her cornflower-blue eyes were bright and open, as if imploring him to plumb their depths and see the truth. A trick of the recessed lighting in the kitchen. Kyla never missed her mark.

She set the glass down and positioned a handful of talons on his arm. "I made a mistake. With Guy. When I told you, you got so mad. I thought that meant you cared more than you'd let on and needed space to get over it."

He could have saved her the suspense if he'd just had this conversation a long time ago instead of avoiding confrontation. "Mad because you cheated on me and lied. I never gave you one reason to treat me that way."

"That's not true." She pouted. "I was lonely, and you were so distant and focused on work. The thing with Guy happened in a moment of weakness. He was there for me."

What a cliché. "You were bored. And guess what? I don't blame you."

Improbably, he wasn't angry about Hansen. Not anymore. He had been detached and passionless with Kyla. When she'd moved on, in hindsight, he'd been relieved. He should have told her.

Kyla's confusion grew as fast as his clarity. "Does that mean you've finally forgiven me?"

"It does. Totally forgiven. You were right, there was a lack of resolution to our relationship. Thanks," he said sincerely. "For forcing the issue. I'm sorry I was so distant."

"It's okay," she said with a delicate sniff and covered his hand with hers. "I understand why you're like that. You're almost a robot. That's why you're a director, not an actor, even though you've got the look. But you stay behind the camera because you can't tap into the emotional layers necessary to be someone different in front of the camera."

Someone different? He was already someone different. The person he could only be because of VJ.

He'd disconnected from life and poured himself into his art, the only defense he thought he had against all the raging things inside. If VJ hadn't blasted his barriers apart, he'd likely have continued being a non-participant in his own story forever.

He'd tried so hard not to be his father that he'd neglected

to be Kris. Only VJ saw through his defenses, demanding his participation, forcing him into the middle of the action. Drawing him out in spite of himself.

"Is that right?" he asked.

She nodded. "You like to tell people what to do. You're a control freak, and it shuts you down inside. I can help you."

"Let me ask you something. How come we hardly ever had sex?"

A stiletto scraped against the Travertine when she half stepped, half stumbled in surprise. "You never wanted to. I assumed you had a low sex drive but were too proud to talk about it. Some macho European thing."

"How come *you* never wanted to?"

"I did. I tried. You blew me off, muttering about edits or a read-through the next day, and you'd disappear inside yourself."

That sounded about right. Excuses instead of intimacy. Justifications instead of passion. He only allowed film to excite him.

Until VJ.

"But I'm okay with that," she purred. Her hand wandered up his arm, toying with his biceps and brushing against his sleeve, as if she had every right to do so. "We'll work on it. So let's put it behind us and start over. I forgive you for that little indiscretion in Dallas and—"

He laughed and removed her hand. "You don't want to get back together. You just want something you can't have, and you can't have me. I'm in love with VJ, and I let her go like a complete idiot. I have to get her back."

Finally, *something* that made perfect, absolute sense. It was so clear now. He loved her, with ferocious terror and awe. She was his passion and had torn that lid off in her unique VJ style, unleashing a flood of emotion and creativity he had hadn't even realized was missing.

She balanced him. He'd been teetering so far in the other direction, the true danger lay in living an unengaged life, not in somehow turning violent overnight. Without VJ, his soul would shrivel back up into that person who wasn't his father, but also wasn't who he wanted to be.

Kyla's eyes widened. "She tried to destroy your career, Kris. You can't be serious."

"If my career is over, it's my fault, not hers." His career was low on the list of concerns at this moment. He'd built it from nothing once, he'd do it again. After settling more important matters. "I should've taken responsibility for the problems in my relationship with you a long time ago. If I had, the fake engagement would have died at the outset, and you wouldn't have had a chance to issue a statement about VJ. You forced her into talking to the press."

That was his mistake for ever mentioning her to Kyla, which he'd only done as yet another way to avoid his feelings. No more autopilot. VJ warranted all of his heart. All of his passion. The answer was so simple—transfer the energy he spent pretending to be something he wasn't into ensuring that the passion he felt for her never died, never changed, and was always a positive reinforcement of his love.

It might be the hardest thing he'd ever attempted. Fear hijacked his lungs, but he squeezed in a deep breath.

He'd make it happen. VJ was worth it.

"You should know better than to cross me," she said, and that was as close to an admission of guilt as he'd get. Her eyes narrowed. "She's a nobody. She'll never fit into our world."

"Then I'll put my creative energy into finding a way to fit into hers. Oh, to be clear, we're through. Finally, completely and forever. Your cab's here."

Without another word, he escorted one of the world's most beautiful and glamorous women out the door and locked it behind her. He had a lot of work to do before he could earn his happily-ever-after.

Somehow, he had to figure out a way to give VJ back the belief in it.

Thirteen

VJ hopped into Bobby Junior's ancient truck, slammed the door and stared straight ahead at the sun rising along the horizon in an inferno of heartbreaking colors. "Stop looking at me like that."

"Sorry." Her brother rested a work-roughened hand on the steering wheel. He started the truck and pulled out of Pamela Sue's driveway to make the long trek to the hospital where Daddy lay recovering. "I don't mean to."

She sighed. This was why she'd waited until this morning to ask Bobby Junior to take her to see Daddy. She'd needed a day to collect herself. A girl could only have so many illusions shattered in a week and losing the one where her oldest brother was still a hero might be the straw.

"You're dying to ask me about it. Go ahead. What do you want to know? How many times Kris and I had sex?"

Fourteen. Counting the times they'd done...other stuff. *Get over it.* She couldn't let the memories unwind or she'd blubber like a housewife watching talk shows.

"No!" Reddening, he shook his head. "I don't even want to think about that." He signaled to turn onto Little Crooked Creek Road and cleared his throat. "I have three kids. I know how they got here. It's different when it's my little sister."

"So, the lurid details are what you wanted to ask about."

It took a full five minutes before he responded. "Jamie…she wondered about the tattoo. Did you really get one?"

"You want me to come over tonight and show it to her? Show the kids?"

"VJ." Bobby Junior frowned, looking a lot like Daddy, and chomped on the ever-present gum he'd traded for chewing tobacco after the birth of his first kid. "You took off with a stranger and ran around all over Dallas, getting photographed and talked about on the news. People are curious. You ask a lot if you expect them not to be."

The folks in Little Crooked Creek could pass judgment with the best of the internet piranhas. Day before yesterday, VJ stepped off the bus and huddled on a bench to wait for Pamela Sue, only to glimpse Mrs. Pritchett caning across the street to avoid VJ. Two weeks ago, they'd shared a pew in church. VJ had held the hymnal for the eighty-year-old woman since her arthritis flared up in the August heat.

"Well, I'm sorry I caused such a ruckus trying to have a life." She laced her arms across her chest but it didn't bandage the hurt. "You can say it. I got what I deserved. I let a guy have the milk without buying the cow and then he left to go back to his real life in Hollywood. Can't expect to grow an oak tree with okra seeds, right?"

Kris's business card was burning a hole in her pocket. He'd written his cell-phone number on the back in swirly numerals and left it on the coffee table of their—his—hotel room. No message, no indication of why. He'd probably left it accidentally. With no intention of pulling it out until she could write him a check, she'd tucked it into her bag. As a memento of what happened in real life when she forgot that fairy tales were for books.

"That's not what I was going to say." His back stiffened, pulling away from the cracked bench seat. "Daddy was bad after you left. Worse than normal. Went off on a tear, throwing furniture around. Mrs. Johnson called the sheriff when he drove through her flowerbed at midnight. I had to pick him up, still drunk, from the clink."

Bobby Junior's quiet condemnation dug into her stomach with claws. She'd walked out on her responsibilities. Lots of people had to deal with parents and life and real hardships. They didn't leave. "I guess that's my fault, too, same as the heart attack."

"Daddy's heart attack wasn't your fault. Yeah, he got a shock seeing you on TV and hearing the things people were saying. But the doctor said it was the stress of Mama and a year of hard drinking. I would have told you that if you'd come around instead of hiding out at Pamela Sue's."

"I'm here now. I'm being a good daughter and going to see Daddy, aren't I?"

Wounds from the night she left Little Crooked Creek were still fresh and coupled with the new ones, she couldn't have done this any sooner. All of yesterday had been spent in the fetal position on Pamela Sue's bed, alternately bawling and staring at the wall.

Then Daddy had taken a turn for the worse, and she'd forced herself to push back the grief. What if he died before she saw him again? She didn't want to have to live with that. He was still her father.

The shoulder where she'd stopped to check out the sleek Ferrari flew by in a flash. Just like her relationship with Kris. Relationship—or whatever it was called when a person blinks and the highlight of her existence vanishes, leaving only a sharp memory too vivid to erase and too painful to enjoy.

She'd only meant to drool over the car. Not the driver. Or

his hands. His mouth. The way he opened up when he was inside her and his soul spoke without any words. And when he did talk…her eyelids fluttered closed and time stopped while she ached.

She missed Kris, and it was a slow, agonizing death instead of the difficult, but eventual, recovery she'd hoped for.

Bobby Junior took a deep breath, jerking her out of her misery. "Why didn't you tell me what Daddy did to you?"

"Which part?" she asked, too surprised he'd found out to answer right away.

His hands were clamped so tight on the steering wheel, veins popped. "When I picked up Daddy from the sheriff, he was babbling about how he'd driven you away. I finally got him to tell me he'd taken all your money." Bobby Junior paused for a beat. "And that he hit you."

She shrugged. "What difference would it have made if I had told you?"

"What difference—" He thumped the seat between them, startling her with the force. "You could have stayed with me and Jamie. Let us help you get your money back. You're so independent. There's nothing wrong with asking for a little help. Why didn't you?"

Her throat hurt from the twinge in Bobby Junior's voice. How selfish she'd been to leave without thinking how others might take it. She probably should have told her brothers about Daddy hitting her, too, but she'd been so sure no one would take her side. "I don't know."

"I do. You're just like Mama. Both of you take charge. The whole time Mama was sick, you did what had to be done. I don't know where you found that grit. Then she—" His voice broke and he swallowed. "She died and all of us were lost. Except you. You took care of the funeral. Daddy. The boys. Everyone except yourself. I'm surprised it took so long for you to break. Woulda been nice if your rebellion had been a little safer and lower profile."

"Pamela Sue made me promise to use condoms." Which wasn't everything she wanted to say but her throat closed.

The blush, not quite gone anyway, flared up and spread from his cheeks to his neck. "Glad to hear it," he said gruffly and tapped her chest. "But I meant safer in here. You're different. Your shoulders are heavier."

"I grew up. It was past time. I have to face reality, not live in a fantasy world where an exciting man sweeps me off my feet, only to disappear at midnight."

All of a sudden, it didn't seem so devastating to be back in Little Crooked Creek, still broke, but not in such a bad place after all. Some maids became princesses, and some women just became self-sufficient. When she'd left the first time, options were hard to come by and the one promising excitement and escape won. Now, because of Kris, she had the wisdom to evaluate opportunity openly, honestly and without a coating of fairy dust. That's what strong women did. Like Mama. Like her.

"Want me to kick his butt? I'd like to think you still need me for something." Her brother's affable gap-toothed grin settled her heart. Not completely, but along with the gift of absolution, it went a long way. He ruffled her hair like he had for as long as she could remember.

She smiled at her brother and patted his arm. "Thanks. That means a lot."

Downtown Van Horn unrolled through the windshield as Bobby Junior drove down the main street lined with adobe-plastered stores, family-owned Mexican restaurants and dust. West Texas still wasn't for her. She'd find a way to get back to Dallas and start building a life on her own terms. A life based in reality.

He pulled into the hospital lot and parked, then threw an arm around her shoulders to walk with her into the lobby. They sat by Daddy's bedside for a few hours, talking to each other, talking to Daddy without expectation of a response, smiling at the nurses. Daddy woke up once and squeezed VJ's hand. It was enough. She'd find a way to forgive him. Not today, but eventually. Some hurts went too deep to heal easily.

When the truck pulled into Pamela Sue's driveway, her friend sprinted out and opened the door. She pushed VJ to the center, then bounced onto the vacated seat. "What took you so long?" she asked, breathlessly. "We have to go down to Pearl's. Drive, Bobby."

"What's at Pearl's?" he asked, as he shifted into Reverse and peered at the rearview mirror. "I got to get back to the garage."

"It's a surprise for VJ," she said. "Drop us off and ske-daddle."

VJ gave Pamela Sue a one-eyed stare. "A surprise like pin a scarlet letter on VJ or more like a surprise public flogging of VJ?"

When Pamela Sue had picked her up from the bus station, VJ'd asked to visit Pearl first, to apologize for leaving her former boss in the lurch. Pearl was a marshmallow, so she wouldn't be the one pinning or flogging, but as for the rest of the town, it was anyone's guess.

"Neither. Wait and see." In a very un–Pamela Sue way, she kept her mouth closed clear through the single stoplight in the center of town. Right before Bobby Junior turned the corner at Pearl's, she asked, "Are you sure you don't want to come in, Bobby? You might be sorry you missed it."

Now VJ was really curious. Oh. Everyone had missed her birthday. Surprise party, of course. She whimpered. Normally, she'd love that but with folks' dirty looks and general hostility, attendance would be slim.

But then she caught sight of the parking lot at Pearl's. It was full. Jam-packed, with cars and trucks lining the street for a block, and people streaming through the front doors.

Eyes wide, she glanced at Pamela Sue. "It *is* a public flog-ging. I'm suddenly feeling very feverish."

"Just get out." She hooked elbows with VJ and hauled her

out of the truck the second Bobby Junior braked at the curb. The engine shut off, and Bobby Junior swung out of the cab.

"Can't stay but a minute," he said in concession.

All three of them trooped inside. The diner was dark—the kitchen, the dining room, entrance—but the rustle of people was unmistakable. The lights flashed and everyone yelled, "Surprise!" but there were no decorations, no cake and no balloons.

Instead, a line of people stood in the middle of the room, each holding a single yellow sunflower. Confused and a little weirded out, she turned to Pamela Sue. "What is this?"

"Take the flowers," she said, which was no answer at all, and dragged her toward Mrs. Johnson, who was at the head of the line. VJ trailed after Pamela Sue, only because their arms were still hooked.

Mrs. Johnson extended the flower, which had a rectangle of white attached to it with a silky ribbon, and said, "I liked the red dress."

A compliment. Not a judgmental put-down. Mystified, VJ gripped the sunflower, held it to her nose and inhaled the fresh fragrance. The dress hung in the back of the closet at Pamela Sue's. Another memento she couldn't toss. "Thanks. I liked it, too."

"Read the card," someone in the audience urged.

Intrigued, she flipped the card and took in the words. Her stomach seized up like an overheated engine. The card shook so hard in her trembling fingers, it was a wonder she held on to it. "I can't. It's Greek. I don't know how to translate it."

"I do," Kris said from behind her.

She spun and oh, *yes*. There he was, in the flesh. Clad in black, ebony hair falling against his cheekbones, arms crossed and one hip leaned gracefully against the discolored wall. Beautifully, sinfully gorgeous and—

Dear Lord. Every person in this room knew they'd been

intimate. Frozen, she stared at him. Couldn't move, couldn't breathe. One hand flew up to cover her mouth.

Kris straightened and strode toward her, eyes fluid and searching and beguiling. He stopped a couple feet away but didn't touch her.

His phone buzzed.

The only thing she could think to say was, "You went to the communication dark side and started carrying your phone in your pocket?"

With a wry laugh that almost broke the tension, he pulled it out and pitched the phone at the closest table. "I kept hoping you might call, and I didn't want it to go to voice mail."

She was the person too important to leave a message?

"What are you doing here?"

All around them, fascinated faces watched her and Kris, blurring into a ménage of colors as it crystallized.

He was here. In Little Crooked Creek.

"I'm doing what I should have done in Dallas when you said it was time to get back to reality." He edged closer, his sensual aura overwhelming. "My reality isn't the same anymore. You destroyed it and gave me something better. A reality where fairy tales come true. I'm here to recapture that reality."

His voice washed over her, flowing through the coldness inside, heating her thoroughly. She must be asleep. Dreaming. Tentatively, she reached out and flattened a palm against Kris's chest. Solid. Warm. Amazing. Real. It took every ounce of will not to sink into his arms.

This was all wrong.

"Kris." She shook her head and snatched her arm back. "You don't want that. You never wanted anything other than to make movies, and I ruined that."

The taut lines around his sculpted mouth softened. "You're wrong. I was wandering around in the desert, lost, and didn't even realize it until you found me. You showed me how to tap into my emotions. To tell the story from my heart. Without you, my career is nothing. I'd abandon it in a second if that would prove it to you."

"No! I can't let you do that," she said fiercely and took a step back. He was too close, and her will was only so strong. "You shouldn't even be here. Go back to Hollywood and get photographed a bunch with Kyla so people forget about me. Then maybe you can still make *Visions of Black*."

"You're the only person I want to be photographed with." A camera, a huge professional number like from a movie set, appeared in his hands from its hiding place under a table. He pushed some buttons and positioned it carefully on the scarred Formica tabletop. Suddenly, the camera was on them both, recording.

Kris took her hand and squeezed, so she couldn't move out of range. "This time, everyone, especially the media, will get the story right. Once upon a time, there was this guy who had all these chaotic, extreme emotions inside, and he was so afraid of letting those things control him, he pretended he didn't feel anything at all. Then he met this extraordinary woman who really got that. And this guy fell in love with her but couldn't figure out how to get past being that same guy so he let her go. Now he's trying to get her back."

Kris was in love with her? Definitely a dream. "How does the story end?"

"With a translation." He nodded to the card hanging from the sunflower still clutched in her fist. "It says, 'The first time I saw you, you reminded me of a living sunflower. Beautiful and open.'"

With a firm hand, he guided her to the next person, who held the next flower. Her third-grade teacher, Mrs. Cole, smiled and handed off the bloom. "I'm jealous you got to stay in such a fancy hotel," she said with a wink.

Coupled with Mrs. Johnson's nice comment, it warmed her. Not everyone thought she was the devil incarnate. These people were here to support her. They were here because Kris had asked them to be. He was rescuing her from the bad press, because that was what he did.

Kris leaned in, brushing her ear with his lips and as her lobe burned, he said, "This one reads, 'The second time I saw you, your hair smelled like coconut, and I couldn't get the scent out of my mind.'"

Where was he going with all this loveliness? Before she could blink, Kris shuttled her to the next flower, held by Pearl. "This card says, 'I nicknamed you my desert mirage, a shimmering, gorgeous fantasy rising up out of the bleak landscape.'"

A nickname. *Oh, no.* "The stages. You have all the stages written down on these cards."

Impishly, Kris smiled and handed her another flower. "'The Scrambler. Then the Ferris wheel.'"

He was reading the cards in public. Great balls of fire. *In public.*

"Everybody out. Now." She turned to address the room at large before Kris could start on the next flower, which undoubtedly read: *You exposed your breast, showed me the butterfly tattoo and I tasted it in the elevator.* "I appreciate everyone coming out today. Your support means a lot. But some things are best done without an audience."

Grumbling, everyone shuffled to their feet and filed out slower than lizards molt. The flower bearers laid the stalks in a pile on a nearby table. Pamela Sue grinned and hustled a glowering Bobby Junior out the door. VJ made a mental note to thank her later for taking care of all this.

Finally, they were alone.

Alone, with Kris. She never thought she'd see him again, never mind while he spouted romanticisms in that gorgeous voice.

"I wasn't going to read them all aloud," he said. "That's why I wrote them in Greek."

"What else do the cards say?" she asked, her throat raw with emotions too big to process.

"Lots of things. Like, how I love being your guinea pig. Six-forty-five, which is what time I watched the sunrise while I held you. This one." He pulled a bloom from the stack and swept it across her cheek. "This one says, 'Love, passion and friendship. You gifted me with all three, and I want to spend my life giving them back to you.'"

He dropped the flower, pulled something out of his back pocket and held it up. Her lungs collapsed.

A ring box.

Hesitantly, he fingered a lock of her hair. "I didn't put it in a big box and let you unwrap it. Our relationship is based on honesty. I didn't want you to have to guess. So you know right up front that I'm asking you to marry me."

"Why?" she blurted out because her brain was stuck. Her pulse was stuck. Everything was stunned into immobilization.

His stormy eyes roamed over her face. "There's only one reason to marry someone, or so you've thoroughly convinced me. Because I love you and can't live without you."

God Almighty. Kris had been possessed by aliens. "Eh." She waved it off. "You're only suffering from a hormonal imbalance."

Without missing a beat, he flipped the hinged lid and took the ring, holding it out between two steady, golden fingers. "It's inscribed. Will you read it?"

Gingerly, she accepted the pale circle of metal—Holy Heaven, it was a huge, beautiful square-cut diamond exploding with fire—and read the inscription carved into the platinum. Her knees turned to jelly.

Stage Seven is Forever.

When she couldn't speak, he said, "At Casa di Luigi, you told me I'd hit all the stages. But I missed one. Happily ever after." He plucked the ring from her fingertips. "Will you allow me to put this on?"

This wasn't solely a rescue, some elaborate scheme he'd invented to save her reputation. He was balancing the scales, legitimizing their relationship. Transforming her with his magic-wand-engagement-ring into Mrs. Demetrious.

"You're crazier than a drunk June bug." Or she was. She hardly knew which way was up. Was this some kind of setup? A different approach to publicity? "What's happening with *Visions of Black?*"

"It's a mess, but I don't care. Resolving it is meaningless unless I fix us first. I can't function without you. I can't think, can't concentrate. I need you more than I need to breathe. Please."

He was truly hurting. The evidence was there, in his rigid stance and the pain in his tumultuous expression. Hurting, because he was in love with her, like head-over-heels, Romeo and Juliet, take-a-bullet-for-her in love. Refusing him might result in as much of a gutting as his lost career. What was she supposed to do?

Once, when she was still blinded by stupidity and had an overinflated sense of her ability to read this profound man, she'd have known what to say, how to act. He'd destroyed that in Dallas, and she didn't know how to get it back.

"VJ, I messed up by not grabbing what we had." Clearly disconcerted, he exhaled and shoved his free hand through his hair. "But I'm not afraid anymore. I'm on this side of the camera, in the middle of the scene with you, exactly where I want to be. Begging you to believe in me, to believe in happily ever after again after I broke your heart. What can I say to convince you I'm sincere?"

"That was a pretty good start," she mumbled, her heart too busy duking it out with her brain to come up with a better response. "You can't marry me. We've known each other barely a week."

He cupped her chin, lifted it. The touch of his fingertips on her face almost split her in two.

"The length of our acquaintance is irrelevant, *agapi mou,*" he said, drawing her into his melty-brown eyes. "There's been something between us from the first. You feel it, too. You knew immediately you didn't want to marry that other guy. Why can't I be certain in an instant that you're the one?"

Where had this stuff *come* from? He'd blown far past romance instruction, *far* past any romance novel, into territory she'd never dreamed existed. With no experience and no clues, she didn't trust herself, didn't believe she could ever fathom the mind of Kristian Demetrious. What if she was wrong? What if it wasn't real love? What if—

In a flash, the answer came to her. With the smallest bit of dawning hope, she asked, "What kind of car do you have? At home?"

"What? A BMW SUV. So I can haul around equipment."

German. Still foreign and complex and incomprehensible.

"And a '67 Mustang," he continued as an afterthought. "I only drive it occasionally. It's the quintessential American car, symbolic of my U.S. citizenship. What does this have to do with anything?"

A Ford. Kris had a Ford in his garage.

"With a 428 V-8 engine?"

When he nodded, tears finally burst the dam and flowed down her cheeks. It was the first engine she'd ever touched, the one she'd learned everything from. She could take the entire thing apart and rebuild it. One-handed.

The coincidence didn't mean anything. Not really, but it broke her resistance. Her greatest emotional need was the heart of this man, and he was spilling it out, passionately, with soul-wrenching truth. Offering her something real, tied up with a fairy-tale bow, and asking if she was woman enough to accept.

"And you're crying because?" he asked.

"Because I love you. Put the ring on, Kristian."

The storm clouds finally cleared from his eyes as he slid the circle of forever onto her finger. Then he kissed her. It was joyous, magical, right.

Almost.

She pulled back. "Um, can you turn off the camera? I'm about four seconds from stripping you, and a sex-tape scandal might not be the best move for us."

His rich laughter took up residence in her heart, and she believed again. Not in a fantasy, but in real, true love.

Epilogue

Kris tossed the phone onto the island in the middle of his kitchen. *No way* had that just happened. He barged into the master bathroom, raring for a confrontation, anticipating it, because he never had to pretend he was emotionless ever again.

Coconut-scented bubble bath hit him at the threshold and ignited that primal reaction that hadn't faded. At all. His mind drained of everything except for the scene before him. VJ soaked in the tub, spread out appetizingly, with her eyes closed, hair wet and pure bliss in her smile. The diamond on her third finger caught the light and refracted, splintering through his heart.

She'd moved into his condo only a month ago, sliding into it as if she'd always been there. Her presence alone lightened the darkness of the decor as if he had a private sun all his own. Only a month, and already the preproduction work on *Visions of Black* was done. Brilliantly, and largely due to VJ, his stellar new production assistant.

Love was the greatest muse of all. How had he ever created without her? How had he ever lived?

She popped an eye open and regarded him steadily, shamelessly naked and gorgeous.

"Are you going to watch or get in?" she asked, her voice husky. "If it's the former, I should move some of these bubbles."

In a slow, sensuous scrape, she swished them from her breasts and the red butterfly peeped up from the foam. That butterfly—the color of passion and permanent. Every waking moment, he labored to live up to what it represented. To be worthy of the faith she'd had in him from the beginning.

Familiar quickening spiked through his groin, but he crossed his arms instead of flinging clothes to the floor. "I'm not falling for that again. Figure out a different way to distract me because—" With a sigh, he turned his back to the provocative sight of his soon-to-be-wife. "Never mind. It still works."

VJ laughed. "What am I trying to distract you from this time?"

"Kyla called. A warning might have been nice." He tried to sound stern and failed. "She was letting me know, oh-so-casually, how excited she was to start shooting since you talked her into taking a percentage of profits instead of the upfront fee her contract called for."

What a relief. A huge, gigantic relief to have that albatross off his shoulders. The film was all downhill from here.

"What? I'm not allowed to rescue you occasionally? Too bad if you don't like it. That's stage eight, by the way, and I'm bound to think of a few more," she said with a little splash, as if she'd risen from the water, perhaps exposing the butterfly fully. "Wedding's in three days. Last chance to back out."

"No way, *agapi mou.*" He twisted and ripped off his T-shirt, followed swiftly by the rest of his clothes. He stepped down, sank into the water filling the enormous garden tub and spooned VJ into his arms. Definitely his favorite position. "You're stuck with me. I gave up half my bed for you, after all."

"It's only fair. I gave up a half of a condo in Dallas for you. Though I have a feeling Beverly Porter and Pamela Sue are going to kill each other before too much longer," she said drily and settled back into that place only she fit. Wet cinnamon hair splayed across his chest, warming his skin and his heart.

Now. He had to join with this amazing woman who had saved him, and within seconds, it was a reality. The best reality because it was a combination of passion, love, friendship and a touch of magic.

Happily ever after had a lot to recommend it.

Six months passed in a blur of pleasure. Kris married VJ in a fairy-tale wedding and took her on a two-week honeymoon to Fiji, which was as far out of the state of Texas as he could get. He fell more in love with his wife every day.

He filmed *Visions of Black* on a shoe-string budget like in the old days, and discovered an interesting secret. Turned out when he put his heart into directing, cast and crew alike responded with vivid performances. The media, never hesitant to jump on a good story, devoted a great deal of coverage to the romance between the director and the woman who inspired him.

During the whirlwind of positive publicity following a surprise record-breaking opening weekend for *Visions of Black,* a reporter asked Kris how he knew it was true love with VJ. With a laugh, he said, "She told me, step by step, the secrets of romance. And she keeps telling me every day. Fortunately, I pay attention to the things she says."

* * * * *

0816/05

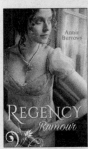
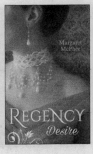

MILLS & BOON®

The Regency Collection – Part 2

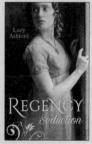

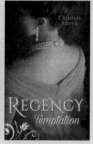

Join the London ton for a Regency
season in part 2 of our collection!

Order yours at **www.millsandboon.co.uk/regency2**